TIME TO ROCK

Peter J. Maida

Copyright © 2022, 2023 *Peter J. Maida*

All rights reserved.

This story is about Freddie MacArthur. He is the lead guitar player for the band Barracuda. It is September 1973, and the band has made it big. Their single, "She's Got the Devil in Her," has hit number one, and their album "Wrecking Ball," is highly rated. With success comes problems and Barracuda had them in spades. They had two concerts left on the "Wrecking Ball," tour when things began to come apart. It all exploded after the last concert, in Detroit, leaving Freddie rushing out of town with a college student named Emily Hicks. While hurdling down the Edsel Ford Freeway they encounter a blue curtain of energy.

This is also a story of Emily Hicks. Emily is a sophomore at the University of Michigan at Ann Arbor in September of 1973. She's a journalism major with great ambition. Emily had just got on the school newspaper, and she was looking for a big story. She gets a tip that Barracuda was having problems and she is offered a way to be backstage at their Detroit concert. Emily pretends to be a groupie and she ends up getting a lot more than she expected. Emily records talk of covering up a serious crime then she is discovered. Freddie helps her escape, and they race down the freeway to the blue curtain.

Freddie's 1973 Plymouth Barracuda rushes into the blue curtain, there is a blinding flash of light, and Freddie fights to keep control of the car. He pulls to the side of the road to catch his breath. They then proceed on Interstate 94 in the early morning hours of September 16, 2017. This is where the story starts. See what happens next and see how this event triggers the rebirth of rock and roll.

Table of Contents

Acknowledgments 1

Part One 1973 2

    Chapter 1: Emily 3

    Chapter 2: Barracuda 19

    Chapter 3: Detroit 37

    Chapter 4: Transition 60

Part Two 2017 69

    Chapter 5: Homecoming 70

    Chapter 6: Names 90

    Chapter 7: Look-Alikes 113

    Chapter 8: Virginia 130

Part Three Time to Rock 164

    Chapter 9: KWTZ 165

    Chapter 10: Barracuda Rising 186

    Chapter 11: Changing Sides 206

    Chapter 12: Radiant Energy 227

    Chapter 13: There is Someone Else 249

    Chapter 14: Tachyons 276

    Chapter 15: Cindi, Anita, and Mickey 298

    Chapter 16: Impact 318

    Chapter 17: A Dark Night for Walking 340

Acknowledgments

I would like to thank my son David Maida for telling me about the hammer and pull guitar technique. It became a special part of this story.

Part One

1973

Chapter 1: Emily

It was September 1973, and Emily Hicks had just started her sophomore year at the University of Michigan. Emily's major was journalism, and she spent her freshman year lobbying for a position on the student newspaper, The Michigan Daily. Being in the newspaper was an honor in many ways. U of M started the first student newspaper back in 1857. She finally landed a spot, but now she was feeling like it was just after the nick of time. The Paris Peace Accords were signed two months earlier, and this semester was expected to be a lot quieter and more orderly. That was great news for the university but bad news for Emily.

Emily Hicks was a petite green-eyed young lady with shoulder-length chestnut hair and Audrey Hepburn features. She liked to be stylish in her dress without being too fancy. She never cared much for the hippie look.

She had a plan. She wanted to be an anchor on a major news network. Her hero was Barbara Walters. She was convinced that Barbara would be the first female anchor, and she wanted to follow in her footsteps. To do that, there would be a lot of barriers to push through. She would have to stand out from the beginning, and the beginning was now.

The university newspaper office was filled with students milling about and getting ready for the first organizational meeting of the year. When Emily entered the room, someone called out, "Red alert. Captain, there's a Romulan on the bridge." Emily was used to the puns about her being from Romulus, Michigan. In fact, she enjoyed the popularity it gave her.

Emily called, "Stand down; I have two war birds cloaked and ready to power up their disruptors."

That brought a laugh from the group. The senior manager of the newspaper came over, shook her hand, and said, "Welcome; I'm Dave, and we are just getting started."

The discussion of how things worked went as Emily expected. Being the newest member, and a sophomore, they had her penciled in for fact and grammar-checking copy; that wasn't Emily's plan. She didn't react to the assignment. It was a fair job for her to receive, but she planned to do more than check facts on other writers' copies. She would find a big story, a scoop, somewhere.

Emily left the meeting and headed for her second lecture of the day. Her mind was racing, trying to come up with a lead on a story. Then she heard her sister call to her, "Hey Emily, wait up."

Emily slowed down, and Sarah caught up. Emily asked, "Don't you ever get tired of this place? You spent four years here, and now you're back for more."

Sarah Hicks was taller and rounder than her sister. She was full figured, but not overfull, and her short black hair and solid brown eyes seemed to be made for business, "This is the first semester that they offered a computer science course. I want in on the ground floor. My business degree will help me get in doors, but I believe a computer science degree will really make things happen."

"You were always way better at math than I am, and that computer stuff seems to be a whole lot of math."

"That's why I really think I will catch on quickly. It is mathematical algorithms, and I do like that stuff. If I thought women could make a good living in engineering, I would have taken that instead of business. Anyway, I wanted to ask if you were going home this weekend. Mom wants to have a birthday party for dad, and she asked me to see if you would be there."

"Of course, I'll be there. I have no other plans. Can I catch a ride back with you; the bus is really a pain."

"Sure, I'll see you Friday around six outside of your dorm."

"Sounds good, Sarah; see you then."

The week went by as expected. The lectures were easier to follow now that Emily had a year of listening to them under her belt. She also had perfected her note-taking skills. The year was just starting, but she felt more comfortable and confident in her ability. She was also less awkward socially, and some of her freshman friends were back.

"Hey Romulan," Bobby Baxter caught up with her as she left her last lecture. "So, what are you up to tonight? I was thinking we could go to Hank's Bar for a beer. Paul is going to be there, and he said he knows someone that hangs with Barracuda. We may be able to score some tickets to their Detroit concert."

"Oh, Bobby, I'd love to, but I can't. It's my dad's birthday, and I really have to go back to Romulus for the party. I hope Paul can get you a ticket."

"Do you want me to see if I can get you one? You can pay me back later."

"I'd love to see them, but I think I better hold on to my money for now."

"Okay, return to your home world, but you owe me a night out."

"You got it, Bobby; I'll see you next week."

A few minutes later, Sarah pulled up in her 1968 Chevy Impala. Emily got in and said, "I can't wait until I have one of these."

Sarah started pulling away, and she said, "You know the deal. Mom and dad paid for college as long as we didn't need any other big-ticket items. This car represents three years of summer jobs. Now I can barely keep gas in it. Sometimes it gets gas instead of me getting food."

"That's one way to keep your girlish figure."

"Well, it's no fun trying to write lines of computer code when your stomach is growling."

Romulus, Michigan, was halfway between Ann Arbor and Detroit. It was less than an hour's drive from campus across the Edsel Ford Freeway. They arrived at the Hicks homestead just before seven, and their mom Shelly had their dinner waiting for them.

She hugged them as they came in the door, saying, "How are my two college girls?"

Sarah answered for both of them, "We're fine, mom."

Emily added, "And starving."

After a week of grabbing food when they could, the young ladies dove into mom's pot roast like lions on a downed zebra. Shelly tried to start the conversation, but the girls kept their mouths full of food.

Henry Hicks came in and kissed each of his girls on top of the head, and they continued to eat. He sat down, and Shelly brought in his dish and hers.

The girls came up for air long enough to say hello to their father. Henry laughed and said, "Keep eating; you are both too skinny. I think your mom better start driving your meals to Ann Arbor before you two fade away. When you need a breath, tell me what's going on."

Finally, Emily was ready to talk. She said, "I got on the school newspaper."

"That's great," Henry said, "that should help you with your journalism classes."

"I'm sure it will, but I want more than that from my work there."

Shelly asked, "What more do you expect, dear?"

"I expect to get my byline on some big stories and have something to show people when I head out in the world."

"Now that is forward-thinking," Henry said, "good for you."

"Yeah, that's great, but being the new one on the paper, I am assigned to fact and grammar checking."

"Well, that makes sense," Henry said, "someone has to do it, and you're on the bottom of the totem pole."

"I know it does, but I can't wait to be assigned a story. You know newspapers or magazines are not going to be chomping at the bit to hire a woman reporter. I'll need a knockout resume from the start, and I have three years to get it. I can't wait."

Shelly said, "Well, I'm afraid that you will have to, dear. Just study hard, and I'm sure you will be successful."

Henry let that be the final word on that subject and turned to Sarah, "How about you? Are you getting the hang of that computer stuff? I wish I had one of those things at the store. I swear our bookkeeper failed second-grade arithmetic."

Sarah smiled and said, "It is going great, dad. I am beginning to write in COLBOL, and I see how it works. I like this course a lot more than I liked my business courses."

"That's good," Henry said, "you got A's in those courses, so this one should be a breeze."

Shelly brought in the dessert, and the girls once again dove into the food.

Later the girls sat on the bed in Sarah's room in their pajamas and talked about boys and more about their plans. Emily said, "There's a guy in my journalism classes named Bobby. I know he likes me, and I'm going to go out with him."

"That's great," Sarah cheered, "what's he like?"

"Oh, he's a great guy. He's really nice. He wanted to try to get me tickets to the Barracuda concert in Detroit, but I told him no. I didn't want to spend what little money I had left on a concert ticket."

The name of the band sparked a memory of something that Sarah had just heard, and she told Emily, "I heard that Mickey Hardstone may be leaving the band."

Emily was shocked, "Mickey is leaving the band? Where did you get that? I hadn't heard about that."

"Nobody's talking about it."

"Then how do you know?"

"Do you remember Betty Rother? She was my best friend in high school. Well, I've kept in touch with her, and she told me."

"How did she know?"

"Well, Betty got a little crazy for rock bands. She has become, well, I guess the best way to describe it is that she has become a professional groupie with Barracuda. She's right in with the band. She said something was going on with Mickey. Now, I said he might be leaving."

"I want more. This can be my first big story. What else can Betty tell you?"

"I don't know. She was in Denver with the band, but I think she was planning to come home and drive from here to their concert in Chicago."

"Is she going to be home this weekend?"

"Yeah, I'm going to have lunch with her tomorrow."

"I want to go. I need to know what she knows."

"I thought you wouldn't be into entertainment-type news; that's not what Barbara Walters does."

"I have to start somewhere, and this would be big on campus."

"Okay, then we'll see her tomorrow."

Emily had a hard time sleeping. Her mind was racing. This was the first time she would essentially be interviewing someone for the purpose of getting a story. She would need what Betty knows and the name of someone that could corroborate her story.

They met Betty at the food court in the mall. They got their food and sat down. Emily let the two friends chat for a few minutes, and then it was Sarah that got the ball rolling, "Emily has landed a place in the U of M newspaper, and she is really interested in what you know about Barracuda. They're really hot now, and they are really big on campus."

"Well, they are hot," then Betty smiled and said, "in more ways than one."

"Okay," Sarah said, "this is a school newspaper. Let's keep the rating better than R. Emily wants to practice her interview skills, so let her ask you questions like you're a witness or something."

"Sure. Okay, Emily, fire away."

Emily got out her notepad and started, "How long have you been with the band?"

"It has been a little over a year. I went to their concert in Omaha, and I caught Don's eye. It wasn't hard. If you have a reasonable body, you can catch Don's eye. Anyway, he invited me backstage, and I have been hanging out there ever since."

"Can you tell me a little about the members of the band?"

"Well, they're all from the same town in Virginia. They've been together since high school. Mickey Hardstone is the leader of the band. He keeps them together, and he is the one with the business sense. The girls love him. When he flashes those pale blue eyes at you, you will melt; trust me. His rugged good looks and his styled blonde hair make him look like a model. He isn't into the long hippie hair. He works on his hair more than I do. He likes the girls and the booze; scotch is his favorite, but his real love is money and how to make it. He's always working on one scheme or another.

Ryan Witowski is like Jekyll and Hyde sometimes. He is all personality on stage. He doesn't just sit back in the dark, keeping a beat. He insists that there are lights on him, even if they make him sweat like crazy. He does his drumming, sitting, standing, and sometimes dancing. They claim Rick does the stage antics. He doesn't do any more than Ryan. The off-stage Ryan is quite different. He is generally miserable and complains about one thing or another. The place is too hot, or the place is too cold, or they didn't bring in the right kind of snacks. He doesn't seem to be happy unless he is complaining about something. His shaggy red hair and deep blue eyes tend to make him look like someone that should be angry."

Betty paused and then said, "Don Foster has magic fingers."

Sarah interrupted Betty's lecture, "Keep it clean, Betty."

Emily complained, "Sarah, you're treating me like I'm ten years old. I know what sex is, and I don't blush that easily."

Betty smiled and continued, "As I was saying. Don has magic fingers. I have never seen a person that could zoom over a keyboard the way he does and hit every note and chord perfectly. He is amazing. Off stage, he keeps all of the ladies very busy. How should I say this without ruffling anyone's sensitivities?"

Emily spoke up, "You won't ruffle mine."

Betty continued again, "Don loves to be a lover. He loves women, all women, and he intends to dedicate his life to making love to as many women as he can. He wants to sleep with a thousand different women before he's forty."

Sarah was annoyed, "Shall we do the math on that? Foster is what, about 27? That gives him about thirteen years to sleep with a thousand women. There are less than five thousand nights in thirteen years. He would have to sleep with a new woman every five nights. If it was just sleeping with a woman, I could see it, but sleeping with a thousand different women, that's not going to happen."

Betty just smiled and said, "Well, he is surely having fun trying, and he seems to have a lot of candidates. He is a darn good-looking guy, and being six foot, three does attract the girls.

Rick Santora is the loose cannon of the band. You never know what he is going to do on stage or off. He is the long stringy hair, tie-dyed hippie of the group. Sometimes I wonder if he ever washes his hair at all. It's always just hanging there, looking greasy. His brown eyes might have been pretty if they weren't red all of the time. The guy is a one hundred percent druggie. He will drink, smoke, or take anything, and he does it on a regular basis. I don't know how he keeps himself together to perform, but he does. Once on stage, he is a dynamo of energy, jumping around and swinging his bass guitar in the air. He and Mickey somehow synchronize and put on quite a show.

Then there is Freddie. Freddie MacArthur is definitely the musical brains of the group. He writes most of their songs, and he runs the practices. His lead guitar work is the best in the business; I don't care what they say about people like Ritchie Blackmore or Jimmy Page. Those Brits have nothing on him.

Freddie is also the healthiest member of the band. His black hair is quite thin, and he generally has it in a ponytail. His hazel eyes rival Mickey's in their ability to look right through you. He also has some muscle to him. He's not skinny like the other guys. That's probably because he doesn't hit the booze and the drugs like the other guys. He will do his share of drinking and carousing, but sometimes he is just as happy sitting in his hotel room working on his music. He will write a bunch of pages and then have someone make him copies on a mimeograph machine, and then he would mail the copies to his mother. That's how important his writing is to him. I would say if there was a member of Barracuda that was the marrying kind, it would be Freddie."

Emily was impressed, "Well, thanks for that. That was quite a detailed description of the boys. Now I want to get to why I'm really here. Sarah said you mentioned that Mickey Hardstone was going to leave the band."

Betty got a bit defensive, "I didn't say he was going to leave. I said it looked like he was thinking about it. After their last concert, a new guy showed up. Mickey gave him the pass to hang around with the band. He is definitely an agent or someone that acts like an agent, and he isn't the one the band normally uses. I know this guy is making the other guys nervous. I definitely know that he is making Don nervous. Don is the one worried that this guy is trying to convince Mickey to go out on his own. That's where I got the idea from."

"Then you don't know for sure."

"I don't know anything for sure, and I think I might have said too much already. You go quoting me saying stuff like that, and I will find my ass thrown out. I'll end up being just another fan in the audience again."

"I won't do that. You haven't said anything definite, so I wouldn't quote you. I also would like at least one more source before I make any statements."

"Well, don't hold your breath on that. I can give you the names of some of the other girls and even the names of some of the roadies, but none are going to risk their position to give you a story."

Emily was disappointed, but she said, "I understand. You have given me some great stuff, and I'm sure I can use it. Thanks for helping me out."

"Not at all. I remember back in high school. You used to want to tag along with us. We had to find clever ways to ditch you."

"And you did, every time."

"Yeah, I guess we did, but you have grown, and now you're ready to tackle the world. Well, I've got things to do before I make my way to Chicago. The boys will be there on Thursday. They like getting in a few days before a concert. They like to get a hold of their new Barracuda's and cruise around town before they get down to business."

"Their what," Emily asked.

"Their new Plymouth Barracudas. They each have one rented and available when they get to town. It is kind of a signature move of theirs. They have their own colors. Mickey's is banana yellow; Ryan's is black, no surprise there; Don's is emerald green; Rick's is royal blue; and Freddie's is candy apple red. They also paint their initials on the rear bumper. The rental company doesn't mind. I'm sure they make a ton of money renting a Barracuda driven by a Barracuda. Anyway, I have to go."

Emily was disappointed. This wasn't a scoop. Most of what Betty told her could be found in fan magazines. There were a few tidbits that she could pass to Dereck, the entertainment section coordinator, but it certainly wasn't anything that would get her a byline. She would have to look somewhere else.

The sisters returned home after doing a little shopping. They had to get themselves ready for their father's birthday party. Their dad was celebrating his forty-fifth birthday, and mom had been cooking all day.

When evening came, the guests began to arrive. They would have a house full of friends and family. Many of their friends were people that worked for their father at his store in Detroit. Others were from the neighborhood.

There was plenty of eating and drinking, and there was a grand chorus of Happy Birthday. Henry was still quite fit, and he had no problem blowing out the candles. The music was mainly fifties do-wop and even some big band selections.

While moving around the party, Emily was stopped by her Uncle Bernie. He was her mother's older brother, and he never missed a chance to have his opinion known. He started, "Young lady, maybe you should consider changing your major. Why don't you take business like your sister? There are plenty of jobs in the retail industry for young ladies before they settle down and marry."

"Uncle Bernie, I have no interest in business. I want to be a journalist, and that's what I'm going to be."

"You shouldn't fill that pretty little head with ambitions that can't be realized. Women have no place in the newsroom unless they are delivering copy and coffee to the reporters."

"Barbara Walters is being quite successful in the newsroom. She is very accomplished, and she will be an anchor one day, and so will I."

"Barbara Walters is a disgrace to womanhood. She is taking a good job from a man who could be supporting his family. She won't be an anchor. They will get rid of her sooner or later. There is an order to things, and no woman should try to turn over the apple cart."

"Barbara Walters is a fine reporter and a brave woman. She will be an anchor, and she will turn over that apple cart. She has to because some of those apples are rotten. Now, please excuse me."

Emily walked away, fuming a bit, and then she heard her father behind her, "Stick to your guns, baby girl. You are the future, and he is just an old blowhard."

She turned around and hugged Henry, and said, "I love you, Daddy."

Sarah came by, and she turned to Emily and said, "We have to fight old boys like Uncle Bernie. I've found out that there is a chapter of the National Organization of Women on campus, and I heard that Betty Friedan herself would be stopping by later in the year. I'm going to join up, and I think you should also. I'm going to read her book, *The Feminine Mystique* before she arrives. They say that book started the new women's movement."

Emily was still staring at Uncle Bernie as she said, "You bet I want to go. Tell me when and where." Then she thought that the women's movement might be the story she was looking for.

Sunday was a lazy day. Emily didn't want to do anything but sit around the house eating party leftovers and watching old movies. In the middle of the afternoon, the phone rang. Her mother called to her, "Emily, it's for you."

Returning to her old teenage habits, Emily continued to watch the movie and called out, "Who is it?"

"I don't know. She just said that she had some information for you."

That got Emily's attention, and she jumped up and moved to the phone in the hall. She answered, and the voice said, "Hi, Emily; it's Betty. I wanted to make sure no one knew that I called. Your sister will probably hate me for this, and I would rather not feel her wrath until I have to."

"Why would she be angry? What more can you tell me?"

"It's not what I can tell you; it's what I can do for you. I can't get you more information, but I am pretty sure I can get you backstage for the Barracuda concert in Detroit. It would be a perfect setup for you. All you would have to do is play a groupie for two or three days, and you will be free to suck up as much information as you can. You probably know that Detroit is their last concert on their 'Wrecking Ball' tour. After that concert, they will all be heading home to Virginia for a while. The last place they will want groupies to show up will be in Virginia, so they would expect you to disappear the morning after the concert."

It sounded like a big break, but Emily was a little nervous about the whole groupie thing, "What exactly would I have to do as a groupie?"

"Emily, you said that you weren't that naive. Haven't you ever had a little fun with a guy?"

Emily looked around to make sure her mother wasn't in earshot. She answered honestly, "I'm not completely innocent. I have had some experience, but it was with my steady boyfriend at the time. We thought we were in love. I never did it just for fun."

"You may not have to now if you are clever enough. If you don't want to go along with the fun, then I suggest that you find some way to stay away from Don. In any case, think it over. I will be leaving for Chicago on Wednesday, and I need to know by then if I'm going to get you a pass for the Detroit concert."

"I will, Betty, and I appreciate you thinking of me. I will let you know before you go, I promise."

Emily hung up the phone and pondered the idea. She would be right in with the band. She could find out all kinds of inside information, but what would she be willing to do for it? If she wasn't willing to do what was needed to be done, would she be clever enough to avoid it for up to three days?

Sarah came down from upstairs and asked, "Who was on the phone."

Emily hated to lie, but she did, "Just a girl from school who wanted to tell me about a lecture that was rescheduled. Speaking of that, I better go over some of my notes; I should be getting a pop quiz soon."

Emily moved quickly up the stairs to her room. Sarah looked at the TV in the living room. She could tell that the movie wasn't nearly over, that made her wonder what Emily was up to.

Before the sisters knew it, they were back on campus, hitting the books. Both girls were blessed with almost photographic memories. They studied dutifully for tests, but as long as they listened to the lectures, it was hardly necessary.

Emily did pass on some of the information to Dereck, but she held some back. She was still pondering Betty's offer, and she wanted to keep the big story, just in case. She got points from the editor for the information, but he also gave her a little lecture, "Emily, this is a student newspaper. It isn't *Rolling Stone*. We publish articles about the students and life here at U of M. There can be stories of the outside world, but they would have to be something special, and they have to relate somehow to the school."

Emily acknowledged his point and proceeded to do her fact and grammar-checking work. She thought, "He wants something special. Well, maybe I can give him something special."

The next day Emily took time off from class to go with Sarah to sign up at the local chapter of the National Organization of Women. There was a woman there giving a talk about the choices women make and that sometimes it is the peer pressure from other women that make them cave in and give up their ideals. She finished by saying, "Women must have respect for themselves before they can expect men to respect them. If you do not want to be demeaned, do not allow yourself to be demeaned."

Emily thought of the speaker's words as she left the meeting. She told Sarah, "You know the lady was absolutely correct. We will do things that will undermine our own dignity to win favor or to be more popular, and it's wrong."

"You're damn right it is," Sarah said, and that's why, though Betty is still a friend, I can't accept the position she puts herself in just to be close to people that have found a little fame. It is demeaning, and frankly, it is embarrassing to other women."

Emily saw the connection, and now she was thinking of another angle for a story. The story should not be about the band. The status of a rock band like Barracuda was really irrelevant. What it should be about is how these women grovel at their feet. She could expose the world of the groupie and how they are treated. Now Emily was determined to go. She would find a way to keep them off of her until she had the story that she wanted.

That night she called Betty and told her that she wanted to go. Betty spent almost an hour on the phone explaining how things worked. To keep their place, they had to make at least one of the band members happy, and it was up to them to define the word happy. Emily planned to keep moving and hoped each member thought she was spoken for by another member. If that failed, she would choose the one that was less repulsive and give him a little test. She would accept his advances, but when they were in his room, she would ask him what he thought of her. That should be a major turn-off, and he would do one of two things. He would either attack her to get what he wanted or he would throw her out and find someone more fun-loving. She was hoping for the latter, but she planned to bring something along in case he chose the former.

This would be an expose on rock stars and their treatment of women. It will also focus on what some women will do for a little fame. She knew the Michigan Daily might refuse to publish it. She also knew if it was published, that she could end up getting a lot of hate mail, but she felt it was something she had to do.

Chapter 2: Barracuda

The band Barracuda was zooming up the charts. Their album, "Wrecking Ball," was the most talked about album in the business, and their single, "She's Got the Devil in Her," just hit number one on the charts. Freddie MacArthur was Barracuda's lead guitar player, and his skill had gotten noticed. He was being compared to Hendrix and Clapton.

It was the night of the Chicago concert. The band, the roadies, and the groupies were all backstage relaxing. Mickey brought in a copy of the latest *Rolling Stone* magazine with Barracuda on the cover. Everyone gathered around to look at the article written about the band. There was a paragraph about Mickey and his talent and one about Freddie and his guitar work. They called Freddie the maestro of the screaming guitar. Don and Ryan also got a few lines. Rick was mentioned almost in passing in a single line, and they misspelled his name.

Rick stared at the article in disbelief. It was like he didn't matter at all. It was his energy on stage, not to mention his solid bass work, that made the band work. What really got him was that no one looking at the article protested. No one else saw how he was treated, or maybe they just didn't care. Rick was angry, but he tried to hold it in, but Rick was never good at that. He wandered away, unnoticed by everyone. He went to the one place where he always found pleasure. He went to his stash of cocaine hidden in one of the trunks. He fired himself up, and he was more than ready for the concert. He would show them. He would show them on stage.

The warm-up band finished its set, and it was time for Barracuda to take the stage. They held back just a minute longer, listening to the crowd chant their name. Mickey smiled at the boys and then led them to the stage. The crowd roared as soon as they appeared. They hooked up and went right into a high-energy tune called "Rabble Rouser."

Rick hammered on his bass and jumped in the air to the delight of the crowd. He and Mickey played off each other like they always did, and then Rick flew off on his own. Mickey stared for a moment and then turned back to the crowd to get their attention. The crowd turned to him, and Rick settled down.

During their one ballad, "A Dark Night for Walking," Rick seemed to have completely calmed down, and Mickey released a mental sigh of relief. When it was over, Mickey talked to the crowd giving them the standard lines about how great it was to be in Chicago and that it was one of their favorite places to play. They played several more tunes from the "Wrecking Ball" album, and Rick seemed to be fine.

Then Ryan cracked his drumsticks together three times, and the band fired into their number one hit. "She's Got the Devil in Her." The crowd came to their feet, and the energy was electric. This fired up Rick again, and he began to dance around. He was in a full cocaine buzz and began to stumble around, nearly knocking over amplifiers and microphones. The crowd started to laugh at him, and that only made things worse.

Rick bounced close enough to Don for him to say in his ear, "Settle down, drug boy, or I swear to God I will cripple you when this concert is over."

That did bring Rick down a notch, and that was enough to get them through the concert without a disaster. They finished their sets and did two encores, and they were off.

Rick stumbled off the stage, and Don grabbed him as soon as they were clear of the public, "What is your problem, man? We're on top, and you're trying your best to screw it up."

"Get off me, you big prick. The concert is done. Go back to your harem and leave me alone."

Don brought back his arm, but Freddie was standing nearby, and he stopped him, "Don, he's wasted. He probably wouldn't feel the punch until tomorrow, and then he'd wonder why his jaw was so sore."

Don let Rick go, and he stumbled away. He turned to Freddie and said, "Then we better get some goddamn control over him, or he is going to screw us out of the best thing of our lives. It has happened to other bands, and it can damn well happen to us. Where the hell is our fearless leader? He wants to be the boss so bad; why isn't he here to fix this?"

They looked around, and Mickey was nowhere to be found. "Where the hell do you think he is?" Ryan stepped into the conversation. "He's off in a corner somewhere with his new best buddy. He's getting ready to screw us; I know he is."

Freddie tried to calm the guys down, "Look, I will find Rick and see what has wound him up this time. Tomorrow we all need to have a talk with Mickey. He can't keep this up. Tonight let's try to bring it down a bit. We have one more concert on this tour, and then we can go home and relax for a while. I'm sure if we can get Rick through Detroit, he will have time to get straight before we're needed in the studio. We'll find Mickey tomorrow; does that sound good?"

Don and Ryan grumbled an agreement, and they started moving to the limo for the trip to the hotel. As Don was walking, Betty slid up to him. He put his arm around her and says, "Old Betty Eveready, you are just the person one wants to see tonight. I need a lot of tender loving care, and I know you can provide it."

"I sure can, baby, and I have more good news for you. I have a new girl for your collection."

"Really, is she young and pretty?"

"That she is. She's a nineteen-year-old college sophomore, and she is dying to meet you."

"Well, now, bring her along. The more, the merrier."

"She's not here now, Donny; she'll be in Detroit, but she will need a backstage pass."

"No problem, sugar."

Don called to Roger Mendez, their chief roadie, and said, "Hey Roger, give sweet cheeks here an extra backstage pass for Detroit."

Don turned to Betty and said, "You go fetch the pass and meet me in the limo; I think it's time we stained that backseat a little."

"I'll be right there, baby."

Freddie was happy to see Rick in their limo, though he was really wasted. Freddie tried to talk to him, "Rick, you have to settle down. Just hang in there for one more concert, and then we can go home."

"Yeah, like you care. You proved you don't care; you all proved you don't care."

"Rick, you should get some rest."

That was all Freddie could get out of him. When they finally got to the hotel, Rick stumbled out of the limo, and Freddie followed. At that moment, a group of fans broke through the barrier and surrounded Freddie. He tried to look past them, trying to see where Rick went, but he was gone. Security finally arrived, and Freddie broke free, but Rick was nowhere to be found.

Rick was well out of control. He sat in a corner in a men's room, mumbling, "No one understands. No one cares. They all think I'm a loser. People laughed at me. Well, if they don't care, I don't care." He grabbed his cocaine stash, a bottle of whiskey, and he headed for his Plymouth Barracuda.

Freddie spent an hour looking for Rick, and when he couldn't find him, he decided that he had better get some professional help. He got to a pay phone and called Pete Chiles. Pete was their main security guy and fixer. He had gone back to the hotel when the concert was over, "Pete, Rick is really high, and he's gone. He's out in the city somewhere."

Pete asked, "Does he know anyone in town? Are there places that he would go?"

"No, he doesn't know Chicago at all. I have no idea where he would go. Pete, he's really high, and his Barracuda is gone. He could end up in jail or worse."

"His is the blue one, right?"

"Yeah."

"Okay, Freddie, I'm on it. Get everyone back to the hotel and make sure they stay there."

The first thing Pete did was step into his hotel room and call his old friend Gina, "Hey Gina baby, it's Pete Chiles; how have you been?"

"Pete, I haven't heard from you in a dog's age. I know it's not my good looks that made you call. Do you have someone that needs a place to rest?"

"Your looks always make me call, but yes, I think I will. Are you at the same place?"

"Yes, I am, but the rates have gone up since we last did business."

"That's no problem, baby; these people can pay. I'll let you know when to expect us. Oh, and have Doc Jenkins around; I think he will also be needed."

"Will do; see you soon."

Pete had a team of eight people for personal security for the band. He called them together and got them moving. He left Jack by the phone in the hotel room. All teams would check in with Jack every thirty minutes. Pete sent the others out in sets of two. One went with him, and the search was on.

At two in the morning, Rick roared through the streets of Chicago. The lights of the city were just a blur, and he turned onto Michigan Avenue. The roar of the Barracuda's engine echoed through the city. Rick was barely in control of the car. It swerved in and out of his lane and side-swiped a Toyota Corolla just before East 28th Street, sending its side mirror flying onto the sidewalk.

The changing traffic light at East 26th Street didn't slow him down at all. Then he saw her, a woman in the crosswalk, in the middle of the street. The look of horror on her face as the car's bright lights illuminated the last minute of her life. Rick could do nothing but stare as he felt the car strike the woman's body. He saw her bounce off the car, and he panicked. He hit the gas and roared away.

Without knowing how, Rick ended up on the side of the road at the end of East Roosevelt Street, down by the lake. He just hunched over the steering wheel and cried; the woman's face forever burned into his mind. The front seat of the car was a mess of cocaine and spilled whiskey. Rick looked like a tragic clown with tear trails running through the cocaine powder on his face. He passed out with his forehead on the steering wheel and the car idling.

Pete had his people roam the city looking for a brand new royal blue Plymouth Barracuda with the initials R.S. painted on the rear bumper. Pete and his partner were in the company van. They drove down Michigan Avenue and saw the police and an ambulance at the East 26th Street intersection. Pete slowed, rolled down his window, and asked a police officer what had happened.

"It's a hit and run. Someone laid into a woman and kept going. It didn't look like he even tried to stop."

"That's a shame. Do you have any idea who did it?"

"Nothing yet, but I think it was some whacked-out hippie partying after the concert at the International Amphitheater."

As they drove away, Pete told his partner, "I've got a bad feeling about this."

At 3:45 in the morning. Two of Pete's team saw the tail lights of the Barracuda at the end of East Roosevelt Street. They pulled up to the car and saw Rick passed out in the driver's seat.

One told the other, "Get out and see how he is; there is a phone booth back up at Michigan Avenue; I'll call Jack from there."

By four in the morning, Pete pulled up in the Van. He got out and asked, "How's he doing?"

The man answered, "We gave him the standard shots. He is stable for now, but a doctor better look at him soon."

"That's all setup. Get him in the van, and then start cleaning up this mess. We'll need to get the car to the body shop tonight. Find someone that will do it fast and keep their mouth shut."

The man was surprised, "You didn't look at the car. How did you know that the bumper was banged up and the light was out?"

"A cop up at Michigan and 26th told me, now get going."

Pete stopped at the phone booth at the Michigan corner and made three calls. First, he called Jack and told him to tell the other teams to return to the hotel. Next, he called Gina and told her that he was on his way and to have the doctor waiting. Then he called Freddie, "Freddie, your boy is in a bad way. I'm taking him to a place where he can rest and have a doctor look at him."

"That's great, Pete. I really appreciate this."

"Don't get too happy yet. The headaches of this stunt have just begun. I'll tell you the details when I see you, but you better call the record company. This is going to cost more than you guys can pull out of your pockets."

Daniel Murphy was the detective assigned to the hit-and-run case. He arrived at the scene at 3:30 in the morning. He looked at the position of the body and at the street. He asked the officer on the scene, "That's not where she was struck?"

"No sir, her purse was in the middle of the street, right in the crosswalk."

"And there are no skid marks at all?"

"No sir, the bastard didn't even try to stop. Detective, I'm sure it was some goddamn hippie roaming stoned out of his mind."

"You may be right; they have been advertising that Barracuda concert since the fourth of July. I'm sure there were plenty of stoned-out freaks on the streets tonight."

It had been five years since the 1968 Democratic Convention and the riots. The Chicago Police were slammed by the press for trying to keep order, and not all of them had gotten over the bitterness.

Daniel Murphy looked at the woman and asked the officer, "Who was she?"

"Sheila Ferretti, she was a nurse at Mercy Hospital. She must have just finished her shift and was crossing the street to get to the bus stop."

"And the bastard just ran her down. I want this person. That car must have been hauling ass to have knocked her so far from the crosswalk; that means it didn't leave the scene undamaged. We have to look around; there must be debris from the car right here under our noses. Then we need to check every body shop in town. Whoever did this will not want that car on the street in that condition.

This crime will not go unsolved. If the person we catch is a long-haired freak, he is going to try to escape, and I'm going to have to use excessive physical force to restrain him."

"Hit him once for me, detective."

Pete met Freddie back at the hotel. Mickey and the rest of the band were with him. Pete explained, "You guys have some real trouble on your hands. It looks like Rick got himself completely wasted and ran over some lady over by the hospital on Michigan Avenue. I've got him in a safe place, and he's being treated. The car is being cleaned up and fixed. This is all going to cost a bundle. As I told you before, Freddie, you need to call the record company."

Mickey complained, "How the hell did this happen? You know how Rick gets; wasn't anyone keeping an eye on him?"

Don got right in his face, "We were trying to deal with it, but where were you? Were you in your hotel room cozying up to your new boyfriend?"

Mickey came to his feet, and Don just sneered, "Go ahead, take a swing."

Freddie had to be the peacemaker one more time, "Settle down, guys. We have a mess here that we have to deal with. Mickey, when this is over, we need to talk. Right now, we have to see how Rick is doing and find out what happened to the woman."

Pete said, "I'm afraid she's dead. I passed the scene. They weren't treating her; they were examining her body. This is hit and run and vehicular homicide. Rick didn't even try to stop. If they catch him, he'll never see the light of day. As I said, we can clean him and the car up. There will be no physical evidence to tie him to the crime, but I'm going to need cash and a lot of it."

Mickey said, "We'll get you the cash first thing in the morning."

"Can we do this?" Freddie asked, "Can we cover up a murder?"

"We have to," Ryan said, "Rick is a pain in the ass, but I don't want to see him in prison for the rest of his life. It's not murder; he didn't mean to kill the woman."

Freddie agreed, "Yeah, I don't want to see him in jail either."

Don added, "Locking him up won't bring the woman back, and it isn't just Rick that will be screwed; it will be all of us. I don't know if our rep will survive a hit and run."

"Okay," Freddie said, "I get it. We'll get you the money, Pete."

"That's not all that we need. We need an alibi for Rick. One of you has to swear that Rick was with you tonight. We have to cover all of the angles. If someone asks, we need to be sure that we have an answer."

"That would be odd, wouldn't it," Ryan asked, "that after a gig, two of the band members would wander off together. Everyone knows that after a gig, it's party time. We are either together or off having fun with some of the groupies. Wouldn't it be better if a groupie said that she was with him?"

"Do you want to risk your futures on the word of a groupie?"

No one answered, and Pete continued, "In fact, no one else should know about this. Freddie, I think you are going to have to come up with an alibi for Rick. I know you have been looking for him, so you are the only one that wasn't involved with anyone but the band and my team. The rest have been with people that we don't want to involve in this. Freddie, I think it's up to you."

"What am I going to say? Everyone knows that Rick and I are friends, but we have completely different interests. We don't spend a lot of time together."

"Think of something. You must have a common interest that would be believable in this context."

Don called out, "Gambling; I know you and Rick like to play cards on occasion."

Freddie said, "Play cards after a concert; that isn't very believable."

"You'll have to sell it," Pete said.

Ryan added, "Freddie, remember you owe Rick. He gave you an alibi when that woman accused you of rape last year."

"I never met that bitch."

"Yeah, but you needed an alibi for that night, and Rick gave you one. It's time to return the favor."

"Okay, but how would I know about any card games around here?"

Pete said, "I'll take care of that. I'll find a game, and I'll even get some of them to swear that you played."

Freddie looked confused, shrugged his shoulders, then asked, "Then what do you need me for?"

"For realism Freddie, Rick would not have wandered out and found a game by himself. This will work. I will get you the details."

Mickey said, "I guess I better contact the promoters and cancel the Detroit gig."

Pete put his hands up and said, "Whoa, you can't do that. If you cancel, you will have to explain why. If you say that Rick had taken ill, that will arouse suspicion that he had a problem on the night that woman was killed. Chicago detectives are pretty damn smart. You don't want anything to lead them to you. You have to leave Chicago on schedule and arrive in Detroit on schedule.

We will have Rick fixed up in a few days, and we'll get him to Detroit. He will be ready for the concert. Okay, that's enough for one night. Just get that money to me; the people I deal with don't take credit cards."

Freddie didn't like this at all. He wasn't a good liar, and he hated to be part of covering up a crime, but this was Rick. He knew Rick when he was a chubby eighth grader with plans of being an astronaut. They've been through a lot together, but where did he go wrong? When was reality not enough for him? Freddie couldn't put his finger on when it happened, and that made him realize that he hadn't paid much attention to his friend. Then he thought, "Maybe no one had. Still, a woman died crossing the street, and he was going to see that the person responsible got away with it. He wouldn't sleep at all on that night."

No one gets up early the day after a concert. People began dragging themselves out of their hotel rooms just after noon. Betty walked with Patty out of the hotel. She asked her, "Was Rick as weird as Don was last night? Don disappeared for a while, and when he came back, all he wanted to do was sleep. Jenny was with me, and we were both ready to play, but he just said he was tired. I have never seen Don turn down a roll in the hay, especially not from two girls."

"Betty, I can't tell you about Rick because I never saw him. I waited in the room, but he never showed up. I think he must have gotten wasted and wandered off somewhere."

Betty thought, "Old Rick must have really screwed up this time."

When they got to the bus, Betty started to get on, and Don said, "Where the hell do you think you're going?"

"Come on, Don; you're heading to Detroit. You'll be going right past my hometown on the Edsel Ford Freeway. You can just drop me on the side of the road."

"Not this time, baby. We have business to discuss."

"Oh, come on, Donny, I can sit on your lap, and we can talk about the first thing that pops up."

"I said no. Now get your ass out of here."

"Well, aren't you being a buzz kill this morning. Maybe it's because nothing killed Rick's buzz last night."

Don grabbed her and growled, "Look, you little slut, we have business. We don't have time to give your cheap ass something to do. Now get out of here and find something to do with your clothes on for a change."

Don pushed her away, saying, "Go on, get lost, and don't show up in Detroit until Friday; maybe I'll be ready for you then."

Betty was upset as she tried to pull herself together. As she started walking away, Freddie stopped her, "Hey Betty, don't take it personally. We have a problem that we have to work out, and we have to do it alone."

Betty was now crying. She said, "I thought he liked me. I'm not talking about love or anything, but I at least thought he liked me."

"He does, Betty. I know he does. Look, here are a couple of hundred bucks. Buy yourself something nice and catch a bus home. We'll see you before the concert. Everything will be fine then; you'll see."

Betty took the money and said, "Thanks, Freddie. You are special; all the girls say so."

Freddie smiled a bit and said, "Tell them to stop by before we leave, and we'll see that they are taken care of also."

When Betty walked away, Pete caught up to Freddie. Freddie asked, "Are you going to get your money?"

"Yeah, the record company is wiring it to my account; everything will be taken care of. That was a damn smart move stopping Betty like that. The last thing we want is some pissed-off groupie running her mouth all over the place. There was no way to stop them from finding out that Rick wasn't around last night, but we don't want them spreading the story all over the country."

Pete joined the band on the bus, and they were on their way. Mickey announced, "The money will be transferred today, and it's coming right out of our royalties. We can't keep doing this. After this tour, changes are going to be made. Rick isn't even that great of a bass player; we can dig up a session guy that plays twice as good."

Freddie was surprised, "You want to throw Rick out of the band? We started this band in his basement, for Christ sake."

"I'm sorry, Freddie, but when we get to this level, the band is a business, and he is costing us money. He damn near cost us the whole thing. We just can't risk losing it all because of him."

Ryan spoke up, "If it was just the money, I wouldn't think of it, but he's getting too dangerous to have around. We all may pay for his problem sooner or later."

Don said, "Rick needs to get out, and he needs to get help. We don't have to abandon him, but I think he needs to get away from this life before it kills him."

"Or us," Mickey added.

Pete cautioned, thinking of his conversation with Freddie, "This is a tough time for everyone, but we have to be careful how we react. It was the right move making sure no outsiders were on the bus on this trip, but we have to be careful how we treat the groupies and the roadies. They know a lot more than we think they do, and we don't want any rumors starting."

Don scoffed, "They know when they have it good. They're not going to say anything to ruin the free ride we're giving them. They know they can be easily replaced."

Freddie couldn't think like that, "Don, they are people. Sure, they're taking advantage of our success, but we are taking advantage of them, also. They are paying for their ride, and they shouldn't be abused."

"Well, Freddie, the humanitarian. You were always the bleeding heart. Fine, you can be all nice to them, and I'll just screw them."

Pete took back the conversation, "Rick should join us on Thursday. He will be fixed up, but his problems aren't over. He is seriously addicted, and I agree with Don. He needs real help. I am having Doc Jenkins come along with him, just in case.

After the tour is over, he needs to check into a hospital somewhere and go through withdrawal. That won't be easy, but it's the only way that you will be able to trust him as part of the band. Getting him through Detroit will be hard enough."

Freddie turned to look at Mickey, "Speaking of after the tour, are you sure you plan to be in the studio with us after we take a break?"

"Yeah," Don jumped in. He had been waiting to have it out with Mickey on this subject for several days, "What is that agent, or whatever he is, offering you, and are you going to take it?"

Mickey knew this was coming, and he tried to explain, "Danny is just giving me some options for the future. There may come a point in the future when I may want to try something on my own, but that is in the future."

Don didn't like that answer, "So what are we supposed to do, sit around hoping that one day you won't flush us all down the toilet? We agreed back in Rick's basement that we would stay together forever."

"That was when we were kids. This is big money now, and we all need to treat it like a business."

Ryan grumbled, "Now I can see why it is so easy for you to drop Rick; he is only the first one of us you plan to drop. Maybe we need to have this out after Detroit. I say we get one of the lawyer types to draw up a contract that legally keeps this band together."

"I won't be shackled to this one kind of music and to this band forever. I have other things I want to do, other songs I want to sing. We all need to grow, and I will not be held back by a piece of paper. I won't sign anything, and if that ends the band, so be it."

Don spit out, "You selfish little bastard."

"Now wait," Once again, Freddie tried to bring some common sense to an argument. "I have had some of the feelings that Mickey has. We can't force each other to do only what is good for the band. How about this? We can take a little longer getting our next album out. Mickey, you can take the extra time to record some single tracks for an album of your own. I'll even help you write the songs. You can have it both ways, and we can keep the band together."

"There will have to be a contract about that," Ryan said.

Freddie asked Mickey, "How about it, Mickey, would you sign a contract that gives you the freedom to record on your own but still requires you to record and tour with the band?"

"Yes, I would. That's all I want is to be free to sing what I want to sing."

"Good," Freddie said, "Now I'm sick of all this serious bullshit. I'm going to take a nap."

Pete let Freddie rest for a while, and then he had another subject to talk about, "Freddie, I got a call before I left. A friend of mine has located a card game that plays in the basement of an Irish pub less than a mile from the hotel.

Freddie just said, "Great."

Pete finished by saying. "I'm going to rent a car when we get to Detroit, and I'm driving back to Chicago. I'm keeping the same room for a couple of days at the hotel. Give me a call on Tuesday, and I should have some real details for you."

Daniel Murphy was at his desk in the squad room when he looked up to see his partner, Steve Anderson. Steve had just returned from his vacation, "Well, partner, did you have a good time."

"Yeah, the wife and the kids love going to the farm in Indiana. It was a great change from the noise of the city. I slept like a baby. Her brother is a good guy, and we always have a great time there. Hey, I hear we caught a hit and run."

"Yep, right on Michigan Avenue. From what we collected last night, it looks like the car involved is missing a headlight, at least. The pieces that were found are being pieced together. We're hoping that we have enough to give us some information about the car."

As he was talking, an officer stepped to his desk and handed him a report. Daniel continued the conversation, "Okay, this is a preliminary report on the headlight pieces. It looks like there was enough to tell us the car is Mopar, probably a Plymouth or a Dodge, and it is a car, not a pickup truck or anything else."

"That's a start, I guess. That still leaves us with a lot of ground to cover. What about body shops?"

"They're being checked. I hope the guy wasn't smart enough to drive it out of state."

At that point, the officer from the scene appears, "Detective, we've caught a break. It isn't a big break, but it's a break. While we were checking the auto body shops, one shop owner told us that a guy came in first thing this morning. The driver's side of his car was dented and scraped, and the mirror was torn off. The man said that his car was sideswiped during the night. And get this; the car was parked on Michigan Avenue two blocks from the crime scene."

Dan got to his feet and told the officer, "Make sure no one touches that car; it is evidence is a police investigation."

"That's already been done, sir."

"Good job lad; I won't forget this."

The young officer just smiled as the two detectives rushed out of the squad room.

Detectives Murphy and Anderson inspected the damaged car. Steve said, "Who buys these cheap Japanese cars anyway. We shouldn't let them in the country."

The major clue they were seeing was sparkling blue paint streaked on the red Toyota. Daniel said, "That is a mighty fancy shade of blue. I don't think you will find that on many Dodges or Plymouths."

The owner of the shop heard the statement and said, "That looks like the new super royal blue. It just became available this year. If I remember right, it is only on muscle cars like the Charger, the Roadrunner, and the Barracuda."

Daniel looked at Steve and said, "Now we're getting somewhere."

Chapter 3: Detroit

Betty returned home and spent Sunday and Monday fuming over the way she was treated. She did appreciate what Freddie did for her, but she still couldn't forgive Don for how he made her feel. She thought Don liked her. She thought that she was somehow special. He now convinced her that, to him, she was no more important than a paper napkin. She was to be used and thrown away; well, Betty Ann Rother will not be thrown away that easily.

Emily had given her the number of her dorm, and on Tuesday evening, she called. After a minute of searching, Emily was found, and she picked up the phone. Betty said, "I got you a pass."

"That's great, Betty. I really appreciate this."

"I also may have a great story for you."

"Did you find out something about Mickey leaving the band?"

"No, this is about Rick. I think he got himself really wasted after the concert on Saturday. He wasn't at the hotel, and I bet he was at a hospital or something being worked on. I don't think he was even on the bus going to Detroit. The whole band was in a really pissy mood Sunday morning. Something happened, and it's all about Rick."

"Okay, that's good stuff."

"Emily, I want you to get these guys. I want you to tell everyone what they're really like."

"Has something happened?"

"Yeah, but I don't want to talk about it right now. Maybe I'll tell you on the way to Detroit. Can you be ready by noon on Friday?"

"Sure, I'll skip my Friday classes. There is a bus that will get me back to Romulus before noon."

"Don't tell Sarah, I know that she will freak out."

"I won't. We get so busy during the week that most of the time, we don't talk until Saturday. I'll get home, grab a few things that I want to take with me, and meet you at the food court at twelve-thirty."

The wheels were turning in Emily's head. She had come up with a way of getting some real information, but she had to know one thing first, "Betty, does security go through your bag before you go backstage?"

"They probably should, but they don't. One of these days some pissed-off groupie is going to show up with a gun and start shooting."

That's all Emily needed to know.

"Okay, and thanks again, Betty. I'll see you on Friday."

"That sounds good, Emily; I'll see you then."

Emily got into bed. She was so excited that she couldn't think of sleeping. Something happened to Betty. Something that could fit right into the kind of story she was hoping to write. The idea of playing along with the guys to get information was gone from her mind. She would not be anyone's plaything. She would have to be clever enough to keep their hands off of her until she got what she wanted.

Emily had a thought on her way to a lecture on Wednesday afternoon. She stopped at the National Organization of Women chapter and had a talk with Annie Shimko, the manager of the chapter, "Miss Shimko..."

"That's Ms. Shimko; unless I tell them, no one should assume my marital status. In most cases, my marital status would be irrelevant to the conversation."

"Ms. Shimko, I am Emily Hicks. I signed up last week. I am also on the staff of the Michigan Daily, and I am about to gather information for a story. The story is going to be about how the women that follow rock bands are treated. I know someone in that world, and

I believe she is being abused. That person has gotten me backstage with Barracuda for their Detroit concert. If I get the information I believe I will get, it can expose what is really going on and how those women are treated."

"That's great. I will look forward to reading about it, but what does that have to do with me?"

"The manager may refuse to publish the story. He is only looking for things happening on campus. That's not the way the paper used to be. If they refuse to publish it, I was wondering if you could help me get the truth out."

"You are a sophomore, aren't you?"

Emily nodded, and Annie Shimko made her point, "Are you sure the paper wouldn't publish it because of its content or would it be because you're a sophomore and sophomores don't write stories? I was on the paper myself for a year until I found better things to do."

"Does it matter? If I find proof that women in that world are being abused, would you help me get the story out?"

"It would have to be real abuse. I'm not interested in some twit that wants to waste her life playing patty cake with rock stars."

"This is more than that; I'm sure of it."

"If you bring back something real, I will consider working with you."

"Thank you, Ms. Shimko; I will get something."

On Thursday night, Pete brought Rick to the hotel in Detroit. He made sure that they got up to the band's rooms without being seen. Pete had cautioned them several times over the last few days about how they should act around Rick. They all got the message. He also told them something that was actually really good for them. Rick doesn't clearly remember what happened in Chicago, so, at least for now, he isn't very depressed over the whole thing.

Mickey stepped up and hugged Rick, and asked, "How are you doing, man?"

Rick's eyes were still a bit glassy, and his speech came out slow, "I don't know, man; it's all been a blur. I lost almost a whole week."

"That's okay," Freddie said, "you're back now, and we're going to rock the house tomorrow night."

"Yeah," Rick said with a slow-rising smile, "yeah, I want to do that."

"Okay," Mickey said, "let's get something to eat, and then you can relax a little."

Don said, "I'll call Patty. She's waiting for you in your room. Have something to eat, and then she'll take good care of you."

Pete got an irritated look on his face, but no one seemed to notice. The band was happy with the result, but Pete warned them that Rick was still very fragile.

Mickey said, "We'll keep him away from the booze and drugs."

An older man appeared and said, "You can't do that. You must control what he consumes, but he must have alcohol and cocaine. He has been stabilized. He is still addicted. Unless you want him to go through withdraw on stage, you must provide what his body needs until he can get to a proper treatment place. Just control how much he consumes. I will give you specific numbers on that."

Pete introduced the older man, "This is Doc Jenkins. He handles things like this. Take his advice."

Emily got up Friday morning, told her roommate that she would be gone for the weekend, and headed to the bus station.

Sarah had finished her one morning lecture, and she had to go across campus to her lecture that was scheduled for just after lunch. Sarah had to pass Emily's dorm, and she knew that she was free that time of day. She stopped by to see if she wanted to get some lunch. She knocked on the door of Emily's dorm room, and her roommate opened the door, "Oh, hi Sarah, Emily's not here."

"Did she go to lunch somewhere?"

"No, she got a call a couple days ago. Right after that she told me she was going to skip her Friday classes and go home. She said she had something going on. Didn't she tell you? I thought it was a family thing."

"She went home? Do you know who was calling?"

"Not for sure, but I thought I heard Emily call her Betty."

Sarah's eyes widened, but she held her temper and said, "Thanks, Olivia; I'll catch up with her and see what's going on."

Sarah was talking to herself out loud as she left the dorm, "If Betty is trying to make a groupie out of my little sister, I am going to seriously kick her ass." She ran back to her own dorm, jumped in her car, and raced toward the Edsel Ford Freeway.

Emily got home, and the first thing she did was grab her mother's big container of black pepper. She found a plastic bag and poured a quantity into the bag. This was going to be her body protection. Then she ran upstairs and changed into something a little more casual and more like a rock fan. She got together what she needed and put them in her large carpetbag-type shoulder bag. She brought a notepad, pens, and a new cassette tape recorder. That's what she really came home for. She had several tapes, and she planned to get some good recordings. She put the recorder in the bag and carefully taped the microphone at the top, just out of sight. She started down the stairs, but she was met halfway down by Sarah, "Where do you think you're going?"

"I'm going to get a story."

"You're going to Detroit, aren't you? Betty is getting you in to be with the band, isn't she? Emily, the girls that spend time with the band, are being used by them, and you know what I mean by being used. You are not going to put yourself in that position."

"That's my decision. I'm nineteen; I can make my own decisions."

"You're a kid, and I won't let you do this."

"Get out of my way."

"No."

Emily pleaded, "Please, I promise those guys will never touch me."

Sarah stared at her for a minute, and she said, "You better be home Sunday evening and back to class Monday morning, or there will be hell to pay. Where are you meeting Betty?"

"We're meeting at the food court at twelve-thirty."

"Okay, before you go anywhere, I'm going to have a few words with my old friend."

"Please don't get mad at Betty. I asked for help, and she is trying to help."

"You still don't understand. Betty has been my friend since grammar school. We have done a lot together, but we went in different directions. My best description for her lifestyle is that she is a free spirit. Others would describe her with much stronger words like whore, or prostitute. She sells her body to the band; that's the price she pays for their attention. She doesn't seem to mind now, but some day she will. Someday the endless party life will come crashing down, and she'll have nothing."

"I know, Sarah. That's exactly the story I want to write. I want to expose how these girls are lured into the endless party and, how they get hooked on drugs, alcohol, and sex, how they end up being toys for the band's pleasure. I'm not going to fall into that pit; I'm going to shine a light on it."

"And you think they will just let you do that?"

"They won't know it was done until they read about it."

"You're taking a hell of a risk."

"I can do it. Please, Sarah, this is what I've been looking for. It is also what we have been talking about. This is Uncle Bernie, only worse."

"Okay, you go, but if you're not back by Sunday evening, I going to Dad and then to the cops if I have to."

"I'll be back. I promise."

Betty spent her time Friday morning doing a little shopping. She was spending the cash that Freddie gave her and a little more of her own. She felt a bit guilty about using Freddie's cash but not guilty enough to stop her. She wasn't at the mall. She was visiting an old friend who dealt with just what she needed. She bought methamphetamine powder, the kind that can be mixed in with food. She had plans for the drugs, and they weren't for her. She tucked the powder in her purse and thought, "Now let's see what kind of fun this cheap ass can have with her clothes on."

When Betty got to the food court, she was surprised to see Sarah there with Emily. Sarah didn't give her a chance to speak, "Betty, I am going to trust my little sister's judgment on this, but if anything happens to her. If she ends up high or used, there won't be a rock big enough for you to hide under. Do you understand me?"

"I'll watch out for her, Sarah; I promise. Something happened that has changed my attitude. This is my last time being with the band. I want to help Emily get her story."

"What you do is your business; just get Emily back here safe." With that, Sarah left, still not happy with the situation.

They caught the bus to Detroit, and Betty told her a little about what happened to her on the trip. Emily asked, "So he grabbed you. Do you think he might have hit you?"

"I don't know. He was pretty mad, and I don't really know why. I must have struck a nerve when I mentioned Rick being buzzed out the night before."

"Rick must have caused some real trouble to have him so upset."

"It wasn't just him. All the girls said they were all miserable that morning. All but Freddie, he's always nice to us. He wasn't miserable, but he sure wasn't happy either. Something bad happened after the concert, and I'm sure that Rick caused it."

"I don't care what was on their minds. They have no right taking it out on women, especially not physically."

As soon as they got through security at the arena, Emily found a restroom. She was really happy that the pass got them through without having her oversized bag checked. In the stall, she did two things. First, she took out the tape recorder, put in a tape, and set it to record. She hoped the microphone would pick things up clearly from the top of the bag. Next, she pulled out the black pepper and poured some into her hand. She stared at it for a moment, and she counted to three. On three, she threw the pepper in her face. She quickly became flushed, her eyes got red, and she started to sneeze.

She came out, and Betty said, "What happened to you."

Emily smiled and said, "Instant illness. Now let's see who is eager to put their hands on me."

"Very clever; you're going to make a great investigative reporter."

Emily was on a mission, but it didn't stop her from becoming starstruck when she laid eyes on Mickey Hardstone. He was sitting at a small table drinking a beer. There was a blonde woman on one side and a brunette on the other, and neither was keeping the hands off of him.

Emily stared like she was a schoolgirl. Then she sneezed again, and they moved on.

Don Foster walked up, put his arms around Betty, and said, "Hey, Betty baby, I was in a weird mood on Sunday. I was just running my mouth. Everything is good now. What do you say that I show you how much I missed you with a nice mustache ride?"

Betty smiled and said, "Oh, you know how much I like that baby; I'm ready when you are."

Don looked past Betty and said, "Who is our new friend?"

"This is Emily; she is a friend of mine from my hometown. Don stepped around Betty and started to reach for Emily, and she sneezed in his face.

Don yelled, "What the hell?" That got Freddie's attention.

Emily started her act, "I'm so sorry. This cold just came up on me all of a sudden. I didn't know I had one; I promise."

Don growled, "And now you intend to make us all miserable."

Then he just called out, "Will someone throw Typhoid Mary out on the street before she infects the whole place."

Emily froze; she didn't expect that response. It looked like her clever move backfired in grand style. Betty tried to change his mind, "Don, sweetie, she'll take a pill and she'll be better in no time. She is a pretty young thing isn't she?"

"There are plenty of healthy, pretty young things around here. Get rid of her."

"Oh please," Emily pleaded. This is a dream of a lifetime. Please don't send me away."

Don just smirked, "Like I care."

Then Freddie's voice was heard, "Wait, Don, you can stay away from her. It's a cold. It's not like she has the plague."

Freddie stepped up and turned to Emily, and asked, "What was your name again, darling?"

Betty was right. One look into Freddie's hazel eyes, and she was entranced. She barely got out, "I'm Emily."

"Emily, I'm Freddie. Would you stay and be my date after the concert?"

Emily tried to keep control of her tongue, "I . . . I . . ., I'd love to."

"Good, just hang around here for now. The boys and I have to talk over a few things. We'll be back in a few minutes."

Don wasn't finished, "Oh, there goes old bleeding heart, Freddie."

Freddie looked at him and said, "Don, you can be dumb as a damn stone sometimes. Now there is something we need to go over before the show. We are meeting in the backroom over there, so let's go."

The girls watched them leave. Betty paid particular attention to Rick and where he set down his whisky bottle. Emily was also staring. She was watching Freddie walk away.

Finally, Emily said, "You're right. Freddie is different."

Then she asked Betty, "You're not forgiving Don that easy, are you? I mean, he didn't even apologize."

Betty smiled. She saw her chance to make her move. All she had to do was distract Emily just for a few minutes. First, she responded to Emily's question, "Oh, don't worry about me. Despite what it seems, I'm not that gullible. I think Rick needs a better drink."

Emily didn't quite know what to make of that response. Then she pointed to the tall slim black haired woman that appeared in the room, "Who's that?"

Betty smiled again. She had her distraction. She answered, "Oh, that's Patty Grundy. She is Rick's main squeeze. I bet she can tell you a lot about what's going on."

Betty called Patty over and introduced her to Emily. Then she excused herself to use the restroom. Patty said, "So you're from Romulus also."

"Yep, I'm a Romulan."

Patty laughed, and Emily said, "It is a great icebreaker when I meet people at U of M."

"You go to Michigan; that's a great school."

"It is, so how long have you known Rick Santora?"

"I've been Rickie's companion on the road for about four months. It's not exclusive or anything, but I'm the one that he can count on."

"How's he doing?"

"Why do you ask?"

"There were some rumors going around school saying he was a bit out of it during the concert in Chicago."

"He's fine."

"Oh, didn't mean to imply anything. It must be great spending so much time with him."

"It is, especially last night."

"Why was last night so special?"

"He was different last night. Normally he would want a quickie, hard and fast, and then he would drink some whiskey and do a few lines. In an hour, he'd want to do it again. After that, he would be too out of it to know that I was there."

"That didn't happen last night."

"No, he had some stuff, but he just wanted to cuddle. He didn't even want sex. He just wanted me to hold him. It was nice. It was really nice."

While Emily was busy, Betty moved over to the table and quickly snatched Rick's whiskey bottle and dropped the meth powder into it, and returned it. She moved away as quickly as she came. She thought, "Have a nice concert, boys."

In the backroom, Mickey was telling Rick, "Rick, we think it is best if we cut Rabble Rouser and Devil's Due from the playlist. We also think it may be better if you didn't move around on stage tonight. You've been sick, and we don't want to cause you any problems."

Rick was surprised, "Hey man, those are my two best songs. I have that great bass run in the middle of Devil's Due. That is the one time I can get noticed for my guitar work."

Freddie tried to help Mickey, "You can't push yourself right now."

Rick's entire demeanor changed, and he turned angry, "That's all bullshit. You don't care what state I'm in. You're trying to cut me out. You want me to disappear."

Mickey answered, "No, that's not it at all. We don't want a lot of pressure on you right now. You need to recover."

"Screw you, Hardstone. I know what you all think of me. You made it clear when that Rolling Stone article came out."

Now Ryan spoke up, "Rick, that was last week. We looked at the article together. No one said anything about you."

"That's right, Ryan; no one said anything. They had a whole paragraph talking about how great Mickey is. There was another paragraph calling Freddie the maestro of the screaming guitar. They had a few lines talking about Don's keyboard work and Ryan's drumming style, and what did they say about me? They said, and I quote, 'Richie is good at following Mickey's lead in their onstage antics.' That was it. Nothing about my guitar work, and they even got my goddamn name wrong. That pissed me off, but what really got me is that not one of you complained about that. Not one of you spoke up and said anything about it. Now I know why. You don't think I am any damn good. I guess you never have."

They almost said it in unison, "Rick, that's not true."

Then Mickey took over, "You're one of us. If we missed how much that article upset you, then we are really sorry."

"You still don't get it, Mickey. The problem is not how much the article upset me; it is that it didn't upset you at all. Nothing changes, goddamn it. If you want a change, you will have to throw me out of the band. Now I have a bottle of whiskey with my name on it."

Rick got up and left, and Freddie just said, "Oh shit."

Don said, "Man, I didn't think he would pussy out so much over one damn article."

The other three stared at him in disgust, and Freddie was the first to say it. Don, how did you end up being such an asshole? Not only are you an asshole, but you're also a stupid asshole."

"Screw you, MacArthur. If you want to give him a shoulder to cry on, be my guest. I'm sick of tending to him like he's a two-year-old."

"Just like you're not smart enough to treat the groupies with a little respect for one goddamn night. Pete told you to be careful around them. He said they know more than you think they do, and we shouldn't give them any reason to tell stories."

"Is that your excuse for being such a candy ass around them?"

"No, I'm a candy ass around them because of my upbringing. You come from an intelligent and a very civil family; what the hell happened to you?"

"I don't have to take this shit. I'll run the keyboard tonight and then will see what happens after that."

Mickey got back into it, "Calm down, Don. We'll get through this."

Don got up and said, "Yeah, we will, and then we'll see what happens." Then he left the room.

Friday was a busy day in the squad room. It was getting late in the afternoon. Daniel came in and found Steve reading the newspaper at his desk, "You don't have time at home to check your horoscope?"

"Angie just called. She said that I should check out the entertainment section and the story about the band Barracuda. I talk to my wife about our cases. I don't get into details, but sometimes I find it useful to bounce things off of her. She is really quite smart, and she has an eye for details. Sometimes she asks questions that I wouldn't think of asking. Anyway, she just called me up, and the story is rather interesting."

"Why is a story about a noisy rock band interesting?"

"Well, the rumor is that their bass guitar player, a guy named Rick Santora, got really high after their concert here in Chicago, and he had gone missing for a while."

"Really, what else did they gossip about?"

"The paper tried to get a quote from someone, and they were stopped by the band's head of security. Would you like to guess who that is?"

"It must be somebody we know."

"It is none other than Peter Chiles."

"He's the Philly ex-cop that went to the other side."

"Yep, the guy who was head of security for that big-shot banker when he was charged with raping a seventeen-year-old girl. All of the evidence amazingly disappeared, including the rape kit from the hospital. After that, Chiles was rumored to be a fixer, and he started his own business."

"Boy, I would really love to nail that bastard on something."

Then something flashed in Daniel's mind, "Wait, wait, my daughter told me something the other day about the band. She is always rattling on about one rock band or another, so I was only half listening.

Daniel got on the phone with his wife, "Amy was saying something about the band Barracuda the other day. Something about some crazy thing they do in every city they play in. What was it?"

"Daniel, she sat right there and told you. You need to pay more attention to your children."

"I will, I will, but what was she talking about?"

"She said that Barracuda has a set of brand new Plymouth Barracudas rented and waiting for them in every city they play. It's kind of a thing to make them stand out. I think it is a publicity stunt; they want people to notice them. Amy was also talking about the British bands like Deep Purple and . . ."

"That's great, dear; I'll talk to her about it when I get home. I'll see you then."

Daniel hung up the phone and said, "I love Liz dearly, but you can die of old age waiting for her to stop talking."

"What about the band?"

"Well, it seems to that the band rents brand new Plymouth Barracudas in every city they play."

"Well, now, things are getting interesting. Maybe that's why we struck out checking every registered new Charger, Roadrunner, and Barracuda in the state. I think it's time we contact Hertz, or maybe Avis is trying harder."

Steve had Avis on the phone, and the man was telling him, "They were shipped out."

"Why were they shipped out?"

"The company doesn't rent Plymouth Barracudas in every city. If the distance to the next city they play is short enough, we just have the cars driven to that city, and Detroit is an easy drive. I'm sure the band has them by now."

"Why would the company go to all that trouble just to rent five cars?"

"Are you kidding? They make a ton of money renting Barracuda's Barracudas to kids. It's a gold mine."

Steve hung up and told Daniel, "We need to take a trip to Detroit."

The detectives gathered information. They got a picture of Peter Chiles and a description of the van that he was driving in Chicago. Daniel said, "Okay, let's go."

"It's rush hour. We're not getting out of this town in a hurry. Why don't we call our wives and plan to be gone until tomorrow. We'll get some dinner and head out in an hour or so?"

"They'll be finished with their concert by the time we get there."

"You know those rockers. After the concert, they drink, get high, and screw their brains out until sunup. They have no idea we're on to them. We have plenty of time to get there."

"Okay, how about steaks and Joey's?"

"That sounds good to me."

Rick had drunk half of his bottle of whiskey before the band got back to the table. It was clear to everyone that the boys were not in a good mood, and everyone left them alone. Emily had just slipped into the restroom and put in a second tape in the recorder when things started happening at the band's table.

It was lucky for her that the girls wanted to be close as they could to the band. If the band had noticed how close they were sitting, they would have chased them away. Emily had her bag on the table when things started to happen.

Freddie went to Don, and Don growled, "Stay away from me, MacArthur, or we're going to have it out right here."

"Don, look, maybe we all have to grow up a little. Mickey is right when he says that we are now partners in a business. It's a business that is making us a hell of a lot of money. Besides that, Don, we've been friends since you let me cheat off you in Mr. Chamber's algebra class. We have some real problems. Can we just get past the shit from earlier?"

"You are the peacemaker, aren't you?"

"We have to keep this together, or it will all disappear."

Freddie reached out his hand and said, "Come on, do it for Mr. Chambers."

That made Don smile; he reached out his hand and said, "Okay, for Mr. Chambers."

As they shook hands Rick stood up and began to waver around. He said in a dazed voice, "Guys, something is happening to me," and then he collapsed.

Patty screamed, "Ricky," and she ran to him.

Freddie stopped her, "Patty, let us take care of him. We'll let you know how he's doing."

Mickey was calling for Doc Jenkins.

The doctor was there in a minute, and he examined him. He determined that he could be moved, and he was carried into the back room. In the confusion, Emily was able to slip away and drop her bag just outside the backroom door.

As the doctor examined him, Ryan asked Mickey, "How much of that stuff did you give him?"

"I gave him exactly what the doc told me to give him; don't try to pin this on me."

Freddie said, "Maybe we let him drink too much whiskey."

The doctor said, "This isn't whiskey or cocaine. This is something else."

Ryan questioned, "How could it be something else? How could he get something else; one of us was with him the whole time?"

Jenkins concluded, "Then someone else did it."

Mickey asked, "Are you saying he was dosed?"

"It's the only answer."

Don said, "The new girl. It must be her. She shows up, and Rick gets dosed."

Freddie said, "We'll check her out but don't start attacking her before we know something for sure."

Don looked at Freddie and said, "You keep defending that little piece of fluff. Do you have a thing for her or something?"

Mickey jumped in, "Freddie just wants you to stay calm. We don't want this to get any worse. Doc, can you get him on his feet for the show?"

"I think so, but the best I can promise is that he will be able to stand and hold his guitar, but after that, he needs to go to a hospital."

"Okay," Mickey took control, "we have about an hour before the warm-up band takes the stage. We need to rearrange the stage to have Rick away from the lights and propped up somehow. We are cutting Rabble Rouser and Devil's Due. Don, you're going to have to work your bass keys to cover for Rick; his amp will be turned off. Ryan, we're going to need more antics from you to distract from Rick. We'll keep this one short; just one encore, and we're off. If we screw this up, we'll be rolling the dice on the future of our second album."

Ryan looked at Rick and said, "First the hit and run, and now this. I'm sorry, Rick has to go. He's going to have us all in jail."

Freddie said, "He didn't do this, Ryan. He was dosed."

"Who would want to dose him? The only thing I can think of is if someone knew the person he ran over and was trying to get revenge."

Mickey found that absurd, "Come on, Ryan, that's at least a million to one shot. Someone in our entourage just happened to know the woman that Rick hit."

"No, maybe Don is right; maybe it's the new girl. Maybe she knew the woman and has been planning her revenge since last Saturday."

Don now felt vindicated, "Let's find that little bitch and get it out of her."

"Not now," Mickey ordered, "we have to get ready for the show. We need to go over everything that has to change. Especially you Don; you have to go over every tune on the playlist and figure out how to throw in a bass from your keyboard. Ryan, you need to think about what extra you can do to help with the distraction, and Freddie, you'll have to move more toward the center stage for your guitar cuts. I'll have to talk to Roger Mendez about adjusting the staging, and I'll need to move more on stage also. We've got very little time if we're going to pull this off."

The doctor said, "Go ahead and take care of business. I'll need some time to get Rick on his feet. We're lucky the dose wasn't larger; it could have killed him."

Before they left, Mickey went to Pete. I want everyone at the hotel after the concert. I want to rent one of their conference rooms or ballrooms, whatever they are. Then I want everyone in there when we get there."

Pete said, "I'll see to it."

The band left the room and moved quickly in a different direction. Don stared angrily at Emily as he went toward his keyboard. Freddie really had nothing additional to do, so he did start his own investigation.

As he moved toward their table and he spotted Emily moving away quickly. She had gotten nervous over how long the band was in the room. She decided to grab up her purse while she could. She was heading back to the girls, but she didn't make it.

Freddie caught up to her, "What the hell were you doing over here?"

"I . . . just thought I could pick up a souvenir from your table."

"Really, and what did you pick up?"

"Nothing; I didn't see anything I could pick up."

"And were you by our table the last time we left it?"

"No, I wasn't. Why are you asking me all these questions? What's going on?"

"Maybe Don is right. Maybe I do treat you girls with too much respect."

"What the hell does that mean? Don is a pig. I thought you were different."

"And I thought you were here to be with us and not here with your own plans."

Emily thought he had figured her out, but then he said, "Why did you do it? What has Rick ever done to you that you would do this to him?"

"Do what? Wait a minute; what do you think I did?"

Freddie walked over to the table and picked up Rick's whiskey bottle, and held it up to the light. He could see some residue that had settled at the bottom of the bottle. He turned back to Emily and demanded, "What did you put in Rick's bottle? Tell me, damn it!"

"What, nothing. I was never near Rick's bottle. You think I put something in his bottle? I couldn't do that to anyone."

"Then where were you the first time the band had a meeting?"

"I was talking to Patty Grundy. You can ask her. I was with her the whole time."

Patty was sitting not too far away, crying. Freddie moved Emily over to her. First, he said, "Don't worry; the doc is fixing Rick up. He will be on stage with us."

Then he got to it, "Patty, I need to know something. Were you talking to anyone when the band had our meeting earlier?"

"Yeah, Betty introduced me to Emily. Betty went off, and we had a nice chat. I was telling her how nice Rick had been to me last night. Now he's lying in there; what's going on?"

"You said Betty went off; where did she go?"

"To the restroom, I think."

Freddie looked at Emily and said, "Maybe I jumped the gun a bit."

"Yeah, maybe you did, and it was more than just a bit."

"Hey, someone dosed a good friend of mine and damn near killed him. Where's Betty?"

Emily got right back in his face and said loudly, slowly, and distinctly, "I don't know."

Freddie marched away, and Patty said, "You shouldn't talk to him like that. He can have you thrown out of here."

"So what? He's not a God, and this isn't heaven. I won't grovel for anyone."

"You're not a groupie, are you?"

"If I have to reduce myself to being treated like an animal, I will never be a groupie."

Emily walked away from Patty, and Betty's words echoed in her mind, "I think Rick needs a better drink." Betty was alone during that time. She had the opportunity. Getting something to put in the bottle was no problem, so she had the means, and she must have taken Don's abuse even harder than she let on, and that would give her the motive. The question in Emily's mind was, what would she do with this speculation?

Roger Mendez worked hard under Mickey's direction to rearrange the stage. They had Rick to the far right. He would only have to take a few steps to be in position. There was a heavy prop in the dark behind him to lean on, and he could easily be taken off the stage if it looked like he might collapse.

Doc Jenkins was an expert at getting drugged people on their feet temporarily. He had done it for many of the big bands and made a good living at it. What happened to the person afterward wasn't his problem.

The warm-up band was finishing. It was time to go on stage. As Black Hawk left the stage, they passed Mickey, and their leader asked, "What the hell happened to the staging man?" Mickey didn't answer.

This was the toughest show of their career. Don worked the keyboard feverishly, and he did an amazing job covering the bass lines. Pete Chiles was just off-stage talking to Rick the entire time, trying to keep him animated enough not to look dead.

Ryan nearly drove himself to exhaustion, adding more drum work and jumping around every chance he could.

It seemed to work; the crowd didn't react to Rick's stationary position. Later some of the entertainment writers would say that it seemed that he was subdued because of the reaction he got from the crowd for his antics in Chicago.

It worked. They made it through the concert. Now it was time to get Rick more help and to find out who had dosed him.

Chapter 4: Transition

It was a temporal anomaly. It was something that humanity could not conceive of in 1973. It would be another three hundred years before they understood the complex combination of forces and energies it took to create such an entity.

But it was 1973, and a temporal anomaly would briefly skim the surface of the Earth. It would go unnoticed by all but a few people. Some were indirectly affected, but only three would enter the temporal corridor and leave their present life for one in the twenty-first century.

Don caught up with Mickey as they walked to the limos, "The bitch is gone. She must have slipped out."

Pete was keeping pace with Mickey. Mickey turned to him and said, "Find Betty; she couldn't have gotten that far. Find her and get her back here even if you have to drag her scruffy ass back from the dumb ass little town she comes from."

The trip to the hotel in the limos did not have the usual party atmosphere. The vehicles were quiet, and there was no drinking or drugs going on. Patty was once again upset, "Why can't I go to the hospital with Rickie?"

Mickey answered, "We all need to be at the hotel. There is something we have to get straight, and no one goes anywhere until we do."

Lainey, Mickey's blonde companion, complained, "But you're going home tomorrow. This is our last night to party for a long time."

"We'll party later; this won't take very long. Just deal with it."

Freddie was in the second limo with Emily, Ryan, and his companion Sheila. Sheila was the only one who didn't notice much difference. Ryan always seemed to be in a foul mood. Emily asked Freddie, "What's going to happen when we get to the hotel?"

"We're all going to sit down and have a chat."

"You want to find out who drugged Rick."

"You're damn right I do."

"I thought that was figured out."

"We need to be sure."

"And then what will happen? If you find out, what will you do to that person?"

"I don't know, but it won't be pretty."

"Freddie, what do you mean by not pretty? You're not a thug; you're a musician."

"I'm not a thug, but Pete has plenty of thugs, and they are on our payroll."

"If you let that happen, you are a thug."

"You know you are pretty damn opinionated for someone who just showed up. If you weren't needed at the hotel, I would throw your ass out of this car right now."

"Would you bother to ask the driver to stop? Look, Freddie, this is not you. From everything I have heard from the girls and from everything I've read, you are thoughtful and respectful of other people. Violence is not in you."

"It is now. Okay, Miss Judgmental, who is the closest person to you right now in your life?"

"It's probably my sister Sarah."

"What if you saw your sister collapse and nearly die? What if you could find the person that did that to her? What would you want to do?"

"I would want to kill that person, but . . ."

Freddie interrupted her, "There are no buts about it; that's how anyone would feel."

Emily continued like he hadn't spoken, "But I would hope there would be someone there to bring me to my senses."

Freddie didn't have a response, and the rest of the ride was quiet.

Betty did it. Emily was sure of it, and then she ran. Emily never thought she would be caught up in this kind of business. The abuse of women was a serious subject, but this was criminal stuff. She was afraid, but she didn't want to show it. Despite her fear, she kept the recorder going. She knew this would be the last tape; she couldn't possibly put in another one. Actually, she wished she could get rid of it. She didn't really know any of these people, and she didn't know what they would do to her if they found it. She wanted to gather information for a story, but now she may have evidence that could send people to jail. Yeah, she was scared, all right.

Pete's people herded everyone into the large third-floor conference room. Mickey stood at the head of the table as everyone sat down. He started, "Everyone here knows our story. We've been together since high school. We have paid a lot of dues to get to where we are. We are brothers. We fight now and then, as all brothers do, but we are brothers. Someone has hurt one of our own, and we want to know who it was. We have a good idea, but we want to know what you know, and then we can all have our farewell party."

Patty yelled, "You are keeping me from Rickie for this shit. You know damn well I love Rickie. Let me the hell out of here."

Jimmy Breslau was a roadie. He spoke up, "That new bitch had a pretty damn big bag. She could have brought all kinds of shit in with her."

Emily cringed, but she had to fight the fear. She stood and yelled back, "I was checked out. I wasn't anywhere near the band's table. Where the hell were you?"

Don didn't like Emily from the start, and he still didn't like her, "You didn't do it, but it looks like it was your friend that did. Maybe you helped her. Maybe you brought the stuff in for her."

Emily was trying to think. She had her bag under the table. As she talked, she reached into her bag and managed to pour the remaining pepper into her hand, "I didn't bring anything in that could hurt anyone. If Betty did it, I had no idea what she was planning. If anything, she brought me as a distraction so she could do her dirty work. I had no part in it."

Emily just had a feeling that she might need the pepper, and it didn't take long for her feeling to be proven correct. Don leaned on the table and said, "In that case, let's see what's in your big bag. Come on; dump it out on the table."

Emily jumped up and screamed, "NO, you keep your hands off my bag."

Ryan was closest to Emily, and he made a grab for her bag. Emily yanked it away, and the microphone flopped out into view.

Don yelled, "The bitch is a plant!"

Emily was already on her feet, so she dashed to the door. One of Pete's men stepped up to block the door, and Emily threw the pepper in his face. He backed up, rubbing his eyes, and Emily ran down the hall.

The floor exploded in chaos. Pete was out hunting down Betty with several of his people. No one thought they would need people to chase someone around the hotel. Freddie was out of the door first, and he ran down the hall. When he got to the end of the hall, he saw the stairway door just closing. Freddie ran into the stairway. He could hear Emily crying below him. He called out, "Emily, stop; I won't hurt you." Freddie just heard her crying and her footfalls on the stairs.

It was long before cell phones, but the security team did have walkie-talkies. Emily kept going until she got to the bottom of the stairs. The exit door led to the parking garage, and she burst through it in a blind panic.

She ran right into the arms of a waiting security man. He held her tight as she struggled. The man said, "You're not going anywhere but back upstairs."

The motion did turn the man away from the door. Freddie came through the door and jumped on the man's back. The action made the man release Emily, and Freddie yelled, "EMILY, RUN!"

Freddie was strong, but he wasn't trained. The man gave him a horse kick to the groin and two elbows to the ribs, and Freddie released him and staggered back. The man turned and gave him a right cross before he saw who it was, and then he pulled out a revolver and said, "I'm going to get that little bitch, and you better stay out of my way."

Emily was running up through the parking garage toward the exit, and the man gave chase. Freddie looked the other way toward the reserved area containing the band's Barracudas.

The man yelled to Emily, "Stop running, little girl, or I'll shoot you in the back. You'll never see it coming."

As Freddie got to his car, he saw Emily duck between two parked cars and the man coming up quickly behind her.

Emily was crouched between the cars, almost in a fetal position, as the man came toward her.

Suddenly the red Barracuda screeched to a halt in front of her. Freddie pushed the door open and yelled, "GET IN!"

Emily stared for a second and dove into the car. Freddie sped away, hearing the gunfire as he did.

Daniel and Steve were in Detroit. They drove down a street, and Steve said, "There's the hotel up ahead."

At the next intersection and a black van with New Jersey plates turned in front of them. Daniel said, "Well, well, if it isn't Mr. Peter Chiles himself. This should be interesting."

Behind them was a car with two Detroit detectives in it, and behind them were three patrol cars. They followed Pete Chiles to the hotel. Just as they approached, Freddie careened out of the parking garage and rushed down the street.

Daniel was torn on who to chase until he saw Pete Chiles exit the van dragging a young woman by the hair. He pulled over, and the procession behind him did the same, blocking the exit from the parking garage.

Daniel and Steve jumped out, and Daniel called out, "Chiles, let her go, turn around and put your hands on the van." Steve went around the van and got the driver out.

Pete let Betty go, and she started to run. Then Daniel said, "Oh no, sweetheart, you're not going anywhere."

Cars slammed on their breaks to avoid hitting the police cars in front of the parking garage exit. One of the Detroit detectives called out, "Round them up. No one leaves this hotel tonight."

Then he called to Daniel, "I'll get an A.P.B. out on the red Barracuda."

Daniel called, "I've got the license number, and the car also has something written on the back bumper."

Freddie turned onto the Edsel Ford Freeway, heading west. Emily was still crying, "Please don't hurt me."

Freddie said, "Calm down; I'm not going to hurt you. If you give me your recorder, your tapes, and all of your notes, I might be able to get you out of this."

Emily just pushed the bag away from her and said, "Take it. Take it all. I just want to go home."

"You and Betty are from the same town, right?"

"Yeah, Romulus, it's right down the freeway."

"Okay, I'll get you there, and if we're lucky, that will be the end of it."

"Thank you."

"What were you doing? Are you with a fan magazine or something?"

"I just joined the Michigan Daily."

"Is that a town newspaper?"

"It's the student newspaper for the University of Michigan. I'm just a sophomore, so they wouldn't give me my own byline. I thought if I could get a big scoop they would make an exception."

"So you thought you could get a big story out of us."

"Actually, the story was going to be about Betty and her friends and how bands like yours treat the women that follow them."

"Well, in that case, Don must have made your day. You know not all musicians are like Don."

"I know they're not, and I was going to be fair."

"What else did you record about our private business?"

"I don't know; I haven't had a chance to listen to the tapes."

"Then you'll never know, and that's good. I can tell everyone that you have no information to offer anyone, and that should keep you safe."

They drove in silence for several minutes then suddenly, flashing lights appeared behind them. Freddie sped up, and Emily was confused, "They're the police. Just pull over, and you can hand me over to them and be on your way."

"I'm sorry; I can't be sure you won't claim I snatched you and take back your bag."

"I won't, I promise."

Freddie looked in the rearview mirror at the police car just as an eerie sparkling blue curtain crossed the highway. Emily screamed, "FREDDIE, LOOKOUT," and she threw herself down to avoid going through the windshield.

Freddie looked up just as the car rushed through the curtain. There was a blinding white flash. Freddie slammed on the brakes, and the car skidded across the lanes. He lost control for a second, but he got it back quickly and brought the car to a halt on the side of the road.

Freddie leaned on the steering wheel for a moment, and then he got his wits about him. He grabbed Emily's bag, pulled out her wallet and tossed it to her, and jumped out of the car. He threw it over the guard rail down into a gully. Then he waited for the police car to catch up.

Emily called to him, "Freddie, what are you doing?"

"I was going to hand you over to the cops. Then I will go find your bag and make sure I got rid of it properly when I have a chance. I have a pretty good idea of where it is down there. It shouldn't have taken more than a couple of minutes for them to show up, but there is no sign of them."

"Maybe they gave up and turned off."

"They were gaining on us. I thought they would have been on us as soon as I stopped the car, and there wasn't any place for him to turn off. The car just disappeared."

"Freddie, please take me home. You can come back a look for my bag later if you feel you have to."

Freddie was getting back in the car when another car zoomed by. They couldn't see it well in the dark, but it seemed oddly shaped, and the tail lights looked very strange. Freddie pulled away and then continued down the highway.

Emily asked, "What was that thing that we went through?"

"It looked like someone was playing with a laser light show and ended up shining it across the road. I've seen them at concerts, but I don't know if it is possible just to set one up anywhere."

"Well, it was crazy. They shouldn't do that kind of thing. They could get someone killed."

"I agree with that."

After another mile, they came upon the big green interstate sign. It read, "Interstate 94 West Chicago."

Emily looked at it and asked, "Now, where did that sign come from? This is the Edsel Ford Freeway."

Freddie answered, "Technically, it is interstate 94. Maybe they decided to change the name."

"Well, then they changed state law and put up the signs since this afternoon when Betty and I came this way on the bus."

Then Emily saw a sign that gave her some relief. It told her that there were thirteen miles from Romulus. In just over ten minutes, they saw that exit for Shook Road, and Emily let out an audible sigh of relief, and she said, "I'm home."

Part Two
2017

Chapter 5: Homecoming

Freddie and Emily got off the interstate, and Emily felt better seeing the auto dealership and the grocery store. Things were familiar again. That was until they stopped at a traffic light. A 2015 Nissan Rogue pulled up next to them. They stared at it as if it came from outer space. It was like no car they had ever seen before. The driver of the Rogue was equally shocked. He never thought he would see a mint condition 1973 Plymouth Barracuda. Emily said, "Just get me home; I'll direct you."

A few minutes later, they drove onto the driveway of the well-kept little house on Craig Street. The headlights of the Barracuda illuminated a brand-new Cadillac CRS in the driveway. The two sat and stared at the vehicle for a moment, and then they got out of the car. Freddie planned to just drive away, but somehow he couldn't. Things were odd, and he didn't want to leave Emily alone. He followed her to the door, and Emily tried to put her key in the lock. The key didn't fit.

Freddie said, "It looks like your parents changed the locks."

"They wouldn't do that without telling me, and they sure wouldn't purposely leave me locked out of the house." Emily knocked on the door.

It was almost five in the morning, and the sky was beginning to lighten. While Emily knocked on the door, Freddie looked around the neighborhood. Between the lightening sky and the street lights, he could now see all of the cars on the street. As Emily knocked, Freddie wondered out loud, "Is your town some kind of test area for experimental cars or something?"

"No, of course not," Emily said, and she continued to knock.

"Then, we're in the Twilight Zone."

Emily was about to turn around when the porch light came on, and Emily heard her mother's voice, "Who's out there so early in the morning?"

Emily thought her mother's voice was a bit odd, like she had gotten a cold. She answered, "Mom, it's me; open the door."

"Who is this? How can you be so cruel; on today of all days? Go away, you evil child, or I'll call the police."

"Mom, what's wrong? Why won't you let me in? What is that thing in the driveway? Where is your Chrysler Imperial?

"Stop, stop, please don't you have any mercy. My Emily, my dear sweet Emily, taken from me so long ago on this very morning; and here you are torturing me. Why, why are you doing this?"

Emily began to cry, "Mom, it's me, Emily. I haven't been lost. I'm sorry for not telling you I wouldn't be home. I thought Sarah would tell you."

"Evil, you must be the evilest child. I am calling the police. Leave here now, or you will be thrown in jail."

"Mom, please!"

"Shame on you for doing this to an eighty-three-year-old woman. I'm calling the police right now."

The porch light went out, and Emily started hysterically slapping at the door with an open hand. Freddie reached for her, saying, "Come on; let's go. We'll come back when we figure this thing out."

Emily just sat in front of the door crying and repeating over and over again, "The world has gone insane, the world has gone insane."

Freddie eased her up and got her back in the car. As he got her in, a car pulled up, and a boy threw the newspaper out of the window. Freddie picked it up, and he couldn't believe the headline. It read, "North Korea Tests New Long-Range Ballistic Missile."

Freddie mumbled, "North Korea?" Then he saw the date on the paper, September 15, 2017. He dropped the paper and just mumbled, "Oh my God."

Freddie picked up the paper and got in the car. He was shaking and confused, but he had to keep it together until he and Emily could sit down somewhere. He had no idea where he was going, but he knew he had to get her out of there. He tried to bring her down to Earth a bit. Steadying his voice, he asked her, "Where can we get some breakfast?"

Emily answered through her sobs, "There's an IHOP about a mile and a half away. Just go left out of the driveway, go down two blocks, take a right, and go to the second traffic light. It will be on the right."

Freddie was hoping to God it was actually there. As he drove, one thing flashed in his mind, "Forty-four years."

Then he had another thought, "We've got to be tripping, man. Maybe Betty dosed everyone, and we are now just feeling it. It's got to be LSD or something." He kept gripping the steering wheel harder and harder trying to make sure it was real. Car after strange-looking car passed them as they drove. By some miracle, the IHOP was there, and he kept it together long enough to park the car.

As they got out, they saw several people staring at his car. Finally, a woman asked, "Where did you get that great old car? It must be worth a fortune."

The only thing Freddie could think of saying was, "I got it recently."

A younger man going by said, "OMG, that car is the bomb."

Freddie said, "It's not a bomb, man. It's a really cool car."

"That's what I said; it's dope; it's the bomb."

Other people had little rectangular metal things, and they were flashing lights at the car. Freddie just got a hold of Emily, and they went into the restaurant. When they sat down, Freddie grabbed Emily's hand and asked, "Can you feel my hands?"

"Yes, of course, I can feel your hands. Oh, I see you are hoping that this is a dream; so was I. If it is, we are having the same dream, and it's not a dream. It's a nightmare. Freddie, wake me up; please wake me up."

"Emily, something happened to us; it must have been that thing we went through. If this is real, we've come a long way."

"We're here in Romulus, but it is all wrong somehow."

Freddie laid the paper on the table and carefully said, "We didn't come a long way in the distance; we came a long way in time. Emily, Romulus isn't wrong; we are."

Emily stared at the paper, and she couldn't form words; they were all stuck in her throat. She looked around at the way people were dressed and how so many of them were either staring at little metal rectangles or were talking with them pressed to their heads. This was not her Romulus; she was lost.

She put her head down on the table, and Freddie tried to give her some perspective, "We are in shock. Think of what would happen if someone from 1929 showed up in 1973. Think of all the things that are different between those two years. That person would be paralyzed just as we are. We have to take it slow and learn. We're like children in this world."

Emily lifted her head and said "Future shock."

"What?"

"Future shock" is the name of a book that was big on campus. It was written by Alvin Toffler in 1970. It explains that technology is changing the world so fast that some people can't keep up. They become unable to function. He called it future shock."

"That is a perfect description. We have to recognize that and move forward slowly."

Emily nodded and then added, "This is not a dream, drug-induced or otherwise. You can't read in a dream, that part of your brain isn't working, and I can read that newspaper just fine."

Freddie picked up the menu and was again hit with multiple shocks, the pictures on the menu, what the menu was made of, the variety of the choices, and most of all, the prices. He said, "My God, I could eat steak for a week for the price of a couple of eggs in this place. I'm sure glad I always carry a lot of cash."

The server appeared and asked, "What can I get you?"

Freddie thought, "Well, at least that sounded like normal English."

Then he said, "Two eggs, ham, toast, and coffee, please."

The server turned to Emily. Emily couldn't focus on the menu, and she just said, "I'll have the same."

When the server left, Emily asked, "What are we going to do next?"

"We have to go back to your house. You have to convince your mother that you are her daughter."

"Oh, thank you, I thought you were going to say that we needed to stay away, so we didn't sound crazy."

"That is a risk, but we need someone. We need help. No matter how hard we try, we will not be able to function without help. We are like children; we need to be taught. Your family is our best hope."

They ate their meal and prepared to return to Emily's home. Freddie always went by percentage when leaving a tip, so the server didn't get stiffed. Freddie took the bill up to the cashier. He pulled his wallet out of his back pocket. It was a large black leather wallet with the red Barracuda band emblem on it. A silver chain secured it to his belt loop. He pulled out two twenties and handed them to the cashier with the bill.

The cashier looked at the bills, then at Freddie, and said, "One moment, sir,' and she walked away. Freddie could see her talking to someone that must have been the manager. The cashier returned and said, "Boy, I heard of retro, but you are one hundred percent. If that wallet of yours was original, it would be worth a ton of cash. That ancient money threw me for a minute. Anyway, here's your change; have a nice day."

Freddie was happy he didn't have to respond. As they turned to leave, they found an older man staring at them. He said, "Forgive me for staring, but you two look just like the two young people that were lost forty-four years ago. In fact, it was forty-four years ago today. I mean, you are identical. I knew Emily Hicks, and I was a huge fan of Barracuda; I was at their last concert in Detroit. You have the look right down to the hair styles and the clothes. That wallet is a very nice touch. So what's the angle? Why have you gone out of your way to look like them on the anniversary of their disappearance?"

Emily's mind was racing. Who could this old man be?

The man pulled out his cell phone, and the two watched in amazement while he poked at it. Then he turned it around. The screen had a picture of a newspaper with Freddie and Emily's pictures on the front page. He said, "See, you two are perfect."

Then he poked at a bit more and turned the screen around again. There was a picture of Emily when she was about twelve. She was with Sarah and some boy, and she had a bandage on her right arm. He said, "See, I knew Emily. I dated her sister Sarah for a while in high school, and if I didn't know any better, I would swear that you, young lady, were Emily Hicks."

Freddie was trying to come up with a response, but his mind was blank. He thought that they were in big trouble, and then the man gave them an out, "You're professional look-a-likes, aren't you? What, did some agent send you here to find work? I thought they made contact first and then sent the talent. In any case, I may have a job for you; if you are interested."

"A job," was all Freddie could blurt out.

"Yes, my son is a marketing manager for the local classic rock station. They put on a show every year around the holidays, and he has been contacted by some writer that has a story about Barracuda. He said it could be turned into a rock and roll play. You two would be perfect for the leads."

Freddie started mumbling something about just getting into town and needing to find their bearings, and the old man just shoved a card in his hand and said, "This is my son's card at KWTZ; give him a call when you get settled, I'm sure he would love to talk to you."

Freddie and Emily thanked the man as they moved as quickly as they could out of the door.

The old man watched them get into the brand new 1973 Plymouth Barracuda, and his expression changed. He made two calls. He called his son and told him that he just ran into some people that might help him get his ratings up. Then he called his old friends at Romulus police headquarters, "Rosie, this is Barry Batali; how have you been?"

"Barry, it's good to hear from you, you old goat. What have you been doing with yourself?"

"Living the good life; not like you working stiffs. Rosie, I need a favor."

"Sure, Barry, anyone that put in over forty years in this department is deserving of a few favors."

"Thanks, Rosie; there is a mint condition 1973 Plymouth Barracuda driving around town. I was wondering if the patrol officers could watch out for it. It has Illinois plates, and I believe they are expired. Ask them not to pull the car over yet; just see where it goes."

"Do you think they're up to something?"

"I don't think what is going on is criminal, but it is odd, and I would like to know a little more."

"You got it, Barry; I'll get it out to everyone."

"Thanks, Rosie; the place never had a better police captain."

"You were always a sweet talker Barry. I'll give you a call if they come up with something."

It was the middle of the night in Bueno Vista, California, when Sarah Hicks Rutherford's phone rang. Sarah reached blindly for the phone. Finally, she got it and mumbled, "What's so Earth shaking that I have to be bothered in the middle of the night?"

Her mother's voice was trembling, "Sarah, please come home; I need you."

"Mom, what's wrong? What happened?"

"Some young woman knocked on my door very early this morning. She said she was Emily."

"Mom, Emily wouldn't be young. Emily would be sixty-three years old."

"I know, Sarah, but she kept crying and begging me to let her in."

"You didn't let her in, did you?"

"No! I'm an old woman, but I haven't lost my marbles yet. But Sarah, I peeked when they were leaving."

"Did you say they?"

"Yes, there was a man with her. The woman looked just like my Emily, so young and so beautiful, and the man looked like that rock and roll man that was lost with Emily. Why are they doing this, Sarah? On the day I lost my baby girl, why are they doing this to me?"

"It's some kind of scheme to get money from you, Mom. Don't worry; I'm on the way. Do you remember my friend Tim?"

"Yes, he's a nice young man."

"He will be there very soon, and a few other nice young men. They will keep you company until I get there. I should be there by noon."

"What if they come back?"

"Tim and his friends will take care of them. We'll make this girl take a DNA test, and then we will turn her over to the police."

"Okay, Sarah. Thank you; you always take such good care of me."

"And I always will, Mom. See you soon."

Sarah jumped out of bed with her phone in her hand. The first person she called was her head of security, Tommy Eversol, "Tommy, get a hold of Tim and a few more of your people in Detroit. Tell them to get over to my mother's house in Romulus and keep her company until I get there. Pack a bag, you're going with me."

Next, Sarah called her personal assistant, "Jimmy, have the plane warmed up and bring the car around; I'm going to Romulus. I also want the staff of one of my laboratories rounded up and waiting for me by the plane."

Sarah Hicks Rutherford was one of the most powerful women in the country. She had turned her business and computer science degrees into an empire. She developed some of the first banking and commerce applications, and she just grew her power from there. Sarah was considered to be the Einstein of business computer applications.

Her fortune was vast, and her influence considerable. She wanted to build a fine estate for her mother in Bueno Vista, but her mother wouldn't leave her little house in Romulus.

Sarah was sixty-six years old and semi-retired. She could not bring herself to completely give up the reigns. She worked when she wanted and for as long as she wanted. The rest of the time, she worked with her charities. She happily joined Warren Buffet and Bill Gates in pledging half a billion dollars to charity.

Her husband of thirty-two years, Sam Rutherford, died of a heart attack in 2012, and she couldn't imagine anyone that could replace him. She has had many potential suitors, but they all paled in comparison to Sam.

Sarah hadn't missed a step. She always considered her health a priority, and her endurance and dexterity would put women twenty years younger to shame. She was up and dressed in a few minutes. She threw a few things in a bag and started down the stairs of her sprawling California home. Housekeepers greeted her as she passed; she greeted each of them pleasantly, stopping to chat now and then. All of her staff thought she was the best boss. They respected her, and she respected them.

Sarah moved quickly out of the front door and into her waiting limousine.

Freddie and Emily returned to Emily's family home. Her mother watched as they pulled into the driveway. On the drive back, Emily tried to think of things to tell her mother that only the family would know. Things that might make her mother believe the impossible.

Emily moved toward the door and knocked again. She didn't have to wait long for a response. Her mother warned, "My daughter is sending people to protect me. They will be here very soon."

"Sarah, Mom, is Sarah here?"

"She will be soon, and when she comes, she will fix you for good. She will see that you get what you deserve for being so cruel to her mother. You better go. Her friends will be here any minute. If they catch you, they will take you away."

"Mom, please, something happened. Freddie was bringing me home, and we went through something. I know it all sounds impossible, but it's true. We went through something that took us out of 1973 and put us here now. Please believe me."

"You talk crazy. We will see. If you stay here Sarah's friends will come, and they will take you. They will give you a DNA test, and that will prove your lies. Then it will be off to jail for the both of you."

That got Freddie's attention, "Emily, maybe this wasn't such a good idea. We better get out of here."

"Wait, Freddie; this may be just what we need."

Emily called to her mom, "Is this test supposed to prove who I am?"

"It will prove you are not Emily, and they will force you to take it."

"Mom, I want it. I want the test. I will stay right here, and I will let them take me. I want the test to prove that I am Emily. Mom, do you remember Dad's birthday party? You made that big cake with lemon frosting because it was his favorite. Do you remember Uncle Bernie telling me that I shouldn't try to be a journalist? Do you remember what Daddy said to me? Do you remember he told me to stick to my guns?"

"Since my Emily disappeared, everyone has learned all about our family. Your dad or I could have mentioned that to any one of the hundreds of reporters that we talked to. All of those times they came, all of the pleas we made begging to let our little girl come home, all for nothing; my heart still breaks."

Emily was crying again, "Mom, it's me; I've come home. I will stay right here. I will allow these men to take me, and I will prove to you that I am Emily."

Emily turned to Freddie and said, "You can leave if you want to, but I am staying, and I am going to take this test."

"I'm here, Emily. I won't leave you."

Emily smiled at Freddie with a warmth that made everything right just for a moment.

It took only another few minutes for a car and a van to pull up in front of the house. Six men got out, rushed up and grabbed them, and started moving them to the van. Shelly Hicks opened the door and cried, "No, please. Bring them into the house. They can stay here until Sarah comes."

Tim said, "Mrs. Hicks, Sarah told us to get them away from you."

"No, please, Tim, bring them in. You can watch them, but I want to talk with them a little longer. Sarah said that she would be here for lunch. I want her to see this girl."

Tim got on his phone to get approval from Sarah. She approved, and everyone moved inside.

Emily spoke up, "I am Emily Hicks. I know you think I'm some kind of criminal, but I'm not, I swear. My mother said there was a test that could prove who I am. I want to take it."

Tim asked, "Girl, what's your angle? The only way you can fool a DNA test is to have someone in the lab working with you. Well, lady, we won't be sending this result to a regular lab. Sarah Hicks Rutherford has rented a local lab, and she is bringing her own people to do the analysis."

Another man turned to Freddie and said, "I suppose you are the great Freddie MacArthur who disappeared when he was on top of the rock world."

"Yep, that's who I am. Give me a guitar, and I will rip out 'She's Got the Devil in Her' like I had done it on stage yesterday. Oh yeah, I did do it on stage yesterday."

The man said, "I ought to smack you for being stupid enough to say that to my face."

Freddie stood right up to him, "If you keep your buddies out of it, I'd like to see you try."

Freddie and the man stood face to face, but Tim stopped things right there, "Sit down, John, and you, too, whoever you really are. We aren't going to turn this into a brawl in Mrs. Hicks' home. Ms. Rutherford said to do this quietly."

Shelly Hicks came over and took Emily's hands, and looked her in the eyes. She started crying, which made Emily cry again. Shelly said, "You look just like my Emily. You have the same sparkle in your eyes, the same little turn of your mouth. I know I'm a foolish old woman, but I wish in my heart that the test proves you are my Emily."

"It will, Mom, it will, you'll see. It will be another test that you can put on the refrigerator like you did with all of my spelling tests. You put every spelling test I ever took on the refrigerator. You wanted me to enter the national spelling bee, but I really wasn't that good."

Shelly looked at Tim and asked, "How can she know so much if she isn't my Emily?"

"Criminals are very smart these days, Mrs. Hicks. Don't let her fool you."

Hours went by in relative silence until a large SUV appeared in front of the house. Two men jumped up and rushed out to move their cars. The SUV pulled up, and the driver jumped out, ran around the vehicle, and opened the passenger door. Sarah stepped out. The rear door opened, and a large, powerful-looking man stepped out and took Sarah's arm. He led her to the door and inside the house.

Sarah entered the house and went to her mother. She hugged her and asked, "Mom, are you alright? Did these people upset you?"

"I'm fine dear, but look, look at her."

Emily stood, and Sarah stared at her. Emily looked at her sister and instinctively moved to hug her. Three men quickly jumped in her way, and Sarah said, "Oh please, child, keep your dramatics to yourself."

Emily backed off, Sarah nodded, and the men sat down. Sarah walked over and examined Emily and Freddie. She nodded approvingly, and she said, "This is fine work, fine work indeed, and my compliments to the doctor that put you two together. This must be a complex scam that you're running, but I'm afraid you wasted a lot of money for nothing. I'm not impressed, and you are both fools to think that I would be."

Freddie just sat quietly and shook his head. If they decided not to bother with that DNA test, then he was sure he would be looking at a serious beatdown before going to jail.

Emily looked at her sister and smirked, "I see you've got yourself some money. From the way these guys grovel at your feet, I'm sure it's quite a lot. You say you're not impressed; well, neither am I. You can scare other people, but you can't scare me. I still remember you climbing into my bed and hiding behind me because you thought you saw a spider. You were nine, and I was only six, and still, you hid behind me."

"Cute story; well-practiced; I'm sure it was part of some interview somewhere."

"Well, how about this. Did you ever tell Mom that you drove me to the mall to meet Betty? Did you tell Mom that it was you that gave me the idea for the story in the first place? Oh yeah, did you ever seriously kick Betty's ass like you said you would if I didn't come back?"

Sarah stared at Emily, and she finally said, "Shut up. Just shut up, you little bitch."

Their mother looked at Sarah and asked her, "Did you send her off that day?"

Sarah answered, "Mom, that was a long time ago."

"But she is right; you never told me. If you didn't tell anyone else, then how would she know?"

"This is a trick, Mom, and I will prove it."

Emily jumped back in, "Yes, the test. Just tell me what I have to do. Do you want blood? Is it a series of examinations? Whatever it is, I want to do it, and I want to do it now. As you loved to say when we were kids, 'put up or shut up.'"

Sarah turned to the big man and said, "Tommy, take the swabs and get them to the lab. The people at the lab are standing by."

As Tommy carefully took a large Q-Tip type swab out of a plastic tube, Sarah said, "I am in full control of this process. I rented a lab right here in Detroit, and I have my own people doing the test. There will be no tricks. It will take no more than an hour to get the results. Your time is up, missy."

When Tommy was finished with Emily, he swabbed Sarah and Shelly for the comparison.

Emily set her eyes on her sister and asked, "When did you become such a sour old bitch?"

Two men stood, and Freddie stood to stop them. Sarah ordered, "Settle down, boys; this little nobody and her boyfriend will be off to jail by dinnertime."

Emily kept talking, "I guess this was what Annie Shimko meant when she talked about empowering women. She meant that they could turn women into grumpy old men. You know she was going to help me get my story out if the school paper wouldn't publish it."

"Yes, I knew that she was going to help Emily. Everyone knew; she told the world about how Emily was going into the lion's den for a story. She made a lot of mileage on the connection with Emily. It got her known nationally in the organization; like you didn't know that."

Emily's defiance suddenly drained away. Her whole expression changed. She looked at her mother and asked, "Where's Dad?"

Sarah jumped right in, "My father died of a stroke four years ago. I was wondering when you were going to pull that out."

Emily dropped back in her chair and just started crying. That only angered Sarah further, "Stop it. Stop it right now. Do not make a mockery of my father's death with your little performance."

Emily screamed through her tears, "Go to hell! You are just a mean bitch. I should have told Mom all of those little secrets that you told me. Maybe I should have told her how I caught you and Barry Batali making out on the back porch. I should have told her that, after he left, you pushed me down the porch steps when I threatened to tell. She never knew that's why I had to go to the emergency room and get the stitches in my arm."

Through Emily's grief and anxiety, a thought flashed in her mind, "So that's who the man was at the IHOP."

Shelly Hicks looked at Emily and then at Sarah. She asked Sarah, "Tell me truly, did you push Emily down the steps that day?"

"Yes, Mom, I did." Sarah looked at Emily, and tears came to her eyes.

Emily was also crying, and she said, "You see me now, don't you? You see that it's me."

Sarah's voice became softer, "Emily, how could this be?"

"I don't know. We were driving down the Edsel Ford Freeway, oh, I guess you call it interstate 94 now, and we drove right through this weird blue curtain. There was a flash of light, and then things started to change."

This time it was Sarah that moved. She put her arms around Emily. Their mother joined them. Everyone left the room to give them some privacy.

In the other room, everyone stood quiet for a few minutes. Then Tim looked at Freddie and asked, "Are you really the Freddie MacArthur?"

Freddie was getting tired. They had been up all night, and the confusion of the day had taken its toll. He looked at Tim and said, "That's what I've been trying to tell you."

"Wow, my dad is going to freak out when I tell him that I met Freddie MacArthur. When I was nine, I started listening to the eighties hair bands . He must have told me a million times that shredders, like Eddie Van Halen, couldn't carry Freddie MacArthur's guitar case."

Sarah entered the room and ordered, "Your father will never know. Listen up. Not a word that was spoken in this house will be repeated. If anyone repeats a word of this, I will see to it that the rest of their miserable lives will be a living hell. Do you understand me?"

Everyone acknowledged the order. A few minutes later, Tom entered the house with a large envelope in his hand. Everyone watched as he handed it to Sarah. Emily was nervous. She knew who she was, but she didn't know how this test worked.

Sarah opened the envelope and looked at the papers inside. She looked up and announced in a shaky voice, "There is no doubt about it; this is Emily; my little sister is home."

Even with all that had happened to that point, the men in the room, excluding Freddie, stood in shock at the news. The women hugged each other one more time.

When they stepped back, Emily and Sarah had the same thought. They looked at their mother, and Sarah asked, "How are you doing, Mom?"

"How am I doing? I have my little girl back. This is a wonderful day, more wonderful than I can imagine."

"I know, Mom, but it's also quite a shock."

"Oh, don't worry so much; I come from strong stock." Then Shelly Hicks got an excited look on her face, "We have to celebrate. I want to make a big pot roast for everyone."

The men smiled at the older lady and tried to tell her to relax. Sarah told her that she would have a grand dinner brought in, but Shelly Hicks would not hear of it, "No, no, you keep your fancy chefs for another day. Emily is going to get her mother's cooking, and I'm going to be singing while I make it."

"Okay, Mom, is it okay if I have sandwiches brought in for lunch?"

"Yes, get some good ones. It will be an all-day celebration."

"Meanwhile, make a grocery list, and Tim will get everything you need for your feast."

"Sarah turned to Tim and said, "Make sure that everything is of the finest quality."

Tim had to smile at the joy as he said, "Yes, Ma'am," and he stood ready for the list.

Sarah dismissed all of the other men except Tommy. His job was just beginning.

Shelly Hicks was just bubbling over with happiness, and her daughters just soaked it up. She made a list and sent Tim on his way, and then she announced, "Everyone out of the kitchen; I have some planning to do." Before they left, she had to run over and hug her daughters one more time.

In the other room, Sarah got down to some business. She talked to Freddie and Emily, "Of course, no one will ever believe that this happened. We could show them the DNA test, and they'll just claim it was faked. The truth is, though it means you really can't be you, it also means that you can live normal lives once you get acclimated. You will need new identities. It will take some time to work that out.

Also, you can't stay in Romulus, and you certainly can't be seen coming in and out of this house. That would definitely cause confusion and speculation. I can get you a couple of nice suites near St. Clair Shores. There is a very nice hotel there called Hotel Les Flots Bleus. You should be very comfortable.

Emily asked, "Then what?"

"Then you will have to lay low, so to speak, until we have your new identities ready. I know that's probably not what you wanted to hear, but it is best."

"No," Freddie said, "That's exactly what we need. We need a quiet place where we can slowly begin to adjust."

Emily said, "It's future shock."

Sarah got the analogy and smiled. Freddie added, "It's also because I'm damn tired. I've been awake since yesterday morning."

"No," Sarah said, "You've been awake for forty-four years."

Emily remembered Barry and changed the subject, "We ran into Barry Balti at the IHOP this morning. I didn't know it was him until we talked about him earlier. He thinks we are people that he called look-alikes, and he offered us a job."

Sarah responded, "And that's why you have to get out of town. I don't know how much you remember about Barry. I was sixteen and in my rebellious phase. Barry was the cool bad boy at school, and we dated for a while. We just kind of got bored with each other after a while. After school, he was drafted, and he went to Vietnam. When he came back, he was a different person. He got into the police academy and made himself a great career as a police detective. He is considered one of the best detectives Romulus ever had. They say he could always tell when something wasn't right, and he would stick to it until he figured it out. Old Barry might be a problem."

Sarah turned to Tommy and said, "Have someone check on his activity. Let's see if he is getting curious."

Chapter 6: Names

The dinner was one of the most joyous occasions that any of them had ever experienced. Emily and Sarah told more stories, and Shelly added several of her own. It would be the only time in history that anyone would find a time traveler and one of the most powerful women in the country in the kitchen, washing dishes and doing it with a smile.

Later, Sarah had Tim fetch a guitar, and Freddie put on a little show. Everyone thought that he was just a hard rocker, but he played and sang some beautiful ballads. He also played an extended version of the great instrumental "Classical Gas." When he was finished, everyone applauded, and Sarah went to him. She said, "Now that we know it is really you, I want to thank you. This is a thank you, I never thought I would have the opportunity to say. Thank you for keeping Emily safe. The whole story of what happened in the hotel that night came out over time. Everyone knows that you risked your life to get Emily out of there. So, thank you, Freddie MacArthur; I am forever in your debt."

Freddie was a bit embarrassed. He said, "I knew she wasn't a groupie, and she didn't deserve to be hurt to cover up all of our faults."

"He did more than that," Emily stepped into the conversation, "he is here because of me. He was driving me home after he got me away from those people. If he didn't do that, he would have had a full life with his band."

She looked at Freddie as if she realized what she was saying for the first time, "He didn't just risk his life for me; he gave up his life for me."

Emily's look was special. Freddie never really knew how the heart was related to affection until that moment. Her look was making his heart pound. He answered, "I had no idea this would happen. Giving up my life wasn't voluntary; it was an accident."

"In any case," Sarah ended the subject, "I have my little sister back, and you kept her safe. I am in your debt."

Sarah turned to talk to Emily, and Tim leaned over and whispered, "You're a golden man. She has only used that phrase twice in her life. When she does, she means you are set for life. You have a permanent income and an unlimited expense account. You have to figure out how things work, but you don't have to worry about getting a job."

Freddie thought about that as the conversations went on around him. He was twenty-three years old. He should be sixty-seven, but he was twenty-three years old. It wasn't a matter of money. He needed something, and he knew what it was. He needed his music. He needed to play, and he needed to play for an audience.

Sarah and Emily returned, and Sarah said, "There is one thing that needs to be decided now, if possible. I know this is not easy, and I don't know how you feel about it, but you will need new identities. I think it's best if you can come up with new names now so Tommy can get started as soon as possible."

Freddie and Emily looked at each other. They heard Sarah say new identities, but it hadn't sunk in as to what that really meant. It would be another familiar thing gone. This was harder than they could have imagined. They had so much taken from them and now they would have to give up the last thing that defined them. They sat in silence for a few moments until Sarah said, "We can create names for you if you like."

"No," Emily said, "I just need a minute."

Freddie started, "Okay, I'll be Frank McAlester; I don't want to lose my initials."

Sarah said, "Frank McAlester, it is."

Finally, Emily said, "I'll be Elizabeth Richards."

"You're using Mom's maiden name."

"Yes, it feels like family."

"Good."

Sarah turned to Tommy and said, "Would you get this started, please?"

The big man answered, "Yes, Ma'am," and he stepped away to make a few calls.

At the end of the day, Shelly Hicks didn't want her daughters to go. She held onto them for a long time. Finally, they said goodbye. Tim had everything set up at the hotel. Elizabeth Richards and Frank McAlester were checked in. He handed Emily and Freddie their room keys, and the two just stared at the piece of plastic they were handed.

Sarah said, "It is a key. You just slide it in the slot and pull it out, and the door will open. Freddie said, "This is like Star Trek stuff."

Tim said, "There are a lot of things that you will think are Star Trek stuff. The writers of that show didn't think technology would move as fast as it did."

Emily and Sarah looked at each and said in unison, "Future shock."

Freddie would drive his car, but Tim would be his navigator. Sarah wanted Emily to ride with her in the SUV so they could talk more. Freddie was almost thankful that he was driving in the dark. The darkness would conceal the landscape, and he had enough shocks for one day.

Sarah sat in the back of the SUV and just smiled at her little sister. Emily looked around the car, feeling the soft leather seats, and she said, "You always were brilliant. Not many people would get a degree and then go back to school to get another because they had a vision that it would be important. You got it right."

"It seemed like a good thing to do. I owe it all to Mom and Dad. When I asked Dad if I could stay in school to learn computer science, he didn't hesitate. It wasn't until years later that I found out that he used the money he and Mom were saving for a trip to Hawaii to pay the tuition. Dad was the best."

Tears were in Emily's eyes again as she said, "He's gone. I can't believe I missed all those years with him. I hate it, Sarah. I hate it. I missed everything. All those years when I could have been a part of your lives, I missed everything."

"I know it's hard. It was hard on us not having you there. Mom set a place at the table for you for years, hoping you would walk through the door. The day that everyone gave up the search was. . ."

"No, please, Sarah. It breaks my heart. I don't want to imagine Mom and Dad like that."

"Okay, Emily."

Freddie and Tim drove behind the SUV, and Freddie asked, "I guess Sarah has millions?"

Tim laughed, "Millions? Ms. Sarah Hicks Rutherford is one of the most powerful people in the country. She doesn't run a company or a corporation; she runs an empire."

"She started right there in Romulus; how did she get so rich?"

"First, she is really smart; I mean really, really smart. Also, she has what they call the knack. She has a sixth sense of how things are going to go in business and in the world. It started when she was a kid, and she decided computers were going to be the big thing. This was back when computers were big clunky things that filled up a room."

Freddie asked, "Isn't that what a computer is? It's just a giant adding machine."

"Not anymore," Tim said, and he pulled out his cell phone, "This little thing right here has more brain power than a thousand of the big computers of the seventies, and it is a thousand times faster. I won't try to explain it all to you now. It will take time, but you will learn."

Freddie got the subject back to Sarah, "So she somehow knew this was going to happen."

"Not exactly that, but she could see the stages. Back when computers were big, there was a computer company called Digital Equipment Corporation, or DEC for short. DEC was the in-computer company. IBM was still number one, but DEC was the fair-haired boy. Everyone wanted to write apps. Well in those days, they were called programs for DEC computers."

Tim interrupted himself when he saw the look on Freddie's face, "Apps are what make the computers work. Trust me; I'm sure Ms. Rutherford will have tutors come by and explain it all to you."

Freddie acknowledged that "Okay, so what did Sarah do?"

"Well, around the same time, something new was showing up. Things were getting smaller. The new thing was called a personal computer or a PC. Companies like Apple, Microsoft, and Hewlett-Packard appeared. Ms. Rutherford refused to renew her contracts with DEC and instead made deals with Apple, Microsoft, and Hewlett Packard." Everyone thought she was nuts and that she had just sent her company down a rat hole. A year or so later, DEC was in the tank, and Apple, Microsoft, and Hewlett-Packard all had taken over a big chunk of the market. That's what's called having the knack.

She did that over and over. She still runs a major tech corporation, but she has also diversified. Now she has her own line of cell phones, she has a controlling interest in several resorts, and she is even a major bondholder for several small towns.

The small-town thing was a no-brainer for her. She would find a small town that was struggling, most often because a company pulled their factory out and sent it to China, but that's another issue. Anyway, when Ms. Rutherford knew that she needed to build a new company headquarters, distribution center, or factory somewhere, she would find a struggling town, buy up the municipal bonds for pennies on the dollar and then drop the new structure in the town. The town would be revitalized, the people would love her, and she would make enough profit on the investment to pay for building the new structure.

The most remarkable thing about it is that she did it all without cheating or screwing over anyone except for people that tried to screw her over. In that case, she can be quite ruthless. There is nothing out of her reach."

All Freddie could say was, "Wow."

Barry Batali's phone rang just as he was heading to bed. He answered, and the man said, "Hey, Barry, it's Chip Langston; how are you doing?"

"Just great, Chip. Do you have something for me?"

"Yeah, your nose is still good. There is something odd going on. That Barracuda, which is one fine car, by the way, was parked all day at the Hicks place on Craig Street. That is odd, but to top it off, who happens to stop by with her entourage but Ms. Sarah Hicks Rutherford herself. As usual, they blocked the whole damn street.

Just a little while ago, everyone left. Cindi was given the word, and she picked them up on the way out of town and tailed them to this fancy hotel outside of St. Claire called the Hotel Les Fots Bleus. It looks like they are staying there."

"Yeah, and I bet Ms. Money Bags is footing the bill. Why would the Hicks family be interested in a girl impersonating their daughter?"

"I have no idea, but there isn't a law against it."

"You're right about that. I appreciate all you've done, especially Cindi for being out there on her off hours."

"Cindi loves jerking Ms. Rutherford's chain whenever she can."

"Why is that?"

"I don't know. It was something that happened when she was a kid."

Barry wanted to ask more but just said, "Have Cindi and all the rest come by Stoney's Monday night, and I'll buy everyone a few rounds."

"Will do, Barry; we'll see you then."

Barry thought, "I believe I feel the need to see beautiful Lake St. Claire, or at least to get close to it."

The cars pulled up at the hotel. Sarah's SUV didn't stop at the front but pulled around to the side. Tim showed Freddie where to park, and everyone got out. Sarah said, "You will find some clothes in your rooms and some other things. Tommy and I will be back tomorrow, and we'll do some real shopping. Get some rest."

Tim shook Freddie's hand and said, "It was great to meet you. You are still a rock icon."

Freddie answered, "I'm sorry you can't tell your dad."

Tim said, "Yeah, me too," as he walked away.

The two were happy to see that hotel lobbies and elevators worked the same way. They made it up to their rooms, and they pulled out their room keys. They looked at the instructions, and after several tries, they finally got the doors open.

They looked at each other one more time, and Emily said, "Thank you, Freddie, for everything; you are a good man."

Then they said good night and entered their rooms. Freddie managed to take the time to get his clothes off, and then he collapsed on the bed.

It was well after noon before Freddie thought about opening his eyes. He was still half asleep, and he thought, "Man, it's quiet. Where the hell is everyone? I should at least hear some groaning from someone. There's nothing; I don't even hear Jenny, and she snores like a freight train. Did they just take off and leave me here?"

Freddie's eyes opened, and he said out loud, "Oh yeah, they're all dead or really old. Man, this sucks."

He looked around the beautiful suite from his bed. He had been in suites just and nice, but in the morning, the carpet would be covered in empty whisky bottles, various forms of food, and several bodies. The air would be a combination of stale cigarette smoke, alcohol, and the contents of at least one person's stomach.

The rooms were sparkling clean, and the air was fresh; it was like an alien world. Slowly Freddie got out of bed and went to the bathroom. It was different but not unrecognizable. He showered, which felt really good. The dresser drawers contained underwear, something called boxer briefs. He actually liked the idea. There were undershirts and socks that looked fairly standard. There were blue jeans and pullover shirts in the closet. He chose at rust color shirt to go with the blue jeans. They had guessed well on the sizes, but the shirt was a little too big.

He was looking in the mirror, wondering what the world would think of him, when the phone rang. He turned and looked around the room. He could hear it ringing, but he couldn't find the telephone. Finally, he saw the blinking light on the little piece of plastic and metal by the bed. He picked it up, but it kept ringing. He looked it over and over, and it still kept ringing. He was about to throw it against the wall when he saw the green call button. He pushed the button, and the ringing stopped. He looked at the phone again, and he heard Emily's voice coming through, "Freddie; Freddie, are you there?"

He figured out where the voice was coming from, and he put it to his ear. He said, "I'm sorry, it took me a little while to figure this damn thing out."

"I just figured out how to call you. I tried to call my mom, but it refused to ring; I don't know what I'm doing wrong. Anyway, you're finally up; are you decent?"

"Ah, yeah, I just got dressed."

"Good, open the door; I'm coming over."

He opened the door, and Emily glided in. She looked around and said, "Isn't this place fabulous? I've been up for an hour, and I've been exploring."

"Yeah, the place is pretty nice."

"Oh, I forgot; you're a rock star. I'm sure you've been in places a lot fancier than this."

"I was a rock star. Now I'm Frank McAlester, and I don't know what I am yet."

"Oh, sorry, Freddie; I mean Frank."

"I guess we'll have to get used to using those names. What do you want to be called, Liz, Lizzy, or Beth?"

"Oh boy, I have to think about that."

Freddie pondered a moment. Then he said, "I don't think you're a Lizzy."

"Yeah, neither do I. I'm thinking Beth."

"Okay. It's nice to meet you, Beth."

"And it's nice to meet you, Frank."

Freddie went to the window, saying, "It is a really nice spot. Everything is so green."

He scanned around, and he spotted someone walking around his car, "Hey, someone is screwing with my car."

He moved quickly to the door with Emily right behind him.

They got down the elevator and out the door quickly, and Freddie dashed to his car. He called as he approached, "Hey, what are you doing, man?"

The man turned, and he saw it was the guy from the IHOP. Emily had called him Barry something. Barry answered, "I just admiring it. It's in mint condition; why do you have old plates on it?"

"I haven't gotten around to replacing them; what do you want?"

"I just wanted to see if you had contacted my son yet."

"No, we are working some things out."

"I can see that. If you can stay here, you must not be hurting for money."

Emily joined the conversation; "Look . . ." She had to stop. She almost blurted out his name. It would have been very hard to explain how she knew his name. She started again, "Look, mister, we will contact your son when we're ready and if we feel like it."

"Okay, I was just curious."

Emily was not through with him, "You came all the way out here from Romulus because you were curious? How did you know where we were?"

"This is very important to my son. He really needs your help. To answer your question, I have friends."

"So you had us followed," Emily charged.

Freddie said without thinking, "Damn, the country has turned into a police state. They watch you everywhere you go. I bet there are cameras everywhere."

Barry kept up the pretense, "My son has a deadline. They need to start work if they are to be ready by the holidays. You two are perfect."

Emily repeated, "I said we'll let you know."

Barry turned back to the car, saying, "This sure is a great car." He stopped when he saw what was written on the bumper. He turned, and suddenly he grabbed Emily's arm. Freddie pushed him, and he immediately released her.

Barry straightened up and asked, "What's going on here?"

Emily answered, "What's going on here is that you are a nosy old man who is not helping his son at all."

Barry ignored that answer and asked, "How did you know to write that on the bumper of the car?"

"The members of Barracuda always wrote their initials on the bumper of their cars."

"Yes, they did, just their initials. The only time Freddie MacArthur wrote FM's Cuda on his car was in Chicago. They had the same cars in Detroit. That car wasn't moved from its parking spot at the hotel until it zoomed out of the parking garage the night he and Emily Hicks disappeared. Very few people knew that's what was written on that car, so I'll ask you again, how did you know to write that on the car?"

Freddie was getting madder by the minute, "If it was such a secret, how did you know?"

"I was in my second year on the force when we got the call to start the search. The state trooper said he was behind them, and then there was a flash of light, and they were gone. Everyone thought the car exploded, but there wasn't a hint of debris. Nothing was ever found. Only a handful of people knew what was written on that bumper."

"No one but you and a hundred other cops knew about it. Now I'll ask you; why don't you get out of here before I kick your ass."

"Okay, that was a clever response. Then I'll ask you, young lady, how did you get that scar in exactly the same place Emily Hicks has a scar, and why are you chummy with the Hicks family?"

Emily was saved from answering by two men coming up, getting between Barry and Emily. One turned and asked, "Ms. Richards, is this man bothering you?"

Emily didn't respond to her new name immediately. Freddie jumped in, "We caught him walking around my car; I think he was planning to steal it."

"Relax," Barry said. He pulled out his identification and said, "I'm a retired Romulus police detective. I spotted this car, and I noticed that the tags were expired. I was double-checking before I called it in."

One of the men looked, and he couldn't believe how old the license plate was. He turned and said, "Sir, your tags expired forty-two years ago."

Freddie had to think fast. He said, "Damn, I'm sorry. I used this car in a show, and I forgot to put its street tags on it when the show was over."

"I guess you had better do that as soon as you can."

"Yes, of course, but what was this guy doing out here in the first place?"

The manager of the hotel hurried to the scene. She seemed quite nervous over the entire situation, "Mr. McAlester, Ms. Richards, is everything alright."

Emily charged, "I think this man is following us."

One of the men said, "Ma'am, he's a retired police detective."

The manager turned to Barry and said, "Please leave. If there is something to report, go report it and bring back someone who is still on the force."

Barry moved away, and Freddie called out, "And tell your son to screw himself and his job."

101

When everyone left, Freddie said, "He suspects the truth, but I don't think he can make himself believe it."

"He will keep digging," Emily said, "Sarah said that he never gives up."

Less than an hour later, Tim returned. He was driving a red Dodge Challenger, and another security man was in the passenger seat. They parked, and Tim explained what was happening, "Ms. Rutherford wanted me to pick you up and bring you to her in Dearborn. She didn't want to draw any more attention to you by meeting you here.

Freddie, I mean Frank, Ms. Rutherford would like to trade cars with you. She would like to give you the Dodge for your Plymouth. I'm sorry, I know that car probably means a lot to you, but she thinks it also attracts too much attention. They don't make the Plymouth Barracuda anymore though there are rumors that it may appear again in a year or two. The Challenger is the closest we could find. It is your decision, of course."

Freddie walked over to the Challenger and stroked the hood. Then he looked at the Plymouth Barracuda and said, "That car isn't even mine. It's a rental. I bet AVIS was crying in their beer when they lost that car. Anyway, I have no great love for it. I just hope I can drive the modern version of a car."

"Driving is the same. The Challenger will have more bells and whistles, and I'll go through them with you. If you didn't show up for another ten years, then things might have been different. We're getting close to cars that drive themselves."

"Hell no," Freddie said, "not with me in it."

Tim laughed and said, "A lot of us feel that way."

Freddie traded keys with the other man, and the man went to the Barracuda. He put Michigan plates on the car and drove the Barracuda away.

Future shock struck again, and the two-time travelers stared at the key that wasn't a key. Tim explained, "Cars have what they call keyless entry now. You just keep that in your pocket, and when you get close to the car, it will know it's you, and it will allow you to unlock the doors and start the car."

Emily said, "Trading cars is really a good idea. Someone found out we were here, and I'm sure he tracked the car."

That got Tim's attention, "Someone knows you're here?"

"Yes, it's that Barry guy that my sister and I talked about yesterday."

Tim excused himself and called Tommy. The two were getting used to people talking into what they now knew was a phone of some kind. After a minute, Tim reached out to give the phone to Emily, "Tommy would like to talk to you."

Emily took the phone carefully like she was holding an alien artifact. Slowly she put it to her ear and said, "Hello?"

"Ms. Richards, how do you know that Barry Batali tracked you?"

"He was here just a little while ago. He made a big deal about the plates on the car being expired. He had a point; they had been expired for forty-two years. Freddie, I mean Frank, told him that those were show plates and that he had forgotten to put the street plates back on before he started driving. We think he knows who we are, but, for the moment, he can't make himself believe it. He knew we were at my mom's house, and he knows my sister was there."

"Okay, Ms. Richards, Your sister would like to meet you and Mr. McAlester as soon as possible. Are you ready to leave now?"

Emily looked at Freddie and asked him, "Are you ready to go?"

He nodded, and Emily got back to Tommy, "Yes, we're ready."

"Okay, Tim will bring you to a mall in Dearborn; you will meet Ms. Rutherford there. Someone will pick up your things; you will not be returning there."

Emily speculated, "I'm sure Barry had his friends in the police department following us. I would think his friends are watching us now."

There was a pause; Tommy seemed to be thinking, then he returned saying, "Excuse me for one moment, Ms. Richards."

Emily waited a minute or so, and Tommy returned, "I believe you're right, and I apologize for not dealing with this soon enough. It will be taken care of, but I must change the plans. Please remain where you are until I call, and could you please put Tim back on the phone."

She handed the phone back to Tim, and Tim listened. He acknowledged Tommy's orders, and then he made another call, "Larry, change of plans; Tommy wants you to take the Barracuda to the Dearborn Mall. You will pick up Ms. Rutherford and take her for a ride."

It took a few seconds for Larry to realize what Tim was saying. Tim coaxed, "Larry, Ms. Rutherford is waiting."

Finally, Larry said, "Yes, yes, of course."

Freddie asked, "What was that all about?"

"We're going to complicate Barry Batali's life and little bit and, at the same time, make sure no law enforcement officers in the state help him with his little quest."

Tommy informed Sarah of the situation, and then he said, "I beg your pardon, Ma'am, if I have overstepped my authority."

"How would you have done that?"

"I have started in motion a plan that will require personal involvement by you without your permission Ma'am."

"I have made you chief of my security because I trust your judgment. I am not an expert in these matters; you are. Tell me your plan."

"Ms. Rutherford, I have told one of my men to bring the Barracuda here. I think he should take you on a little drive on Interstate 94 west, as far as the Illinois line, if necessary. My people and I will follow at a discreet distance. I have a feeling that Batali's friends will follow the Barracuda."

"So, we're going to catch them following the Barracuda. What good is that going to do, and why is it useful for me to be in the car?"

"Ma'am, before you leave, I think it would be good if you contacted someone in the governor's office to complain about being under police surveillance. If I may suggest, I believe you should be quite indignant."

"Well, Emily did say that Batali asked what I was doing at my mother's house. I don't have to act; I am actually rather upset about that. Yes, a call to the governor's office is in order. Wait, I get it. You are baiting them. You are expecting someone to tail the Barracuda, and you want to catch them."

"Yes, Ma'am, I am hoping the embarrassment to the governor's office will get the knuckles of some of the police chiefs in the area smacked. After that, I don't think Batali will be getting any more favors from his friends for quite some time."

"We're running a sting; I love it, Tommy. To hell with someone in the governor's office, Tommy; get the governor on the line."

"Yes, Ma'am."

Tommy got on the phone. After a moment, he said, "Ms. Sarah Hicks Rutherford for the governor."

Sarah's name made many people jump, including the governor. He was on the line in less than a minute. Tommy smiled and handed the phone to Sarah.

The governor started, "Good day Ms. Rutherford. What may I do for you today?"

"Governor, sir, you can tell me why I am being treated like a criminal in my home state."

"You have been treated like a criminal, Ms. Rutherford?"

"That's right, governor. My mother called me yesterday morning and asked me to come home. You know yesterday was the anniversary of my sister's disappearance?"

"I know, Ms. Rutherford, and we all still mourn your loss."

"Thank you for the kind words, governor; I just wish the law enforcement people in this state would have the same compassion."

"Why, what has happened?"

"For reasons beyond my understanding, they have had me under surveillance since I entered the state. I'm sure you realize that my security people are professional. They spotted their actions. I could have had them simply take countermeasures, but I would rather do things above board. I would like your office to determine why I am being treated like a criminal. I know that law enforcement has noted the time I arrived and my mother's house, the time I left, and where I went after leaving my mother's house. I find this action highly insulting. Am I suspected of any wrongdoing?"

The governor was shocked and quite nervous about what this could mean for his political ambitions, "Ms. Rutherford, rest assured that I will get to the bottom of this, and please accept my most sincere apology."

"I know that you can't control every law enforcement officer in the state, and I would not have bothered you if I didn't know that there was more than one jurisdiction involved in the surveillance."

"My office will contact every police department in the state; I promise you. No one will bother you again."

"Thank you, governor; I knew I could count on you."

Sarah looked at Tommy and asked, "Okay, what's next?"

"Now we wait for Larry to bring the car. They won't get the word out to everyone that is looking for that car immediately. I believe that you should have Larry drive you through Romulus, then out onto Interstate 94 going west. I will have my people doing a tag team surveillance keeping the Barracuda in their sight. They will know if it picks up a tail. When it does, we'll let you know, and you can call the governor and tell him that someone is following you right now."

"You want the cops to pull over the cops. Won't they just contact them and tell them to back off?"

"It depends on the vehicle. If it is a marked police car, we'll just video the event and note down the identifying information. If the car suddenly breaks off, we will have enough information to have the governor rain down the fire. If it is unmarked, we will stop it. We'll box it in and force it to stop."

"How are you going to know for sure the Barracuda is being followed?"

"When we suspect you're being followed, we will ask you to have Larry pull off the interstate and go to the nearest gas station. If the car follows, we will know for sure."

Sarah was excited, "This is an adventure; I can't wait for Larry to get here."

"It will take a few more minutes, and I'll need that time to get my people in position and ready to go."

It took forty-five minutes for Tommy to get everything set up. When he was ready, Sarah opened the car door and sat in the passenger seat. She looked at the interior, and she said, "My, my, I may just have to keep this beauty."

Then she turned to Larry, "You are Larry?"

Larry was very nervous. His voice shook a bit as he answered, "Yes, Ma'am, and it is an honor for me to drive you, Ma'am."

Sarah smiled at his nervousness, and she said, "Relax, Larry, you're just taking an old lady for a drive; now let's be off."

The fire did rain down from the governor's office to the mayors, to the police commissioners, and all over the detectives and officers. Detectives Cindi Baveroski and Eric Volstad were outside their normal lunch spot when they got the word. Eric said, "Oh boy, I guess we better back off of Barry's little quest."

As they got in the car, Cindi growled, "That just pisses me off. Money Bags makes a call, and everyone jumps like trained dogs." Then they got a call on the radio, "Detective Baveroski, we just spotted that Barracuda you were looking for. It's on 94 heading west, just passing Shook Rd."

Cindi acknowledged the call and started the car. Eric asked, "You're going after it, aren't you?"

"You're damn right I am. The brass didn't say anything about chasing down an old car with expired plates. We're going to pull his ass over and ask him a few questions."

"But he must be a friend of Sarah Hicks Rutherford. You're about to piss off a billionaire."

"Then she should have told her friend to get a proper registration."

"Nice and easy, Larry," Sarah instructed as Larry drove the Barracuda west on 94. "Keep it to the speed limit. We don't want to give them any legitimate reason to pull us over."

Sarah's phone rang. She brought it out, and Tommy told her. "You have a tail, ma'am; it's a few cars behind you. Please tell Larry to take the next exit. There is a gas station half a mile north on the right. I have two teams ahead of you. They will be in position. One will be at the gas station, and the other will fall in directly behind you when you come off the exit."

"Okay, Tommy, see you soon."

Larry said, "I heard the instruction."

Sarah couldn't help it; she just started giggling. "This is such fun. I have made up a whole speech in my mind. If they don't ask any questions, I might have to give it to them anyway."

The Barracuda had a black SUV come up behind them as it came off the exit. A few seconds later, Cindi brought her car off the exit. Eric said, "I don't like this. Where did that SUV come from?"

Eric got on the radio as he stared at the license plate on the SUV, "I need a plate run. It's a Michigan plate, AK6-982; it's a black Ford Explorer."

Cindi watched the Barracuda, and the SUV pull into the gas station as the voice on the radio reported. The SUV belongs to a security company called Max Protection. It's out of Detroit."

Eric acknowledged the information, and Cindi pulled into the gas station. Suddenly she found herself boxed in by the SUV and another one that had been parked a few feet away. The security team jumped out, took positions, and waited.

Cindi rolled down her window while Eric was on the radio calling for backup. Cindi showed her badge and her gun and called out, "Back off; we're on police business. Move away now."

No one moved as a third SUV entered the gas station. Tommy stepped out and walked to Cindi's car and said, "We are Ms.

Rutherford's security detail, and you have been following her for a few miles. We could only assume that this was a kidnapping attempt."

"We weren't following Ms. Rutherford. Do you see a limo around here anywhere?"

Sarah tried to keep a straight face as she stepped out of the Barracuda. She said, "I don't always ride in limos, my dear. I am upset. I was assured that the harassment that started yesterday would be ended."

Cindi was beyond surprised, but she wasn't the type to back down, "No harassment was intended, Ms. Rutherford. We had a report about a mint condition 1973 Plymouth Barracuda driving through town with expired plates. It was our duty to find it."

"Detective, would you please step out of the car so that we can converse properly."

Tommy opened the door, Cindi stepped out, and Sarah responded to Cindi's statement, "You are saying the entire police force was mobilized to find a car with expired plates. Who reported this heinous crime?"

"One of our officers saw it but lost it in traffic."

"And that's when the dragnet started."

"Not a dragnet; we just put out a BOLO."

"And it was just a passing police car that spotted the fugitive car in my mother's driveway? Why did the officer not stop and simply issue a citation?"

Cindi knew she was in trouble, "He didn't want to disturb the gathering. He did see your SUV parked out front."

"How nice of him, then why not pull him over after he left instead of tailing us to the hotel?"

"Again, he didn't want to disturb you."

"If that is the only reason, why was he reporting my every move? What evil deed have I been suspected of doing?"

"Nothing Ms. Rutherford; we were after the car, not you."

"This BOLO was issued because of an expired plate. That is rather odd in itself. What is odder is that this car doesn't have expired plates."

Cindi stepped into the car and saw the up-to-date Michigan plates on the car. Cindi stated, "Those plates were changed. There were expired plates on the car."

"They were show plates on the car detective. The owner just forgot to take them off before driving. The show plates expired in 1975; who would have forgotten to renew their registration for forty-two years?"

Cindi didn't have an answer, and the silence was broken by five police cars rushing into the gas station. The security people spun around. Sarah called out, "Stay calm, holster your weapons, and raise your hands."

Tommy added another touch to the plan. He tipped the local TV station to the event, and the police were quickly followed by a news crew. Sarah stepped out with Cindi; now, she felt like she was really on stage. She called, "Ladies and gentlemen, this is all an unfortunate misunderstanding. The detective and I have worked it all out."

Everyone relaxed, and police cars pulled away, but the news people wanted more. Sarah loved it so much that she came up with another story on the spot, "As I said, it was a misunderstanding. Someone saw me in the passenger seat of that great old car and was afraid I was being kidnapped. The detective and her partner rushed into the gas station to save me. Though it was a false alarm, I appreciate their courage and their effort on my behalf."

Cindi was surprised and found herself a bit tongue-tied when the microphone was turned to her. She did finally make a statement, and Sarah politely asked if she could be excused from any more questions.

When the reporters left, Cindi had to ask, "Why did you cover for me like that? I thought for sure you were going to demand my head."

"Because you are strong and fearless, you remind me of my little sister Emily. She was like that; that's why she was with Barracuda. I know you are wondering, and the answer is yes, there is a connection between Emily and this 1973 Barracuda. This isn't the Barracuda that disappeared that night, but it is another Barracuda that Freddie MacArthur drove during the tour. It had been preserved, first by AVIS and then by the subsequent owner. I'm sorry; I tend to babble at times. I heard you tell the reporters that your name is Cindi Baveroski?"

"That's right."

"Good; I wanted to be sure I had it right when I talked to the commissioner."

That statement made Cindi suck in her breath, but Sarah eased her mind, "Oh no, I just want to tell him that the force needs more good people like you."

After the detectives left, Tommy asked, 'Did you call the governor from the car?"

"No, I forgot to; now I'm glad I forgot. She's a fine detective. It is always better to make a friend instead of an enemy."

Sarah hadn't made a friend. She didn't recognize Cindi's name. If she had been going by her maiden name, Cindi Harrison, she might have remembered. Then she might have realized that Detective Cindi Baveroski would not let up. Her anger was too deep.

Chapter 7: Look-Alikes

Emily, Freddie, and Tim had just finished a snack at the restaurant when Tim got the call. They all got up and headed for the SUV. Freddie said, "I guess Sarah brought the hammer down on the cops."

"Yeah, the plan worked well. Tommy is pretty damn clever himself, and Sarah is smart enough to handle things without making serious enemies."

They arrived in Dearborn just a few minutes after Sarah. The security team moved away and discreetly controlled the area. Sarah never dressed lavishly, but she was dressed even more casually for their trip to the mall. She wanted to walk around with Emily without being noticed.

As they entered Macy's, she asked Emily, "You had told me that Barry assumed you were actors looking for work?"

"Yes, he said we were something called look-alikes and that he assumed some agency sent us to Romulus to look for work."

"You know that isn't a bad cover. You might not recognize the term, but people have been making a living by looking like celebrities for years. They've always been in Vegas, but they seem to be a bit more popular now. Everyone knows them as look-alikes. Some of them are quite remarkable in the resembling of the actual stars."

"That's perfect."

Sarah turned to Tommy, "Tommy, find an agency that works with look-alikes and set them up."

Freddie entered the conversation, "I was thinking; the offer from Barry's son may still be useful. It would give us a reason to be in Romulus, and the look-alike deal would answer the questions about why we look like people everyone thinks are dead."

Sarah turned back to Tommy and asked, "Tommy, please have the agency reach out to KWTZ and convince them to grant our two actors an interview."

Tommy was already on the phone with his people in California, but he responded promptly, "Yes, Ma'am."

Emily found the styles to be different but not crazy. Yes, there were some crazy styles, but there were crazy styles at every age. Everyone laughed when Freddie told them how much he liked the idea of boxer briefs.

In the middle of the shopping spree, Emily was hit with a thought, "Freddie, you never talk about your family. Where did you grow up?"

"I grew up in Fairfax, Virginia; everyone in the band did."

"You have to find your family."

Freddie had been thinking about them, but he didn't know how to fit them into his new world. His brother Steve would be sixty-three. His sister Dorothy would be sixty-one, and Mom and Dad would both be in their nineties. He didn't want to face it, but the odds were that they were gone. Finally, Freddie answered, "I don't know. I don't know what I would say to them."

"You will say exactly what I said, "That you're home and that you love them."

"How? I don't know where I would even find them. They've had full careers and probably families of their own. A whole life has gone by."

"I know, Freddie, I have cried over what I have missed, especially missing my dad, but you have to see the people you love. Believe me; it is worth the effort."

Sarah joined, "You do, Freddie. Believe me. I am so happy that you helped bring Emily back to us. Just give us a few more days.

Driving that far could be difficult for you, and flying or taking the train would require you to show a picture ID."

"Man," Freddie said in frustration, "when did this country get so damn paranoid?"

"We're not paranoid, Freddie; someone really is out to get us. They are called radical Muslims, and they committed some terrible terror attacks in the United States. The worst was the attacks on September 11, 2001. It is referred to as nine-eleven. Terrorists crashed commercial airliners into the two tallest buildings in New York, another into the Pentagon, and another was going for the White House. The White House was saved by a group of very heroic passengers. Instead, the plane crashed in rural Pennsylvania. The Pentagon was seriously damaged; the twin towers of the World Trade Center were completely destroyed. The attacks killed thousands of people. It surpassed Pearl Harbor as being the worst day in American history. Since then, no one gets on a plane without being searched and having proper identification."

Freddie and Emily were struck silent for a moment. Then Freddie said, "Man, I never would have believed that something like that could happen. I saw a news report a little while ago; well, what seems to me was a little while ago, it was announcing the completion of the World Trade Center. I think I'm happy I wasn't around for that."

Sarah said, "I wish I could have skipped it also, but that's the reason for the security. You will see more security everywhere. Because of that, we need to make sure you have ironclad IDs before you go anywhere. It will be a few more days."

Emily asked, "How ironclad do they have to be?"

"Very," Sarah answered, "you still don't understand the power the internet has put in the palm of everyone's hands."

"Yeah," Emily remembered, "Barry poked a few buttons, and he showed us the headlines in the paper of the day we went missing. I didn't know how he did that."

"Information is available instantly; all people have to do is type your name into the device and search through the common information. If they don't eventually find the information that you gave them, you will be caught. It takes more than making some documents these days, but we have experts that can handle it; it will just take a few days."

Emily was amazed at the mall. The entire structure had changed, and she was taking it all in. Freddie had gone to the big mall in the Washington area at the time. It was Tyson Corners Center. They were just completing a brand new mall right in Springfield when he left on tour. There were stores they recognized and some they had never heard of. They kept Sarah busy with questions about what happened to this store and what happened to that store.

Finally, they arrived at a cell phone store. Sarah announced, "It's time that you two had your own phones."

They picked out the phones, and they got their first lesson in their use. When the clerk asked for the billing details, Sarah handed the clerk her identification and said, "Just bill everything to me."

The clerk looked at the information, and her eyes opened wide. She looked up and asked, "Are you. . ."

"Yes dear, and they are buying Rutherford phones, so I think you know I'm good for it."

"Yes, of course, Ms. Rutherford; the store is yours."

"Yeah, I guess it is, isn't it."

Sarah told the time travelers as they caressed their phones. I'll give you enough to get you started, and then I'll send someone to your hotel to give you full instructions. Consider this your real introduction to the twenty-first century."

They left the mall late in the afternoon. Emily and Freddie were dropped at an Embassy Suites in town, and Sarah went back to her accommodations.

Freddie sat in his room. His thoughts were now on his family. How did it all turn out for them? He knew Steve was in college before all this happened. He was a physics major; he was always the smartest kid in the family. Dorothy was no dummy herself. She was in high school and getting decent grades, but Dorothy had a wild streak. He was afraid that she might end up in the groupie world. Maybe that's why he could never abuse the girls.

"What happened to them," he wondered.

He was afraid to think about his parents. They could still be at home, but what were the odds? Dad was in pretty good shape, but he smoked like a chimney. He was an electrical engineer, and he worked for Defense Systems Incorporated. DSI developed a new technology for the Navy. Mom stayed home and took care of everyone. Mom was a little heavy, but otherwise, she always seemed healthy. They could be at home.

Sarah told them to dress up. She said that they would be going to Faraday's. Emily told him that Faraday's was the finest steakhouse in Detroit. Freddie put on the suit that the ladies helped him pick out. It took him a while to remember how to tie a tie. There isn't much call for wearing a suit when touring with a rock and roll band.

He had just finished dressing when he heard a knock on the door. He opened the door, and there was Emily smiling at him. Freddie just stared. He had seen hundreds of women with knock-out bodies but no one as elegantly beautiful as Emily. Her dress flowed over her body like a work of art, and her face was just radiant.

Emily said, "Why don't you look sharp in your new suit."

It took a moment for Freddie to respond. Emily said, "Earth to Freddie, come in, Freddie."

Freddie snapped out of it, and he stumbled through a response, "It's been a while. I had forgotten how stiff these things were. I feel like I'm in a suit of armor."

"Well, you look very nice, sir."

"And you look so beautiful."

The tone of Freddie's voice made it clear that he was serious. Now it was Emily's turn to take a breath.

Chip Langston called Barry that night. Barry picked up the phone, and Chip started right in, "Barry, old buddy, you really stirred up a hornet's nest."

"I thought Rutherford might flex her money muscle. What did she do go crying to the commissioner?"

"Try the governor, my friend. The sky turned brown over every police station in the state if you know what I mean. His anger made the Mayors angry, and their anger made the commissioners angry, and now we're all feeling the heat. On top of that, Cindi managed to pull over your mint condition 1973 Plymouth Barracuda, and Ms. Sarah Hicks Rutherford herself was in the passenger seat. That turned into a circus with her security, police backup, and a news van."

"Oh boy, I'm really sorry I caused that much trouble. Is Cindi getting through it? They're not coming down too hard on her, are they? If so, I will come in there and straighten them out."

"No, amazingly enough, old Money Bags praised her and talked her up to the commissioner. She is going to end up ahead of the game."

"Oh, the lady is smart; I'll give her that."

"She also had an explanation that covered all the bases, including the car. It sounds good if you don't look too close; believe me, no one is going to look too close."

"Well, maybe I will."

"You'll have to do it on your own. We can't get anywhere near her or anyone she is remotely connected to, and they are serious."

"I understand; again, I'm sorry for the trouble."

"It's okay, buddy; we'll see you Monday night."

Barry was pacing in his family room when his wife came in, "I haven't seen you do that since you left the force. What are you pondering?"

"I'm pondering the impossible."

"You're still thinking about that girl that looks like Emily Hicks."

"She doesn't look like Emily Hicks; she is Emily Hicks, and her friend is Freddie MacArthur."

"Barry, maybe we should take a vacation. Maybe we should go to the beach or on a cruise."

"Yeah, I know, you think I've gone off the deep end. Maybe I have. I just remember the old Sherlock Holmes quote, 'Once you eliminate the possible, whatever remains, no matter how improbable, must be the truth.'"

"Well dear, I would have to say that you have not made all of the possible impossible yet, because the improbable is not possible."

"Look at the picture. I took this before I talked to them at the IHOP. You went to school with her; tell me that isn't Emily Hicks."

"Didn't you tell me that you thought they were look-alikes from California or somewhere?"

"Yes, I did; that was before I saw the writing on the car and the scar on her arm. Those two things could be created, but what are the odds?"

"They are better odds than people appearing out of nowhere after forty-four years. There weren't many people that knew what was written on the car, but it wasn't a state secret. During the search, a lot of cops knew, and at least some of them told their families. It could have gotten around. The scar could be a coincidence, or it's a fake."

"If what was written on the bumper was known, why wasn't it part of any of the hundred or so documentaries on their disappearance? If Twenty-Twenty didn't have it, no one would."

"You know what this is, don't you? You miss the mystery. You miss cracking the case. I could see it from the first time you told me about those two. You haven't been this excited about something since you left the force. Don't give up, Baby. Find the real reason for this mystery."

Barry's wife left the room, and Barry remembered something he was told recently. Another blast from the past appeared in town just a few weeks ago. Betty Ann Rother was back and living with her brother. She was down on her luck again; it seems her life hadn't changed much. No one knew what had happened to the guy she was supposed to be married to. He would track her down. He was sure that, for a few bucks, she would be happy to help him find out more.

The restaurant was beautiful, with linen tablecloths and fine crystals. Everything served was a creation of the chef, and the wine was top drawer. Freddie realized that the wine was the first alcohol he had had since they left Chicago; Detroit was too crazy to think about drinking. He thought, "I guess that proves I'm not an alcoholic."

Sarah proposed a toast to family foundations and meeting new friends. That brought Emily back to Freddie's family, "Freddie, I think we should go as soon as we can."

"Oh, you don't have to go with me. You should stay here and be with your family. Your mom is such a wonderful lady and she wants as much of your time as you can give her."

"My mom would want me to be with you. I wouldn't be with my family if it wasn't for you, and I want to help you reunite with yours."

"I guess it will be some time. After we have all the paperwork we need, we still have to buy tickets, and I don't think they have seats available on the same day you buy a ticket."

Sarah broke into the conversation, "I was thinking about that. There isn't any reason for you to go through all of that. You still need proper ID for travel, but you don't have to deal with getting tickets, going through the terminal, and dealing with the lines."

Emily asked, "Why not?"

"I'll take you."

Freddie was confused, "Are you going to drive us all the way there in your limo?"

"No, I'm going to fly you all the way there in my airplane."

Emily was happy she wasn't sipping her wine because she would have to spit it all over the table, "You have an airplane?"

Sarah turned to Freddie and asked, "You and your band traveled from place to place in your own bus, didn't you?"

"Yeah, I spent many hours in that thing."

"Why didn't you use public transportation?"

"It would have been a mess and not very safe. I don't want to sound like I thought we were special, but the fans would have been all over us."

"Then it was a matter of security and not ego."

"Yeah, we needed to get from place to place in one piece."

"People in my position have the same problem. I can't just wander into large crowds without being very careful. My plane is just like your bus. I can make some calls. There are a few people in Washington that might benefit from my paying a visit. The plane can do double duty. Since I will do a little business, I can even write off the trip."

Freddie was back to his favorite word, "Wow."

"I have some business to take care of in the next few days. It will take a little more time to get your IDs together, so this is what I propose. I will send a tutor by to give you more details about the technology that you need to understand. In a few days, you should be able to handle your phone, the internet that it is connected to, and other things like your television. Once you understand those things, all the information of the last forty-four years will be at your disposal."

Emily and Freddie returned to the hotel. They still held their phones like they had found the greatest treasure of their lives. When they got up to their rooms, they turned to say goodnight. Freddie turned to find Emily right in front of him. She kissed him, and he responded by putting his arms around her.

When they stepped away, Emily said, "I got tired of waiting. You've been too nervous or polite to make the first move, so I decided to make it for you."

"I'm very happy you did, but are you sure this isn't just a survivor thing? You know, two people with a common problem."

"We'll see, but that isn't what my heart is telling me."

Freddie put his arms around her again and said, "Then I am very happy to agree with your heart's analysis of the situation."

Emily stopped him right there, "Goodnight, Freddie. Let's do this one step at a time, shall we?"

Freddie smiled and acknowledged her request. She kissed him one more time, and they entered their rooms.

The next few days were a blur of instruction. Ellen Crenshaw was a wonderful tutor. Before the time travelers knew it, they were making calls using Bluetooth, taking pictures and videos, looking things up on the internet, and buying things online. There were many glitches and confusions, but their understanding moved forward, and the amazement never ebbed. The future was becoming less shocking by the hour.

Freddie asked Ellen, "So we don't have a station on the moon?"

"No, I'm afraid the space program took a nosedive. We had the space shuttle, which did some wonderful work in orbit. We have an international space station that has produced some great things.

The most exciting events in space were the probes sent to the other planets and the space telescopes that have brought us some great pictures of the universe. The probes have sent us pictures from most of the planets. No probe lasts long enough on Venus to send us a lot of pictures. Also, telescope technology has advanced greatly. It has allowed us to find planets around other stars."

"Wait, you are saying that there are other Earths out there?"

"We haven't found a planet like Earth, but we're getting close."

"So they think one is out there?"

"Oh, they think there are a lot of Earth-type planets; the question is, will we ever find one? It is a very large universe. Even if we do find one, it is likely to be too far away for us ever to get there."

Emily wanted to know more about the state of the world, "You said that the Soviet Union is gone and that we do a large amount of business with China. They were our two scariest enemies. Does that mean we are closer to world peace?"

Ellen tried to explain, "I'm afraid not. The Middle East now has many radical groups that have threatened to do all kinds of destruction in America. We know they are supported by some of the Middle Eastern nations, and we haven't quite figured out how to deal with them."

"They are the religious extremist that caused the tragic event in 2001?"

"Yes, and they claim it is on religious grounds, but it is far more complicated than that, and it isn't something that can be fully explained in the time that we have. And the Middle East isn't the only problem. Russia is no longer communist, but it isn't a great friend either. The world had a chance in the nineties to make great strides to mend the fences between the East and the West, but it didn't happen. The Cold War ended, but I'm afraid it is in the process of restarting. China is a major trading partner, but we are still at odds with them politically. There are many issues that can still bring us to the brink of war with China. This is all too complicated to resolve in a few days. I'll just have to answer your question by saying; I'm afraid the world may be a more dangerous place now than it was during the Cold War."

Ellen finished her final lesson and said her goodbyes. The time travelers thought about all they had learned, and they were deciding how to use this newfound knowledge. Emily started, "I'm calling Mom. Now I know that I should have been putting in all ten digits to make it work; I can talk to her. It's funny that we would have to use an area code to call someone a few miles away, but I guess it's necessary."

Freddie heard Emily start talking to her mother. The happiness in her voice made Freddie smile. He considered looking for information on the band. Up till now, he had the excuse of not having access, but now it was all there on his phone. He decided to do it. He knew deep inside that the story wouldn't be good, but he had to know. He found out he was right quickly with the title at the top of the search list. It was Barracuda, a Rock and Roll Tragedy. He didn't want to see what it was going to tell him, but he opened the link.

After he and Emily left the hotel, the police rounded everyone up. Rick spent quite some time in the hospital recovering from the drug overdose. When he recovered, he was charged with leaving the scene of an accident and vehicular homicide. He was in prison for fifteen years, and it ended his music career. The last report they had on him was that he went home and was living in the old homestead. Freddie wondered, "Could he still be there?"

Peter Chiles was charged with several crimes, including obstruction of justice. They threw the book at him. He received the maximum sentence for all crimes. Many thought it was because he was a good cop who went to the other side. The other members of the band were charged as accessories but received suspended sentences.

Mickey did go on to have a reasonably successful single career, but the cloud of that night always hung over him. When this documentary was shot, he was in California, and he still performed at small venues in the LA area.

Don did join another band, but he never hit the big time again. He died of pneumonia brought on by his battle with AIDS. He died at age forty-seven.

Ryan dropped off the grid. He gave up his drums and sunk the money he had left into being a naturalist. One day he went on an expedition in New Guinea, and he was never seen again. He had cleaned out all of his accounts and bought up all sorts of the things needed for living in the wild. It looked like getting lost was purposeful. His body was found in a shallow grave deep in the jungle. No one knew how he met his end. When he was last seen, he was fifty-three years old.

Finally, he saw what they said about Freddie MacArthur, "Freddie disappeared along with Emily Hicks, a college student studying journalism. According to Emily's sister, Ms. Sarah Hicks Rutherford,

Emily was doing research for a story on the life of a groupie. Freddie supported her dramatic escape from the Detroit hotel, and they were never seen again. Rick Santora had claimed that he was with Freddie that night in Chicago when the woman was struck and killed, but Freddie wasn't there to back up his story. Many thought the loss of Freddie was the end of Barracuda. Mickey might have been the leader, but Freddie was the anchor of the group. Without him, they spun off out of control. The disappearance of Freddie MacArthur and Emily Hicks remains one of the greatest unsolved mysteries of our time."

There was plenty of footage from their concerts and some taken on the bus and backstage. What really surprised Freddie was what was said about Betty Ann Rother, "Though many accused her of putting the drugs in Rick Santora's whisky bottle, it couldn't be proven. No one actually saw her do it, and Rick's whisky bottle was discarded before it could be tested. Betty Ann Rother moved on to a punk rock band called Wicked Licks, but it was short-lived. She wasn't quite trusted, and she finally left the groupie life. She held various jobs, moving from one part of the country to another. At last report, she was married and living somewhere in Louisiana."

Freddie sat and watched a video of him and the boys playing, and he couldn't believe that they would never do it again. To him, it was less than a week since they were on stage together, but it was forty-four years ago. Barracuda, and all of their music, were gone. Suddenly Freddie felt an aching need to play a guitar and a great sadness for what will never be again. He just sat in the chair with his head in his hands.

Emily ended her conversation with her mother. While she talked to her, she could hear the story that was being told about Barracuda. She went to Freddie, put her arms around him, and said, "You need to go home."

Tommy called Emily and Freddie and asked them to join him, Tim, and Sarah at the Hicks homestead. Shelly Hicks was overjoyed to have everyone back for another meal. She made a big pot of soup, homemade bread, and a chocolate cake. Friday evening's chatter picked up where it left off, and everyone again was filled with happiness.

After the meal, Tommy pulled the time travelers aside and handed them each an envelope. In it, they found a driver's license, a birth certificate, a passport, several credit cards, and a stack of documents related to education, medical records, and employment history. Tommy suggested that they study the documents and commit the information to memory. He also showed them their internet trail. It included a Twitter account, a Facebook page, and an Instagram account. There were cleverly created pictures of them in places they had never been, with people that they had never met. The people would swear to know them if they were asked.

Freddie looked over the information and said, "Well, you sure covered all of the bases."

"I wanted to be thorough."

Emily asked Sarah, "When can we go to Washington?"

Sarah answered, "In a couple of days if you like. I have talked to a few people, and I am set up to see them at my convenience."

Emily asked Freddie, "Are you ready?"

Freddie was surprised that they could leave so soon, "I wanted to see what the internet could tell me about my family before I went there."

Emily volunteered, "We can do that in a day."

Emily announced, "We're off to Virginia."

Sarah wanted to bring up one more point, "I was thinking of another issue. This isn't one we need to deal with any time soon, and you need not have a big role in what I want to plan. I am a tech person; it seems some people have dubbed me the Queen of Tech. I have lived with an analytical mind my entire life. Your appearance after forty-four years is probably one of the greatest mysteries in human history. There are questions. Has it happened before? Will it happen again? What kind of power would it take to cause such an event, and could we control it?

It is a mystery that we should at least make an attempt to solve. In addition to my other interests, I have created SHR Laboratories specifically to search for the next breakthrough that will improve the human condition. I want the mystery of what happened to you investigated. I don't think it will take up much of your time."

Freddie and Emily not only agreed but were happy to hear that people may one day be able to explain what happened to them. That discussion ended the evening. Emily and Freddie returned to the hotel. They stopped at the hotel bar for a drink. They needed a minute to, once again, take a breath.

Freddie said, "Things keep moving so fast. It has only been a few days, and it seems like I have been on some kind of roller coaster for weeks. You think I would be used to this kind of pace from touring, but this is different. Can we slow down for an hour or so? Maybe we can take a walk?"

"That would be great, Freddie. I know what you mean. I feel like I can't breathe sometimes, and it scares me. I still feel outside of this world, like I'm a visitor. Being with Mom and Sarah is great, and this may sound crazy, but sometimes the only one that feels real is you."

They left the hotel and just walked about the landscaped grounds and the parking lot. They weren't interested in site seeing; they just wanted to feel the peace and quiet of the night. Emily took Freddie's hand, and Freddie felt her touch stabilize him just a bit. He looked up at the stars that he could see in the glare of the city and said, "At least they're still there. I loved to look at the stars when I was a kid. I guess I thought that I grew out of that, but maybe I just traded it for more destructive nighttime pursuits."

Emily looked around and said, "I hope Sarah can find someone that can explain how this happened. Maybe that would help make this feel more real."

They stopped, and Freddie had to ask, "Is that why you have feelings for me? Is it because I'm your only connection to your previous life?"

"Freddie, it isn't because of what happened. It is because of who you are and how you have always been toward me; before and after this, whatever it is. It's not the world, Freddie; it's you." They stopped in the middle of the lighted parking lot and kissed.

Chapter 8: Virginia

The next day Freddie and Emily searched the internet. The first information hit Freddie hard. Both his parents were gone. His father had a stroke four years ago, and his mother just seemed to waste away and died two years later. Emily said, "I'm so sorry."

Freddie just sat back for a moment and said, "I guess I'm not surprised at what happened to my mother. Mom and dad were inseparable; I guess she just couldn't live without him.

So many years, so much life that we've missed. So many people are gone forever. It's not just my mom and dad; it's Don and Ryan. Those guys were like brothers to me. In the last few years, in our time--not in this screwed-up time, I was closer to them, Mickey and Rick, than I was to anyone. Mickey and Rick are alive, but they're in their sixties, and I can't tell them who I am anyway. I was just with them; now they're gone. They're all gone. What's the point in going back there?"

"Let's find the rest of your family. Who else can we look for?"

My brother Steve and my sister Dorothy should be in their sixties. They don't have to be in Virginia; they can be anywhere."

"Well, let's find out. We can start with your brother; he should be easier to find."

They searched for Steven MacArthur and found quite a few in Virginia. After a process of elimination, they found Dr. Steve MacArthur. He was a retired theoretical physicist living in Occoquan, Virginia. Emily said, "Listen, this could be him. It says he graduated from the University of Virginia and went to graduate school at Brandeis University in Boston, and he grew up in Fairfax, Virginia."

Freddie was reading with her, "That's him. I remember that he was starting his senior year at the University of Virginia when the Wrecking Ball tour started."

"Okay, then there is a reason to go to Virginia. Now, what about your sister?"

They continued searching, and they found Dorothy Amherst. Her maiden name was MacArthur, and she grew up in Fairfax, Virginia. It said that she was a retired paleontologist who spent her career doing fieldwork for the Smithsonian. She was married with two children and three grandchildren. She and her husband, Richard, lived in Sarasota, Florida. Freddie was happy to hear it. He said, "I guess she settled down a bit after I left. The last thing I heard, she was in high school giving my parents fits with her antics."

He also found out that Rick Santora did return home to Fairfax. Despite the availability of drugs in prison, Rick stayed clean and returned home a different man. He got into public service work. Being a somewhat famous person that burned himself out on drugs made him quite a catch for drug prevention groups. He married and had two boys. His boys were grown and gone, and his wife died of cancer three years ago. Soon after, his mother passed away, and that's when Rick returned to the old homestead.

After reading that, Freddie sat back again. Emily asked, "Are you thinking of seeing Rick? What would you say to him?"

"I would like to tell him that I didn't bail on him on purpose."

"Actually, Freddie, that is one reason I'm happy that you are here. From what that documentary was saying, he expected you to lie for him. You could have ended up in prison also."

"He was Rick. Yes, I would have lied for him. I had already been asked, and I was planning on doing just that, but I wasn't there. He went to prison because I wasn't there."

"No, he went to prison for getting high and running down a woman and leaving her to die. I know he was a lifelong friend, but what happened to him wasn't your fault; it was justice."

"The point is moot. He probably wouldn't believe me anyway. For that matter, how am I going to get my brother to believe me? How do I even approach him?"

"We'll work it out. Maybe we should have asked for more time. I guess I wasn't thinking when I said we were ready to go. We do know that the DNA thing seems to be foolproof."

"Yes, I know. I just have to think a little."

Emily had a thought, "Wait a minute, didn't you say that your brother was a theoretical physicist?"

"Yeah, it said that he just retired. I think they said he worked at the U.S. Naval Research Laboratory."

"Then he would be just the person Sarah may want to talk to. Whatever happened to us can't be just magic. There has to be some science behind it, and that science must be physics. I think Sarah can help you to convince Steve."

Freddie got a funny look on his face, and Emily asked him what was wrong. He tried to explain, "Please don't think that I'm not grateful for everything Sarah has done. I am eternally grateful, but it seems that she is doing everything. She completely supports us. She is helping us get over the future shock, and she protects us from everyone, including the cops. I don't know; maybe it's a man thing. I guess I am feeling like a helpless child. I can't even meet my own brother without her help."

"You're right. I guess I don't feel it as much because she's my sister, and I would expect her to do things for me. We aren't taking anything that we didn't need to take. We couldn't have made it without her."

"Oh, I know that, Emily. Believe me, I do. I just need to take one step on my own. I think your idea of Steve getting involved in the mystery is great; if he is interested. I think Sarah should talk to him about it, but can we try to approach Steve on our own first?"

"Of course, we can. You can do it yourself if you like."

"No, I will need you there. You said that there are times when I'm the only one that feels real to you. Well, there are times when you are the only thing that keeps me anchored to this new world of ours. I need you with me."

Emily just rested her head on his shoulder for a minute.

Barry watched the house where Betty was supposed to be living. On Sunday evening, he finally saw her returning home. She was driving an old 2009 blue Ford Fusion, and it clearly didn't look like it was maintained properly. Barry noted the plate number, then he got out of his car and moved to intercept her before she got in the house. He called to her, "Betty Ann Rother, it's me, Barry Batali."

"Betty turned and watched Barry approach. Finally, she asked, "How did you know that I was here?"

"I saw you one day, and I just guessed that you were with Buddy. How've you been?"

"Just Dandy, I'm rolling in the dough; I'm just living with my brother to give him some company."

"Look, I may be able to get you some quick cash and get you involved with something that you might be interested in."

"Last thing I heard, you were a cop. You still seem like a cop to me. What do you want with me?"

"I'm not a cop anymore; I'm retired, but I do have a mystery to solve. It might be worth a few bucks to you if you could help."

"Okay, I'll bite. What do you want me to do?"

"There is a young woman in town that looks, talks, and acts like Emily Hicks. She even has a scar on her right arm exactly where Emily had her scar."

"The one she got when Sarah pushed her down the stairs."

"Yeah, that's the scar."

"So there is a really good Emily Hicks impersonator in town; what do you want from me."

"I want you to find out if she is an impersonator."

"What else could she be?"

"I think she's the real thing."

"Damn, Batali, and they told me that I was burnt out on drugs."

"I know. I sound like a nut job, but you have to see her and talk to her. You knew Freddie MacArthur fairly well, didn't you?"

"Yeah, don't tell me that he's here too."

"He is. It's like they appeared after forty-four years and just finished their ride home. They appeared on September 16th, exactly forty-four years after they disappeared."

"Geez, shields up, Captain; we're about to encounter a temporal anomaly."

"Maybe they did encounter a temporal anomaly."

Betty smiled, "Okay, Barry, what's this really about? Whatever looks I had are long gone, so I don't think you are trying to get into my pants like you did back in high school; so what do you really want from me?"

"I want you to follow her and see what she does. Later I want you to introduce yourself and see how she reacts. She has a relationship with Shelly Hicks and Sarah Hicks. Sarah is supporting them, from what I hear. Why would she allow them near her mother, and why would she be supporting them if the girl wasn't her sister? Here's a hundred bucks. If you can figure out how to talk to her and you can get me some information, I'll give you another four hundred. Forget who I think she is. If you want another four hundred, you will talk to her and report back to me. Here's my cell; call me when you have something."

"How am I going to find her?"

"I don't have that information yet, but I'll have it soon. Give me your number, and I'll call you when I have it."

Betty looked at the money and said, "Sure, what the hell; here's my number. If she was the real Emily Hicks, I would have some words for her. I thought she was going to write a story about the band. It turns out she was going to write about us poorly exploited groupies. That righteous little bitch would have told all our secrets."

It was time for them to go. They traveled in the limousine to the airport; they passed the terminal and into a special hangar. The plane was waiting for them there. Tommy directed transferring their luggage to the plane, and the passengers were greeted by the attendants as they bordered. Freddie said, "Yeah, we had our bus to ride in, but it wasn't anything like this."

Sarah said, "It will just take a couple of hours to get to National Airport. There will be a car waiting for you, and you have reservations at the Hyatt Regency in Arlington. I suggest that you not travel on interstate 95 anywhere near rush hour. You will find it a very frustrating experience."

Freddie commented, "Then nothing has changed."

Sarah continued, "You have my number and Tommy's. Let me know if Steve is interested in helping us. Let Tommy know if you have any problems that he can help you with. Oh yeah, there are a hundred thousand dollars in your California Bank checking account.

If incentives are needed to get their attention, feel free to use that account."

Freddie and Emily sat quietly, looking out of the window while Sarah went over some paperwork. Freddie said, "From up here, it all looks the same."

Then he noticed the firm grip Emily had on his arm. He asked, "Are you okay?"

"Yeah, it's just that I've never been in an airplane before."

"This is only my second time; I guess I think after all of this time that they have this pretty much figured out."

"Yeah, I'm sure you're right, but I'll just hold on if you don't mind."

Freddie put his hand over hers and said, "I don't mind at all."

Tommy got off his phone and gave the time travelers some news, "You are clients of the Whitford Talent Agency in Burbank, California; you will get more details about the agency later. Your agent is Amanda Janloan, and she has contacted KWTZ. She has sent them your resumes and your pictures. If you recall, your resumes are in the information that I gave you. The station has agreed to bring you in for an interview. You should contact them when you get back."

They thanked Tommy for the information and then realized that they had spent very little time looking over the information that he had given them. They spent the rest of the time looking over what they were able to put on their phones.

National Airport had changed since Freddie saw it last, but at least it was still in the same place. Before they left the airport, Freddie had to take his first step to meet his brother. He brought out his phone, and Emily asked him, "Do you know what you're going to say?"

He gave her a half smile and said, "No, not really. I don't even know if he's home. Maybe I shouldn't have complained. Maybe I should have let Sarah take the lead on this also."

"No, Freddie, we can do this. Sarah will support us later, but we will meet Steve first."

Freddie thought another minute and said, "You think I would have done this back in Dearborn? If he tells me to get lost, we would have wasted a lot of jet fuel for nothing. Okay, here goes."

Freddie punched in the number, and part of him hoped that he wouldn't get an answer, but he did. A man answered, and Freddie's voice was shaky, "Steve, is this Steven MacArthur?"

"Yes, who am I speaking to?"

"Steve, you are not going to believe this. It's Freddie."

"Freddie, who?"

"Steve, it's your brother."

Steve MacArthur laughed, "Yeah, and I'm the tooth fairy. Goodbye, loser."

"Wait Steve, please wait, it's me, your guitar freak brother."

"Who told you I called my brother that. Did Dorothy put you up to this?"

"No, it's me, and I can prove it. I'll take a DNA test. You pick the time and place."

"If it's you, where the hell have you been for forty-four years?"

"It's been forty-four years to you but not to Emily and me."

"Are you saying that Emily Hicks is with you?"

"Yes, she is and her sister, Sarah Hicks Rutherford brought us here from Detroit. Something crazy happened, Steve; I don't know; I can't explain it. There was a flash, and we left everything behind. We didn't live the last forty-four years, Steve; we somehow skipped them."

"You skipped the last forty-four years. You know if you're going to scam someone, you need to come up with a better story."

"Let us come to your house. We'll prove it to you. Please Steve. We are just figuring out how to live in this new world. I just found out that Mom and Dad are gone. You and Dorothy are all that I have left."

"And I suppose the famous and powerful Sarah Hicks Rutherford will bring you here in her limo."

"Not now, but she does want to talk to you about how this could have happened. I don't want her to convince you. I want you to know me, and then she will talk to you. Please just let us come to your home. I want to meet your family. I need my family, Steve."

"Okay, come to my house, but I will have my sons here, and my wife will be ready to call the police."

"That's fair enough, and find out where we can have a DNA test done. I want to do that as soon as possible. Please find someone that can be discreet. We can pay for their discretion."

"When will you be here?"

"We're at National Airport."

"In traffic, you're probably about ninety minutes away. I'll be waiting, but I am not at all convinced."

"I understand. Steve, it's good to hear your voice."

"Yeah, we'll see."

Steve MacArthur hung up the phone, and he had to take a few deep breaths. His wife Cathy went to him and asked, "What's wrong."

"That was someone that claimed to be my brother Freddie. He's coming here from National Airport."

"This is crazy; why would you agree to such a meeting? He's a scam artist or worse. I think we should have the police here. They can just take him away when he gets here."

"No, not the police, not yet; I want to convince Steve Junior and Eric to get out of work and get here as soon as they can. If they hurry, they can be here before these people get here."

"You said they; who is with this guy?"

"He claims he's with Emily Hicks, and they were brought here by Sarah Hicks Rutherford."

"The billionaire?"

"Yeah, Emily Hick's sister is Sarah Hicks Rutherford."

"And that's why you want to talk with this guy?"

"No, I want to talk to him because he sounded just like Freddie. The tone in his voice, the inflection, and the little lisp that I used to kid him about; I heard it all in his voice."

Cathy had to pause for a moment, and then she said, "I'll call Steve; you call Eric."

Freddie got behind the wheel of a Cadillac CTS, and they just marveled at its style and all the gadgets. Emily remembered their lessons about the Global Positioning System or GPS. She put the address into the car's GPS, and the map came up. They were surprised at the clarity of the voice giving the directions. Freddie said, "I thought it would sound more like a computer. It sounds like a real person."

They drove south on Interstate 95, and Emily said, "I hope we get a chance to see the monuments while we're here."

"Oh, we have to do that. Every American should see the monuments. When you see them, you can feel the pride in your chest."

The GPS got them safely to his brother's home in a beautiful development in Occoquan, Virginia. They stared at the homes on the lazily curving suburban street, and Emily commented, "These homes are beautiful. I've never seen anything like them."

Steve's home was at the end of a cul-de-sac. There were two cars in the driveway, so they pulled up in front of the house. As they got out, they saw two men standing on the porch; neither was old enough to be Steve. One called out, "If you have come here to run a scam on my father, you better rethink your plan."

Freddie called as they walked toward the house, "Just let me speak to your father."

Eric was the taller of the two and stepped forward, "Not until we think you are worthy."

Freddie didn't like his attitude, "I didn't know my family had become royalty. I'm sure my brother can make his own decisions."

"Don't call him that."

Steve came out the front door and stared at the young man on his front lawn. He couldn't believe what he was seeing. He told his sons, "My God, it's him. It's your Uncle Freddie."

"Dad, he's younger than us; how can he be your brother?"

Freddie said, "We want your dad to help us figure that out."

Eric yelled, "Bullshit! If you are Uncle Freddie, tell me the one place that my grandpa took my dad and Uncle Freddie that both of them would never forget. Where was that?"

"RFK Stadium for the Beatles concert. That was freaking amazing. We couldn't hear a thing over the screaming, but just to see them was a dream come true. Steve, remember how we tried so hard to get our hair to look like theirs, but every time it got long, Mom would make Dad take us to the barber. We yelled and cried. I think you even threatened to run away once."

The brothers looked at each other, and then Steve Junior came right back, "You could have found that on the internet or something. Dad told a lot of stories about his brother when he went missing."

Steve told his son, "I may have mentioned going to see the Beatles, but I never said anything about threatening to run away. I know I didn't."

Eric said, "Dad, you could have forgotten. These two are pros. They spent a lot of time getting the look down. I remember the pictures and the videos. They worked really hard on the look. I'm sure they have plenty of stories to tell you."

Freddie got back into the conversation, "I told your father that I want to take a DNA test. I know that is the only way to really prove that I am Freddie MacArthur. You can have the test done anywhere you like, and we will pay as much as it takes to have the results expedited."

"Really," Eric said.

"Yes, let's do it and end all this jabbering."

"Okay, it will cost ten thousand dollars. My dad said that creature behind you is Emily Hicks, and her super rich sister is funding your little trip."

Freddie rushed forward and grabbed Eric, and pulled him off the porch. Everyone started yelling, and young Steve went to his brother's aid. Before he was pulled off of Eric, Freddie told him, "Nephew or no nephew, if you insult Emily again, I will knock your teeth out."

Emily screamed, "Freddie, please, calm down. We can prove it right now. Give them access to our checking account. Remember how Ellen told you it worked?"

Eric stood and said, "Well, I guess I struck a nerve. I don't see you pulling any big bills out of your pocket."

Freddie calmed down and tried to steady his voice, "You will need to get an app from the Bank of California. Get that and let me know when you have it."

The older Steve came off the porch. He walked up to Freddie; tears were in his eyes. He said, "I never thought I would see you again."

Steve Junior called, "Dad, this can't be him."

"It's him, son; it's your Uncle Freddie. We will take the test to be sure, but I know my brother. Call it a miracle, call it magic; call it what you will, but this is your Uncle Freddie."

Eric called out, "I have the app; now what?"

Freddie directed him, "Go to the login screen and type in this username. Freddie dash Emily with the F and the E capitalized."

"Okay, that's done."

"Now you need to type in 1973 dash 2017 for the password."

Eric typed it in and stared at the screen. He stared so long that his brother had to ask, "Eric, what do you see?"

Eric said in amazement, "There is a checking account with a hundred thousand dollars in it."

"Bullshit," young Steve couldn't believe it. This is a setup. There probably isn't a real Bank of California. It's all a fake."

Freddie ignored the complaint and asked Eric, "Do you know your own information well enough to set up an online transfer of funds?"

"Yeah, I do."

"Okay, set up a one-time transfer of ten thousand dollars from that account to your account."

Young Steve yelled, "Don't do it; they just want your account information."

Their father pulled out his phone and said, "If you won't do it, I will. If it is a scam I will cover your loss."

Freddie said, "I'm the one trusting you. There is nothing stopping you from transferring all of the money to your account."

Eric said, "Okay, Dad," and he set up the transfer and reported, "Well, at least it looked like ten thousand dollars was deducted from the account."

Everyone waited until Eric accessed his own checking account. Again he just stared at the screen and then reported, "Damn, I have ten thousand dollars more in my checking account than I had this morning; holy shit!"

Freddie said, "That may not prove that I am Freddie MacArthur, but it sure proves I'm not here after anyone's money."

Steve hugged him again, calling out, "It's my big brother; he's come home!"

The brothers just looked at each other, and then Eric said to Emily, "Then you really are Emily Hicks."

"Yep, that's me."

"And Ms. Sarah Hicks Rutherford, is really your sister?"

His brother cut in, "Of course, she's her sister. Every story we saw made a connection with the Queen of Tech. That's where the hundred grand came from."

"He's right," Emily said, "that's where the hundred grand came from."

Eric was now embarrassed; he said, "Oh, I'm so sorry for calling you a creature."

Emily smiled and said, "This is an impossible event. No one could blame you for trying to protect your father. Emily tried to explain how they got to 2017, and what she said didn't make any sense even to her.

Finally, she said, "My sister wants to fund an effort to investigate what really happened. We don't know if it is possible to even get started, but she would like your dad's help figuring it out."

Eric called to his father, "Dad, did you hear that? Ms. Sarah Hicks Rutherford wants you to study the event. That's fantastic!"

Emily said, "Sarah will talk more about that when she sees you."

That statement made Eric swallow hard, "Are you saying that your sister will come here?"

"Yes, she brought us here from Detroit, and she wants to discuss what can be done. She wants your father's input."

Freddie stopped the conversation, "Nothing gets done until the DNA test is done. I'm ready to be swabbed; where can we go."

Young Steve volunteered, "I'll find a place."

Freddie's brother announced, "Let's all go inside and have some drinks. We'll get to the lab as soon as we can."

Eric added, "With ten grand as an incentive, I'm sure we'll be able to wait right there for the results."

They went inside, and Cathy was waiting. Freddie and Emily were now used to the look of awe on the faces of people that learned the truth.

Freddie smiled and said, "Cathy Belcher, well, I guess it's been a while since someone called you that. How's Joe? You know we had classes together at Robinson."

Cathy tried to get enough air in her lungs to say, "He is well."

"Uncle Freddie," young Steve just smiled at him, "I wanted to be just like you. I begged and begged until Dad bought me an electric guitar. I really wanted to learn "Rabble Rouser," but I couldn't ever get that jamming intro right."

Freddie said, "That was the key to the song. I spent more time working on that intro than I did on the rest of the song."

"I still have my guitar. I'm sure it's all out of tune, but there should be extra strings in the case. I'll call Becky, that's my wife. She can bring it and the kids."

The talk of the song sparked a memory in old Steve. He told his brother, "Mom refused to allow us to throw anything of yours away. When she died, I didn't have the heart to do it either. It's all in a storage facility in Springfield, including your desk with everything in it."

Freddie was shocked, "Are you saying that all of that music that I wrote and sent back to Mom is still around?"

"Yeah, Dorothy and I kept everything there. All of your papers are protected in plastic. She comes in from Florida a few times a year, and we'll find ourselves over there looking at your things and talking about our big brother."

Now tears were in Freddie's eyes. He said, "I want to see her, but I want this test done first."

Young Steve announced, "There's a lab up on Oxen Hill Road in Fairfax. I told them to name their price. They will take us as soon as we can get there."

Freddie said, "Let's go."

Everyone moved toward the cars. Freddie and Emily took Eric with them, and Steve and Cathy rode in Steve Junior's car,"

"Eric told Freddie, "There is a branch of my bank right down the road. Stop there, and I will get what we need in cash. I do believe expediting the results made this a bit of an under-the-table kind of transaction."

They made the stop, and then they were on their way. It took several minutes to get there, and there was actually someone waiting for them.

Steve asked his son, "How much did you promise these people?"

"I promised them four grand on the spot, and maybe I'll give them another five hundred if they're speedy."

"Then the rest goes back where it came from."

"Oh no," Freddie said, "The rest is a down payment to cover what you have been shelling out for that storage facility all these years. You won't be transferring money back. You'll be taking more money out."

"That's not happening, big brother. It was no burden on Dorothy or me. And as I said, we loved having it around."

Cathy was able to get Emily alone, and she was excited to ask, "So, what was it like being with the band? Did you really see the concert from backstage?"

Emily didn't think this was the time to get into any great detail, "It was great. Those guys were amazing on stage. I never saw anyone play the guitar like Freddie."

"What about Mickey? I remember how cute he was in school. I was just a freshman, so he wouldn't look at me. I actually followed him down the hall once. And that voice; he sang like an angel."

"Mickey was a first-class hunk. Did you use that word, hunk, I mean?"

"Oh yeah, that he was."

The technician came out and took the samples; Eric handed him the four thousand in cash and said, "There is another five hundred in it for you if you can get us the results in less than an hour."

The man said, "You got it, pal."

While they waited, Steve got on the phone with his sister, "Dorothy, you've got to come home. Something amazing has happened. It's a miracle. Freddie is here. Yes, it's really him. You and Richie have got to get here as soon as you can. I don't know, pay for a damn first-class ticket, drive all night, or catch the train; do whatever it takes."

Freddie waved his hand, and Steve handed him the phone; he said, "Hey, Pokka Dot, are you still stashing your weed under the mattress?"

Dorothy screamed; Freddie took the phone away from his ear so everyone could hear. Eric called out, "Put her on speaker."

Freddie remembered the etiquette and asked Dorothy first; then he put her on speaker. They all heard her say, "Since you want to tell old stories, do you remember how you used that against me? You made me be your lookout while you snuck Irene Ferantaerra up to your room. I've never got the sound of that bed squeaking out of my mind."

"Can you get here, baby girl? I can't wait to see you."

"You're damn right. I'll get there. I have something I want to say to you in person. Now get off my phone. I have some calls to make."

When Dorothy hung up, Steve said, "I didn't know she had a stash of weed. She couldn't have been more than twelve years old when you were dating Irene."

"She was twelve, and that wasn't the only time I used that against her. I blackmailed the crap out of her, and I feel that I may be receiving a little payback when I see her."

The conversation went on non-stop until the door opened, and the man came out with the papers. Everyone stood and stared at the man until he said, "There is no doubt about it; you two are brothers."

A great cheer rose in the room, and Eric slapped another five hundred in the man's hands. They all danced out of the building like the characters from the Wizard of OZ dancing down the yellow brick road.

The older Steve called out, "There will be a big party at my house tonight. Gather your families. This will be one for the history books."

Emily had to stop everyone in their tracks, "Wait one minute, please. There is something we must think through. What would happen to Freddie and me if this was made public? The likely answer is nothing because no one would believe it. The person that does let it out will likely be considered a fool or maybe insane. If someone actually believed it, Freddie and I could end up in a lab somewhere, spending the rest of our lives having our cells analyzed. We need to keep this in our own families. My family is doing this. In fact, my sister is giving us new identities. For the sake of all of us, you need to do the same. Yes, bring in the family but caution them, especially the kids, of what can happen to them if they start spreading this story around."

Eric said, "The lady has a point. I don't need anyone questioning my stability; my security clearance is up for review this year."

The older Steve said, "We will keep it to ourselves, but we are going to have a hell of a party!"

Everyone cheered, and they headed for the cars.

The chatter continued in the car until Emily's phone rang. She answered by saying, "Oh, hi Sarah."

Eric made a gulping sound and whispered to Freddie, "Is that. . ."

Freddie just said, "Yes, it is."

The only sound in the car after that was Emily's conversation, "No, his brother is in another car with his oldest son. His other son Eric is with us. Yes, he's an electrical engineer like his grandfather was."

Eric's eyes widened, and he whispered to Freddie, "Is she talking about me?"

Freddie tried not to laugh, and he answered, "It sure sounds that way."

Emily was saying, "Yeah, everything went great. Freddie was just super. No, I don't think they would mind, but I'll ask them."

Emily turned around and asked Eric, "Do you think your dad would mind if my sister and a few of her people joined the party tonight?"

Eric started mumbling, "Your sister?"

"Yes, my sister."

"Ms. Sarah Hicks Rutherford wants to come to my father's house?"

"Yes, our two families have a common interest. Can I take that as a yes?"

"Ah, ah, yes, of course, yes. We would be honored. Please, please tell her yes."

Emily got back on the phone and said, "Yes, Sarah, you may join us tonight. Do you know where it is? Okay, we'll see you soon."

Eric had his phone out, and he tried to be coherent, "Mom, Sarah Hicks Rutherford is coming to the house tonight. Yes, Emily's sister. Yes, the Queen of Tech. She's coming."

Emily interrupted Eric to say, "Please tell your mother that she doesn't have to do anything special. My sister is, and always has been, a real person. Your parents' house is beautiful, and she will love it."

Eric got back on with his mother, "Mom, did you hear Emily? No, Mom, you don't have to stop and buy new silverware."

The party was grand indeed. It took quite a while for everyone to understand what was going on, and many had to see the DNA results before they actually believed it. When Sarah arrived, young Steve and Eric ran out and moved their cars to let the limousine park in the driveway.

When she entered, there was a clear hush to the conversations. Tommy escorted Sarah into the house. Several other members of Tommy's staff were discreetly positioned around the house. Sarah called out, "Please continue," but all eyes were on her.

Finally, she said, "Thank you for inviting me. This is a most exciting time for both of our families. I would caution all of you that this is best kept within our families. Freddie is a fine man; all of you know what he did to help my sister. You can be proud of him. Now I just want to mingle and meet all of you."

The party was a great celebration that went on for hours. During the festivities, Sarah found the older Steve, and he led her to a quiet room. They sat down, and Sarah started, "I am known to be a fairly analytical person, and I have a great respect for science. What happened to my sister and your brother wasn't magic and it wasn't divine intervention. It was some sort of phenomenon, and I think it will take a theoretical physicist to understand what it was if there is any understanding to be had."

"And you want me to see what I can find out."

"You and your staff will find out, Dr. MacArthur. As you may know, I created SHR Laboratories to work on the cutting edge of science. I don't think there is anything more cutting-edge than this event. I will instruct the head of the laboratory to recognize you as the head of this new project. It's up to you where the office will go and who will be employed there. We can staff the office with scientists and engineers from our staff, or you can bring in your own people, anyone you like. If your sons want to work on it part-time, that would be fine also."

"Wait, wait, Ms. Rutherford, please let me catch my breath. Are you saying that you are going to fully fund a project to research what could be some kind of temporal anomaly?"

"See you have educated me already. That is the proper term for it, a temporal anomaly. Yes, I do. I want to know, and I am hoping that you will be able to give me the answer I seek."

"I certainly will try, Ms. Rutherford."

"Call me Sarah; we're almost related. Now I want another piece of that German chocolate cake."

"There is one thing, I won't take money for this work, and my sons won't either. This is a labor of love. It's for family. If it wasn't for Freddie, I would never have gone to graduate school, and my sister would not have finished college. It was the money that he sent home that made our lives possible."

"Alright, there will be no salary for you or your sons. The kids out there are your grandchildren, are they not?"

"Yes, they are Johnny, Kate, and Melony."

"Well, I will see that they get into the college of their choice, providing their grades are suitable, and the tuition, books, accommodations, and anything else they need will be paid in full. I'm big on family, and I love kids."

Marry Ann, young Steve's wife, brought in Steve's electric guitar. She was a bit sheepish, but she asked Freddie, "I have heard Steve try and try to get 'Rabble Rouser' right. Can you show him how it's done?"

Freddie liked nothing better than playing for an audience. He picked up the guitar and plugged it into the amp. He had to spend several minutes tuning the guitar. He told his nephew, "This is a lively instrument. You should respect it."

After a few more adjustments, Freddie announced, "My apologies to everyone, but it's going to get loud in here for a few minutes."

Everyone cheered, and Freddie turned to young Steve and said, "The secret to the guitar runs in 'Rabble Rouser' is getting down the hammer and pull; that's what makes it a crowd pleaser. You have to pluck the string hard with your right hand and then let the left hand take over. The finger in play hits the string hard like a hammer and then pulls on the string. Doing this will let you make the run without plucking the string again. Raise your right hand in the air like you're performing a magic trick. It's done like this."

When it was over, Eric said, "Now that was music. It's not like the crap they have now. It's like the freaking disco era all over again."

Freddie asked, "What was the disco era?"

"Oh, Uncle Freddie, be happy you missed it. It was just like now. All everyone wanted to do was dance. No one cared about the music. There weren't any real bands, well there were a few, but most of the big songs were singers with an automated beatbox behind them; there were no musicians at all. It is the same way now. There is stuff they call music, but it isn't done by musicians. It's crap. Maybe you should bring back real music. Real music came back after the disco era; maybe you can save us from the Hip Hop era."

"I think it will take more than one guy with a guitar to do that." He said that, but inside, he was thinking that he was just given the mission that he had already given himself. He would do it, and it would start at KWTZ.

The party went on well beyond midnight. For Freddie, it was still early, but the older suburbanites were fading away. It ended, and everyone began to leave.

Steve and Cathy walked Sarah to the door, and Steve said, "It was an honor to meet you, Ms . . ., I mean Sarah. Thank you so much for what you plan to do, and I promise I will do everything I can to get some information about this mystery."

"I am happy to have had a chance to meet the MacArthurs. You have a fine family, and I'm sure we'll be seeing more of each other." Tommy led Sarah back to the limousine.

Freddie and Emily moved toward the door, and Steve called out, "Hold on, big brother; where do you think you're going?"

"We're going to a hotel and get some rest."

"The hell you are. Have you checked in to the hotel?"

"No, our bags are in the car."

"Good, you call that hotel and cancel your reservation; you're not going anywhere. We have two rooms right upstairs, and we'll feed you like no restaurant can. You have returned to us after all this time, and we're going to keep you as long as we can." Freddie hugged his brother one more time, and Cathy took them upstairs.

The next morning Cathy had a hearty breakfast ready. The doorbell rang, and Cathy went to the door. Steve sat down and asked his guests, "So, what are your plans for the day."

Freddie answered, "I think I would like to wander around the old neighborhood and see what it looks like. Maybe I'll go up to the old high school and check it out."

A voice came from the hall, "You're not going anywhere, guitar boy, until I have a few words with you."

Freddie jumped up; Dorothy came around the corner and stopped in her tracks. She called out, "Holy shit, you found the freaking fountain of youth!"

Freddie smiled and said, "Something like that."

Dorothy ran into his arms as her husband Richard stood there with the same confused stare that the time travelers had gotten so used to.

Richard and Emily were introduced, and everything was retold for Dorothy and Richard, and then Freddie asked, "I don't know if I want to know the answer, but what things do you want to get straight?"

Dorothy started, "I have been waiting a long time to tell you this. What the hell kind of a badass rocker were you? You were supposed to spend your money on booze, drugs, women, and ripping apart hotel rooms. What the hell did you do? You sent your damn money home for other people to spend. You were an embarrassment to your profession."

Then she hugged him again and said, "Once I knew it really was you, I knew I had to say this. I really screwed up badly while you were on the road. The money that Mom and Dad had saved to send me to college went to cover my legal problems. If it wasn't for the money you sent home, I wouldn't have the life I have right now. You gave me back the future that I threw away."

Freddie held on to his sister for a few moments and said, "I'm just happy that it worked out. To tell you the truth, I was scared for you. I saw a lot of girls that followed the bands. By thirty, they are burnt out, worn out, and used up. I was afraid that you could fall into that life."

"I might have, but Mom and Dad never gave up on me, and neither did you."

Steve called, "Hey, what about me?"

Dorothy said, "Oh, Steve, you're just a pain in the ass, and everyone knows it."

Steve gave her an over-exaggerated disappointed look, and she put her arms around him and said, "I love you too, middle brother."

Everyone stepped back, and Dorothy said, "We're dog ass tired. We've been driving all night. Freddie, get the hell out of here so I can get some sleep."

Freddie had to tell her as she headed upstairs, "I'm happy a college education and a profession in the sciences haven't changed your colorful vocabulary."

Dorothy said without turning around, "Screw you, Freddie."

Emily said through her laughter, "Sarah will love her."

Freddie turned back to Steve and asked, "What's the old neighborhood like?"

"I haven't been in King's Park West in years. From what I know, there are some changes, but almost everything is about the same. What about you, Emily? Are you going with Freddie, or would you like to do something else?"

"I'll go with Freddie. After that, Freddie promised to spend a couple of days showing me the sites of Washington."

"Yes, you must do that. There is a lot more to see than there was in 1973. Check out the Vietnam War memorial. It is something to see. There is this big wall with the name of every American that died in the war on it. I found Roger Stern's name. It's amazing how just seeing the name on that wall makes you feel. I can't imagine how it is for guys seeing the names of comrades they lost in battle."

Freddie was surprised, "They actually gave those guys some credit. I was against the war, but I didn't think it was right to blame the soldiers for the decisions of the politicians. I'm happy that they got the honor they deserved. We'll check it out."

Later, Freddie and Emily cruised up Commonwealth Boulevard, and Freddie would point out places he remembered. As they passed Pumphrey Drive, Freddie spotted an older man cutting his front lawn. He hit the brakes, causing the seat belt to lock and making Emily call out, "Freddie, what was that for?"

Freddie backed the car up, pulled it to the curb to a place where he could still see the man, and put his window down. Emily asked again, "What are you doing?"

"I think that's him."

"You think that's who?"

"That's Rick."

"Do you mean Rick Santora?"

"Yeah, that's where he lived when we were kids, and they said he went back there. I can see him. I can see Rick in that old man."

"What do you want to do?"

"I don't know."

"I don't think it's a good idea to try to talk to him. What would he think?"

The old man looked up from his lawn mower and saw the car at the corner. He looked closer and saw the face of the man looking at him. His heart began to pound, and he collapsed in his freshly cut grass.

Emily cried, "Oh my God," as Freddie started the car and rushed to the scene. They got out and went to him.

Freddie turned the man over and saw that he was breathing. Neighbors rushed out to see what had happened, and they began to gather around. The man opened his eyes and stared at the young man supporting him. He said in a voice that clearly registered his shock, "Freddie, how is this possible? How can you be here?"

Freddie and Emily could feel the eyes of the neighbors on them. He heard the name Freddie MacArthur whispered by someone. Their identities could not be made public. He helped Rick to his feet and said, "I'm not who you think I am."

"You are, you're Freddie MacArthur, but you can't be. It's been too long."

"I'm an actor that looks like Freddie MacArthur. I'm sorry to have caused you distress. We were in the area doing research on Barracuda. There may be a play opening based on the band, and my friend and I want the parts of Freddie and Emily."

The gathering seemed to buy the story, and with Rick on his feet, they began to drift away. Rick now stared at both of them. He still couldn't believe the images in front of him. He said, "It's not just your look; it's your voice and your stance. How can you mimic Freddie so perfectly?"

Freddie hated to keep up the pretense, but he did, "I worked very hard, looking at film and talking to people. That's what we're doing here. I want to know all I can so that I can be ready when casting begins."

Then Freddie asked, "Are you who I think you are? Are you Rick Santora, Barracuda's bass player?"

"Yes, but that was so long ago. Though it was a time of my greatest adventure, it was also a time of my greatest folly and my greatest pain."

"Would you mind talking about that time with my friend and me?"

"I will tell you as much as I can. Most of it, especially the last two concerts, was a blur. It wasn't until weeks after that last concert in Detroit that I learned that I was dosed. I thought it was strange. Anyone that was paying attention would know that I was killing myself; I didn't need any help. But I suppose you really want to talk about Chicago."

"No, not if you don't want to. Why don't we go get some lunch? Where would you like to go? I know you always loved steak and cheese at Pizza Bazzano."

Rick paused for a moment; then he said, "I don't ever remember telling anyone that, and I don't think the other boys did either. But I guess someone did; maybe my mother. Anyway, yeah, I loved to, but they closed the place about a year ago. After being open for almost fifty years, it was closed. There are plenty of other places for subs. I can finish this up later. Just let me put the mower around back."

Freddie watched Rick push the mower, and Emily could see the pained look on Freddie's face. She asked him, "You want to tell him, don't you?"

"Yes, I do. I want to tell him how much I missed him and the boys, but I won't. I'm afraid of what it would do to him. But I want to know more about what happened after we left, and I want to do something for him. I don't want to just give him money. I want to find out what would make his life better."

"I said it before, and I'll say it again; you are a good man Freddie MacArthur."

They found a place quickly, and they were there in a few minutes. They ordered their subs and sat down. Rick said, "It's been a long time since someone was interested in Barracuda. You know they call us one of the greatest tragedies in rock and roll history. I guess we really did go down in flames. Freddie disappeared. I was rehabbed and then marched off to prison. Don couldn't break his sex habit, and it killed him. The only ones that came out of it halfway sane were Mickey and Ryan.

Freddie asked, "Didn't Ryan end up dead in the jungle somewhere?"

"No, that's one of those fake stories. You can't believe everything that you read on the internet. I have a suspicion that he planted that story himself. I'll get a note from him now and then. Of course, I keep it to myself; at least, I did until now. He's probably going to be pissed if he finds out I told you."

"We'll keep his secret. We are only getting the background to get into character. Where did he end up?"

"Why do you need to know stuff about a time after Freddie and Emily disappeared? How is that going to help you understand their characters?"

Freddie had to think fast, "The more we know about the band, the better we will react if the audition requires a scene with band members."

"Okay, well Ryan is . . .; oh hell, he's going to kill me anyway. Ryan is somewhere in Montana, living in a cabin way up in the mountains somewhere. He won't tell me more than that. He has a wife and a slew of kids, and he is living under another name, and now, he has grandkids. He had sold a bunch of band stuff before he left and squirreled the money away. He didn't spend it all like all the stories say he did. He actually learned a few investment tricks from Mickey, and one of the companies he invested in was a little company called Apple. Ryan and his clan aren't going to starve any time soon."

Freddie tried to hide some of the absolute joy he was feeling hearing those words. Their lunch was served, which created a break in the conversation. Finally, Freddie had to know, and he asked, "Rick, how did you feel when you found out that Freddie wasn't there to back you up? If he had been there to corroborate your story, you might not have gone to prison. Some say he bailed on you."

"Hell no, that's not the way I feel. I might have for a little while, but that was before I came to my senses. He would have done it if he had been there. I didn't ask him, you know. The plan was concocted by Pete Chiles, and Freddie was pressured to go along with it. I was in a haze the entire week. I can't honestly tell you if Freddie and I talked about it at all. When I was lucid, I wanted to turn myself in. I just kept seeing that poor woman's face in my mind. I still see it; it's with me every day. Pete and the band wouldn't let me; Pete said I owed it to the band to finish the tour. I couldn't do it anyway; I was too scared. When the cops came, I told them what Pete told me to say, but Freddie was never found to back me up."

"Then why don't you blame him for not being there?"

"This is terrible to say, but losing Freddie saved my life. If I hadn't gone to prison, I would have been dead. I wouldn't have lasted the fifteen years I served in prison if I had been on the outside. Betty Eveready should have killed me with the meth in my whiskey, but somehow I lived through that. If I had been on the outside, I would have finished the job."

"But the tour would have been over, and you would have had time to get yourself together when you got home."

"That wouldn't have happened. I had a cocaine dealer right here in Fairfax on the line waiting for me to come home. There would have been no stopping me. Prison saved my life, my wife Marsha gave me a reason to live, and my work after prison gave me a real purpose. Keeping kids away from that poison was the most gratifying work of my life. I hate to say it, but losing Freddie saved me."

Freddie had to force himself not to hug his old friend. A weight had been lifted from him, and he couldn't be more grateful.

Emily emphasized what she had been telling Freddie from the start by asking, "Everyone said that Freddie MacArthur was a good man. What do you think?"

Rick looked at her and said, "Freddie MacArthur was the best."

They finished their lunches and drove Rick home. After dropping Rick off, they drove up to the old high school, but Freddie had already gotten far more than he ever thought he would get. By mid-afternoon, they drove back to Steve's house.

When they arrived, the two couples were there to greet them with an idea. Dorothy spoke for everyone, "Freddie, let's go to that storage facility. We want to look things over, and then we want you to have the key."

Freddie said, "I'd love to do that, but I'll take the key if I also get the bill. You know I can afford it."

Dorothy turned to Steve and said, "The man has been home one damn day and started acting like the big brother again."

Freddie answered, "You bet, Pokka Dot, I'll always be your big brother."

Steve opened the garage-type door, and Dorothy said, "There it is. All of your crap, it's the greatest pile of useless crap ever stored anywhere."

Freddie came right back, "Except maybe your stash of weed, your pack of cigarettes, and your list of boy's phone numbers that were under your mattress."

Freddie browsed the old things for an hour, and it reminded Emily that she had not been in her old room. She wondered if her mother had left any of her things in there.

Finally, Freddie lifted out several binders containing music sheets protected in plastic covers. He looked at them in awe.

Steve said, "Mom protected them with her life. She carefully tucked everything you sent in the plastic covers and put them in the binders. She threatened us with slow, agonizing death if we ever disturbed them."

Freddie just hugged the binders for a minute with tears in his eyes. When they left the storage facility, Freddie was still holding the binders to his chest.

They enjoyed the evening with Steve, Cathy, Dorothy, and Richard and got to bed early for a change. Freddie had his first good night's sleep since entering 2017. For the next two days, they were tourists in Washington, DC. They felt what Steve said they would feel at the Vietnam War memorial. Each found a name of someone they knew. It was a strange and sad feeling. Seeing the memorial to Martin Luther King and the African American Museum showed them that progress had been made to achieve liberty and justice for all. Freddie was pleased about how easy it was to get around on the subway system. There were only buses the last time he was in town.

They flew back to Detroit on Saturday, and their interview with KWTZ was set for Monday morning. They arrived at their rooms. Freddie kissed her and stepped away, but she caught his hand. She smiled, and no words were needed. She opened the door, and they both entered.

Betty got a late-night call from Barry, "My son just called me. They will be at the KWTZ radio station at nine on Monday morning."

Betty had to ask, "Do you have everyone working for you?"

"It's a long story. They will be there, and they will be in a new red Dodge Challenger."

"I guess your cop friends got you that information."

"Don't worry about me. You'll know where they'll be. Get some information if you want to earn money."

After she hung up, Betty got another call. This one wasn't one she wanted to receive. The deep male voice said, "Betty, ole girl, you left New Orleans in a hurry. Didn't you think we'd come after you?"

"Hey Jackie, I was just coming up here to gather your money. I was going to be back there in a few weeks."

"Don't try that scam bullshit on me, girl. I know your style. I've watched you screw over guys too many times, including that idiot that was dumb enough to marry you. I'm coming for my money. You will either give it to me or you'll be taking a ride in the trunk of my car. Do you get where I'm coming from?"

"Yeah, sure, Jackie, I have it for you. When will you be here?"

"You'll know when you feel my hands around your throat. Don't try to run off on me. If I have to chase you again, no amount of money will save you."

Jackie hung up, and Betty was shaking. She had to get the rest of the money from Barry, and then she needed to get more, a lot more.

Part Three

Time to Rock

Chapter 9: KWTZ

Freddie and Emily spent the rest of the weekend studying their information packets. They were becoming confident that they could be Frank McAlester and Elizabeth Richards.

Freddie also spent time looking at the music sheets. It was still very weird to him. These sheets had been preserved for so many years, but he remembered writing some of them no more than a month ago.

Freddie went out and bought a beautiful Fender Stratocaster and an amplifier. He couldn't believe that tiny box could give him the sound that he wanted, but it did. He would take it with him on the interview.

It was past midnight as the clock moved into early Monday morning. Freddie was sound asleep, but Emily was staring at the ceiling. She wasn't worried about the interview; she was worried about her life. She was falling in love with Freddie, and that was wonderful. She didn't mind helping him with what he called his mission, but where was she? Where was her life going? Music was Freddie's life, not hers. She loved the excitement, but she needed her own purpose. She needed to go back to school.

The time travelers arrived right on time for their nine o'clock appointment. They were shown to the office of Tony Batali, the marketing manager for KWTZ. He greeted them, and everyone sat down. Tony started, "Well, my father told me that you were the image of Freddie MacArthur and Emily Hicks, but I wouldn't have ever believed you would be identical. The resemblance isn't all-natural, is it?"

Freddie remembered the story that he told to Rick, and he elaborated on it, "Not entirely, though we did get work as Freddie and Emily before the surgery. We wanted an edge on the competition."

"That was a heavy investment just to get a part in a possible movie."

"Yeah, it turned out to be a big mistake. We're still paying the bills, and the project died on the vine."

"Well, I guess their loss is our gain. Beth, have you had any acting experience?"

"My experience is playing this part. We have done several events around the country. It's all in our resumes."

"Yes, I read your resumes, but how deep have you gone into the character?"

"Excuse me, Mr. Batali, but I find the question a bit odd. I thought this was a promotion of KWTZ."

"It is, but it's a big one. To tell you the truth, the future of this station may be riding on it. As you might suspect, the people around here know the Hicks family. Emily's mother still lives on Craig Street, and her sister, Sarah Hicks Rutherford, visits often. This keeps Emily's memory fresh in their minds. They will see Emily in you, but the whole thing will be a bust if you don't seem genuine to them."

"We have researched our characters, Mr. Batali. That's the main reason we were in Romulus. We also just returned from Virginia, where Frank added more knowledge to his understanding of Freddie MacArthur. I believe we can be considered authorities on Emily Hicks and Freddie MacArthur."

"That is good to hear. Frank, I see you brought a guitar with you; that's good. We had one here for you also. We have a studio set up with a recording of "She's Got the Devil in Her" with the lead cut out. This recording was from their concert in Denver in late August 1973. We would like you to provide the lead for the performance. We know this is something that can't be done cold. Take some time to get used to the setup, and let me know when you're ready. Excuse me one moment," Tony picked up the phone, "Sheila, we're ready."

He turned back to Freddie and said, "Sheila is one of our interns. She'll take you to the studio and show you how it works."

Freddie had done this kind of thing a million times in the studio, but he didn't want to seem too experienced. He allowed Sheila to lead him out of the room.

Tony turned back to Emily, "So, Ms. Richards, tell me a little about how you two became a team."

Emily and Freddie spent quite a bit of time working out these details. Emily was ready with an answer, "An agency put us together. They had a retro thing going on; it was a "Couples of the Rock Era" show. It seems that people have gotten it into their heads that Freddie and Emily were together even though they only knew each other for a day. There was a Sonny and Cher couple, a Captain and Tenniel couple, and several others. The idea seemed to work well. It got us several other jobs, so we stuck with it."

"Is it still just a business relationship?"

"I don't see the relevance of the question, but no, it has become more personal over time."

"I didn't see Frank's Barracuda in the parking lot."

"He doesn't have it anymore."

"He sold a mint condition 1973 Plymouth Barracuda?"

"I guess you had a nice conversation with your dad. To answer your question, yes, he got an offer he couldn't refuse."

"From Sarah Hicks Rutherford; why was she so interested in Frank's car?"

"Why don't you ask the question you really want to ask? You want to know why we were at the home of Shelly Hicks while Ms. Rutherford was there."

"The connection did peak my curiosity."

"Does it peak your curiosity or your father's?"

"Ms. Richards, I don't know how things are done in California, but here the interviewer asks the questions."

"The interviewer is supposed to ask relevant questions, Mr. Batali."

"This is out of character. Emily Hicks would not be so challenging; she was a girl of the seventies."

"First, I wasn't speaking in character; I was speaking for myself. Second, it looks like you don't know that much about Emily Hicks. She and Sarah were members of the National Organization of Women. Believe me; she would challenge you."

"Are you refusing to answer the question?"

"No, I'll answer it, but not because I feel pressured. There is something that you should know about Frank and me. We don't like being jerked around. We have walked away from jobs because we weren't respected. We were even dropped by an agency for walking away from a job. Frank can make his own decisions, and I will make mine. Here's your answer; take notes for your father. As we said earlier, we came into town to do some research. Unknown to us, we were seen by Shelly Hicks in a shopping mall. Don't ask me the name of the mall; I don't know it. It seems we gave her quite a shock. It turned out that she went home and called her daughter and asked her to come to Romulus. She told her about us, and before we knew it, we were stopped on the street by two guys who asked us a bunch of questions. I guess they were impressed because they told us to be at the home of Shelly Hicks before noon, and we were there. I was shocked when Ms. Rutherford came in the door. We sat down and talked, and later she offered Frank twice the going selling price, a new Dodge Challenger, and accommodations at that fancy hotel if he sold her the Barracuda on the spot. That's the story."

"Where did Frank get the Barracuda?"

"I don't know. He had it when I met him. Now, Mr. Batali, the next question better be relevant, or I'm walking out of here."

"Okay, Ms. Richards, I think that's enough questions for now. Let's see how Frank is doing."

They could hear the music as they came down the hall. Someone had put the outside speaker on, and several of the staff gathered around to listen. As they reached the studio, Jimmy Bee, the morning D.J. grabbed Tony. He was babbling with excitement, "Tony, my man, you're signing this guy for the show, right? You've got the contract ready, right?"

"I'm working on it, Jimmy. I'll let you know who I choose in plenty of time."

"What do you mean, who you'll choose? Are you out of your freaking mind; listen to him."

Tony stepped into the studio and asked Freddie, "Are you ready?"

Freddie nodded, and Tony called, "Sheila, from the top."

Freddie also had a mic for background vocals. Listening to the boys play and hearing Mickey's voice was weighing on him. If he closed his eyes, he could almost see them. Don's fingers would be a blur on the keyboard while his eyes constantly scanned for girls to wink at. Ryan twirling his sticks and attacking the drums like Keith Moon. He could see Rick working the bass and the crowd and Mickey slaying the girls with his voice. They were all there in his ears and in his mind. He smiled as he crushed the guitar cut in the middle of the song, and he hit the backup vocals on key and on time.

Jimmy Bee was elated, "Yes, yes, he's the man. He is Freddie MacArthur. Goddamn you, Tony, sign him right now. This idea of yours will be a mega-hit with him on board."

"I agree," Tony heard a deeper voice behind him. It was Art Williams, the station manager. He added, "You won't find anyone better."

"Art, can we move this discussion to your office?"

Art agreed, and Tony turned to Emily and said, "Please excuse us for a few minutes."

Emily agreed, and they moved down the hall to Art's office.

Sheila entered the studio and said, "Mr. McAlester, I'm a big Barracuda fan. My mother told me my grandma went to their concert in Cleveland, and she was just blown away. I have heard a lot of Barracuda covers, but none nearly that good; could you do a little bit of Wrecking Ball off the top of your head?

Freddie was twenty-three, but suddenly he felt very old, but he also loved the praise. He smiled and said, "Anything for a Barracuda."

Emily watched through the window and thought, "At least one of us is having a good time."

Art, Tony, and Jimmy entered Art's office; Jimmy closed the door and said, "What's with the pow-wow man? This is a no-brainer."

Art asked Tony, "What's the problem?"

Tony answered, "Frank is perfect for Freddie MacArthur; there is no doubt about that, but I don't know about the girl."

Art asked, "Why not? She's a perfect Emily Hicks."

"She's an arrogant bitch. I asked her a few questions, and she started giving me a hard time."

Art asked, "What about her qualifications? She clearly has the look; what does her agent say about her?"

"Well, of course, the agent is going to play her up; that's their job.

"So she is qualified, and her looks are right on, but you are negative because she didn't smile at you enough."

"She was rude and even insulting."

"Tony, you've lived here all of your life. You know the people we're going to get at our holiday bash. We're going to get the old timers with the old money. They will want to see an Emily Hicks that looks like Emily Hicks, and you're not going to find a better match than the girl that is out there right now."

"I won't put up with any crap from her."

"If this show of yours doesn't boost our ratings, you will be putting up with crap from the lady at the employment office. Hire both of them, Tony, while we still have jobs."

The meeting broke up, and Tony led Freddie and Emily back to his office. They sat, and Tony got to it, "Okay, we would like both of you to be part of our 'Rock the Holidays' show that we will perform on December 16th. You will be paid the standard performers rate. I'm sure your agent will want to do some negotiating, but our rates are quite firm."

Emily was still not happy with Tony, and she had to remind him, "We will review your offer and discuss it with our agent."

"Wait," Tony wasn't very happy himself, "who do you think you are? You have nothing else going; I suggest you take the offer."

Freddie asked, "Let's see the offer in writing. I'm sure we can settle this right now."

Emily gave Freddie an annoyed look, and he wasn't sure why. Tony handed them the standard performer offer, and Emily said, "This is fair for doing the show."

"There may be other promotional spots if we feel you have the appeal."

Freddie opened his mouth, but Emily was quicker to respond, "If there are, we will require payment for each one unless you would like to negotiate a full package now."

"Okay," Tony groaned, "we can make up a contract that will boost your payment by twenty percent and require you to support all promotional efforts."

Emily was satisfied, "That sounds fair. What do you think, Frank?"

Freddie was a bit perturbed at Emily's dominance of the negotiation, "Well, I'm happy that someone asked me my opinion. Yes, I think that would be fair."

Tony finished the conversation, "Fine, wait a few moments, and I'll get it all in writing for you to look over."

Freddie and Emily signed the contract, and then Tony started to explain what he had planned, "I was contacted by an agent a few weeks ago. She said her client had written a musical of sorts based on the last two concerts Barracuda did in September of 1973. She said this guy was an insider and that he had some real history in his work. She also said that there was artistic license used to make the story a bit more dramatic."

Freddie asked, "Who is the playwright?"

"She said his name was Roger Mendez. We contacted Mr. Mendez, and we have a copy of his play. It is actually quite good, at least in our opinion. There is a lot of music that depicts the Barracuda concerts in Chicago and Detroit, and there is also a big part for you, Ms. Richards. This will really test your acting skills. The play will focus a great deal on Emily using her tape recorder to try to get her story and the clever way she avoided Don the Letcher."

Freddie almost came out of his seat when he heard his friend describe it that way, but he maintained control. He asked, "This is a real play, then?"

"Yes, three acts long. I think he tried to pitch it in New York, and he didn't get very far. We're getting it for a song. I guess he's hoping the exposure will make it more appetizing to the entertainment world. Part of the deal makes Mr. Mendez the director of the play, so he will be calling the shots. You will be getting scripts tomorrow and Freddie, you'll be introduced to the rest of the band tomorrow."

They left the building, and Freddie had to ask, "What was your problem with Tony?"

"You didn't hear the third degree that he laid on me. He was digging for information for his father. He threatened to turn us away if I didn't give him more details. I gave him the details. I gave him the ones that Sarah coached us on, but that's not the point. He thought he could pressure me because I'm a young woman."

"Couldn't you have sucked it up just once? This is important. This is how we make something for ourselves."

"This is how we make something for you. Where am I in this vision of yours?"

"You are there with me."

"Where, I don't have any musical ability. What will be my job?"

"You can do whatever you want to do. You can handle the business."

"If I wanted to handle business, I would have been a business major in school."

"Then I don't know what to tell you. You really don't need to find a job. I'm sure your sister will set you up to do whatever you want to do."

"I don't want to be dependent on my sister any more than you do. Freddie, I will do this little play thing with you, but then I want to go back to school. I'm going to start the process of being accepted at U of M for their winter semester. I will take Sarah's help for that."

"And you will be staying in Ann Arbor?"

"It's too far to commute from here, and I don't know where your plans will take you once this play is over."

"But what about us? We anchor each other?"

"We will just need to feel more independent in this world by then."

"Then that's it. In a little over a week, we go from being strangers to being friends to being lovers, and now we're back to friends."

"No, Freddie, you know better than that. What I feel for you is real. I don't want to lose that, but I can't just be here on the sidelines. I need to have a purpose, and it has to be a purpose of my choosing."

"Okay, we have a lot of time. You don't need my permission to go to school or to do anything else you want to do. Just don't forget about me."

Emily hugged him and said, "How could I forget about the great Freddie MacArthur?"

"You may not be able to forget about him, but you might be able to forget Frank McAlester."

They sat and ate lunch quietly. They didn't seem to know where to take the conversation. Freddie changed the subject just to get them talking, "I don't know if you remember Roger Mendez."

Emily toyed with her salad and answered, "The name is familiar. Wasn't he on the road crew?"

"He was the crew manager. Those guys were always around backstage and at the hotels. They were kind of invisible when we didn't need them to do something. I bet Roger was in earshot of a lot that went on, and we didn't notice him. He could have quite a lot to say in this little play of his."

Emily thought about Roger, "He really doesn't know anything about me. How will I appear in this play of his?"

Then she responded to Freddie, "Yeah, but how much of it will be true?"

The conversation trailed off again, and they finished their lunch in awkward silence.

Dr. Steve MacArthur was invigorated with his new mission. He knew that, in the beginning, he would have to act more like an investigator than a scientist. These days all investigations start with an internet search. Just dropping Sarah's name here and there got him access to places that were solidly secure.

He began looking for anything unusual that happened on the night of September 15, 1973, and the early morning of September 16, 1973. It was a long and frustrating process. After days of staring at web pages, he found his first clue. The National Weather Service reported an unusual atmospheric disturbance that seemed to appear from high in the stratosphere. It descended and skimmed the Earth somewhere west of Detroit. Steve told his wife, "The man that discovered the anomaly was Dr. Edmond Steinberg."

Cathy was also searching. The two never thought that they would invest in those snooping sites where one could get personal information, but they did; they paid for all of them. After several minutes of searching, Cathy called out, "I think I found him. I have a Dr. Edmond Steinberg, a retired meteorologist formerly a chief scientist with the National Weather Service. I have an address and a phone number. Let's try to give him a call."

Steve punched in the number, and he got an answer. Steve asked, "Is this, Dr. Edmond Steinberg?"

"Yes, and who am I speaking with?"

"This is Dr. Steve MacArthur. I'm a theoretical physicist, I am working in association with SHR Laboratories, and I am trying to gather information on an anomaly that occurred in the early morning hours of September 16, 1973. Do you remember reporting some unusual meteorological readings on that date?"

"Yes, I do. That was one of those things that one never forgets. It was very strange. It was there, and it wasn't there. One second the barometric pressure would be zero; I mean really zero, and the next, it was normal. Everyone thought it was just a glitch in the equipment, but it never had a glitch before that date, and it never had a glitch after that date. It was something, but with the limited technology of 1973, we had no hope of finding out exactly what it was. Maybe they will have better luck now."

"Why do you say that? Are they going over the old files and applying new techniques?"

"No, it happened again last week forty-four years later on exactly the same date and exactly at the same time. I have a friend still working, and she had to call and tell me about it."

Steve looked up at his wife for a moment. She could tell by the look on his face that he had just found something. He asked Dr. Steinberg, "Would you give me your friend's name? We may be able to assist her in solving this mystery."

"I don't know how the National Weather Service is treating this information. I wouldn't want to get her in any trouble."

"Could you tell me what division of the National Weather Service would handle this kind of thing?"

"Well, I guess that's no big secret."

Steve got the information, hung up, and he answered Cathy's unspoken question, "Something did happen in 1973, and it happened again last week at exactly the same time. This was some kind of temporal transition; my God, it was real!"

Cathy asked, "Can you get more information about what happened last week?"

"Dr. Steinberg doesn't want to risk getting his friend in trouble, but there may be another way."

He punched in the National Weather Service number that Dr. Steinberg gave him. After a few rings, he got someone on the line. He tried to sound as official as possible, "This is Dr. Steven MacArthur with SHR Laboratories. We had been studying a phenomenon that occurred in the early morning hours of September 16, 1973. Several of my colleagues and I believed this might be a reoccurring event, and we placed some monitors in the general area. We believe we might have detected something, and we were hoping that you could tell us if you detected anything unusual in the early morning hours of September 16th of this year."

The woman on the line was a bit suspicious, "How did you know about the event in 1973?"

"We have access to your historical files; you may verify that. We understand that the phenomenon occurred very briefly, and the one small area went from being normal to something akin to the vacuum of space and back again, and it occurred somewhere west of Detroit."

"And when did you start monitoring for a reoccurrence?"

Steve never knew he was so good at spinning yarn on the fly, "Just two years ago. That's when we started this work. It's been on the back burner until recently."

"Before we can confirm or deny any information, I would need to be able to verify who you are and if SHR Laboratories is really doing research in this area."

"Of course, you may contact Dr. Sam Stevens; he's the director of research. He's the one that authorized me to call." Steve remained calm on the phone while he furiously scribbled a note asking Cathy to call Sam Stevens at SHR and have him ready to confirm his research.

Cathy went into the other room and made the call.

Steve tried to stall the woman for just a few minutes, "May I ask your name?"

"I'm Dr. Rachel Mandachinco, and I am the team leader in the division. I will contact Dr. Stevens; please stay on the line."

While Steve waited on the line Cathy came in and gave him a thumb's up. A few minutes later, Dr. Mandachinco came back on the line. Okay, Dr. MacArthur, give me your email address, and I'll send you a file. Please handle it carefully. We would rather not have this event turn into a media circus. I have been directed to pass all of our information to you and that you and your team would take it from here. Frankly, I'm happy to have it off my plate. We have a lot of real weather issues to deal with."

Steve gave Dr. Mandachinco the information, and he hung up. He chuckled and said to Cathy, "They are officially turning the investigation over to my staff and me."

Cathy kissed him and said, "I am happy to be your staff."

A few minutes later, the file appeared in Steve's email. Steve studied the information, and Cathy asked, "Have they been able to add anything new?"

"Yes, there are more data readings, but the big information is that they have geographic information down to the millimeter. They know exactly where the phenomenon skimmed the Earth. I know exactly where Freddie disappeared in 1973 and where he appeared last week."

Cathy had a thought, "If we know that, we can determine if anyone else experienced any unusual events. We can start looking at newspaper articles and police reports if we can get them."

Now it was Steve that kissed Cathy, then he told her, "You are as brilliant as any colleague I have ever worked with. Let's start looking."

Freddie and Emily left the resturant, and Emily asked, "So what now. I don't feel like going back to the hotel and studying Beth Richards."

Freddie suggested, "Let's go into Detroit. We haven't seen the city since we got here."

They drove into the city, and they were shocked at what they saw. Emily just stared at street after street of bordered-up buildings and collapsing infrastructure. She said, almost in awe, "My God, what has happened? It looks like something out of a war movie."

Freddie was just as shocked, "I don't know. I remember riding down this street on the bus on the way to the hotel. It looked like a regular street. There must have been more riots or something."

"But when would that have happened, and why would the city leave all of these streets looking like this?"

"I have no idea. Our lessons focused on technology and social media, and interaction. I think we need lessons in history and maybe politics."

Emily kept staring and said, "I think you're right about that. Let's go back to the hotel. I think I've seen enough."

As they got to the hotel, Emily's phone rang. She talked for a minute, and then she told Freddie, "Sarah wants us to meet at Mom's house for dinner tonight. She is planning to go back to California tomorrow."

Freddie said, "Good, your mom's cooking is far better than anything at the restaurant."

Before entering the lobby, Emily stopped Freddie, "Freddie, I'm not sure what words to use. We've only known each other for a week and a half, but I have never felt closer to anyone. I can't imagine being in this world without you. I don't want to hurt you or be away from you, but I have to do something."

"You're going to school," Freddie said, putting his arms around her, "you're going to school, and you're going to be the best damn journalist in the business. Emily, you were right. You need your own life with your own ambitions. I want you to be happy. Ann Arbor isn't that far away. I'll drive to you when you can't drive to me. It will work out. Seeing my family and knowing that I have them is great, but they are not you. It has only been a week and a half, but it has been a hell of a week and a half. Many people don't live that much in a lifetime. Emily, I love you. Love is the only word that fits, and I can't avoid saying it because the world would think it was too soon."

Emily just smiled and held him tight.

Everyone gathered for another one of Shelly Hicks' great meals. Shelly felt like she was ten years younger. Her girls were with her, and the world seemed brighter. She had a spring in her step, and she even whistled a tune now and then.

She refused to let anyone help her serve, but she did delegate the dishwashing to Emily and Sarah. Everyone devoured her chicken pot pie. It was the biggest chicken pot pie that anyone had ever seen. Tommy had three helpings, and Shelly hugged him and said, "I love to see a man with a good appetite."

After dinner, Sarah chaired the meeting, "I'm leaving tomorrow. Sometime soon, I want all of you to come and stay at my place in Bueno Vista, and that includes you, Mom."

Shelly scoffed a bit, "Oh, flying in the air isn't for old people."

"You've done it before, Mom; you'll be fine. I want you to come. You can have a nice rest from the chores."

Emily coaxed her mother also, "We can have a great time exploring California. I've never seen the ocean; it would be great."

Shelly patted Emily's hand, which she had held since she sat down, and agreed, "For you, Emily, I will go."

Sarah complained in jest, "Yeah, for her, you'll go."

Shelly said, "And for you, I would walk through fire."

Sarah hugged her mother and said, "I know you would, Mom."

Emily changed the subject, "I am going to apply to U of M for the winter semester."

Sarah was happy to hear it, "That process is even more complicated than it used to be; let me grease the wheels for you a little bit."

"Okay, but Freddie and I have been talking, and we think we have to start handling things on our own."

"As soon as you have more understanding of what's going on. I think you need more instruction. You have, for all intents and purposes, walked onto an alien world, and you have only been here ten days."

"On that, we agree," Emily said, "in fact, Freddie and I took a drive into Detroit, and we couldn't believe what we saw. What happened to the city? Were there more riots? Was there some kind of disaster? It looks like the neighborhoods have been in ruins for many years; why hasn't anyone cleaned it up?"

Sarah responded, "This is why you need more instruction. It wasn't riots or a disaster; it was worse than that; it was economics. I guess in 1973, the most popular foreign car, outside of the luxury cars, was the Volkswagen Beetle. That all changed in the late seventies and early eighties. Cars from Japan flooded into America. They were cheaper, and the quality was high, and they were driving the big three American car makers out of business.

The American car companies couldn't compete on prices because the economy in Japan and the lifestyle of the Japanese people allowed them to pay their workers far less than we paid ours. They made their cars in a cheaper environment and sold them in an expensive environment. It was a big win for them. The American companies only had one answer if they were to survive. They had to build their cars somewhere else, somewhere where the living wage wasn't so high. Slowly they moved all assembly plants away from the United States and put them in Canada and Mexico. It worked for them. It saved their companies, but it destroyed the economy of Detroit and many other towns in the country. It is easy to label the auto companies as the bad guys for leaving so many to suffer in poverty, but, in my opinion, they had no choice. Others disagree and do blame them. I just think that if they had stayed, they would have gone under, and the people would still have been without jobs. The whole thing is really tragic, and there doesn't seem to be an answer to the devastation that was done to Detroit."

Freddie used his favorite word again, "Wow, I guess the future didn't turn out all that great after all."

Sarah answered, "Not for everyone. That is just one example of why I say you have a long way to go before you understand your new world. You need to start getting into the world, and going to school and working for KWTZ are great starts, but there is still so much more that you need to learn. I will set up another tutor for you. I'm sorry if you think I am treating you like children, but I feel this is necessary. It is your life, so if you would rather not, I will accept that."

"We need it," Emily said, and Freddie agreed, "We still see things every day that we either don't understand or can't figure out how they came to be. Heck, there must have been a bunch of laws passed that we don't know about. Just allow us to coordinate with you on the date and times for the lessons."

"That's great; I'll do that. Now on another subject, I got a call from the director of SHR Laboratories. Freddie, it seems Steve is already on to something. He has gotten some information from the National Weather Service that proves something did happen in the early hours of September 16, 1973, and at the same time ten days ago. What you experienced was a real phenomenon, and there is evidence of it. I'm sure Steve will have more to tell us soon. I do believe your brother was the right man for the job."

Freddie smiled with pride and said, "He was always the smartest one in the family. I think I'll give him a call."

The evening came to an end, and there were hugs all around. Even Tommy got his share of hugs. Shelly told him, "You are welcome anytime. I love to have a man around with a good appetite."

Everyone laughed, and Tommy said, "Mrs. Hicks, I have been all over the world, and I have never had better meals anywhere."

Shelly hugged him again, and then she told Sarah, "You keep him; he's a good man."

When Freddie and Emily arrived back at the hotel, Freddie began to voice something he had been thinking about for most of the evening, "We need to get out of this hotel and rent our own place."

Emily smiled and said, "Did you say our own place?"

"Yes, I did; our own place. I thought we could start with a nice little apartment somewhere until we know we could handle something bigger. I also thought that we could rent this place somewhere between Romulus and Ann Arbor; that would make commuting more reasonable."

Emily put her arms around him, kissed him, and said, "Your thoughtfulness is one of many things I love about you."

Freddie got Steve on the phone, "Little brother, I hear you are already making progress."

"Freddie, it's amazing. I never thought I would actually find something and find it so fast."

"Well, don't keep me waiting; what have you found out?"

"I now have documentation that proves that something actually happened on September 16, 1973, and it happened again on

September 16, 2017. Actually, it didn't happen again. It was one event that happened in two time periods simultaneously.

We still have no idea what it really is, but we can guess by its effect that it somehow breaches the time/space continuum. Star Trek has used the term for many years, and now I use it to describe this phenomenon. I call it a temporal anomaly."

"That's amazing. You are a great scientist, my brother."

"This wasn't science, this was investigating, and your sister-in-law has been a big help."

"Then you tell Cathy that I am truly grateful. Did you find out anything else?"

"I now know that the anomaly descended into the atmosphere, skimmed the Earth, and ascended again. I don't know how or why it did it, but I know its path."

"Did it cross Interstate 94 more than once?"

"No, just once; it crossed the highway at two twenty-three on the morning of September 16th."

"Then you know exactly where and when we were shifted in time."

"Yes, I told you the when. The where is 14.3 miles east of the Shook Road exit off the interstate. That's where it happened to you. It is such a momentous event, and there isn't a spec of evidence that it actually happened. I'm sorry that this thing stole your life from you."

"I know. Maybe you can find a way to detect it so that, if it happens again, people can be warned."

"I also want to present enough evidence to prove that it was a temporal anomaly. Once I do that, you can be Freddie MacArthur again. No one will be able to doubt who you are."

"That would be great, Steve. Thank you for doing this for me."

After Freddie hung up, he told Emily all that Steve had discovered. Something about knowing exactly where it happened was important to Emily, but she couldn't figure out why. After pondering for a minute, it came to her, "Freddie, if we know where it happened, then we know where you threw my bag with my tape recorder."

Freddie looked at Emily. He feared what bringing those tapes to light might mean, "Are you sure searching for your bag is a good idea? You don't even know what was on those tapes."

"The whole story is out. The tapes won't get anyone into trouble."

"Then why do you want them?"

"The tapes and other things in the bag can prove who we are. There are other things in the bag. Personal things that I would like to get back."

"Okay, we'll look for the bag as soon as we can."

Barry called Betty Monday night and asked, "Did you see them? Were you able to get any information?"

"No, I missed them. I guess they got there early or something,"

"My son told me that they were hired, so they will be there at the same time tomorrow. Try to get there a little earlier, so you don't miss them."

"You know this is a pain in the ass dragging myself out of bed early in the morning just so I can watch two impersonators walk into a radio station. To think that they are anything else, sorry Barry, but it's just whacked."

"Betty, do you want the four hundred or not?"

"Yeah, yeah, I'm going to do it, but I still think it's whacked."

Chapter 10: Barracuda Rising

Freddie and Emily arrived at the radio station bright and early the next day. They didn't notice the old Ford Fusion parked a few spaces away. Betty was as shocked as everyone when she saw them. She had her window down, and she was lucky enough to be in earshot to hear the conversation as Freddie and Emily walked to the door, "After we are finished here, I want to look for the tape recorder. I think we should have a good chance of finding it. That thing was on that whole day in Detroit. I really want to hear what was recorded."

Freddie agreed, "I have to admit I am curious about what is on those tapes. I hope it isn't too hard to climb into that gulley."

Betty heard the conversation, and she thought, "Could they be talking about Emily's tape recorder? That thing was supposed to have disappeared with her. How the hell could it show up after forty-four years, and why do they think the tapes would still be good? This is getting weird. Maybe Batali isn't so crazy after all."

Then she had a flash in her mind. Despite forty-four years of drug use, Betty still remembered that day. She remembered telling Emily that Rick needed a better drink. She didn't know if that would be enough evidence to open the case. Then she thought, "Hell, the statute of limitations had run out long ago, but how much would backstage tapes of the last concert of Barracuda be worth? Maybe enough to get me off the hook with Jackie. Little girl, I want those tapes."

Betty got on the phone with Barry, "You need to be able to tell me when these two will be leaving the station."

"I have no idea when they will be leaving. They are likely to be there all day."

"Then you're going to have to get your inside man to give you a heads up when they're leaving. I can't sit here all day."

"Did you see them this morning?"

"Yep, and they definitely look like Freddie and Emily."

"Did you talk to them?"

"Not yet; I want to check them out a little first. That is a fine car that he's driving."

"He was driving a mint condition 1973 Plymouth Barracuda."

"No shit?"

"No shit. Now that Barracuda is owned by Sarah Hicks Rutherford. Of course, they came up with a perfectly good explanation for that, and no one dares to validate it."

"Well, you have gotten my attention. Give me a heads-up when they're leaving. I want to be there."

"You are very motivated all of a sudden."

"I guess you are a convincing fellow."

Freddie and Emily were officially processed, and they were led to the conference room. In the room, they found Art, Tony, Roger Mendez, and four younger men.

Roger and the four young men had a shocked look on their faces that Freddie and Emily were so used to seeing. Tony made the introductions, "guys, this is Frank McAlester, and the young lady is Beth Richards. They are look-alikes that will be playing Freddie and Emily."

"Damn." Roger said, "I've seen some look-alikes on the web, but I have never seen anyone this good. I knew Freddie for quite a while, and I remember Emily; you two are them."

Freddie recognized Roger easily. The years were very good to him; he looked older, but he didn't look all that different.

Tony introduced the men, "As you might expect, you are talking to the playwright, Roger Mendez."

Freddie and Emily shook his hand.

Roger looked down when he shook Freddie's hand, then he looked back up and said, "Such detail; you even have that little skull and crossbones on your wrist."

Then Tony introduced the young men, "These guys are the Barracuda tribute band. They call themselves Barracuda Rising. From right to left, we have George Fisher, the keyboard man, Bobby Deeds, the bass player, Andy Porter on drums, and Jimmy Sherman does the vocals."

Freddie asked, "You must have a lead guitar if you have been playing gigs?"

Jimmy, acting as the front man that he was supposed to be, answered, "That's Pete Lorenzo. He's out, and you're in."

"I'm sorry he's being screwed."

"Yeah, so is he, but you certainly have a look. I guess we'll see if you can handle an axe like Pete."

Tony broke in, "Oh, he can; you'll see. Pete played in your audition, and he is really good, but this guy is Freddie MacArthur when he has a guitar in his hand."

Freddie was feeling a bit guilty about Pete, "Can't we get Pete into the production somehow? Maybe he could be someone from another band that jams with Freddie or challenges Freddie to dueling guitars. I bet the audience would love it. What do you think, Roger; could you work something like that in?"

Art interrupted the conversation, "Why would I want Roger to go through the trouble of a rewrite so I can spend more money on this project?"

"Because dueling guitars is always a big draw; it will be another marketing ploy. It will be worth the money."

Roger said, "I could do it, but it will cost a little extra."

Art looked at Freddie, and Freddie said, "It's still worth it."

"Okay," Art said, "And, Frank, when this is over, I may want to hire you as a negotiator."

Tony got back to business, "Okay, let's take a look at the script. Everyone should have a copy with their parts highlighted."

The group spent an hour going through the script, and then Freddie and the band moved to a studio to start their work together. When they left the room, Bobby got on the phone. He was clearly talking to Pete Lorenzo. Jimmy stopped Freddie and said, "Man, that was a class move. It's something Freddie would have done himself. Thanks man."

Freddie just said, "We musicians have to stick together, especially in this age."

Jimmy asked Freddie, "Tony said you did a lot of research on Barracuda. We know quite a bit ourselves, but if you know something that might help, just let us know. Okay, let's do this. We'll start with "Wrecking Ball.""

Freddie started out awkwardly with his new band. Some of it was real, and some of it was pretense; he didn't want to look too professional. After several tries, he was killing it. It felt good to be working with a band, but it also brought anguish to him. These guys didn't look anything like his friends, but when he closed his eyes, he could see the boys. He could see them sucking up the screams and cheers from the crowds. He could see the smiles on their faces and that slight look of, how did we get here?

The band was amazed at Freddie's ability. When they finished their short set Sheila, the intern, came in and asked them to return to the conference room. Jimmy talked to Freddie as they walked out of the room, "You have Freddie MacArthur down. How did you get so damn good?"

Freddie told the truth without telling the truth, "I've been working on it for years."

Tony and Art had excused themselves and left the conference room to get on with other station business. While Tony was going over some paperwork, his phone rang. He picked it up and heard his father's voice, "Tony, you need to give me a heads up when Frank and Beth are finishing up there."

"Dad, I can't continue to support your snooping. Frank and Beth are professional entertainers that are working for us now. I think Beth is a pain in the ass, but I think they're going to do good things for us. You need to leave them alone."

"I need to get to the truth of this."

"Why, what truth do you think you are going to find?"

"Please, son, do this for me, and I won't bother you again; I promise."

"Okay, I'll keep an eye out, but this is the last time."

"Thanks, son; I appreciate it."

In the conference room, Emily was trying to make a point about how she should play a scene. Roger was getting frustrated with all of the suggested rewrites, "Beth, you weren't there; I was. I don't care how much research you did. I saw Emily Hicks for real."

"You didn't see her in this scene. This was before she met the band. All you're going by is what you saw in the documentaries."

"And you have better information than that?"

"Yes, I talked to people. One of which was Ann Shimko herself. There is more to the scene in Ann Shimko's office. There is a piece of history that is being missed."

"There wasn't any history made in that office."

"Not made specifically, but there was history being born. When Emily came in, she addressed Ann Shimko as Miss Shimko. Ann educated Emily on the title of 'Ms.' The title of 'Ms.' was not used much at all at that time. Ann Shimko and other members of the National Organization of Women were changing the language and changing people's minds, and I think it's important. It's a small change that has a big meaning."

The band entered the room, and Bobby had to make a comment, "Man, the fur is flying in here. We could hear you halfway down the hall."

Roger grumbled, "It was a small issue. It's been resolved. I hope we can finish this first read-through without any more creative modifications."

Everyone was finding out how much work it takes to get people to say the right lines at the right time. They had hours of rehearsals ahead of them.

A few hours later, Tony returned to the conference room as the meeting was breaking up. He asked, "So, how did it go?"

Roger said, "We managed to stick to the script for the rest of the day."

Jimmy was more upbeat, "It was great, Mr. Batali. We're going to rock the house."

"Excellent; well, I'll see you all tomorrow."

Tony left the room and called his father, "Here's your heads up, and let this be the end of it."

"Stall them for a few minutes."

"What?"

"Stall them."

"Dad, this is getting crazy."

"Just do this one thing, please, and it's the last thing, I swear."

"I'll try."

As Freddie and Emily walked past Tony's door, he stepped out and asked, "Are you happy with the arrangements?"

Emily thought the question was mainly directed at her, so she answered, "Yes, they are fine. Have you set up any promotional spots for us yet?"

"No, we want to be sure this thing is going to fly before we start advertising it."

Freddie spoke in a definite tone, "Oh, it will fly."

"Well, I'm happy to hear that you're so confident, Frank."

Emily tried to start moving again, "Well, it's been a long day, and I'm looking forward to some dinner."

"Can I offer you a quick drink first; I have a little bar in my office."

Emily was all but pushing Freddie toward the door, and she spoke for them again, "No, thank you; I am quite hungry."

Betty almost missed them. She got to the parking lot just as they were leaving. She followed them, trying to be careful.

"So you want to do this now," Freddie asked Emily.

"Yes, the suspense has been killing me all day."

"You do know it is rush hour. We experienced rush hour on Interstate 95. I'm sure it isn't much better on Interstate 94."

"We'll survive; I want to hear those tapes."

"Okay, you're better at that GPS thing. Tell me when we're fourteen point three miles from the Shook Road exit. It was the flash that made me pull over so that should put us at the right spot."

"But we're going in the other direction."

"That shouldn't cause us a problem. I remember I threw the bag directly over the guard rail, and it landed several feet to the right of a tree. It was the only tree around. If I see the tree, I should be able to find the bag."

"Great; let's go get it."

Emily watched the GPS as Freddie drove. Neither noticed the Ford Fusion behind them. Emily counted up, fourteen, fourteen point one. Freddie slowed down and began to pull onto the left shoulder of the road. Betty went past them. Fortunately for her, there was an overpass a quarter of a mile away. She went under the overpass and pulled over on the other side. She got out quickly and walked back carrying a pair of binoculars. She got in position to see Freddie climbing over the guard rail.

"That's got to be the tree," Freddie was saying, "From this side, the bag should be a few feet to the left."

"Be careful; you don't know what else is lurking in that tall grass."

"Oh, thanks for that image."

"I mean, there might be broken bottles and things down there."

Freddie made his way carefully down the slope. At the bottom, he began to look around. He was frustrated. He thought he would find it easily. He called to Emily, "It should be right here."

"It has been some time. Maybe somebody found it."

Freddie looked up the slope and said, "I found it. It didn't make it all the way down."

Betty watched as Freddie picked up the bag and carried it back up the slope. She said out loud, "Be careful with that thing. It's going to bail my ass out of a tight spot."

Freddie and Emily grabbed a quick bite at a fast food joint and hurried back to the hotel. Ellen was scheduled to be there by seven-thirty to start the new set of lessons. Again, they didn't notice that they were being followed.

Betty got out of her car and waited in the shadows. When Freddie and Emily entered the hotel, she hurried to the hotel lobby. She watched as Freddie and Emily entered the elevator, and then she went in. She watched the elevator indicator until it stopped on the third floor, then she moved as quickly as she could up the stairway. Betty was puffing when she got to the third floor, but she got there in time. She saw them go into their rooms, noted the numbers, and she quickly left.

Ellen knocked on Emily's door right on time. They started by talking about the state of the world and the advancements made in individual rights and tolerance for all people. The more she talked, the more they understood why Sarah said that they needed more coaching. Freddie was actually amazed, "You are saying that two people that are in love can show it openly. It doesn't matter if they are different races or religions, or even if they are the same sex?"

"That's right. It took a very long time and the sacrifice of many people. As you know, from witnessing the civil rights struggle and the fight for equal rights for women, the first people to stand up are the bravest and the ones that take the most punishment. We have seen that courage from interracial couples and gay couples. We have seen transgender people refuse to hide who they are. We are coming closer to achieving liberty and justice for all, but we are not there yet. We are now going through a backlash phase, and some of the gains are in danger of being lost."

Freddie considered what he was told and said, "I can understand some people not accepting all of these changes. It is hard for me to believe that they have happened. Coming from a world that used the words queer and faggot; it will take me some time to get used to all of this."

"The difference, Freddie, is you're willing to try, and you're willing to say it is you that has to change. That's all that anyone can expect of you."

"Emily, what do you think of all of this? How would you react if you saw a black man and a white woman together or two men holding hands?"

"To be honest, I think I would be fine with seeing an interracial couple, but I would probably feel uncomfortable seeing two men or two women show affection to each other. It goes against things that were ingrained in me all my life.

My Uncle Bernie must have been going nuts until the day he died. He was not big on change. I'm sure if he saw an interracial couple, he would say something disgusting about what their children would look like."

"That's why this has been such a long struggle. Everyone in your generation had the same lessons taught to them. It is hard to undo the teaching that people received in their formative years. What has to be said over and over, like a mantra, is liberty and justice for all. That has to be the focus. You may still cringe inside when you see things you feel are unnatural, but you can use your intelligence to realize it is their right. I believe it was Clarence Darrow that talked about the fact that, deep down, we are all prejudiced, but it is our intellect that can overrule that feeling."

Ellen covered several other topics, and then she came to language, "I'm sure you have noticed that, though we do still speak English, the language has changed. All of these topics are vastly more complicated than I can make them sound. When it comes to language, I will focus on three main areas. First are titles, mainly of certain professions. These changes happened largely because of the women's movement. The title for a woman is 'Ms.' unless you know the lady and she accepts a title that relates to her martial state."

Emily interrupted Ellen, "I was just having a discussion about that today. I believe I was present at the birth of that title. I know I hadn't heard it until Ann Shimko explained it to me in her office. She ran the chapter of the National Organization of Women at U of M."

"I believe you were. That was about the time NOW started pushing the use of the title, and it worked quite well. All women are now addressed as 'Ms.'

There have been changes to other titles thanks to the women's movement. All titles that used to indicate gender have been replaced. Firemen are now firefighters; policemen are police officers, and so on. Taking gender out of titles went a long way to accepting women in those positions.

The next area I want to talk about is profanity. The use of profane language has always been common, but now it is acceptable by many people in regular conversation. Even the word fuck, or I should say, especially the word fuck. People, especially young people, use it as a common term in all its variations, so don't be surprised if you hear it regularly.

Finally, I should mention the common slang. Being middle-aged, I haven't kept up with all of the new words, but I can give you an idea of how to translate some of the things you might hear. The use of newer communication devices has made a big impact on our language. Texting is the favored mode of communication."

"Yeah," Freddie said, "no one wants to talk. I'm happy you gave us those lessons on our phones, or I wouldn't be able to communicate at all."

"You will remember that I talked to you about acronyms like BRB, which means be right back."

Emily volunteered, "They're using them to avoid a lot of typing when sending texts."

"That's right, well now they are also being used when speaking. People will say BRB instead of be right back. You may hear any of the acronyms that we went over in normal conversation."

Emily added, "Those emoji things really get me. It's like going back to Egyptian hieroglyphics."

"Yeah, it is. Many of us hope it is a phase, but it may not be. Of course, slang words that you might have been used to using would likely sound strange to people today or at least old-fashioned. Things like groovy and out-of-sight are only used in jest. You still hear someone say things like bummer, but not very often. Fortunately, mainline English still works."

Ellen was very talented in her ability to convey her ideas and information. Freddie and Emily were left feeling that they had made another step in becoming part of this new world.

When she left, the time travelers quickly went to the bag and brought out the tape recorder. Fortunately, it survived the impact with the ground, and it was in working order. They listened to tape after tape. Freddie heard himself calling for Dr. Jenkins and the commotion when Rick collapsed. He snarled, "That bitch dosed him, and she got away with it."

"She didn't go to jail," Emily answered, "but she didn't have a great life. The word got out, and no band trusted her anywhere near them. She had nothing else going for her. It actually sounds like she's been paying for it ever since."

Freddie had a thought, "You were talking to her right before Rick collapsed."

"I was, but she got me talking to Patty Grundy, and she slipped away. I didn't see where she went."

"I know, but did she say anything before she left?"

A look of realization appeared on Emily's face, "She did. You're damn right. She did, and I recorded it. It must be on the previous tape."

Emily didn't have time to properly label the tapes, so they had to search to find the right one. Finally, they found it, and they listened. First, they heard Emily say, "You're not forgiving Don that easy are you? I mean, he didn't even apologize."

Then they heard Betty say, "Oh, don't worry about me. Despite what it seems, I'm not that gullible. I think Rick needs a better drink."

Emily said, "I had no idea what she meant by that at the time."

Freddie cheered, "Well, now we have proof that the bitch did it."

"Yeah, but that was forty-four years ago. The statute of limitations has run out long ago."

"Then we will have her tried in the court of public opinion. Everyone will know what she did."

"And how do we explain finding these tapes?"

That question stumped Freddie, and it ended the night's conversation.

In the morning, they returned to the radio station and met in the conference room. They had a full day of practice ahead of them. There were two new people, Pete Lorenzo and a young blonde lady named Sherry Adjenson. Tony introduced them, "Everyone, this is Sherry Adjenson. She is going to play the part of Betty Ann Rother, and this is Pete Lorenzo, and he will be a rival, of sorts, of Freddie."

Sherry was greeted, and the work began for the day. It started with Roger's idea for Pete Lorenzo's part. "Pete would be a rival of Freddie's, one that wants to prove that he is better than him. He bribes some people to get him in during the sound check in Chicago. When Ryan is counting down to go into the intro for "Rabble Rouser," Pete plugs in and jumps into the song before Freddie. He plays a few measures and turns to Freddie. Freddie plays a few measures and turns back to Pete. From there, you guys can improvise for two or three minutes. It will be up to you two to sell it."

Frank and Pete agreed and talked about working out the jam. Then Roger wanted to go over the introduction to the play, "Okay, this is what I'm seeing. The stage is dark, a spotlight is turned on, and Freddie is sitting on a stool with an acoustic guitar. He is strumming out the melody, and he sings just two lines from 'A Dark Night for Walking.' Freddie sings, *"It's a dark night for walking; nothing is going my way. A dark night for walking; it's time to walk away."*

Now, Beth, I didn't see much in your resume about your ability to sing."

Emily was surprised, and she said, "Maybe because I have no ability to sing. I have never needed it before when I played Emily."

"It was just a thought. You can recite the second part of the chorus. It's a dark night for walking; the flags have all been furrowed. A dark night for walking; I think I'll walk out of this world."

Freddie had to ask, "Are you sure you can't sing it or are you just too shy to try?"

Emily gave Freddie a death stare, and he gave her a sly smile. Roger asked, "Would you like to try? We have plenty of time to work on it."

"Oh, I don't think so."

Freddie led the chant, "Sing it, sing it; sing it."

"Okay, but you don't know the pain you are about to experience."

Then she pointed the finger at Freddie and said, "You, mister, are in big trouble."

"Wait," Freddie said, "let me grab an acoustic from the studio."

Freddie returned and started playing the melody, and Roger said, "Frank, why don't you start."

Freddie sang, *"It's a dark night for walking; nothing is going my way. It's a dark night for walking; it's time to walk away."*

Everyone looked at Emily, and she started nervously, *"It's a dark night for walking; the flags have all been furrowed. A dark night for walking; I think I'll walk out of this world."*

Everyone applauded, and Emily was beet red. Roger said, "That wasn't bad. You can carry a tune, and that's all that we need. In fact, I wouldn't want it to be any better."

Emily said, "Thank you, I think."

Roger said, "The singing is in."

Emily suddenly felt panic, "What do you mean on stage, in front of people?"

"That is where we will perform."

Freddie put his arm around her and said, "You'll be fine."

Emily, clearly not totally serious, growled at him, "You might not be when I get you alone."

After some additional discussion, the band broke off to practice, and Emily began working with Sherry.

Pete talked to Freddie as they entered the studio, "Jimmy told me this was all your idea. I really appreciate it. Can I buy you a couple of beers when we're done here?"

"Yeah," George jumped in, "there's an Irish pub in town. We can hoist some pints and sing Irish ditties."

Freddie smiled and said, "That sounds good."

Freddie wanted to add a little to the staging of the band, but he didn't want to sound like he was taking over. He had thought about how to approach them and how he would answer the inevitable question of how he knew so much. He came up with a story, "Guys, I came across an interview with Mickey Hardstone. This one was not widely distributed; it was more of a technical discussion. Mickey talked about the band's movement on stage, and I think we could mimic what they did."

Jimmy spoke for the band, "Do you mean the things he and Rick Santora did on stage?"

"Yes, that and when Freddie would move to center stage and when Ryan would stand when he played. They had signals, and they had timing. Some motions were made at a certain time in songs, and some were done on Mickey's signal. Would you like to try some?"

Everyone agreed, and Pete told Freddie, "Until we start working on the jam, I'm going to try to follow you; my guitar won't be plugged in. I just want to get some of your techniques down, if you don't mind. After this gig, we'll be back in the bars, and I want to channel Freddie the way that you do."

Freddie couldn't help feeling a rush of pride hearing Pete's words, "That's cool, Pete, and we'll work on the jam after we do a run-through of the concert songs."

Sandwiches were brought in for lunch, and everyone gathered back in the conference room. Emily shot daggers at Freddie with her eyes, and Freddie said, "Oh come on, Beth, it was fun, wasn't it? You did a great job."

"It was adequate, just like Roger said. You're just lucky I wasn't laughed out of the room. If that happened, you wouldn't leave this place in one piece."

"Okay, I get it. Oh, I'm going out for a few beers with the band tonight."

"Oh, you are?"

"Yeah, just for a little while. We'll have dinner, I'll drop you off, and then I'll head out."

"You want to bond with your new band?"

"That sounds good. Actually, I just thought that a few beers would be good, but I like your excuse better."

"If you're going to be wandering in after midnight, go to your own room. Don't expect me to get out of bed to let you in."

"I would never argue with a Romulan commander."

"Oh, aren't you cute?"

"I watched Star Trek too."

In Virginia, Eric and Steve Junior joined the search. They were looking for any unusual reports from the early morning hours of September 16th, 1973, or 2017. They found several UFO reports, all describing the same shimmering blue rectangular object. One described it as a blue curtain. Steve and Eric made notes of names and addresses.

Then Eric found a 1973 article that didn't appear in the Detroit Free Press until September 19th. It was buried deep in the back pages. It seemed a woman called the police and claimed a UFO had taken her dog. She said she heard her dog barking, then there was a flash of light, and her dog was gone.

His father had looked for anything about a dog appearing from nowhere recently. He couldn't find anything. Young Steve suggested, "Maybe the person just didn't report it. Maybe the dog appeared in the middle of the night and just wandered off."

The older Steve said, "I think I want to find out."

It took a little digging, but they found a name and a phone number for the people living at the address of the incident. The woman who reported the incident no longer lived there, but they did find her contact information.

The older Steve turned to his wife and said, "How about we take a trip to Detroit? We can see Freddie and do a few in-person interviews."

Everyone had practiced how to approach people. They came up with a little dialogue that they used, hoping the fame of SHR Laboratories would open some doors for them. Eric got on his phone and started calling police stations in the area. He was hoping to get access to old police files if they still existed. He went down the list, and he got to Romulus, "Hello, my name is Eric MacArthur, and I represent SHR Laboratories. We are doing a study of a possible phenomenon that occurred on the morning of September 16, 1973, and we were hoping that we would be allowed to access your police files for that date."

The person on the phone explained the procedure for gaining access, and Eric wrote it down. Eric thanked the person and began to follow the procedure. It didn't take long for the query to be known by everyone in the department. Someone with an interest in that date was not going to go unnoticed.

Betty watched and waited. When Freddie and Emily left the hotel, she entered and went to the third floor. She waited and tried to keep out of sight until the housekeeping staff started making their rounds. When the woman opened Emily's door, Betty wanted to just rush in, but there was no way to do it without getting caught. Betty also found out that the housekeeping staff was not as careless with their access keys as they were on television. She couldn't get in the room, and she left in frustration.

Betty left the hotel, but she returned by late afternoon. She didn't know what she was going to do next. She just sat in her car trying to come up with an idea. Then she saw the red Challenger enter the parking lot. She watched, and she was amazed when Emily got out, and Freddie drove off. This was her chance. She always carried a butterfly knife in her purse for protection; now, it would come in handy. She got out of the car, moved quickly, and entered the hotel just behind Emily. She followed her to the elevator trying to keep her head down. Once they got to the third floor, she closed in on Emily as she reached her door. She poked the knife near her ribs and said, "Open the door and let's go in."

Emily was shocked and petrified. She opened the door, and Betty pushed her in. Emily stumbled and turned around. Her shock grew when she looked at the woman's face. She said, "My God, you're Betty Rother!"

Betty said, "I can't believe he was right, but you are Emily Hicks, aren't you?"

"What do you want?"

"I want those tapes and your recorder. I don't have a rich sister, and I need money, and those tapes are worth a lot."

"How did you...."

"I don't have time to explain. I followed you. I saw Freddie get the bag from the gulley out on 94. That boy still looks good! Now fetch it for me and make sure everything is in it."

"I can get you as much money as you want."

"Sorry, but I'm in a hurry; I'm sure you could get the cash, and if the timing was better, I might take you up on that. Unless you have five grand in cash stashed in this room, I will have to go with the tapes."

"Okay, they're over by the bed."

"Put everything back in the bag and hand it to me."

Emily got the bag together and took it to Betty. Betty reached for the bag and grabbed Emily's hand instead. Emily screamed, and Betty put the knife to her throat and said, "Sorry little girl, but I need to get out of town with the tapes and without the cops on my ass. You're going to have to come with me."

Emily knew if she left that room, she may never come back. She stomped on Betty's foot which made her loosen her grip, and then she pulled away. Betty lunged with the knife and struck Emily in the back as she moved away. Emily groaned in agony and dropped to the floor. Her blouse began to get wet with blood.

Betty grabbed the bag and left the room with Emily bleeding on the floor.

Chapter 11: Changing Sides

Freddie and his new bandmates finished singing along to an Irish ditty, and Pete ordered another round. Freddie asked them, "How did you guys get together?"

Bobby answered, "We were all in other bands in the Detroit area at one time or another. Jimmy and I had left our last band. It seemed like those guys were more interested in scoring dope than playing music. Don't get me wrong, we can party with the best of them, but the music comes first. We noticed just how many Barracuders there were in the Detroit area. Then we found out that they were all over the place, especially in Detroit, Chicago, and the Washington area. After all this time, Barracuda still had fans. I guess old Bob was right; rock and roll never forgets. There is even a chain of bars called Barracuders."

Freddie found his words very satisfying, "But you guys are what, mid-thirties; how did you get so hooked on the old rock and roll?"

"The same reason a young guy like you did, the music man. We want to play music, and there isn't anyone playing music these days. Anyway, Jimmy and I decided to form a Barracuda tribute band. We had been playing a few Barracuda tunes, and we began to learn more. We also wanted to know more about the band. Once we had a handle on what we wanted to do, we advertised on the web for musicians that were into Barracuda and could handle their music. We checked out a bunch of people, and we ended up with these guys. That was about two years ago. We now have regular gigs in the Detroit area, the biggest being at the Barracuders bar. Playing there kind of anoints us as the official Barracuda tribute band. It's been fun, but we still aren't making what we were making in our day jobs."

"Yeah," George jumped into the conversation, "but this is a lot more fun."

Jimmy asked, "How about you? The way you handle an axe, you can't have always been in the look-alike business."

Freddie knew he could handle band questions on the fly, "I was in several bands, and we did fairly well around Sacramento, but no one wanted to leave there, and I did. I went to southern California. I know it sounds crazy just to wander off and see what happens, but that's kind of in me. I got in a pretty good bar band, and I was making enough to eat. Then a guy came into the bar. He told me that people were saying how much I looked like Freddie MacArthur. He offered me a deal to join this look-alike agency out of Burbank. I went for it, and I've been doing that ever since."

"But didn't that kill your chance to play your music?"

"Not entirely. It did kill my band work, most of the time. I've had gigs like this before where I was paired up with a band, but most of the time it was just me and my guitar. That's until Beth came along, and they decided it would be cool to do a couples' thing. You know, like Sonny and Cher. But I'll tell you this, you guys are tight, and you are the best band I've worked with in a long time."

Jimmy once again spoke for the band, "Thanks Frank, we appreciate that."

The songs were sung, and the beer flowed to about ten o'clock. Then Freddie begged his leave. The guys tried to make him stay longer but he wanted to get back and talk to Emily about the tapes. He left the bar and got back to the hotel about twenty minutes after ten. He was sure she would still be up, so he knocked on her door. He waited a minute, expecting to hear her approach. When he didn't, he knocked again, and he listened more intently. Then he heard her weak voice, "Help me, please help me."

Freddie pounded on the door calling, "Emily; Emily, what's wrong?!"

Freddie could hear her voice fading, "I can't . . . Get help."

The panic was rising in Freddie, but he kept enough of his mind to unlock his door and get on the phone to the front desk, "Get up here and unlock 326. The woman is badly hurt and locked in the room."

He didn't wait for a response. He got out his cell phone and stared at it for a second. His mind was racing, "Emergency number, what the hell is the emergency number?" Then he remembered and punched in 911.

He got an answer and frantically called into the phone, 'There is a woman in room 326 of the Embassy Suites on Sherborn. She's badly hurt, hurry. Yes, she was breathing; she talked to me through the door. I called the hotel people. I think I hear them outside now. They should have the door open. Yes, I will."

Freddie rushed out of the door just as the hotel staff opened the door. They saw Emily in a pool of blood. Freddie was frantic. He almost forgot he had the 911 operator on the line. The first man to Emily said, "She was stabbed. She's lucky it isn't very deep, but she's lost a lot of blood."

Freddie stretched his arm forward and said, "Here, I have the emergency people on the line. You can tell them better than I can."

The hotel staff began giving Emily first aid while Freddie paced and pulled on his long hair. He just kept mumbling, "Why did I have to go out? Why did I leave her alone?"

A few minutes later, the EMTs arrived and took over. The hotel man handed Freddie back his phone and said, "I think she'll be alright. If the wound was just a little deeper, she would have been in real trouble."

As they got Emily ready for transport, an EMT turned to Freddie and said, "She managed to lie in just the right position to put enough pressure on the wound to slow the bleeding."

By this time, the police had arrived. Freddie was trying to breathe a sigh of relief when they started firing questions at him. He explained where he had been and who he was with, and they moved on to questions about whom else could have stabbed Emily.

Freddie moved behind the EMTs as they started moving Emily down the hall. He looked back at the police and told them that he had no idea. He got in the ambulance and watched the EMTs continue their work and communicate with the hospital. Emily opened her eyes and called, "Freddie."

Freddie held her hand and said, "Don't speak; just rest. You're going to be okay."

Emily told him, "It was Betty. She wanted the tapes, and she wanted me to come with her."

Freddie was furious, "That scurvy bitch. I will find her."

When the ambulance arrived at the hospital, Emily was taken in for treatment, and Freddie was left to pace the floor. While he paced, he called Sarah and told her what had happened. He didn't want to call Shelly. He asked Sarah to do that. Sarah told him to stay there and she would have people there to support him, and that she would be there as soon as she could.

Freddie paced for another five minutes then Detectives Cindi Baveroski and Eric Volstad entered the room. They introduced themselves, and then they began to ask questions. Cindi took the lead, "You are Mr. Frank McAlester; is that right?"

"Yes."

"And you came into town with Ms. Elizabeth Richards."

"That's right."

"Why did you come to Romulus, Mr. McAlester?"

"What difference does that make? Em… Beth was stabbed by a woman named Betty Rother. She told me that in the ambulance. Ask the EMTs; they must have heard her say it."

"Why would Betty Rother want to stab her?"

"Betty stole her bag. It contained some tapes that could incriminate her."

"Tapes, what kind of tapes did she steal?"

"They were cassette tapes. Beth had them and the recorder."

"What crime would those relics shed light on?"

"While you're standing here giving me the third degree, she's getting away."

"No, she's not, Mr. McAlester; my partner has already called it in. A BOLO is going out as we speak. Now, what crime did Betty Rother commit?"

"The tapes prove that she dosed Rick Santora's drink back in 1973."

"Well, I'm afraid it's a little late to present that evidence."

"I guess Betty didn't know that. She stabbed Beth and took the tapes and the recorder."

Eric finished his calls and commented, "If those tapes are recordings of Barracuda in 1973, they could be very valuable."

"They weren't at the concert. There were recordings of things that happened backstage before, during, and after the concert."

"That will make them more valuable."

Cindi got back into the discussion, "Are you talking about Emily Hicks' tapes?"

Freddie now knew he was in trouble. He had to answer, "Yes, we discovered them as part of our research."

"Where did you discover them? Everyone assumed that they went with Emily."

Freddie tried to get off the subject, "That doesn't matter. Betty Rother stabbed Beth to get the tapes; that's the story."

Cindi raised her voice, "I asked you a question, Mr. McAlester; where did you find the tapes?"

Before he could answer, Tim and three other men came in. A well-dressed man stepped up to the detectives and said, "I'm Nathaniel Evans, and I represent Mr. McAlester and Ms. Richards. Can't you see that this man is distraught? I think he has answered enough questions for tonight."

Cindi didn't like the interruption, "Well, Mr. Evans, you are interrupting an ongoing investigation. Some might call this obstruction of justice."

Freddie yelled, "I told her who did it and why. But instead of finding Betty, she wants to stand around here and ask me irrelevant questions."

Cindi snapped back, "I'll decide what questions are relevant."

Evans said, "No, you won't, detective. It seems my client has given you plenty of information. You can see that he is very upset. You are bordering on harassment."

"Okay, counselor, but make sure your client is around when we call."

The detectives left, and Freddie thanked his new attorney. He explained what happened, leaving out some parts until he got Tim alone.

Tim asked, "How did you know where to look for the bag?"

"My brother is working to find out exactly what happened to us and he was able to figure out exactly where we made the transition. I knew I threw the bag over the guard rail close to that spot."

"So this woman has cassette tapes recorded in 1973 that look like they were just bought at a store."

"Yes, she does."

"Well, I think Ms. Rutherford is going to consider that a big problem. I'm going to check in with her as soon as I know Emily's condition."

At that moment, the doctor came into the room. Everyone stood, and he made his report, "Ms. Richards is stable. The wound has been closed, and she is resting comfortably. She was very lucky. Her attacker must have lunged from a distance. The knife did not go in far enough to damage any organs or sever any major blood vessels. However, she did lose a lot of blood. We'll keep her until she is strong enough to go home. It will probably be just a day or two."

Freddie asked, "When may I see her."

"Give the nurses a few more minutes to get her in her room. Someone will be out to get you."

Freddie thanked the doctor, and he left the room. Tim pulled out his phone and he turned to Freddie, "There's no reason for me to relay information. Why don't you just tell her the situation yourself?"

Freddie got out his phone and selected Sarah's number. Sarah answered immediately, "How's my sister?"

"She'll be fine. She will be in the hospital for a couple of days and then she can be released."

"She won't be there for two days and she won't recuperate in a hotel room. I'm having a place prepared for her and people to tend to her."

"I want to tend to her."

"I'm sure you do, and she will need you there, but I want professionals available, and you need to continue with your life. You need to go back to the hotel; Tim will go with you. Gather your things and Emily's things and check out. Return to the hospital. If Emily has been moved Tim will take you to your new home. It will be much more comfortable than the hotel room."

"I'm not going anywhere until I see Emily."

"Yes, of course. See Emily, and then please start moving. We need to get control of this situation. Now, who was this woman that attacked Emily?"

"It was Betty Ann Rother, the groupie that brought Emily backstage in Detroit."

"Betty? Betty stabbed my sister?"

"Yes, to get a hold of the tapes that Emily made before, during, and after our concert in Detroit. There is incriminating evidence on one of the tapes. It proves that she dosed Rick's whiskey."

"Do you really think that she did this to Emily to get the tapes for that reason?"

"There is another reason. Tapes from that time in perfect condition could be worth quite a bit to news magazine-type shows. They could be a gold mine for her."

"Well, she won't see any money. She's going to pay. Do you know anything else that might help us find her?"

"No, maybe Emily can help when she feels better."

"Okay, I'll be there in a couple of hours."

When Freddie was given the word, he hurried to Emily's room. He wanted to put his arms around her, but he knew he couldn't. Emily smiled weakly when he came in and said, "Do you see what happens when you go out with the boys."

"I know; I'm so sorry."

"Freddie, I was kidding. I'm going to be fine. I'm going to have a vacation for a few days, and then I'll be back on my feet."

"You might have been kidding, but you're still right. If I had been there, this wouldn't have happened."

"Maybe not tonight, but she would have tried another time. Betty is in bad shape. She needs money in a hurry for some reason. She had been following us for a couple of days."

"How the hell did she know that we were even in town, and how did she know how to find us."

"I have no idea. I thought she was in Louisiana. She got the tapes in a way that's good for us. We wanted to hear what was on those tapes, but explaining how we had brand new forty-four-year-old tapes might have been tricky. Betty certainly won't tell anyone where she got them."

"Your sister is having us moved, and she is on the way. You can expect to be hauled out of here any time now. I was being grilled by a detective named Baveroski when Tim, a few guys, and a lawyer showed up. The detective had just painted me into a corner when the lawyer got between us. From her line of questioning, I would say that she was a friend of Barry Batali."

"And that's why Sarah wants us to disappear."

"Yes. Emily, I'll move, but I'm not going to disappear. I want to do this show. These new guys are great, and I think we can really get something going. I don't want to give that up. I know Sarah wants to do her best for us, but I can't live in hiding, no matter how fancy the digs are."

"I understand. I was getting a kick out of playing myself. The whole thing has been a special experience for me. I'll talk to her."

"She'll be here in a couple of hours. She asked me to get all of our stuff from the hotel. Tim is going with me; I think he is going to make sure I do what I'm told."

"I don't think Sarah wants to control you."

"I think she'll do anything to make sure you're safe. She won't leave anything to chance, not even my freedom of movement."

"I'll talk to her; I promise. Why don't you get the things, and I'll get a bit more rest before people start hauling me around."

Cindi and Eric returned to the station, and Cindi was more than a little curious about these tapes and the sudden appearance of one of the most powerful lawyers in the state. This was just another connection between the Hicks family and these two look-alikes. This was far too much of a coincidence for her. There was someone that might know more. Orders or no orders, she was going to get to the bottom of this, and she had to start with her old friend. She selected Barry Batali's number, and it rang. Barry answered, and Cindi got right to it, "A person of interest of yours was stabbed tonight."

"Really, and who would that be?"

"Elizabeth Richards was stabbed by Betty Rother, and Betty made off with some cassette tapes. They are supposedly recordings of the last days of the band Barracuda. What do you think of that?"

"What I think is what I have thought since I talked to those two, but to say it out loud would make me crazy."

"You're thinking that those two really are Emily Hicks and Freddie MacArthur."

"Yes, that's what I think. How is that possible?"

"I might have at least a hint to an answer for you. A story started going around the station that someone from SHR Laboratories wants to get a hold of our files from September 16, 1973. Now we know what the SHR stands for and guess who is representing them. It's a man named Eric McArthur. That roused everyone's curiosity. Well, Eric MacArthur submitted the paperwork to get access to the files, and that gave us enough information to check him out. He's Freddie MacArthur's nephew."

"Do you know what they are looking for?"

"According to him, he is looking for anything unusual."

Barry felt like he was being vindicated. He was now more determined than ever, "Eric got his uncle back, and his uncle is probably younger than he is, and he wants to know how it happened. I need to talk to those two, and you need to find Betty Ann Rother."

"How do you think Betty got wind of those two being in town and what made her seek them out?"

Barry paused. He knew he could be in for some trouble, but he wanted Cindi to know, "I did. I was talking to Richie from narcotics, and he told me that she was back in town. I tracked her down. I thought she could use a little money, so I paid her to get what information she could about Emily and Freddie. She thought I was an idiot when I first approached her, but two days later, she seemed to be really motivated to do the job. I guess now I know why."

"Barry, I'm going to pretend I didn't hear that. My life is complicated enough already. The fact is there is no law against time travel; if that's what happened, my job is finding Betty Ann Rother and locking her up."

"I can help with that. She's driving a 2009 blue Ford Fusion. It has a Louisiana tag; it's Able, Delta, Kilo, 472. The car is beaten to crap. It should be easy to spot."

"Thanks, I'll get that right out."

"Thanks, Cindi; I'm sorry about this. I guess my snooping might have got the girl stabbed."

"Well, you'll have to deal with that one. One warning, Ms. Rutherford has already surrounded those two with lawyers and security people. You're not going to get close to them."

"I won't get close to Emily, but I may be able to have a chat with Freddie. He's actually working for my son right now."

"Just be careful."

Barry hung up, and his wife asked, "Was that about your obsession?"

"I'm not obsessed; I'm curious. I've found out that Freddie MacArthur's nephew is now working for SHR Laboratories and is searching for anything unusual that happened on September 16, 1973. Tell me that's just a coincidence."

"Curiosity doesn't run people's lives twenty-four hours a day; obsession does."

"Well, don't worry. I have a feeling Ms. Rutherford is about to flex her money muscle again. I won't be able to get near them."

"I heard what you said. You are planning to get Tony mixed up in this again. He told you that he didn't want any part of your investigation and that you were causing him problems at work. Barry, you can't do that to your son."

"I know, but the station is my only shot at getting to Freddie."

"It's Freddie now, is it? I thought his name was Frank. Look, you are not going to buck a billionaire like Sarah Hicks Rutherford. You'll just ruin our lives and maybe your son's."

"Then you just want me to give up."

"No, there is another way."

"What other way?"

"If you can't beat them, join them. If SHR wants information about that date, they probably wouldn't mind help from someone who knows his way around and can expedite things for them. Contact this nephew and offer him your support. I'm sure you will have to sign a nondisclosure agreement, but it would get you to the truth."

Barry kissed his wife and said, "You are the brains in this family."

Freddie and Tim returned to the hospital in time. They were back in the room with Emily when Sarah's people arrived. Ellen was with them. Sarah thought that it would be a comfort for Emily to see a friendly face. Ellen went to Emily and said, "I'm sorry. Maybe I should have spent more time talking about the level of violence that is in society today."

Emily said, "The only one at fault here is Betty Rother. It is good to see you, Ellen."

Freddie came to be with her as the men prepared her for transport. She wouldn't be jostled. The men took her, bed and all. They also moved the IV stand with them. She, the bed, and the IV stand were lifted into the back of a truck. Freddie jumped in, and they were off. No one attempted to stop them. The word was passed from the hospital's chief administrator not to interfere with Emily's transfer.

The interior of the truck was padded, and the bed was secured; it would not move around. The driver knew his cargo was very precious, and he kept the ride slow and smooth.

When the back of the truck was opened, its riders saw that they were on the lakeshore. From the time it took them to get there, they guessed it was Lake St. Claire. They were taken into the private retreat, and the staff was ready to greet them. The doctors, nurses, and management introduced themselves, and they were treated like royalty, which included a procession from the front door to Emily's room. It was impressive, but Freddie felt very uncomfortable. He had been used to being treated special, but that was because of who he was and not who someone else was. Despite all the changes, he still had a nineteen seventies ego, and he didn't like being kept by a woman. The grounds were beautiful, and they seemed to go on forever in every direction to the lake shore. It was a very peaceful place.

Sarah arrived thirty minutes later with her entourage. She rushed in to see Emily, and everyone, including Freddie, gave her the room. Emily assured her that she was fine, but it only slightly eased Sarah's tension. Sarah told her, "I lost you once; I'm not going to lose you again."

"You don't have to tell Mom about this. I'll be up and around in a few days."

"I do have to tell Mom; if she doesn't know already. You were stabbed in a downtown Dearborn hotel; that's news. It will be at every station. I'm going to talk to her as soon as I'm sure you have everything you need, and I'll bet she will be here by lunchtime."

"Sarah, I need to talk to you about Freddie. He can't be locked up in this beautiful place. You said you lost me once, and you don't want to lose me again. Well, Freddie has lost his life once, and forcing him to stay here would make him lose it again. He is back playing his music, and he is beginning to fit in. Please don't take that away from him."

"You love him, don't you?"

"Yes, I do, and he loves me. I want him to be happy."

"How about you? You said you wanted to go back to U of M for the winter semester?"

"Yes, and I also want to finish what I started with Freddie. I want to be part of the show. I didn't know how much fun something like that could be. Freddie actually got me to sing."

"You are going to sing?"

"Just a half of one chorus; it is right in the beginning."

"Oh, I have to see that. We'll work it out."

"Thanks sis."

Sarah stepped outside and went straight to Freddie, "You better get some sleep. You have work tomorrow, and I will make sure that you aren't hassled while you do it. Emily will also be joining you when she is up to it."

Freddie let out a great sigh of relief, and he said, "I am so happy to hear you say that. I had this big speech planned about needing to do things, and you saved me from that embarrassment."

"It wouldn't have been embarrassing. I don't want to take care of you or Emily for the rest of your lives. I just want to smooth a very tough road for you as much as I can."

"And I am forever grateful."

"No, Freddie, I am forever grateful for the love and the caring that you give to my sister."

Freddie was a bit groggy when he entered the radio station the next morning. Everyone was waiting to ask about Beth. He told them that she was resting comfortably and that she would return soon.

Roger asked, "Can she have visitors?"

Freddie hated to say no, but he knew he had to, "I'm afraid they want her to have a little privacy for a while."

Sherry asked, "Can we Skype with her?"

Freddie had to pause for a second. He had to remember his tech and language lessons, and then he said, "Yeah, I'm sure that will be fine."

"Good," Roger said, "let us know when it can be done. I don't want her getting too far behind."

Tony was in Art's office. Art wasn't very happy, "I just got a call from corporate. They impressed upon me that no one in your production should have their work interrupted by unnecessary interrogations. I assured them that the work would not be interrupted. Now I know that your idea is rather unique, and it did garner some interest beyond our little station, but can you tell me why they would have to make such an unusual request?"

Tony knew exactly who they were referring to, and he knew he had to have another conversation with his father. He responded to his boss, "I don't know what they are referring to, but I promise there will be no interruptions or interrogations."

"Make sure that is the case. We are counting on this show, and corporate's good graces, to keep us employed."

Tony went to his office immediately, and he called his father. His father picked up, and he didn't begin with pleasantries, "Dad, after the stabbing last night, I'm sure your detective juices are flowing. I am begging you not to accost Frank McAlester. My job is on the line here. Art just told me that in so many words because corporate told him that."

"I guess Ms. Money Bags got to them."

"Maybe so, but please do not bother Frank or Beth. I hate to make threats. You know I love you and Mom, but if I lose this job because of you, I will move away, and you will never hear from me again."

"I understand, son, and you're right. I promise I won't go anywhere near either one of them. I do it for you, not because I'm afraid of Ms. Sarah Hicks Rutherford. I have had a threat from a far more terrifying woman, your mother. Frank and Beth will not be bothered by me or anyone representing me."

"Great Dad, I appreciate it."

When Tony got off the phone, he went to the conference room. He pulled Freddie out of the discussion and into the hall. There he told him, "Don't worry about my father. He will not be coming around asking questions, and he won't be following you around. He is an old detective, and habits die hard, but he gave me a promise, and I believe him."

"I appreciate that, Tony. I know he and his friends are curious about who we look like and our relationship with the Hicks family, but I just want to get on with this project."

"And that's what you will do."

Barry had the contact information he needed, and it was time for him to change sides. He called Eric MacArthur. He got Eric's wife on the line. He decided to start with her, "Good day, my name is Barry Batali, and I am a retired police detective from Romulus, Michigan. Your husband has submitted a request for some of the police files on behalf of SHR Laboratories."

"That's correct. Do you have some information for us?"

"That's not exactly why I called Mrs. MacArthur. I want to offer your husband my services. I can expedite his request in the department and help smooth over the process for any other requests your husband may have with the department. I'm also an experienced investigator and would be happy to do the leg work on any reports that pique his interest."

"Well, Mr. Batali, that is a mighty generous offer. Let me give you Eric's father's number. He is coordinating this effort."

Barry ended that conversation. He got Steve on the line and repeated his offer. Steve was a little more skeptical, "May I ask what you plan to get out of this?"

"Well, I was hoping for a salary for as long as I can be useful."

"Is that all you intend to get; a little money?"

"The truth is I was going crazy at home. I need something to investigate. I'm always wandering into the squad room at the department. I think I am becoming an annoyance."

"The work that we do is somewhat sensitive. You will have to be vetted before we accept your offer."

"Of course, I can tell you that my career is well documented, including my early years. I was a second-year patrol officer in September of 1973. Reading those old files will spark a lot of memories."

"Did you have any involvement in the MacArthur/Hicks case?"

"Yes, I did. I saw all the relevant information on the case."

"I suppose finding out a MacArthur was interested in that date got your attention."

"Yes, it did. I knew Emily Hicks when she was a kid. I dated her sister Sarah for a while."

Steve had to say, "Well, there's one that got away."

"Yeah, tell me about it. You don't know how many times the boys in the squad room reminded me of that. I will answer your question before you ask it; yes, I called because I believe you are investigating a new angle on the disappearance, and I would love to help."

"This is a scientific angle, Mr. Batali. I'm not looking for my brother. I'm trying to understand what happened to him."

"Then you think something unusual happened that night?"

"You are a good investigator Mr. Batali. You have gotten plenty of information out of me. Give us a day to check things out. We wouldn't want any discovery taken to the press before we're ready."

"I will sign a nondisclosure agreement. I don't plan to benefit from this other than to know what happened and whatever compensation SHR is willing to provide. I can be very useful, I promise you."

"Okay, Mr. Batali, I've got your number now, and I'll be in touch."

Steve got right on the line to Freddie. Freddie was working on his jam with Pete, and he didn't hear the phone. He turned to Cathy and said, "This detective would be a big help in tracking down leads, but I think he's already been working a case, and the case he is working on is discovering to who Frank and Beth really are. I wanted to talk to Freddie, but he's not picking up."

Cathy suggested, "Call Sarah. I'm sure she would know what he's up to."

"You want me to call Sarah Hicks Rutherford just to ask her a question?"

"That is why she gave you her number. She said it herself; we're all in this together. Call her; I'm sure she would want to be in the loop."

Steve selected her number, and it rang a few times. Then Sarah answered, "Steve, do you have something interesting to tell me?"

"Well, Ms. Rutherford . . ."

"Sarah, Steve; call me Sarah."

"Okay, Sarah, we do have some interesting leads. It turns out a dog disappeared during the event, also. We're going to try to track it down."

"That's great! Is that why you called?"

"No, I need your opinion on something, actually someone."

"Who is it?"

"It's a Romulus retired detective named Barry Batali."

Sarah laughed and said, "That guy never quits. I knew Barry in high school. He was a bad guy then, but he turned out to be a good guy and a really good cop. I guess maybe he is too good. He has a strong suspicion that Freddie and Emily are really Freddie and Emily. I'm sure he hasn't figured out how that's possible, but we can't shake him from trying to figure it out. Why are you asking about him?"

"He called. He wants to help us track down clues in the Detroit area."

"Oh, I bet he does. He is just drooling at the chance to expose Freddie and Emily."

"The thing is that he offered to sign a nondisclosure agreement."

"Really, now that is interesting. Let me do some checking, and I'll get back to you. And that is great news about the dog; I hope it leads to more revelations."

Sarah hung up and waved to Tommy, who was across the room. He quickly made his way to her, and she told him, "I want to have a little sit down with my old friend Barry Batali. I want to find out what he's up to."

Tommy volunteered, "We can get that information for you, ma'am; you don't have to deal with him."

"I think I want to. I want to look him in the eyes and get a real measure of him. I'm sure his police friends will be discreetly in attendance, but that doesn't bother me."

"We will also be discreetly in attendance, ma'am."

"I'm sure you will, Tommy."

Dr. Drexel stood patiently waiting for Sarah's conversation to end. Sarah turned to him and asked, "Is there something I can do for you, doctor?"

"Ms. Rutherford, I will need to take new x-rays of Emily. The ones we received from the hospital are just a bit blurry. They are good enough to support the diagnosis, but I would rather have the sharpest picture I can get, just to be sure."

"What would make an x-ray blurry?"

"I don't know. It must be a malfunction in the equipment. I wanted to let you know so that you wouldn't be alarmed when Emily was wheeled in for more tests."

"Thank you, doctor, and I appreciate your thoroughness."

Chapter 12: Radiant Energy

Shelly Hicks was at Emily's side before lunch, "My little girl; my poor little girl."

Emily tried to console her mother, "I'm fine, Mom. I'll be up and about in a couple of days."

"Betty Rother did this to you?"

"Yes, Mom."

"I always knew that girl was trouble. From the first day your sister brought her in our house I knew she was trouble."

Shelly called to her other daughter, "Sarah, I told you she was no good. She got Emily mixed up in that stuff in Detroit, and we lost her for so long, and now she tries to kill her."

Sarah came in with Tommy next to her. Shelly turned and walked past Sarah. She went straight to Tommy and asked, "You will find her for me?"

"I'll do my best, Mrs. Hicks."

"I know you will."

She turned back to Emily and said, "Tommy will find her, and Tommy will fix her."

Emily spoke up, "Mom, Tommy will turn her over to the police."

"Then they will fix her, and she will be gone. She is such an evil woman. She was always evil. She took Sarah's boyfriend, and Sarah still let her come around."

Sarah responded, "She did me a favor, Mom. I was over Barry, and she was more his type. Mom, the chef, is cooking up great clam chowder. Why don't you see how he's doing?"

Sarah helped her mother up. As they walked away, Shelly complained, "He better not use too much pepper. People always use too much pepper."

Ellen came over and sat next to Emily, and she asked, "How are you feeling now?"

"Much better; I feel like I can get out of this bed and start moving around."

"That's the medication talking. They gave you some good stuff. You'll have to give it a day or two before you start moving around. You lost a lot of blood, and you don't want to get that thing bleeding again."

"I really thought I was going to die; it was so scary."

"I bet it was."

"I didn't want to talk about it with Freddie or Sarah or my mom. I didn't want to freak them out."

"You can tell me anything, Emily."

"I'm happy you're here, Ellen. You are more than a teacher. You're a good friend."

"Thank you; I feel the same about you and Freddie. You were lying on the floor for hours. How did you hold on so long?"

"I just kept thinking of the life I had missed, and I was determined that I wasn't going to lose this one. I also thought of Freddie. I knew he would blame himself."

"Freddie is such a thoughtful guy. You wouldn't expect that from a rock and roll icon."

"He was different from his friends. Those guys were like his brothers; they grew up together, but they could be Class A jerks, especially Don."

"All the documentaries said Don was a ladies' man."

"He was no more a ladies' man than a pimp is. He attracted young girls with his fame and fortune then he used them and threw them away. He had no class. He had no style. He didn't attract women; he bought them. He was a pig."

"Wow, I guess I hit a sore spot."

"I'm sorry; I guess you did."

"That's fine Emily. I'm here if you need to vent."

"Yes, I do get angry thinking about Don. People think Rick's drug taking was the band's biggest problem. Don's abuse of women was right up there with Rick's drug abuse. It was Don's verbal and physical abuse of Betty that caused her to put the dope in Rick's whiskey. I know that isn't an excuse for what Betty did, but it was motivation."

"Then I guess Don Foster met a fitting end."

"I know it's wrong to say this, and I would never say it around Freddie, but I'm happy he's dead."

It was midafternoon when Sarah had Shelly taken home. Sarah had a place for her mother to stay, but Shelly Hicks didn't like being away from home. Sarah knew breaking the routine of a woman her mother's age could be dangerous.

Sarah's next stop was a meeting with Barry Batali. She left the limo at the retreat and Tommy drove her in a Cadillac Escalade.

They were meeting at a Ruby Tuesday's close to the interstate. Sarah came in and went to the table. Barry stood and she approached. Sarah sat and then Barry sat. Sarah said, "It's good to see you, Barry. You did well for yourself since those days back in high school."

Barry made sure that she knew that he was not in awe of her, "You didn't do so bad yourself."

"I guess you miss figuring out mysteries."

"It didn't take you long to get to the point, Sarah. I guess I'm not surprised; you were always the direct type. I suppose that you're going to tell me that it's my need to solve a mystery that is making me see things that aren't there. I'm not that irrational. I have gathered the evidence, and I have come to a conclusion."

"What conclusion is that?"

"You know very well what it is, and frankly, I think it is joyous. As I'm sure, you do. Having your little sister back after forty-four years is, well, it is unbelievable."

"Unbelievable is the right word, Barry. That is a story that no one will believe."

"Sarah, I don't want to go to the press with this, and I'm not looking to blackmail anyone. I just want to know in my heart that I was right, and I want to help you figure out how it happened."

"You said you would sign a nondisclosure agreement if you worked with Steve MacArthur."

"Yes, and I meant it. I would like reasonable compensation for my work, but that is all. I just want the standard rate that you would expect to pay. I just want to be part of proving the unbelievable. I just have one provision."

"What's that?"

"I would like my wife to sign an agreement also. She isn't looking for work, but I have never kept anything from her, and I'm not going to start now."

"I guarantee you, Barry, this agreement will be ironclad. There will be no loopholes to sneak through."

"I don't want any; I swear."

"I have had you checked out quite closely, Barry. You were a good cop, and you are a good husband. Your word has been good to a lot of people for a lot of years. I'll have the agreement drawn up for you and your wife."

"Thank you, Sarah. Just being a part of this makes me feel alive again. There is one other thing I want to tell you. I am terribly sorry for what happened to Emily."

"Thank you. My mother just scolded me like she did when I was sixteen. She told me that Betty would be trouble, and she was."

"Sarah, this is not a sympathy statement. This is an apology. I wanted you to hear it from me. I am the reason Betty knew where to find Emily. I paid Betty to follow her and Freddie and to get information for me. I never thought she would do something like this."

"Thank you for telling me. I believe Betty is more unstable than any of us thought."

"I want to thank you, Sarah. I must have been a thorn in your side, and you could have crushed me in a thousand different ways, but you just tried to keep me at arm's length. You are an honorable woman."

"You should get the agreement by tomorrow morning. If you and your wife sign it and hand it back to the messenger, you could talk to Steve by noon. Is a salary of four thousand a week plus expenses reasonable to you?

"Yes, that is very fair."

"Good; once you get started, you will be contacted by the SHR Laboratories human resource people to get your details and get you in the system."

"That's great, Sarah. You know I was ribbed my entire life for letting you get away. I never saw it like that. Even when we were dating, I knew you were out of my league. You were far too smart and too responsible for the teenage Barry Batali. I never resented your success. I celebrated it."

When Sarah returned to the retreat, she found Dr. Drexel waiting for her. She suddenly got a sinking feeling in her stomach. She called out, "Doctor, what's wrong? Did you find something?"

The doctor eased her fear, "No, Ms. Rutherford, there is nothing wrong with Emily, but I have a bit of a mystery. The x-rays I took also came out slightly blurry. I know my equipment is working perfectly. I don't see what could have caused it."

"That is a mystery. Do you think there is something in Emily that is causing it?"

"I don't know."

"Well, let's get another sample from someone else."

Sarah turned to Tommy, "You can use a checkup. Why don't you get a chest x-ray for your health?"

Tommy said, "Yes, ma'am."

Sarah turned back to the doctor and asked, "Please let me know the results as soon as you can."

Freddie returned to his new home by dinner time. A table was set up near Emily's bed so Freddie and Sarah could have dinner with her. Roast duck and fresh vegetables were brought in, and a fine wine was served. Freddie had to comment, "This is some meal. I feel like I should have a fancy suit on."

Emily said, "You were a rock star. I'm sure you had the best of everything."

"We were into extravagance, not elegance. The fanciest meal we had was a big steak and a boat load of French fries."

Sarah said, "Be happy you're off that diet. We have found out a lot about overdoing red meat. People that do that are putting a ticking time bomb in their bodies."

Freddie had to laugh, "Considering what else we were putting in our bodies, red meat was no big deal."

Emily made an observation, "I don't remember you going crazy on that stuff. I don't think you even smoked any weed."

"Oh, I did some weed, and I did some drinking, but I didn't go crazy. I don't know; I never liked the feeling. While others were being all happy and silly, I just felt uncomfortable and disoriented. I would end up being sick. It seemed that I got all of the bad effects of that stuff and none of the good effects."

Sarah commented, "It couldn't have been that much. You haven't done that sort of thing for two weeks now, and you haven't shown any signs of withdrawal."

"I don't miss it at all. I had fun drinking a few beers with the guys last night, but my stomach told me about it this morning. Those outings will be few and far between."

Sarah changed the subject, "We have a new member of our team. Barry Batali is going to help Steve in his search."

Emily was amazed, "Batali? He has caused us grief since the day we got here. How can you trust him?"

"I knew Barry was one of the best detectives that Romulus ever had. He is a bulldog. I just didn't know that he had the vision to imagine the impossible. He knows the truth, and the best way to control what he knows is to have him as part of the team."

Freddie commented, "Keep your friends close and your enemies closer."

Sarah grinned, "Barry isn't an enemy. He never was. He is a good man, just a very curious good man. He is signing a nondisclosure agreement. He doesn't want fame or fortune; he just wants to be part of the discovery."

Emily concluded, "Good, maybe the police will be on our side for a change."

"He will help with that, and he will get a hold of police records a lot easier than Steve can. If there is more to discover about what brought you here, Barry will be a big help in finding it. Speaking of that, in all of the excitement of the last twenty-four hours, I haven't thought of telling you what Steve has already discovered. He told me that a dog disappeared about the same time you did in 1973. The dog was about a mile northeast of the interstate off South Telegraph Rd. in Allen Park."

Freddie asked, "Has the dog reappeared?"

"I don't know."

Freddie didn't know why this news excited him so much, but it did, "Does Steve have an address; I want to see if the dog is there."

"I thought I would let him handle it. This may be a good job for Barry."

"Why wait? If Steve knows where the dog should be, we should get there before something happens to it. Maybe it appeared and wandered off. The longer we wait, the lower our chances to find it."

"Barry will be onboard tomorrow. I will see that he has the information as soon as he signs the agreement. If the dog wandered off, it has had almost two weeks to roam; it could be anywhere. In that case, it would have to be a search for all stray dogs that have been picked up. If it didn't wander off, it will be there tomorrow."

Freddie conceded, "Okay, but I want to know if he finds the dog."

Then Freddie started a new subject. He turned to Emily, "Everyone sends their best. Tony talked to me today about his father."

Freddie had to add for Sarah's benefit, "Tony is Barry Batali's son. He said that his father had promised not to hassle us anymore. I guess now I know why. Also, Roger wants to set up a Skype connection so he can go over a few things with you."

Sarah was surprised, "A Skype connection? You understand about Skype?"

"Yes," Emily said, "Ellen is a wonderful teacher, and she has become a good friend."

"Wonderful. Sorry, Freddie, please continue."

"Roger doesn't want you falling too far behind. I think he wants to add another singing part for you."

"Another part, I don't know. A couple of lines are good. I could easily screw up any more than that."

Sarah had to announce, "Emily Hicks, on Broadway!"

"Oh, don't go overboard or anything, big sister."

Freddie added, "He's serious. He thinks you'll do fine. It is a rock and roll musical, and he thinks we need more music."

"But what will I sing?"

"We're working on that. I have a ballad that would work, but I have to figure a way of getting them to see it without adding to any mysteries."

Emily asked, "You mean from the music you've written?"

"Yes, I would need to have it translated onto generic music sheets. I'm afraid if I show my original stuff, someone will recognize my writing."

Sarah volunteered, "I'll have that done. I can have all of your writing converted to files. That will preserve them."

"That's great, Sarah. Thanks."

Emily was still nervous about the idea of singing a whole song, "Freddie, seriously, I don't think I can do that in front of an audience. I've never done anything like that."

"You'll be great. You proved you can do it. It's just a matter of practice. Music is a talent like many other talents. People use the word 'talent' more for describing entertainers, but it really is just having the knack for something. Sarah, you have been described as being very talented with computers. That's how you got the title the Queen of Tech. Others are talented in crafts, and others, like my brother, in science. The talent is your starting point. From there, you learn and develop your talent. Emily, you proved you have the talent. All you have to do is develop it. We can do that."

"Well, I'm going to need a lot of help."

"You have it. Also, your voice doesn't have to match the music. The music can be adjusted or arranged to match your voice. I noticed that your voice struggled a bit. When singing just two lines, it doesn't make much difference, but with an entire song, I think we need to change the key to fit you better. I can make that adjustment."

Sarah had to comment, "People don't realize that musicians are signal processors. The technology of music can be as complex as signal processing in any discipline. There is some engineering going on here. Emily, you are getting advice from an expert."

Once again, Dr. Drexel waited until Sarah was free, and then he stepped up, "Ms. Rutherford, I have Mr. Eversol's x-rays, and they are perfectly clear."

Emily asked, "Doctor, why did you need Tommy's x-rays?"

Sarah said, "There's nothing wrong, Emily; we just have a little mystery on our hands."

Emily's face changed just a bit, "Was there something wrong with my x-rays?"

The doctor answered, "There is nothing physically wrong with you, Ms. Hicks; there is just something interfering with the x-rays."

Freddie called out, "Check me."

Sarah turned and looked and Freddie and guessed, "You think it might be some residual effect from passing through the anomaly."

"I would like to find out."

The doctor rejoined the conversation, "If it is common to both of you and to no one else, then we will be entering unknown territory. If that is the case, Ms. Rutherford, I'm going to need a lot of help."

"Oh, you will get it, doctor. I promise you that you will get it."

Freddie got up and said, "I will use some recently learned slang. Okay, doctor, let's do this."

By the end of the day, the doctor had Freddie's x-rays and x-rays from two others as further samples. He explained to everyone, "As you can see, the effect only appears on Ms. Hicks' x-ray and Mr. MacArthur's x-ray. Mr. MacArthur's x-rays were significantly more affected than Ms. Hicks'. It is something within them. It is some kind of radiant energy. It is not gamma radiation, or we would have seen damage by now. It is some kind of benign radiation."

Freddie concluded, "It must have come from the thing we went through. We have to figure out what it is and how to detect it."

Sarah said, "I need to make some calls. This is in your brother's field."

Freddie volunteered, "I'll call him right now."

Steve answered his phone immediately, "Freddie, I was just about to call you. We're going to be there on Saturday. Did you hear about the dog?"

"Yes, and that is big news."

"I want to talk to the people who lost the dog and the people that live in the house where the event took place."

"That is important, Steve, but we have something here that can also be really big. We don't know what it means, and we need your expertise to help us figure it out. Steve, Emily, and I are radiating some kind of energy. It's not harmful, so it's not like nuclear radiation, but it's something. It must have come from the anomaly. We need you to try to analyze it."

"That's incredible! Oh, you're going to need a hell of a lot more than me to analyze that. We're going to need people and equipment from SHR. I will need to be part of a team. We'll be there on Saturday."

"Steve, we need you before Saturday."

Sarah got Freddie's attention and asked for the phone, "Steve, it's Sarah. We need you here right now. How soon can you and Cathy be ready to go?"

"Do you mean today?"

"Yes, how long will it take you to be ready to go from right now?"

Sarah could hear him asking Cathy. He returned to the phone, "We could be ready to leave in about an hour and a half."

"Okay, there will be a car at your door in an hour and a half. I'm sorry that you are probably not going to get a good night's sleep tonight, but we need you."

"Don't worry about that. We will be ready in an hour and a half."

"The car will take you to a chartered flight, and it will be ready to go as soon as you get there."

"Okay then. I guess we will see you soon."

Steve hung up, looked at Cathy, and said, "This is absolutely amazing. They have found that Freddie and Emily are radiating energy that can only have come from the anomaly. Sarah wants us there as soon as we can, and she is flexing her billion-dollar muscle to make it happen. We will be driven to a private chartered plane and flown directly to Detroit and driven to see the group. You can bet it won't be a Ford that shows up at our door in an hour and a half. This should give the neighbors a little more to talk about."

Steve and Cathy were at the retreat very early the next morning. They were shown to their suite, and they got some much-needed rest.

The Skype connection was set up. Sarah had Emily's Skype on a giant eighty-inch screen. Emily felt like she was in a movie theater. She thought it was like actually being on TV, and that made her panic about what to wear. She had plenty of choices, and Sarah brought in a beautician to help her with her hair and makeup. Emily complained, "You know I have been doing my own makeup since I was thirteen."

"I don't want you stretching and twisting. That wound is just beginning to heal. Besides, my people tell me Maria is not just a beautician; she is a makeup artist that specializes in preparing people for being seen on camera."

"Okay, but when I get out of this bed, I don't want people tending to me like I'm some kind of fairy princess."

"When you get out of that bed, your ass is going back to work."

The screen came on and a few seconds later, she saw everyone from KWTZ. They all waved and cheered. It was clear they had a good picture on their end. They all wished Emily well, though, of course they called her Beth. Even Art wished her well.

Roger took over and started with a question, "Beth, considering what has happened to you, I thought maybe we should consider a rewrite to take Betty Ann Rother out of the story."

"Roger, please don't do that on my account. She was a part of that incredible day despite her recent actions. I know this is a musical depiction and not a documentary, but I think people would notice if she wasn't part of the story."

"Okay, Beth, I just wanted to get your feelings on the matter."

Beth could see Sherry in the background mouth, "Thank you."

Jimmy needed to say something for the band, "Beth, we're sorry we kept Frank out so long. We are really bummed when we think of you lying on the floor while we were convincing Frank to stay for one more beer."

"No, don't think that way, any of you. I told Frank that I had found out that she was stalking me. I had something she wanted, and she would have gotten to me eventually. The only one at fault is Betty Ann Rother. I'm happy Frank had a good time, and I'm going to join you next time."

All of the band members smiled, and Freddie, as Frank, said, "Have you seen Steve?"

"Yes, he and Cathy are still sleeping. They should be up shortly."

"I wish I was there for that."

"He will need to talk to you as soon as you get home, I'm sure."

Freddie changed the subject, "We're heading into the studio. I was telling Roger about some of the songs that I've written and that I would show him a ballad that might work for you."

Emily started getting embarrassed. She asked Roger, "Do you really think I can do a whole song?"

Roger responded in his business tone, "As I said before; your voice is adequate, and that's just what I want. Emily shouldn't come off as a Broadway star; she has to be real, but it is a musical, and your voice is good for the part. Frank said that he has something that will fit. I'll check it out, and then we can get started.

Okay, guys, you can't just wander off today. I'm sure the concert parts are coming right along. I need people around for the off-stage interaction. Let's start with everyone looking at the Rolling Stone magazine before the Chicago concert."

When Emily had read that part of the script, she was amazed at Roger's memory. Betty and Freddie had talked about that happening, and Roger's description was pretty darn close to what she was told.

The Skype communication worked well though Emily felt a bit on the sidelines, mainly because she couldn't see what was happening outside of the camera view. Also, she just couldn't look at one person and get their attention. It was everyone or no one.

Sarah was smiling from outside of the room. Even through this communication, it was clear that Emily fit right in with the group. Emily's return resolved an issue that had been in the back of her mind ever since Sam passed away. She had no children and no nieces or nephews. There were plenty of cousins and second cousins, but she was not very close to any of them. Her mother was already set to be taken care of for the rest of her life, but her legacy could not be passed backward. Her last will and testament languished unfinished until now. Now she could call her lawyers and have the job done. Not only did she have the one person she would want to inherit what she built, but her sister was also young and could continue the legacy if she decided to have children. She felt a sense of peace that the issue had been resolved better than she had ever hoped.

Her thoughts of the future were interrupted by Tommy, "Ma'am, we've tracked Betty Ann Rother. She is driving south on Interstate 75. She is a few miles south of the route 50 exit."

Sarah pondered, "I wonder what took her so long to get just a few miles away."

"She probably thought she did more damage to Emily than she did. She thought she wasn't identified, so she took her time."

"That was a big mistake; do you have a capture plan?"

"Yes, Ma'am. Our vehicles are in place. We have two behind her and one waiting just before the Monroe exit. The one ahead will be signaled when to pull onto the road. One vehicle will be in each lane. They will catch up to the Ford Fusion and block her from the back and the side. My people are good. They will time it to box her in and force her to the side of the road. They will report when they have her."

"Very good; first, I want those tapes. Then keep her there. I want to give a present of her to a certain detective. Get Barry Batali on the phone. I have a job for him. Tell your people to hold her there for up to two hours. If the police don't show up, take her to the closest police station."

A minute later, Tommy handed a phone to Sarah, "Here he is, Ma'am."

Sarah didn't wait for a hello, "Did you and your wife sign the agreements? Good, I'll take your word for it. I want you to contact Detective Cindi Baveroski and tell her that we will be holding Betty for her at the Monroe exit off 75. I want her to have credit for the capture."

"Why? Cindi is very suspicious of all of the moves you've made in the last two weeks. She is beginning to believe the truth."

"That's exactly why. She's like you. She is a damn good detective, and she doesn't cave when pressured. I admire her, and the department would benefit if she advanced to a higher rank. She doesn't seem to be the type that would be happy to just have it handed to her. This way, the advancement will be done by accomplishment."

"I don't know if she'll see this as an accomplishment."

"Convince her, Barry. We will have Betty on the side of the road just north of the Monroe exit. We'll wait two hours and then I have instructed my people to take her to the closest police station. It's simple; if she is there, she gets the credit."

"Barry, what the hell are you talking about?"

"Cindi, just get in your car and get to the Monroe exit on 75. She is going to be held for you there. You have two hours to get there."

"Barry, have you become a messenger boy for Ms. Rutherford?"

"I've been hired as an investigator, but I was asked to deliver this message."

"What made you go to the dark side?"

"Ms. Rutherford isn't evil, and, for some reason, she has a lot of respect for you. Do you want the collar or not?"

"Okay, but if she gets away before I get there, I will be in a world of hurt for not coordinating with the state police."

"She's not going to get away, trust me."

Out on Interstate 75, the three black SUVs took their positions. They were in constant contact, and they handled the operation with military precision. The trailing SUVs drove side by side on the two-lane interstate. There was a risk that traffic would come up behind them, but the road was clear. The word was passed to the forward SUV, and it pulled onto the road. It made sure that Betty didn't catch him. The two in the rear caught up to Betty. Betty was in the left lane, and the SUV in the right lane came alongside her.

"What the hell," Betty said out loud. She tried to speed up, but the vehicles kept pace with her. Then she saw the SUV in front of her. She had no choice but to come up behind it. Once she was boxed in, the SUVs slowly decelerated and eased Betty off the road. They held the position until Tim got out of the rear SUV and approached Betty's car from the driver's side. He had a berretta in his hand, and he told her to turn off the engine and step out of the car.

She got out, she was searched, and her hands were secured with a tie wrap. Larry went to the passenger side, opened the door, and searched for Emily's bag. After a minute, he called, "I got it," and pulled the bag out from under the seat."

Betty said, "Is that what you want? Do you want the tapes? Fine, you got them. You're not the cops; what do you need me for?"

Larry said, "What I want is to leave you bleeding here like you left that young girl in the hotel room, but I have to follow orders. Now just shut up and relax you may be here for a while."

Tim handed the bag to the passenger in the forward SUV then two of the SUVs drove off, leaving Tim and Larry with Betty. Betty didn't see any reason to be civil, "So you are a couple of Sarah's puppy dogs. I suppose you get on all fours and kiss her ass anytime she shows up."

Tim said, "Boy, for an old hag, you really are a nasty bitch aren't you?"

"At least I'm not kissing anybody's ass."

"Oh, from what I heard, you made a career out of kissing a lot more than ass."

Cindi and Eric arrived in less than an hour. They got out of their car and Tim and Larry held up their hands to show they weren't hostile. Tim said, "Here is your prisoner."

Eric got a hold of Betty as Cindi looked around. After searching the car she returned to Tim and asked, "Where is it?"

"Where is what, Detective?"

"Don't play dumb, where are the tapes?"

"We didn't see any tapes, Detective."

Betty yelled, "They're full of crap. They took them and passed the bag to their buddy."

Tim stayed cool, "I didn't see any bag."

Cindi wasn't happy, "Okay, ID from both of you. Wait a minute."

Cindi pointed at Larry, "I know you. You were driving Ms. Rutherford in that old Plymouth. Tell her that her little gifts are unnecessary and she is not above the law. Those tapes are evidence of a crime, and I want them."

Tim said, "Detective, we were just trying to help. You have your prisoner, so we will be on our way."

Cindi pulled out her weapon and called out, "Hold it right there. Get on your knees."

Tim warned, "Detective, this is a mistake."

Betty laughed and said, "There you go, lap dog. That's your reward for taking the bag."

Cindi called to Eric, "Get that old flee bag in the car."

Tim said, "Well, at least we agree on something. Detective, I believe you're going to need some backup. We're not all going to fit in that car of yours, and the whole thing will be such a waste of time. Our lawyer will be talking to your boss before you get us back there."

Eric secured Betty, and then he stepped back to Cindi and whispered in her ear, "He's right. We'll go through all the trouble of hauling them in, and we will end up getting chewed out for our trouble. Let's take the win and go home."

Cindi lowered her weapon and told Tim and Larry, "Just get out of here, and you tell Beth Richards, if that is her name, that we will want her down at the station to make the ID and complete the complaint."

Tommy got the report from Tim, and he reported to Sarah, "Ma'am, the job is done. I have to tell you, ma'am, that your kindliness toward this Detective Baveroski is wasted on her. The more you do, the more she seems to hate you."

"Maybe you're right, Tommy, but she just reminded me so much of myself thirty years ago."

"She is going to make a stink out of the missing tapes."

"I'm sure she will, but all she has is a criminal's word for what happened to the tapes. I guess I didn't count on Betty being so stupid. I thought she would have been smart enough to claim that she never had any tapes, but there is no telling what a drug-addled mind would do."

"Do you think not having the tapes as evidence will leave the police without a case?"

"If Betty was any kind of criminal, it might be possible, but she's a junkie. I'm sure she left plenty of evidence in the hotel room; she also admitted to the police that she had the tapes, and Emily will testify. She won't get away with it."

Steve and Cathy were up and ready to go after just a few hours of sleep. Sarah had them sit down with the doctor to get all of his information firsthand.

When their discussion was over, they met with Sarah and Emily, and Steve began, "I've said this over and over again; this is amazing. It is there, I'm sure of it. We need a lot of equipment, and we need people that I can work with. I need colleagues that have been working on the cutting edge."

"They are the only people that we hire for the work at SHR Laboratories. Make a list of everything you need and the people with the skillset needed to best help you."

Emily and Sarah could see Steve's mind racing as he took his tablet out of his briefcase. He was talking more to himself than anyone, "We'll need a top relativity person and someone working in quantum mechanics. I sense aspects of both disciplines here. Wait; can this support the work to discover the unified theory?"

Cathy said quietly, "He's in full scientist mode. He may not make sense for the next few minutes."

Everyone smiled, but they were also impressed as Steve raced through possibilities. After another minute, Steve looked up, and his face turned beet red. He said, "I'm sorry, I guess I got a bit cranked up."

Sarah said, "It was a wonder to behold. I said you were the right man for this job. I don't want to do anything second-rate. We just had a Skype connection set up for Emily. Please use it to communicate with Dr. Stevens. I will make arrangements for the transport of them and any equipment that we need. Don't be shy about your demands. If there is the slightest possibility that a piece of equipment will be useful, put it on the list."

Steve's mind was still racing. Finally, he said, "I am definitely going to be quite busy here. Is Barry Batali onboard?"

"Yes, he has already done something for me."

"Good, because he is going to have to track down the dog lead. That is unless you have someone else in mind."

"This is just the thing he is being paid for. I know your mind is racing, but I want to maintain the chain of command on this. He is working for you. I think you should call him."

Steve got right on the phone. Barry answered, and Steve said, "Welcome to our little group Barry."

"Thank you, I am ready to get started with some real work. I suppose you want me to start looking through the police files for the target date."

"Yes, we will want you to do that, but we need you to track down the dog lead first. We need to find the dog. When you have the dog, we need you to take it and get an x-ray."

"What part of the dog do you want to be x-rayed?"

"It doesn't matter. We just need an x-ray of the dog."

"Okay, I'll talk to the people and see if I can find it."

"Thanks, Barry. I hope this will all be made clear. We have research to do."

"This sounds quite mysterious, and you know how I love mysteries."

"This is a big one, Barry. It may be historic. I promise you won't be left out. You will know what's going on."

"Great, I'll get on it."

"After that, you can start checking the records for things on September 16th in 1973 and 2017.

"Of course, you want to see if other things disappeared and reappeared."

"That's correct. My wife and I are in the area. I am working on another development related to the x-ray thing."

Barry got off the phone to find his wife smiling at him. He asked her, "What are you grinning about?"

"You are so alive. It's like someone pumped you up on uppers or something."

"There is no high like the high of knowing that you can be useful."

"You got that right."

Chapter 13: There is Someone Else

Barry drove to Allen Park. As he drove, he knew his return trip would be in the teeth of the Friday afternoon rush hour, and he was not looking forward to that. He made his way to a small house and the end of a small street just east of Interstate 94's South Telegraph Road exit. Barry knocked on the door, and he heard a dog start barking in the backyard. Barry thought, "Yes, this is working out."

A woman answered the door, and Barry started, "Ms. Amber Dermot?"

"Yes?"

"My name is Barry Batali, and I am here regarding your dog."

"It's not ours. We haven't had any luck finding its owner."

Barry wanted everything documented, and he didn't want to put any words in the lady's mouth, "Ms. Dermot, I represent SHR Laboratories, and that dog is of great interest to us if it is indeed the dog we are looking for."

"Did it escape from one of your labs? I've seen what they do to animals. I won't have him sent back to be tortured."

"Ms. Dermot, may I record this conversation."

"Well, okay, but you're still not getting the dog."

"SHR Laboratories doesn't experiment on animals. We believe this dog has encountered an unusual energy field entirely on its own, and we want to determine if it harmed him at all. The energy field is a bit of a mystery."

"That's not the only mystery. The question of how it got in our yard is also a mystery. We have a six-foot fence all the way around, and the gates were secured with locks. The only way for that dog to get in our yard would be if someone picked it up and threw it over the fence. The dog is a German Shepard. It must weigh at least a hundred pounds."

"When did you notice the dog was in the yard?"

"I have trouble sleeping sometimes. When I do, I end up downstairs watching TV or searching on the internet. I was sitting in my chair around two thirty in the morning, and there was a flash of light. I thought it was lightning. When I looked out in the backyard, the dog was there barking like crazy. I was afraid to get near it at first, but it really is a friendly dog. It has a tag on it. It also has a sticker on the tag that is protected by tape. The sticker has the name Skipper on it; it looks like it was written by a child."

"Have you been able to approach the dog?"

"Once we started calling him Skipper, he calmed right down."

"Can you help me get close enough to him to take a few pictures?"

"That should be easy enough."

Barry followed the woman into the backyard. The dog came right up to her, and she began to pet it. Barry began taking pictures. He thought of asking to have the dog taken to the vet for the x-ray, but he wanted to see if he could get more of the story. He asked, "May I stay for a while longer? I believe I can find the dog's owner, and I want to be here when they arrive. I will stay out here with the dog if you prefer."

"I would appreciate it if you did that, at least until my husband arrives."

Amber Dermot went into the house. Barry examined the dog and found two unique identifying marks on his body. He took pictures of them, the collar, the license, and several of the handwriting on the sticker. He figured the woman that made the original call to the police would be in her early seventies. He was hoping she still had a good memory. He punched in the number, and he was surprised to hear a man's voice come through the phone. He gave the man his standard introduction and then asked, "May I speak to Rebeca Michaels?"

"I'm her son; what do you want to speak to my mother about?"

"This is rather unusual and frankly unbelievable, but I'm with your dog Skipper."

"Mister, we aren't nearly that gullible. Skipper disappeared forty-four years ago. No dog lives forty-four years."

"May I send you a few pictures via text or email?"

"If you think it will do you any good, and the man provided the details."

"Okay, you should be receiving them now."

"Hold on while I take a look at them."

The man returned to the phone, and he said, "Very impressive. All of that information was in the newspaper article. I don't know why you went through all of this trouble. We don't have any money for you to swindle us out of."

"I don't want money. As I said, I am with SHR Laboratories. All I want is your account of exactly what happened when Skipper disappeared."

"Dig around in the old newspapers. Maybe you will find it, and don't bother giving me the number of some guy that will tell me that you are for real. That won't work either."

"Okay, how about this? If you and your mother come to the address that I give you, I will give you five hundred dollars."

"You will give me five hundred dollars?"

"Yes, just for showing up and taking a look at the dog. Also, here is the public contact information for the people that live in the house. You will recognize the address. It was where you lived when Skipper disappeared. You may call them and ask them what's going on. You know that the address is to an ordinary house on an ordinary street, and you can easily find out that it belongs to the people I mentioned."

"Hold on again while I look at this stuff."

Barry waited a few more minutes, and the man returned, "Okay, here's the deal. We will be there in about forty minutes. My brother will be in the car. If we don't return in a short time, he'll call the police. He is also an awful big guy, and he may not wait for the police to show up."

"Fair enough, we'll see you in forty minutes."

Barry was taking a chance. He was sure the Dermots would insist that the dog wasn't theirs and that it appeared in their yard on September 16th, but that may not be enough. He was hoping, despite their age, that Skipper would recognize them.

Andy Dermot came home before the mother and son showed up. He was given the story, and unlike his wife, he was willing to hand the dog over to Barry. They waited and forty-two minutes later, Rebeca and Nick Michaels knocked on the door.

Amber opened the door and led them to the backyard. Nick stopped, took a look at the dog, and said, "Okay, we saw it; where's our money?"

Andy asked, "Is that your dog?"

"Of course not; my dog disappeared when I was six years old. How the hell could that be my dog?"

Rebeca Michaels didn't stop. She went right to Skipper. Nick yelled, "Mom, don't!"

She called back, "It's Skipper," and walked right to the animal. Skipper reacted just as Barry hoped. The dog made whining sounds as Rebeca put her arms around it.

Andy Dermot said, "I sure wouldn't go near a dog that size unless I was sure it wouldn't take a bite out of me. That dog can't be forty-four years old, but it sure knows your mother."

Rebeca called, "Look at the tag Nicky; it's your writing."

Nick Michaels was confused, "How could this happen?"

Barry tried to explain, "As I told the Dermots, that's what I'm here for. SHR Laboratories is looking into this mystery. I have documented the Dermot's story of how Skipper appeared in their yard. Now I need to document yours. Do you mind if I record your story?"

"If it gets us out of here with the five hundred bucks, I'll tell you any story you want."

"Then please, just tell me what happened the night when Skipper disappeared."

"Okay, it was late. I remember hearing Skipper barking like crazy. I looked out of my window, and I saw this weird blue light; it looked like a blue curtain. It was moving across the yard. Suddenly Skipper dashed right into it. There was a bright white flash, and he was gone. I told people, but no one ever believed me."

Amber was getting the idea, "You think this dog ran into that light in 1973 and ran out of it two weeks ago."

Barry answered, "That's what we're investigating. It is impossible, and it is unbelievable, but this is Skipper. I need to do one more thing. I need Skipper to get an x-ray. Don't ask me how that is going to help. The scientists just asked me to do it. After that, you can take Skipper home."

Barry got an agreement, and with enough financial incentive, he was able to get an x-ray quickly. The vet complained when he brought it out, "I'm sorry. There must be something wrong with the machine. The x-ray is barely readable. I just did an x-ray an hour ago, and the machine was fine."

Barry excused himself and called Steve, "Steve, I got the x-ray, but the machine screwed it up for some reason. I guess I'll try another vet."

"No, no, Barry; that is great news. Please have that x-ray sent here as soon as you can. Here's the email address."

Barry was confused, but he handed over the five hundred dollars, and he was on his way.

Steve reported to Sarah, and Sarah asked, "Do you think that this x-ray being more damaged is significant?"

Steve was still pondering, "I'm sure it is, but I don't know how yet."

Freddie arrived and went to Emily, kissed her, and asked her how she was doing. She answered, "Just great. The doctor said I could get up and walk around tomorrow."

"Excellent; tomorrow is Saturday, so I will be here to witness the event."

"Speaking of events, it has been pretty exciting around here today. Barry Batali found the dog."

"Really, and he knows for sure that it went through that thing?"

"Yep, amazingly enough, in the middle of the night, one person saw the dog go into the thing, and one person saw the dog just after it came out. To top it off, the dog's x-ray was even more blurry than ours."

"What does that mean?"

"They're still trying to figure that out."

Freddie tried to put into words what he was feeling, "This is good. I don't know why, but it kind of justifies our existence here. We know that something really happened, and it didn't only happen to us."

Emily continued, "I know. Now it is more like we really were victims of an accident rather than we were cast out of our lives for some reason. Between my sister's brains and your brother's brains I think we're going to get an answer. That brings up another question, what happens after that?"

"What do you mean?"

"Well, if they prove that a temporal anomaly did exist and we did run into it, then the world will know who we really are. Our lives will be seriously changed again."

That gave Freddie pause. The only thing he could say was, "Yeah, there is that, isn't it?"

Barry arrived, and he was shown into a large conference room. Steve greeted him and introduced everyone. Barry had to stop to address Freddie and Emily, "Emily, it is great to know that it's you. We all missed you."

Then to Freddie, he said, "Man, I don't know what to say. Now that I know it's you, I feel like I want to get your autograph."

Freddie said, "You can have it, but no one will believe it."

Barry handed over the x-rays. Steve and Dr. Drexel looked at them. The doctor said, "This x-ray shows far more damage than Freddie's or Emily's. The radiant energy must be stronger."

Steve asked Barry, "Do you have documentation of the event?"

"Yep, I have both stories fully recorded. What does this all mean?"

"I told you that you would know everything, so here it is. We are gathering actual physical evidence of the appearance of a temporal anomaly that linked the year 1973 to 2017 for a short period. It came from outside of the Earth, descended, and skimmed the Earth on a path no more than three miles long. Then it disappeared. We have documented evidence in the form of pictures taken by people claiming they saw a UFO and National Weather Service data. We have physical evidence of the effect of the anomaly on Freddie, Emily, and the dog. We are a long way from making any guesses as to the properties of this anomaly or how it could possibly exist, but we damn well know it did exist."

Barry used Freddie's favorite word, "Wow! I never thought I would be involved with something like this. You're right; this can be historic."

Sarah stepped into the conversation, "But it isn't yet. We have a lot of work to do. Help is coming. What we need is to make sure that there weren't any other encounters out there that we have missed."

Barry brought up something that was on his mind, "While I was driving over here, I was thinking about a case that happened on the same night Emily and Freddie disappeared. I wasn't involved in the case, so I didn't get a lot of the details. It would have been the big news that week if it wasn't for Emily and Freddie. This guy out in Allen Park beat the daylights out of another guy in a bar. It turns out the other guy was sleeping with his wife. When he left the bar, he announced that he was going home and his wife was next on his list. Well, the wife disappeared that night. Everyone assumed he killed her. He did have some of her blood on him, and there was some in the house, but it wasn't nearly enough to come from a major injury. They grilled that guy for hours, and he continued to claim that she got away from him and ran out of the house in her nightgown. No one believed him, and he was convicted on the available evidence. Here's the thing about the story. The people at the bar claimed he left around two in the morning. That would put him home right around two thirty. The dog disappeared around two thirty. Now I'm thinking that maybe the guy didn't kill his wife. It's possible he would have if she didn't get away, but maybe she did get away."

That got everyone's interest. Sarah said, "Oh, I think we need to get everything we can on that case."

Barry said, "I'll get it first thing in the morning."

Barry entered the squad room on Saturday morning and found it a different place. People avoided him, and he got looks like never before. He stopped in the breakroom, and everyone suddenly got quiet.

When he approached the coffee maker, Eric Volstad stood in his way and said, "I'm sorry, sir, this coffee is for members of the department or friends of the department."

"Eric, what the hell is going on here?"

Cindi came in and said, "We don't like people that change sides on us."

"Damn it, Cindi, I didn't change sides."

Eric said, "You're now being suckled by Big Money Mama, aren't you?"

"I am doing a job. I'm sorry if you don't like it. You were happy with me coming around and doing favors for you like a trained seal."

Cindi snarled, "Now you do them for her."

Barry looked at her and said, "I don't get it, Cindi. Sarah has been nothing but respectful to you and to the department, and you treat her like she's public enemy number one."

"She peddled her influence right to the governor, I hear. You should know; it was the favor we were doing for you that brought the shit down on our heads."

"Was anyone disciplined? Did heads roll after the deal at the gas station? No, in fact, Sarah complimented the department and especially you on the way you handled yourself."

"Her people took evidence and walked away smiling. I don't like that."

"I don't know anything about that, and I can't believe Sarah would do such a thing."

257

"Well, she did. Mr. Batali, you are just another citizen now, so what are you doing here?"

"Well, Detective Baveroski, I am here to search your records. The request has been submitted properly, and I have a right to access them."

"Oh gee, Mr. Batali, I'm afraid your request was lost in a paper shuffle. You're going to have to submit it again."

"Don't be an ass, Cindi. No one is jerking you around. You know if I have to leave without accessing those records, you will force Sarah to be less polite. Let's not waste my time and your goodwill with your boss."

"Oh, it's Sarah now, is it? Have you rekindled your old high school romance?"

"I'm not playing these games. I would hate to lose the friendship of any of you. I've always been straight with you, and I've always helped you any way I could, but I need to see those records, and I will go to the captain if I have to."

Cindi stepped away and said, "Go ahead and do your little clerical job for your mistress, but don't touch the coffee."

Barry stopped and said, "On second thought, never mind; I won't bother you any further. Just let me say that your righteousness is amusing, considering what I remember about Billy Joe Sheridan. If I remember correctly patrol officer Baveroski took a bag of weed off of her cousin and set him home. Wasn't that evidence in a crime?"

"Just be on your way."

Barry then turned to the squad, "I've known most of you for thirty or forty years. I shared a patrol car with some of you. This is how I'm treated after all that time? I didn't take the goddamn evidence. You know I would never do anything like that. I will be at Stoney's Monday night, so think about how you'll treat me then."

As he left, someone called out, "Get that evidence back if you ever want to share a beer with us again."

Barry decided that he would go to the source for the information on the case. He drove out to Allen Park, and he hoped the word hadn't been passed to them. On the way, he called Steve, "Steve, I need to talk to Sarah."

"She's with Emily right now. Emily is getting out of bed."

"Okay, well, I need to talk to her as soon as she is available."

"Can I help you? Is there a problem of some kind?"

"Yes, there is a problem, and no you can't help unless you can tell me why Sarah had her people take evidence from a crime scene."

"Oh, no, I don't know anything about that."

"I just got effectively banished from the Romulus police station, and I don't appreciate it."

"I'm sure Sarah can work that out."

"I don't want her working that out. I'm losing friends here. Some of them I've known for forty-five years. I want that damn evidence returned to the police."

"You're right; you need to talk to Sarah about that. Then I guess you haven't been able to get at the police records."

"Not there, but I'm hoping that the Allen Park department hasn't been informed of the missing evidence. I'll let you know."

Steve joined everyone at Emily's bedside. Emily was helped out of bed. She started slapping Freddie's hands away, saying, "Would everyone please relax? I'm not a porcelain doll. I'm not going to shatter."

Dr. Drexel said, "Just take it easy, Ms. Hicks."

"Really, doctor, are you this nervous with every patient with this kind of wound? I feel great. I know I have to be careful and treat the wound with respect. Now let me walk around a bit. I haven't even had a look at this place."

Freddie was at her side, and the slow-moving procession followed behind her. After five minutes, she looked at Freddie and said, "Maybe I'm not quite up for a hike yet."

She reached out her hand, and Freddie held her. In ten seconds, a wheelchair appeared, and Freddie eased her into it. He said, "You did great. You'll do a little more each day."

Emily was disappointed, "I want to be with you at the station on Monday. I have a lot to catch up on."

"You will be. You'll just use the wheelchair until you're a bit stronger."

While they talked, Steve got Sarah's attention, "I just talked to Barry. He is very upset about how he was treated at the Romulus police station. It seems that they have thrown him out because of his new position with you. He said it was something about missing evidence."

Sarah asked, "Where is he now?"

"He's on his way to Allen Park. He is hoping that he can get what we need there."

"Okay, when he calls in, let me know, and I'll talk to him."

Barry started out lucky at Allen Park station. He got access to the records, and he came up with information that indicated that Sheryl Ferguson just might have run through the anomaly. He switched his attention to reports from September 16th of this year, and suddenly the computer he was using shutdown.

An officer stepped to the desk and said, "I'm sorry, Mr. Batali, we seem to have encountered some technical problems. I'm afraid the problems will persist for quite some time. We think it has something to do with missing evidence in Romulus."

Barry smiled and said, "Very clever. I get it. I'll be on my way."

The officer just smiled and said, "You have a nice day now, Mr. Batali."

Steve returned to his work. He was amazed at the number of top-flight PhDs that had appeared in a single day, not to mention some of the most sophisticated equipment he had ever seen. He would have never believed that a completely operational anechoic chamber could be set up in just eight hours.

Several of his colleagues were waiting for him to return. They wanted to discuss some possibilities. One idea was right out of science fiction.

Barry returned, and Sarah came out to greet him. He looked at her and said, "You're just the person I need to talk to."

"Yes, Steve told me. I was told that you had some trouble at the police station."

"You might say that. People I've known all of my life are now treating me like Judas. I'm sorry, Sarah, but you've crossed the line. You had your people take evidence from a crime scene, and I can't be a party to that."

"You aren't a party to it, Barry. You had nothing to do with it."

"Tell that to all of my friends. I never thought they would treat me like that. Sarah, I can't be associated with this sort of thing. I can mend some fences if I can return the evidence."

"I'm sorry, Barry, but I don't think I can do that."

Emily had heard part of the conversation and pushed herself to them in her wheelchair. She looked at Sarah and asked, "You took the tapes? Why did you do that?"

"Did you want to explain how you had brand new forty-four-year-old tapes? If they were made public, things would become very difficult. You and Freddie would have to give up everything that you have started, including the work at the radio station. You would be hounded constantly for answers."

Barry jumped back into the conversation, "They still want answers, and Emily must appear at the station to pick Rother out of a lineup and to officially make the complaint. You can bet that Cindi will be ready to have a little chat with you, Emily."

Sarah was getting defensive, "Emily won't be there alone. She will have Nate Evans with her, and he will see that she is not berated."

Barry tried to explain, "Sarah, you have great power and influence, but there are limits. Politicians respond to power and influence, but they also respond to public opinion. Nothing makes a politician more popular with the people than being imagined as a giant killer. You can use your power to squash investigations and pressure judges, but sooner or later, someone will step up to be the giant killer."

"I don't do any of those things. I do use influence, but I wouldn't demand an investigation be stopped simply for my own gain, and I certainly would never pressure a judge."

"Not yet, Sarah, but you are now on a slippery slope into that world. You have to trust me on this. We are talking about my world now.

I said you were an honorable woman, and I believe that. This is out of character for you, but you have now obstructed the law once for a personal reason. The next time you face that type of a decision, it will be easier to bend the law again, and even easier the next time. That's not you, Sarah. Return this evidence and reverse this trend before it starts."

"How could I possibly return those tapes now?"

"I will return the evidence. I'll figure a way to return the evidence without having a trail leading back to you."

"That brings me back to my original problem. Where did Emily get forty-four-year-old brand new tapes?"

"There must be a way to make those tapes look older."

Sarah turned to her chief strategic and tactical strategist, "Tommy, can you help us with this problem? How would you make the tapes look old?"

Tommy stepped to the group and said, "Ma'am, I think the problem is more complicated than that. You could just bang the tapes around to make them look old, but that will diminish their value as evidence. As far as I know, you haven't touched the tapes. No one has. This is good because I'm sure they are looking for fingerprints and DNA on the tapes. They expect to find Beth Richard's fingerprints and Betty Ann Rother's fingerprints. If they can't get that evidence, then, in their minds, their evidence has only been partially returned."

Sarah was becoming frustrated, "If we can't age the tapes. What do we do?"

Tommy started with a question, "Is it true that every report seen and every opinion made about Ms. Emily Hicks indicated that she was very responsible?"

"Yes, of course. Everyone knew Emily was responsible and careful with everything."

Tommy continued, "Then it wouldn't be a shock to find out that Ms. Hicks kept her tapes in a plastic container of some kind to make sure they weren't damaged. We can claim the tapes were in a plastic container. We do have to be careful that the container was one that was around in 1973."

Emily jumped in, "A Tupperware container. Mom had plenty of them, and I was always borrowing one for one thing or another."

Sarah said, "That's perfect. Please continue, Tommy."

Tommy continued, "We can age the container and the bag. We have the capability to do it right. I believe we can pull it off."

Sarah smiled and said, "Thank you, Tommy; you are brilliant."

Tommy said, "Thank you, Ma'am. Let me know when we should get started."

Sarah said, "Let us do a little more talking. The next question is, how do we return the bag without having my people charged with obstruction of justice?"

Barry answered, "That's not a big problem. Anyone can bring it in, but I want to do it."

"Can you do that without implicating my people? They all seem to know that you are working for me now."

"I was going to come up with this complicated scheme, but simple is better. It would work best if the bag could be delivered to my door before dawn tomorrow morning. It can be Monday morning, but then it would be hard to get it to the station before Emily has to go in."

"It can be delivered on Monday," Sarah said, "I will see to it that she is not expected until Monday afternoon."

"Great, then it can arrive Monday morning. Just have someone drop the bag by the door. Jenny goes out to get the paper first thing every morning. It would be best if she finds it and brings it in. I will deliver it to the station and tell them how I got it. I will also tell them that Jenny had picked it up before I could stop her, so they will find her fingerprints on the bag."

Sarah said, "Okay, Tommy, get the bag. My mother still has all of her old Tupperware. You can get a container from her. Let's make this work."

Emily asked, "Won't they be expecting me at the station today?"

Sarah said, "We'll control that. If we say it is Monday afternoon, then it is Monday afternoon. Don't worry; Nate Evans will be with you. You won't have to answer any question that you don't want to answer."

"But I won't be able to go back to the radio station if I'm still too weak to leave here."

"You can go on Monday. Getting there in the afternoon won't be a problem."

Tommy volunteered, "The bag will be ready on time Ma'am."

Emily was still nervous about answering questions at the station, "I think I need to have something to say if I can't avoid the question about where I got the bag. I must have gotten a clue somewhere in order to find it."

Sarah said, "We have to keep this simple. We have too many elaborate stories going on already. I gave you the bag. I thought that you looked and acted so much like Emily that you should have Emily's bag. If they ask you how I got it, just tell them that you don't know.

They have no reason to drag me in just to ask me about the bag. If asked, I will acknowledge that I gave it to you, and that was one reason why one of my overzealous employees thought I should have it back."

Sarah let out a sigh and said, "Now that the crisis seems to be handled for the moment, Barry, did you get any information at all that will help us?"

"Yes, there is a high probability that Sheryl Ferguson went into the anomaly. In Paul Ferguson's statement, he claimed he saw a blue light, and Sheryl was heading toward it. He slowed up, thinking it might be a police car. He said there was a flash of white light, and he never saw her again. No one took him seriously, but there hasn't been any sign of her since."

Steve said, "That sounds like we may have Sheryl Ferguson wandering somewhere around Allen Park in 2017."

Barry gave them the bad news, "They cut my access off before I could check for any relevant reports from this year. We won't get more until I am back in their good graces."

The news upset Emily, "She is wandering around out there all alone. She must be terrified. Even with Freddie with me, I almost lost my mind on that first morning. I still remember sitting in the booth at IHOP and wondering if I was sane. If Freddie hadn't been with me, I know I would have gone off the deep end."

"You're right," Sarah said, "she would likely be acting strangely, and she would be wandering around in her nightgown. It is likely that she was picked up and taken to a psychiatric wing of a hospital or other facility.

Barry is going to be busy dealing with the bag issue. Steve, you are needed here. Tommy is also busy on the bag issue."

Freddie and Emily both volunteered, "We'll do the checking."

Barry added, "I can give you her physical description."

Sarah said, "Good; Steve will give you the standard introduction that he and Barry have been using. Check any place that might treat people in her perceived condition. Check for any woman found in a nightgown that was checked in since September 16th. Tell them that you are representatives from SHR Laboratories and you need to speak with Sheryl Ferguson. If you are stonewalled, let me know."

Freddie and Emily moved away to begin their task. Tommy was off coordinating the fetching of the bag. Steve returned to his colleagues to give them the news of another possible sample to study. This left Sarah and Barry sitting in the room alone.

The room was quiet for a moment and then Sarah said, "I'm sorry that I caused you so much trouble."

Barry did not want to hide his feelings, "This is a real problem for me. With the exception of Jenny and my son Tony, I was closer to no other people on this Earth than the people in that squad room. To have them shun me was the worst thing that has ever happened to me."

"Barry, I'll try my best to fix it, I promise. If this doesn't do it, we'll think of something else."

"I meet them all at a bar called Stoney's every Monday night. I intend to be there on Monday, and I hope things work out by then."

Sarah spent Sunday with her mother. She took her to Detroit to visit an old friend, and they had lunch at her favorite bistro. Shelly Hicks was reveling in having her daughters so close and seeing them so often.

Steve was huddled with his colleagues all day Sunday. Freddie and Emily felt like guinea pigs. Freddie found it quite unsettling to have to stand motionless in the black anechoic chamber for five minutes at a time while some of the most sensitive instruments ever created tried to detect and energy radiating from him. After Freddie, Emily took her turn; for some reason, she was less nervous about the experience. The scientists believed they were close to making their first statement.

After their experience in the dark, Freddie and Emily resumed their task of searching for Sheryl Ferguson. They had contracted several facilities without any luck. The practice made the introduction more polished. Emily punched in the number for the Sandburg Psychiatric Clinic. The woman answered, and Emily started, "Good afternoon, my name is Beth Richards, and I represent SHR Laboratories. We are investigating an unusual energy pulse that was observed in your area. We have information that a woman might have been affected by the pulse. The pulse occurred at approximately two thirty in the morning on September 16th. There actually might have been several energy pulses at that time. Reports are that the woman was at or close to the pulse, and she wandered off. She is twenty-eight years old. She has long blonde hair and blue eyes, and she may possibly be injured from a physical attack. She was dressed only in her nightgown. We believe her name is Sheryl Ferguson. Was there anyone admitted to your facility matching that description on or after the morning of September 16th?"

The woman answered nervously, "There was a woman who was brought to us by the police in the late morning of September 16th. She was incoherent and suffering from exposure. I can't give you more information than that without a warrant or proof of kinship."

"Can you just tell me if she was wearing a nightgown when she was admitted?"

"Yes, and I can't tell you anymore. Please come here in person with the proper documents."

Emily turned to Freddie and said, "I know where she is, and now we have to talk to Sarah."

Freddie and Emily went to Sarah when she returned from Detroit. Sarah listened to Emily explain the situation, and she said, "It would be good if we could find a relative, but that would take time. I believe I can work out a business solution to this problem."

Barry had that feeling again. It was that feeling he got when he thought he wasn't seeing the whole picture. Sarah was being way too nice to Cindi, and Cindi was way too angry with Sarah. There was more to that picture. He spent a few hours on Sunday clearing up that little mystery.

As predicted, Jenny Batali stepped out on her front porch to get the paper and discovered the old beat-up bag sitting by the door. She brought it in with the paper and called to Barry, "Barry, there was an old bag sitting by the door and, before you get smart, it isn't me."

Barry came out and put on a good performance, "Jenny, damn, please set it down."

Jenny set the bag down; she stared at it and asked, "Is it a bomb?"

"No, nothing like that, but I believe it is the evidence that I told you about."

"And I contaminated it."

"Don't worry. I'm sure the bag was wiped clean anyway, but we don't want to open it."

"I know better than that. Will you take it to the station?"

"I will do it first thing this morning."

An hour later, Barry, using rubber gloves, dropped the bag on Cindi Baveroski's desk. Barry said, "Here is your missing evidence. It was delivered to my front door sometime during the night. Jenny picked it up with the paper this morning, so I'm afraid you will find her fingerprints on the bag, but we didn't open it."

"So it magically showed up this morning?"

"No, it wasn't magic. I complained about the situation to the scientist I'm working with, and he must have passed it along to Sarah. I still don't think she knew it happened. I think one of her security people thought he was doing her a favor."

Cindi looked the bag over carefully and said, "I'll get it over to the CSU people and see if they think it still has any value. Don't think that this means all is forgiven."

"Oh, I don't expect that from you." Then Barry addressed the entire room, "Here's the bag. I didn't take it, but I returned it. All I want is a fair shake."

Cindi called, "But you're still working for her."

Barry asked, "Do you want to do his right here in the room?"

Cindi looked him straight in the eye and said, "Yeah, why wouldn't I? I'm not the one with things to hide."

"Okay, why are you so wound up when it comes to Sarah Hicks Rutherford?"

"Because everybody knows that she is a privileged bitch who likes to throw her weight around."

"Really, there are plenty of rich people throwing their weight around here. We elected one of the mayors. Why her specifically? What do you have against her?"

"Nothing; what are you getting at?"

"Oh, I think you know. It is the same reason that she feels this need to help you out. You two have history."

"Bullshit; I never met the woman until that day at the gas station."

"No, but your father did, didn't he? When you were about eight, your father was a tech guy, and he had started his own business. He was doing pretty well in the area. His big customer was the Manchester Furniture store chain. When the time came for the chain to renew their contract with your father, they got a better offer from Commerce Tech out of California, Sarah Hicks Rutherford's company. They provided a more modern approach for a lower price, and the chain went for it. Your father lost his biggest customer and, soon after, his business. Your family struggled to pay off the debts for years. You blame Sarah for the suffering you and your family went through. That's why you want to cause her as much trouble as you can."

"That has nothing to do with this."

"Oh, you damn well know it does. It's also why Sarah is trying so hard to help you out. She feels guilty about what happened, though she has no reason to feel guilty. She proposed a fair business deal, and it was accepted."

"There was no reason that she had to come back here and ruin our lives. She was already rich. She came back here just to prove what a big shot she was and destroyed my father in the process. He was never the same, and he died feeling like a failure. She has to pay."

"And that's the justice you're looking for. You want justice for your father, and you will keep hounding her as long as she or her people are active in Romulus. Cindi, you have to regain your focus."

"Don't tell me what to do, Batali. You're a nobody, an old fart who was feeling useless."

"You are exactly right about that. What I'm not is a traitor to this department or to my friends. You have a right to your hate, I suppose; no one but you can make that go away. Just be careful that the hate doesn't ruin your career. You are a fine detective, and the department is better with you focused on real cases."

"Just get out of my face and keep your opinions to yourself."

"Gladly, we are done."

As Barry walked away, he got several nods, and Jeff Anders said, "We'll see you tonight at Stoney's."

Barry saw the lieutenant standing in his doorway, and he said, "Good day Lieutenant Summers."

"Barry, my name is still Andy."

"Thanks, Andy."

"Do you need access to our files today?"

"No, thank you, I have somewhere I have to be."

As he headed for the door, he heard Andy call Cindi into his office.

Barry went to the Sandburg Psychiatric Clinic to visit Sheryl Ferguson. An attorney named Phyllis Drake would arrive later, and they had an appointment to see the facility's administrator.

He presented himself to the front desk; Barry now had an id card to go with his introduction. He referenced the conversation that Emily had with the facility, and he was led in to see Sheryl. The attendant explained, "When she was brought in, she was wearing just a nightgown, and it looked like someone had knocked her around a bit. She was just babbling about everything being wrong. She kept saying the world was wrong, and she wanted to go home."

"Did she identify herself?"

"No, we haven't gotten anything coherent out of her. We put her picture out to the newspapers and to the TV stations, but no one has come forward to identify her."

"As my colleagues mentioned on the phone, her name is Sheryl Ferguson, and we think she is suffering from more than a mental breakdown."

"You may know more about that than we do, but the law will not allow us to release her to anyone but a relative or a legal guardian, especially in the condition that she's in."

"We will discuss that with Dr. Reese, and we hope to come to an agreement."

Sheryl Ferguson was sitting and staring out of the window. Barry sat across from her at the small table, and the attendant left them alone. Barry was way out of his expertise on this one. He tried to rely on his experience with victims in shock after a violent crime and his dealing with people high on drugs. He started, "Sheryl, Sheryl Ferguson, I am Barry Batali, and I'm here to help you. Sheryl, there is nothing wrong with you, and there is nothing wrong with the world. You have just been gone a very long time. You are like Rip Van Winkle; time has gone by without you in it. I know that doesn't make a lot of sense, and I don't know if you can hear me, but it is the truth. You are not alone. Two other people have experienced the same thing, and they want to talk to you. You have experienced something only two other people in the world have experienced. We know what happened to you, and we want to help you."

Sheryl turned to him and mumbled almost too low for Barry to hear, "It's wrong. Out there, it's all wrong."

Barry realized that she was sedated, and it was unlikely that he would get through to her. He just patted her hand and said, "It's going to be alright, Sheryl. It's going to be alright."

Phyllis Drake arrived right on time, and Barry joined her in the administrator's office. The portly African American man stood, greeted them, and asked what he could do for them. Phyllis took over from there.

"Doctor Reese, I am Phyllis Drake, and I represent SHR Laboratories. We have information about your patient. You know her only as Jane Doe, but her name is Sheryl Ferguson. Her problems are not caused by a mental disorder. She is in shock from encountering an unusual energy source."

Doctor Reese noted the statement and asked, "What kind of energy source was this? We have had no reports of any problems in the area."

"We are trying to understand that, doctor. It occurred just for a short time on the morning of September 16th, and it traveled approximately three miles through this area. Sheryl encountered it, and you are seeing the effects of that encounter on her."

"I assume you are not here just to relay information, or I would be meeting with a medical doctor."

"That's correct. We have two purposes for our visit. First, we would like to propose a mutual provider agreement. We would like your permission to transport Ms. Ferguson to our facility to perform a series of unique tests. These tests will help us understand what has happened to her and to create the best method of treatment. The tests will also give us a better understanding of the phenomenon that has happened."

"This woman is in our charge. We can't let you take her away and perform unique tests on her."

"You are perfectly welcome to assign someone to accompany Ms. Ferguson and observe and even participate in the tests. Your doctor will be briefed on each process and will be consulted on any suggested treatment."

"Well, that seems fair. Is your facility local?"

"Yes, it is on the shore of Lake St. Claire. I promise we will be respectful and take good care of Ms. Ferguson. I have drawn up an agreement for your legal staff to review and, for your cooperation, SHR Laboratories would like to make a donation of one hundred thousand dollars to help your facility with the good work that you do."

"Well, that is truly appreciated. I will see that the legal people examine your document right away. You said there were two things that brought you here. What was the second?"

Barry entered the conversation at this point, "We would like you to perform an experiment here in your facility. The reason we want it performed here is to give you proof that this energy source did appear and that Ms. Ferguson was affected by it."

"That won't be necessary, sir. I don't doubt your word."

"Doctor, our scientists were quite insistent. They said it also eliminated any chance of anything in the environment at our facility giving them a false positive."

"What do you want us to do?"

"Do you have x-ray capability here?"

"Yes, right on premises."

"Good, we need you to take an x-ray of someone of your choice, then x-ray Ms. Ferguson, and then x-ray someone after Ms. Ferguson."

"You believe that the x-ray of Ms. Ferguson will show something unusual."

"Yes, the energy source leaves behind benign radiant energy that damages x-ray photos. This will prove that Ms. Ferguson made contact with the energy source. We will also get an indication of the intensity of the contact. A medical doctor and a physicist from our lab would like to witness the procedure, but we would like your staff to perform it."

"Tell your people that we will be ready at their earliest convenience."

"Thank you, doctor, we believe the world and Ms. Ferguson will benefit from our mutual efforts."

Barry called Steve, and then he told Phyllis Drake, "Well, counselor, I believe our efforts today might have saved Ms. Ferguson's life."

Chapter 14: Tachyons

On Monday, Freddie wheeled Emily into KWTZ, and everyone applauded as she entered. Tony handed her an official welcome-back pastry, and they got to work. Emily was thrilled to be back. The goodwill made her feel another step closer to being part of this world.

Three new people were standing with Roger as he opened the morning meeting. We have made great progress, but we still have a ways to go. As you can see, several more people have been added to our little troupe. Next to me from left to right are: Patrick McDowell, who will play the part of Peter Chiles, Francine Nagle will be Pat Grundy, and Edmond Glass will play Dr. Jenkins. Okay, let's get to work. Let's do scenes involving band members first so they can be excused to continue their practice."

Everyone went through their parts, and Emily was really getting a good feeling about the show. Her smile and enthusiasm were contagious. She started the scene that involved her, Betty, and Pat Grundy. She was still amazed at how accurate her dialog was as compared to the actual words she spoke. The three women sat at the end of the conference table with their scripts in their hands. Roger said, "Okay, the band had just been called into a meeting, and you just watched them leave. Beth, you have the first line; go."

Emily couldn't believe she was about to speak the words that she had spoken forty-four years ago, almost word for word, "You're not cool with Don now, are you? He didn't say he was sorry."

"Okay, Sherry, give Emily a sly smile, then start."

Sherry's Betty had a bit of a Brooklyn accent, "Hell no, I'm not that stupid."

Emily thought that he must have heard the rest of what Betty said. He must have decided to leave it out to avoid possible legal problems.

"Okay, Beth, point to Pat Grundy."

Emily pointed and spoke her line, "Who's that?"

"Sherry, let's see that smile again."

Sherry smiled again and said, "Oh, that's Patty Grundy. She's Rick's main squeeze. If anyone knows about Rick, it will be her."

"Now call Patty over and then walk off stage left. Francine, it's your line."

Francine spoke her line, "So you're from Romulus like Betty."

Emily answered without direction, "Yep, I'm a Romulan."

Roger commented, "Great laugh Francine. It's your line, Beth."

Emily didn't look at the script. She just blurted out word for word what she had said two and a half weeks earlier, "It is a great ice breaker when I meet people at U of M."

Roger called, "Hold up, that's not the line Beth."

Emily looked at the script and said, "I'm sorry, Roger, I don't know where that came from."

"Okay, read it from the script, please."

Emily read, "Yeah, everyone at school calls me that."

Emily thought that Francine must have had some experience. She was so natural in her delivery. Francine spoke her line, "You go to Michigan; that's a great school."

Roger directed, "Beth, this is where Emily starts her questioning. Try to make it sound like an interview."

Emily smiled, thinking, "If he only knew that it didn't take any acting."

Then she spoke her line, "How long have you been with Rick?"

Francine went right into her lines, "It's been about four months. Other girls show up, but I'm his number one."

The ladies just let the dialog flow from there without further direction; Emily read, "How is he feeling?"

Francine was great with the expression when she asked, "Why do you ask?"

Emily had to make sure she read the script, so she didn't repeat her earlier mistake, "I heard he had a hard time in Chicago."

Emily truly admired Francine's ability with expression. Francine narrowed her eyes and said, "He's fine."

Emily tried to remember the slight panic she felt, thinking that she had said the wrong thing as she said, "I didn't mean anything. I bet you love being with him."

They finished the dialog, starting with Francine, "It's great. Last night was special."

"Why was last night so special?"

"He was different last night. Normally he likes doing it fast. It is usually a party thing."

"That didn't happen last night?"

"No, he was in no hurry; he just wanted me there. He didn't even want sex. It was really nice."

Everyone applauded, and Roger said, "That was great. Beth, you're really getting the hang of this.

In the studio, the boys were working on the lead guitar jam. Freddie was telling the rest of the band, "We have to start working together. This jam is going to be a lot longer than the normal intro to "Rabble Rouser," and I think it's best if you guys aren't just standing on stage watching. This band is tight. I think you can come up with a variation to the music that backs us up and gets you into the jam. You will have to go off the music sheet. Are you willing to try?"

Bobby called out, "Hell yeah!"

The jam started, and the energy grew as Freddie and Pete traded attempts to outdo each other. The band did a great job of keeping up and adding to the energy. Finally, the two lead guitars played together, and Freddie started his signature hammer-and-pull technique. He was surprised at how well Pete kept up with him. The music rose to a crescendo, and Freddie and Pete threw their right arms high in the air. On the final note, they slapped a high five.

When the music ebbed, they heard the applause, and they saw everyone in the building pressed against the windows and applauding. Freddie and Pete looked at each other and automatically hugged.

When things calmed down, Jimmy said, "Man, that was freaking awesome, holy shit!"

Freddie was pumped up, "Guys, I want to stay with you after this gig. Screw that look-alike shit; this is what I want to do. We'll make two lead guitars work."

Jimmy said, "You're goddamn right we will; you bet your ass we will."

At the retreat, Steve was working with his colleagues. Dr. Rosencrantz was urging him to take the initial idea to Sarah."

"It's time. We aren't calling this a solution or even a full theory, but I think we should be showing Ms. Rutherford that we are making progress."

Steve was hesitant, "Isaac, there isn't any rush. She has not given us a deadline. She knows how complex this problem is."

Dr. Rayburn also wanted him to go to Sarah, "We really do have something here."

"Okay, let's write it up, and I'll give Sarah a briefing at dinner tonight."

It was time for Emily to go to the police station. Nathaniel Evans arrived at the radio station to pick her up. Freddie wheeled her out, and Evans said, "I'll take it from here."

Freddie didn't like that idea, "What do you mean by that?"

Evans explained, "If you attend, it will give them another target to shoot at, and it would make my job that much harder. Please have lunch with your friends, and we'll fill you in when we return."

Emily touched his hand; "It's okay, Frank. I'll let you know everything that is said."

Freddie stepped back, and Evans wheeled Emily to a waiting SUV.

It just took a few minutes to get to the police station. Nathaniel Evans wheeled Emily in, and she could feel the eyes on her. She was greeted by Lieutenant Summers, "Good afternoon Ms. Richards. This shouldn't take very long. You just have to take care of some paperwork and positively identify your attacker. Emily was taken into the room, and she watched through the window as the women lined up. She picked Betty out of the lineup, and then they moved to the lieutenant's office. Emily noticed that Detective Baveroski was nowhere to be found.

After the paperwork was done, the Lieutenant informed her, "This conversation is being recorded; it's standard procedure."

Emily acknowledged the statement, and the lieutenant asked her a series of questions about how the attack happened and how she ended up being stabbed. When he was satisfied with those answers, he moved on to talk about the bag, "We have your bag, but we will have to keep it until the case is resolved."

Emily acknowledged the statement, "I understand, Lieutenant."

Lieutenant Summers asked the question, "Do you mind if I ask you how you obtained the bag? Everyone thought it was gone with Emily Hicks."

"Ms. Rutherford gave it to me. I guess I look so much like her sister that she has kind of adopted me. She wanted me to have the bag."

"Did she tell you how she came upon it?"

"No, I'm sorry she didn't, and I didn't have the nerve to ask."

"I see. Well, thank you, Ms. Richards; we'll keep in touch."

"Thank you, Lieutenant."

Just then, Evans' phone rang. He answered, and Emily and the Lieutenant could only hear his side of the conversation. They heard, "Okay. No, I'll handle it. Pull up in front and wait there fifteen minutes and then drive away. I'll meet you at the radio station."

When he got off the phone, he asked Lieutenant Summers, "May we leave through the back entrance, and could you please have one of your patrol cars drive us to KWTZ? It seems a gaggle of reporters are gathering out front."

The lieutenant answered, "Of course, this way."

They left the station, and Nathaniel Evans said, "I believe the lieutenant just made peace with Ms. Rutherford."

Outside, an older Hispanic woman waited with the other reporters. This was more than a story for her, and she had a question to ask Ms. Elizabeth Richards. Anita Morales Jefferson was a seasoned reporter who had traveled the world. She was semi-retired, but she decided to spend her last years as a reporter working for her hometown newspaper.

Evans wheeled Emily back into the radio station. She saw Freddie showing Roger some sheet music. Roger looked up and waved her over, "Beth, Frank was just showing me a ballad that he thought would work for you, and I think he's right. It's called "I'm Waiting for Tomorrow." It will seem tragic, considering Emily Hicks didn't have another tomorrow. Frank was about to play for us."

Freddie got his guitar and started, *"I'm waiting for tomorrow; today was not my day. I'm waiting for tomorrow, when things may go my way. Today started so bright, but it didn't turn out right. Tomorrow there's a chance, and maybe I will dance."*

Freddie completed the song, and everyone applauded. Emily looked at Freddie and said, "That was beautiful and sad but with a touch of hope. I just don't know if I can do it justice."

Freddie encouraged her, "You will be fine. We'll work on it, and I'll change the key if that needs to be done."

Then she turned to Roger, "It will seem tragic knowing Emily's fate. Where do you plan to put it in the play?"

"I have decided to add a little embellishment. Actually, everything beyond when Emily ran out of the conference room is an embellishment, so I will have you hide in the parking garage. The lights will go down like you are stepping out of the story. A light will be on you at center stage, and a dimmer light on Frank playing guitar on upper stage right. The song will end, the lights will come up, and you will complete the scene. I also decided to redo the intro at the end so you will sing your lines from 'A Dark Night for Walking' at the end too. The play will end with the light fading on you."

Emily didn't know what to say. She had never done anything like this before, and now she was opening and closing the play. Finally, she said, "This is going to be special for me."

Roger maintained his business-like tone, "That's the way the story should end. I wasn't thinking about who was going to do it."

Steve and Dr. Drexel made their trip to the Sandburg Psychiatric Clinic. They observed the x-ray experiment and brought the results back to the retreat. Sarah joined the scientists as they looked over the results. Dr. Drexel spoke what was obvious to everyone, "Sheryl's x-ray is unreadable. She is definitely radiating far more energy than Emily, Freddie, or the dog."

Sarah asked, "Do you have a theory that can explain that?"

Steve answered, "I do believe we do. We believe it has to do with the length of the exposure to the anomaly. Freddie and Emily went through the anomaly at somewhere around sixty miles an hour. It's likely the dog was running when it went through the anomaly. Sheryl, even if she was running, she wouldn't have been running as fast as a dog. It's possible she wasn't running at all. We think the strength of the radiation is related to the length of time of the exposure."

"That makes sense. Maybe the strength of this radiation will give you some idea of its properties."

Sarah could see the other scientist trying to subtly prod Steve to say something. She asked Steve, "Do you have a suspicion?"

"Steve didn't like announcing a conclusion without more evidence, but he responded, "Sarah, this is a swag."

"A swag, is that a scientific term?"

"Yes, it's an acronym meaning a Scientific Wild Ass Guess."

Sarah laughed and said, "Okay, I'll take it as that."

"All indications are that we can't measure the energy directly. We can only measure the reaction to that energy. We think that it is because we see a reaction before the energy is radiated."

That confused Sarah, "Wait a minute. Are you saying, if it were a flashlight, that you would see the light before the flashlight is turned on?"

Steve answered, "That is a very good analogy. Yes, that's what I'm saying."

"What could possibly do that?"

"It would be something that we have only theorized about. We believe we may be dealing with tachyons."

Sarah had heard the word before but only related to science fiction, "I thought that stuff was only in Star Trek."

"Up till now, it had only been an idea based on other theories. It was like when science first speculated about a black hole. No one knew if one existed, but there were reasons to believe it might. The same goes for tachyons. Tachyons supposedly move faster than the speed of light. In doing so, they break Einstein's rule that nothing with mass can travel faster than the speed of light. Particles with positive mass must travel below the speed of light. Particles with zero mass can travel at the speed of light. You must have a negative mass if you want to go faster than the speed of light. This is where the string theory people go crazy because they end up with a solution where a number is squared, and a result is a negative number."

"Okay, Steve, now you're making my head hurt, but you are saying you think this may be tachyon radiation. I guess I can see why. Something that is moving faster than light within a small area has to distort time."

"That's what we are thinking."

"This is amazing."

"We hope that our observations of Ms. Ferguson will give more evidence."

"She should be here by the end of the day."

Freddie and Emily made it home before Sheryl Ferguson arrived. They wanted to be with her from the first moment. It looked like they would have dinner before anything happened. Emily slapped her wheelchair and said, "I think I can get out of this thing now."

Sarah wasn't sure, "Why don't we see what Dr. Drexel thinks."

"Sure," Emily complained, "we have to be sure the porcelain princess doesn't skin her elbow."

Sarah just smiled and changed the subject, "How is the play going?"

Freddie wanted to break the news, "Roger has given Emily two more singing parts. Emily is closing the show."

"That's great," Sarah cheered, "See, Emily, I knew you would be heading for Broadway."

Emily blushed and said, "Oh, don't start that again."

Freddie had a little news in that area, "Emily, we were so busy that I hadn't had a chance to tell you the latest rumor. It seems someone has been recording some of your rehearsals, and they have passed them around on social media."

"Who would do that? We're still working on it. It will make us look silly."

"I don't know for sure, but I think it was Tony himself."

"Why, for God's sake?"

"He has a feeling that this show is going to be a hit. From what I hear, the people that have seen it agree with him. The station is getting queries from other stations and from New York."

"Oh, come on now."

"I'm just telling you what I heard."

Sarah had to jump back in, "My little sister, on stage. Move over all you Tony award winners."

Emily said, "Just shut up and eat."

It was just after seven thirty when Barry, Steve, and Dr. Drexel led Sheryl Ferguson, Dr. Stiller, and Nurse Jessica Bauman into the retreat. Freddie and Emily were right up front to greet her. Tears came to Emily's eyes when she saw her, "Oh, this poor woman. This could have been me."

"Don't worry, Emily," Sarah said, "she will get the best care."

Emily turned to Steve and asked, "You're not going to start experimenting on her too soon, are you?"

Steve answered, "She will rest and be under the care of Doctor Drexel and Doctor Stiller until they feel she is ready."

Emily stooped down next to the wheelchair and tried to talk to Sheryl, "Sheryl Ferguson, Sheryl, my name is Emily. What happened to you happened to me and my friend Freddie. You're not alone, and we can help you understand what has happened."

Sheryl slowly looked at Emily and spoke in a dazed voice, "Sheryl, I am Sheryl?"

"Yes," Emily said excitedly, "you are Sheryl Ferguson, and something happened to you."

Sheryl once again stared off like she was looking at something far away, "The light, there was a light, and now everything is wrong."

"Yes, the light; Freddie and I went through the light also. We know what happened, and we can help you understand."

Sheryl kept repeating, "There was a light, and now the world is wrong."

Emily couldn't get through to her anymore. She looked at Dr. Drexel and pleaded, "You can bring her back, can't you? Please, you have to help her."

Doctor Stiller said, "Miss, we will do all that we can. You have done very well. That was the first time that she had said her name."

Dr. Rosencrantz passed a wand over her as she was wheeled by. Emily was upset, "Do you have to do that now? She is more than a lab subject, you know."

The doctor apologized, "I'm sorry. I just wanted to get an initial reading. I won't bother her again."

Sarah wanted to know, but first, she spoke to Emily, "Emily, Sheryl's best chance of recovery is if we know as much about how she was affected and if we know it soon."

Sarah then turned to Dr. Rosencrantz, "Were you able to get a reading?"

"Yes, in order to get a reading at all in this environment was amazing, and I got a very distinct reading. If our estimation of the reason for the level's intensity is correct, Ms. Ferguson was in direct contact with the anomaly for a significant amount of time."

"Thank you, doctor; let's let Ms. Ferguson rest now."

"Of course, Ms. Rutherford, we will not disturb her."

Barry paused at the entrance to Stoney's Bar. He could hear that it was very lively inside. He almost decided to walk away, but he pulled open the door and stepped in. He walked into an argument that was getting more heated by the second. It was obvious what all of the yelling was about, and he couldn't let it continue. Stoney was standing behind the bar with a baseball bat in his hand. Barry asked, "Stoney, may I borrow the bat for a minute? If I cause any damage, I'll pay for it."

Stoney handed him the bat, and he banged the bat on the bar until he got everyone's attention; then he called out, "Everyone listen up. Don't be stupid. You are a family. You have each other's backs. You can't damage that respect over me. Some of you accept me, and some of you don't; just agree to disagree on that point. Those of you that don't want any part of me just ignore me, and I will ignore you. I have friends to share a beer with, and I appreciate that. I don't hate any of you, but I won't beg you to like me. Just split up here but not on the job. There you are all family, and I won't get in your way."

Everyone calmed down, and Barry got a beer. After some general bantering, Jeff Anders sat down next to him and said, "I don't think Cindi is finished with you or your boss. The lieutenant came down on her pretty good, so I don't think she will be using department resources, but she is planning something."

Barry said, "Thanks for the head's up."

Barry called to Eric Volstad, "Hey, Volstad, you better watch your partner. If she does anything crazy, it may be a problem for you."

"Go screw yourself, Batali."

"Okay, I'm just saying. If she does something that gets a raft of shit dropped on her head, that may be bad for you. Shit tends to splatter."

"I don't know what you're talking about, Batali. Is the dominatrix holding your leash planning to make trouble again?"

"No, but I have a feeling that I know what Cindi is up to, and it won't take any outside influence to bring down the shit if she goes through with it."

"You don't know shit, Batali. You're the one that said for us to just drink our beers and be quiet. Why don't you listen to your own advice?"

The week was a story of steady progress in the show and with the research. Emily was up and out of the wheelchair and well on her way to a full recovery.

Sheryl Ferguson was slowly becoming more responsive, and the scientists were preparing for their first test. Emily spent as much time as she could with Sheryl. This Monday night was no exception. Sheryl looked at Emily and asked, "I remember someone say, Rip Van Winkle. Did I sleep for a long time?"

"You didn't sleep, but what happened to you, me, and Freddie was a lot like what happened to Rip Van Winkle. What happened to us is that the flash somehow moved all of us from 1973 to 2017. It really happened. The scientists here can prove it happened. It isn't in your mind, and it isn't in my mind."

"Then where is Paul?"

"I'm sorry to tell you that your husband passed away four years ago."

"Paul is gone? He's been gone for four years? I just saw him just a while ago?"

"I'm so sorry, it seems like just a while ago to me also, but it has been forty-four years."

"No, no, it's wrong. It's all wrong."

"Sheryl, please stay with me. We can get through this."

"It's wrong; it's all wrong."

Sheryl had reverted again. Emily once again had to call the attendant and she left the suite with tears in her eyes.

Freddie found her on the lawn staring at the lake. He brought out her coat and put it on her shoulders. Emily just turned around, hugged him, and sobbed into his chest.

Freddie held her and softly said, "I know it's hard. I could feel myself losing it on that first day. We had each other and we had time to think. She was slapped in the face with it. You are helping her; she is getting better."

Emily sobbed, "I know, but it just breaks my heart when she falls back into that terrible dark hole. I can almost feel myself in there with her."

Freddie held her for a few more minutes, and then he led her inside.

Once inside, Freddie's phone rang. He answered, and he heard Jimmy's voice, "Hey Frank, the guys wanted me to ask if you could hang out for a while after rehearsal tomorrow. There's something we would like to talk about."

"That sounds a bit mysterious."

"Okay, we were wondering, how many songs have you written?"

"Oh, I have a bunch."

"Can you hang with us tomorrow and bring what you have? We want to talk about the future."

Freddie had to smirk when he heard the word future, and then he answered, "I think we can do that."

"Beth can come along if she likes."

"She's been working on something of her own at night, but I'll ask her."

"Okay then, we'll see you tomorrow."

When he got off the phone, Emily asked, "Who was that?"

"It was Jimmy; he wants us to hang out after rehearsal tomorrow."

"You're right for telling him that I have something going on. I want to get back here. Sheryl needs support."

"You know that you're not responsible for her. There are plenty of people here that are helping her."

"They're getting paid to help her, and they can't share with her the feelings that I can. I want to be with her."

"Okay," then Freddie had another thought, "You know it's time that you had your own car. You shouldn't have to be depending on anyone else's schedule."

Emily was a little hesitant, "I would like to be able to come and go as I please, but it has been a long time since I drove; even on our timeline, and I didn't do it very much then."

"Then we'll get you lessons and then get you a car. Consider it another step into this new world."

Emily thought of Sheryl and said, "Yes, yes, I need to be more immersed in this world, and driving in it is one way to do it. Okay, I'll work it into the schedule somehow."

"So what kind of car do you want? How about a Corvette?"

"No, I'm not the sports car type, I don't think. I like those big things that Tommy and his people drive. I think they call them SUVs."

"You want one of those monsters?"

"Yes, I think I would feel safe in one of those, and you sit high up in them."

"Okay, an SUV it is, but for tomorrow, let's arrange for you to be picked up after rehearsal."

Steve returned to his suite, and he and Cathy ordered dinner. Steve could tell by the look on his wife's face that she had something to say. He asked her, "Is there something wrong?"

Cathy had been practicing her speech all day, and she was ready, "Steve, I want to go home. I spend most of my time wandering around here or going shopping. Sarah started sending Ellen around just to give me a companion. Ellen is very nice, but I miss my family and friends, and I especially miss our grandchildren."

Steve put his arms around her and said, "I'm sorry, Cathy. I know I've been ignoring you. You deserve better. You are my sounding board. Discussing the events of the day with you helps me clear my head."

"That has happened very rarely in the past two weeks. You work until all hours, and when you come in, you're exhausted. All you want to do is sleep. I want to make a reservation tomorrow and return to Virginia as soon as I can."

"You're right, but I'm going to miss you terribly."

"I'll miss you too. I'll come back now and then; how's that?"

"That would be great. Yes, go home and give my love to the family."

"Thank you for understanding. I love you."

Barry was on his stool at Stoney's, and things seemed to be calmer than they were the previous week. The conversation was more relaxed, and he was happy to see that the battle lines were less distinct. Jeff came and sat next to him. After a few beers and began talking, "Cindi got a hold of the recording made of Beth Richard's talk with Lieutenant Summers."

"What does she want that for?"

"I don't know, but I hear she decided to take a little drive into Detroit. You know she has some friends on the force in town. She's making a move, so you better be ready."

Cindi Baveroski was making a move. She took with her to Detroit the recording of Emily, as Beth Richards, from her talk with Lieutenant Summers, and one of the cassette tapes and the tape recorder from the evidence locker. She met with a friend of hers who worked in the forensics unit of the Detroit department. She showed her the disk and the tape and asked, "Can you get a voice print from these and compare them?"

Her friend said, "I'm sure glad you brought a recorder; I would have a hell of a time hunting one of them up. Yeah, I can do that, but I have to be careful; people have been on the lookout for off-the-books work. I know I owe you one, so I will get it done."

"Great, let me know what you find out. When I come back to get them, I'll buy dinner."

Cindi returned to Romulus and went through her file. She had been collecting information on Freddie and Emily since Barry asked her to check them out. She had pictures of Freddie and Emily from 1973 and pictures of them as Frank and Beth in 2017. She also had pictures of Freddie's 1973 Plymouth Barracuda, including the license plate. She was able to track the license plate, and it belonged to the Barracuda rented for Freddie MacArthur, the one that was last seen roaring out of that hotel in Detroit on September 16, 1973. She had a picture of the car at the home of Shelly Hicks, along with an SUV that was used by Sarah Hicks Rutherford. This was not a vendetta against Sarah Hicks Rutherford. It was a mystery that she intended to solve, and if she threw a little mud on the old bitch, so much the better.

On Tuesday, the rehearsal went well. Roger made an announcement to the troupe, "We will be moving rehearsal to the Pageant Theater. It's time that we begin to mesh your performance with the staging. They have just about finished the props that we need so we can begin to get the feel of the stage."

This would be a very big deal for Emily. Everyone else in the troupe had experience on stage, but this would be her first time.

Everyone got in their cars and made the drive to the theater. As they drove, Freddie could see that Emily was tense. He tried to relax her with a conversation, "This is Roger's first profession. He did a lot of staging for Barracuda. He was the brainchild for most of those shows that we put on. I never recognized how smart he was then."

"We also didn't know that he could write and that he had such a damn good memory."

"Don't get yourself all tense over being on stage. You'll have plenty of time to get used to it."

Emily just stared out of the windshield and said, "I certainly hope so."

When Emily stepped onto the stage, she nearly panicked. She stared at the rows of seats, and they seemed to go on forever. How could she do this?

Freddie came up behind her, put his arms around her, and said, "You know Roger; he is all business. If he thought you weren't doing a great job, you would have known it a long time ago. You have the talent, and you know the part. You will be fine."

"But I'll be here in front of all of those people. I've never sang at all until a few weeks ago."

"If there is one thing that we should be used to in our lives, it's sudden changes. You were a college student in 1973; now, you're a performer in 2017. You handled that change; this will be a piece of cake."

Roger took over, There will be a spot on the stage designated for you in each of the scenes that you're in. You'll just get to the spot and do your piece. There is one thing that you will be learning if you don't know it already; you will be learning to project. Your voice has to carry to the back row without making it seem like you're yelling.

There is a stack of printouts on the table there. Find the one with your name on it. This will be your homework. You are to study the layouts of each scene and where you are in the scene. Study where you enter and exit the stage; you must know this by heart. You will be doing some of the moving in the dark.

Okay, everyone, look at your printout. We will start at the beginning. No dialog right now. I just want you to look at the information, enter the stage from the proper direction and hit your spot. The scenery isn't in place, so you may not hit it exactly. "Let's go, Frank and Beth; you are first."

The more experienced people knew this was coming. The others were surprised at the level of complexity that was added just by being on stage. The musicians were used to the stage but not having to be so exact with their movements as they needed to be in the acting scenes.

By the end of the day, the idea of performing on stage in front of an audience was becoming very real.

Emily's ride was waiting outside the theater. She kissed Freddie and headed back to the retreat. Freddie and the boys found a good place for dinner and sat down around a big table. Freddie brought out his music. He explained, "I really am stuck in the seventies. All of this writing is in the seventies style."

The band members started to take a look at it, and Jimmy said, "It is not just the seventies style; it is Barracuda style. It's like you wrote it for them. I can't wait to try some of this out."

Freddie asked, "You said you had something that you want to talk over with me. I assume it has to do with our plans after this show is over."

Bobby jumped in, "Yeah, we don't want to be just a tribute band. We can do that if it gets us gigs, but we want to do some fresh stuff."

George came in next, "But we don't want any part of the no-musician music that is around today. Heck, what would we do?"

Freddie's face lit up, and he guessed, "You guys want to bring back real rock and roll!"

Jimmy answered, "You're damn right we do. We're hoping this gig will pump up some interest in real music, and then we'll be ready to fill that need."

George didn't want to be left out, "The tune you did for Beth really sounds great, and we're sure the rest of your work will be great."

Freddie couldn't believe it. It was like these guys read his mind, "I was thinking the same thing. This music without musicians drives me crazy. I mean, there are some good singers, and some have some real style, but I can't stand that droning in the background. Check out what I have. I'm not married to any of it. We can decide together what is good and what doesn't work. If any of you have any of your own music to add, I want to hear that."

Jimmy said, "Great, I guess we better start thinking about putting some of our own time in doing all of that. Frank, will Beth be able to handle you being gone a couple of nights a week?"

"I think she'll be fine with it."

George realized something, "That will be just like the tune."

Freddie asked, "What tune?"

"You know, 'Beth' by Kiss. It's all about a guy staying out late practicing with his band while his girl, Beth, is waiting at home for him."

Freddie had never heard the song, and he didn't know of a band called Kiss. He played it off, "Oh yeah, of course," then he made a mental note to do some studying of rock history. This was like a new start.

Freddie felt energized as he headed for his car. When he reached his car Anita Morales Jefferson was waiting for him. He looked at her and asked, "May I help you?"

Anita answered his question with a question, "You are Frank McAlester, are you not?"

"Yes, and who are you?"

"My, you do look like the late Freddie McArthur. The similarity is quite remarkable. My name is Anita Jefferson, and I'm a reporter for the Romulus Summit."

"I do make my living as a Hollywood look-alike, so, yeah, I look like Freddie MacArthur. If you want a story, let me tell you about the show we're going to put on for KWTZ."

"Yes, I know about the show. I just want you to ask Beth Richards a question for me. I have a feeling that I won't get close enough to ask her myself."

"Beth has been asked plenty of questions. I think she needs a break."

"Indulge an old lady, if you would. After all, I'm not even going to get an answer to my question."

"Okay, what's your question?"

"Just ask her if she has ever had measles."

"That's it?"

"That's it, Mr. McAlester, have a good evening."

When Freddie got home, the retreat was quiet. He was as quiet as he could be coming through the door and getting ready for bed. When he eased himself into bed next to Emily, she asked in a sleepy voice, "How did it go?"

Freddie said quietly, "We don't have to get into all of that now. We'll talk about it in the morning."

Emily seemed to be drifting off again when she said, "Okay."

For some reason, Freddie felt he had to tell her about Anita, "There was one thing, though. When I was leaving, a Spanish lady named Anita Jefferson asked me to ask you if you ever had measles. What a weird question."

Emily's eyes shot open, and she thought, "Oh my God, it's Anita Morales."

Chapter 15: Cindi, Anita, and Mickey

Another month had gone by. It was Thanksgiving, and Sarah gave everyone a week off to be with their families. Sheryl had made great progress. The doctors agreed that Emily's support was a major factor. Jessica Bauman didn't have any family, so she volunteered to take care of Sheryl during the holiday. Emily refused to have them spend Thanksgiving at the retreat, and Shelly was happy to make extra room at her table. Sarah tried to get her mother to take it easy, but she insisted on cooking the meal; she did accept Sarah's help with the preparation and clean up.

It was a grand feast featuring the biggest turkey anyone had ever seen. Around the table were Emily, Freddie, Sarah, Tommy, Shelly, Jessica, and Sheryl. Sarah tried hard, but Tommy would not leave her, and she was secretly happy that he didn't. Shelly was also happy to see Tommy; she loved to watch him gobble up her cooking.

Sarah talked to Emily, "So you have less than three weeks before the premiere. How are you feeling?"

"I'm confident, kind of. I still don't know what it will feel like when the theater is full. At least I've had some experience on the stage with people in the audience. Art Williams, the station manager, brought in several groups representing station sponsors to see a rehearsal. He and the groups left smiling, so I guess we did okay."

Freddie had to jump in, "She did great. She was out there all by herself singing her solo, and the audience loved it."

Emily blushed a bit and said, "I wasn't completely alone. I could hear you playing behind me, and that somehow gave me support."

Sheryl suddenly spoke up, "The turkey is beautiful."

Shelly smiled and said, "Thank you, Sheryl; eat as much as you like."

Sheryl looked around, taking in the familiarity of a family home. She spoke to no one in particular, "This is a home. This is where people live."

Jessica responded to her, "Yes, this is Ms. Shelly Hicks' home. Her family has lived here for many years."

Sheryl kept looking around and talking, "Yes, those were years I didn't see."

Emily responded this time, "That's right. They were also the years that Freddie and I didn't see. Shelly is my mother, and this is her home. We will go back to our home soon."

"That's not a home," Sheryl contradicted, "that is pretty, but it is a place to stay, not a place to live. It is not a home."

Now it was Shelly's turn to respond, "Then why don't you stay here?"

"Mom," Sarah was surprised by her mother's offer.

Emily defended the idea, "Why not. I think Steve and the scientists have gotten all they need from her. Mom has room for Jessica and Sheryl."

Sarah tried to explain, "We have an agreement with the clinic. Sheryl is to be supervised by their doctor until they determine if she is ready to be released. Doctor Stiller can't supervise her progress if he isn't here."

Jessica spoke up, "I can give the doctor updates. I believe he is quite pleased with her progress, and I believe this setting will be more conducive to her recovery. I'm sure this is a setting that feels more normal to her. I can understand if you have other reasons for objecting, but I think it would be good for Sheryl."

Sarah looked at Emily and said, "Sheryl will no longer be a walk down the footpath from you. If you want to see her, you will have to come here."

Emily answered, "I'll be able to do that soon. I think I'm ready to do my own driving, and I can't wait to take my new car out. I'll be happy to stop by regularly."

Shelly saw the win-win in this arrangement, "Not only would I have two friends to keep me company, but I would also have my Emily coming home more often."

Freddie had to make a statement, "Everyone has discussed the pros and cons of this idea, but no one has asked Sheryl."

Shelly looked at Sheryl from across the table and asked, "Would you like to stay here with Jessica and me?"

Sheryl smiled and said, "Yes, I would. I would be in a home."

Shelly had the final word, "That settles it then. She will live here."

Then she pointed at Sarah and scolded her, "And there will be no more back talk from you."

Sarah just smiled. Shelly Hicks is one of the very few people in the world that would dare to talk to Ms. Sarah Hicks Rutherford that way.

Later Emily asked Sarah, "I had to sneak out of the police station last month because reporters were waiting outside, but I never had that problem again. Did you do something?"

Sarah answered, "I made some adjustments to your security. I guess they worked."

"I guess they did. Well, almost."

"What do you mean, almost?"

"About a month ago, Freddie was stopped by a woman, and he was asked to ask me if I ever had measles. Sarah, it was Anita."

Sarah was surprised, "Anita Morales Jefferson was here in Romulus? What would she be doing here?"

Now Emily was confused, "I guess she became a reporter; that's what we both said we would do."

Sarah tried to explain, "I wanted to tell you about Anita, but I didn't know how you would react. Anita realized your dream. She became an award-winning journalist. She did some amazing work in war zones ducking bullets and getting the stories. I don't know what would bring her back here."

Emily was thoughtful, and then she said, "Maybe it was me."

At the MacArthur home in Virginia, Cathy put on an equally impressive spread for a holiday. Eric and Steve Junior were there with their families. Dorothy and Richard made the trip with their families. It was a grand gathering.

Everyone talked, laughed, and ate mightily. The main subject was the progress of the research. Steve explained, "We are ready to report that we have our first-ever encounter with a tachyon field. We don't know if the time distortion is a constant effect of the field or if the Earth's gravity well or atmosphere contributed to the phenomenon. We believe if we had data from one more source, then we could write a report."

Steve Junior applauded, "That is incredible, Dad. This is history-making stuff."

"But not Nobel Prize stuff. At least not yet."

Eric said, "Wait until NASA gets that new orbital telescope up; then, we may be able to detect all sorts of things."

Steve almost choked on his turkey. Cathy had to ask him if he was alright. Steve answered, "Physically, I'm fine, but intellectually I'm a total idiot. Not only am I a total idiot, but I have been working with a highly-rated group of Ph.D. total idiots."

Cathy was amused by Steve's response, and she prodded him, "Why are you and your fellow scientists total idiots?"

"Because we have had our heads buried in the sand of particle physics for the last several weeks, and we totally forgot about other angles. No one has contacted NASA to see what information they might have. I don't know what they could have from back in 1973, but I would expect they would have picked up something on September 16th of this year."

Eric asked, "Wouldn't we have heard about it if they did?"

Steve answered, "They may not want to talk about it if they couldn't figure it out. I've got to call Sarah and see if she can pull some strings."

Cathy tried to calm Steve down a bit, "We will be talking to Sarah in a few minutes. Eric has sent up a Skype connection, and we'll be calling at seven-thirty."

When seven-thirty came, the screens came on, and there were introductions all around. After Dorothy's grandchildren were introduced, Sarah immediately extended the college support offer to them.

Dorothy was surprised, and she responded, "That is a wonderful offer, but we have plans in place for them."

Sarah wouldn't take no for an answer, "This isn't charity; Steve and his sons would not take payment for their research work. This is the payment they would have received. Please accept it with our appreciation."

Dorothy acquiesced, "Thank you, but now I need to do something to help."

Steve jumped in, "You can be our liaison to NASA in Florida."

Sarah asked, "Do we need a liaison to NASA?"

"I believe we will. Eric reminded me that NASA is probably sitting on information about an event on September 16th. I am going to contact them tomorrow. Dorothy lives down there in Florida. If we need someone down there to talk to them, it would be nice if it was someone who knew the true reason for the query."

"Could NASA be the final confirmation that you and your staff are looking for?"

"Yes, if we have that, I believe we could publish."

"That's a fabulous idea, kudos to Eric for bringing it up."

Eric didn't say anything. He didn't think he deserved the credit for that one.

Shelly complained, "We meet these nice people, and all you do is talk business."

Sarah laughed and said, "Okay, Mom, I'll get out of the way."

Dorothy brought her children and grandchildren back to the front. This was the first time they saw their Uncle Freddie. Freddie stood in front, and they all told him how happy they were to see him. Then ten-year-old Matthew said, "I watched your concert videos. You play a kick-ass guitar."

His mother yelled, "MATTHEW," and everyone laughed.

It was clear to everyone that Freddie was looking at Dorothy when he said, "I wonder where he got that from."

Cindi Baveroski had her holiday meal with her brother, his family, and her mother. She enjoyed being with her family, but her mind was somewhat preoccupied. She kept wondering why it was taking her Detroit friend so long to analyze the voice prints. She was convinced of what the results would be, and she had been thinking about how to use the information. Could she just come right out and accuse Beth Richards of being Emily Hicks. That didn't sound like a good idea. There had to be a better way.

The dinner conversation eventually came around to the Betty Ann Rother case. Cindi's nephew asked, "Aunt Cindi, does Beth Richards look as much like Emily Hicks as they say she does?"

Cindi answered by saying something she didn't believe, "Well, she is a professional look-alike. She spent a lot of time trying to look like Emily Hicks."

Her brother Mike observed, "It's interesting that she ended up being such a friend of Sarah Hicks Rutherford."

"She said that was because she reminded Ms. Rutherford, so much of her sister."

Mike didn't buy his sister's defense of Beth Richards, "Cindi, give me a break, I have never heard you tow the department line when you think there is something going on, and I know you think something's going on."

Her nephew jumped back in, "Come on, Aunt Cindi, give us something good."

"I don't have anything good to tell you. I have had nothing to do with the Rother case since October."

Cindi's sister-in-law had been quiet. Now she spoke up, "I have something, well not any real information really, but I know that Anita Morales Jefferson is really interested in Beth Richards. I have a friend that temps at the Romulus Summit. The story I get is when Anita Morales Jefferson saw a picture of Beth Richards and she had to know what was going on."

Cindi responded, "That was a while ago. As far as I know, no one connected with Richards has been approached by the media. It seems Ms. Rutherford pulled some strings and shut it down."

Mike got back into the conversation, "You don't shut down Anita Morales Jefferson. She can use her three-name label quite well, and she is really smart. She's had warlords threaten to behead her, and she still got the story. She's not done yet; I would bet you on that."

Cindi's mother spoke in a deep and resentful tone, "Please stop mentioning that Rutherford woman's name at my table."

Cindi thought, "I think my family just gave me my next move."

Anita Morales Jefferson was not sitting on her hands. She knew going at the principles in the story would be met with major obstruction. She was also in no hurry to show her hand. She saw plenty of other paths to obtain information. She focused on SHR Laboratories when she heard that Steve MacArthur had joined SHR and he was working closely with Sarah in the Detroit area. She put out feelers for any SHR activity in the Detroit area, and she got a hit.

She was led to Rebeca and Nick Michaels. She sat in their living room on the day after Thanksgiving, and Nick was telling her, "Yeah, they gave me five hundred bucks just to get us to go to the old house where we lived when I was a kid and to look at a dog."

Anita was taking notes while she asked, "And you now believe the dog in your backyard is Skipper, a dog that disappeared forty-four years ago?"

Rebeca insisted, "It is Skipper. He came right to me the first time I saw him." Then she said, "Come into the backyard. Skipper is a good dog; he won't hurt you."

Anita had a bullet just missing her head; she wasn't worried about a dog. She followed them. Rebeca stopped and dug into a box in the back of the closet and pulled out a paper. She said, "I will show you."

They went into the backyard, and Skipper happily pranced up to meet them. Rebeca pointed, "Look at his collar. Do you see his name written on the dog's collar?"

"Yes, I see it."

"Nicky wrote that on his collar when he was little. I will swear to that in any courtroom. Now, look at this old paper. You see the date. This was Nicky's spelling test. You see, the writing is the same."

Anita stared at the evidence, and she was amazed. She asked, "And Skipper had disappeared early on the morning of September 16, 1973?"

"Yes," Nick said, "I will never forget it. I heard him barking, and I got out of bed. I looked out the window and saw this blue light. Skipper ran into it, and there was a white flash, and he was gone."

Anita was furiously taking notes. She deduced, "I suppose you told people about this, and they didn't believe you."

"I told the police; not only didn't they believe me, but they also didn't care. They were too busy trying to find that rock star, Emily Hicks and Sheryl Ferguson."

Anita had to stop writing for a moment. Then she said, "Sheryl Ferguson, I forgot about her. Her husband killed her that night. That was one heck of a night."

Rebeca said, "My husband knew Paul Ferguson. He always said that he was a mean bastard, but he didn't think that he would kill anyone. And Paul claimed he didn't do it right up till the day he died. They never found her body or even a hint as to where she could have gone."

Anita closed her notebook and said, "Well, thank you very much. You have given me all that I needed."

Nick asked, "Then you believe us? You believe that is really Skipper?"

"Yes, I do, Nick; I may also believe Paul Ferguson's claims."

Anita left the Michaels' home and headed straight to the Allen Park police station. When she asked if she could see the records for September 16th, she got a surprising answer. The desk sergeant told her, "That is a very popular date, especially this year, for some reason."

Anita asked, "Really, who else was asking about it?"

"A retired Romulus detective named Batali. I think he is working for SHR Laboratories now."

Anita noted that and then moved to the records. The records put her on the same path that Barry followed. A chat at the Sandburg Psychiatric Clinic sent her to the Lakeside Retreat. It was late afternoon when she drove up to the locked gate and pressed the button. She stated her business when requested, "I would like to speak to Sheryl Ferguson."

There was a slight pause, and then the voice said, "I'm sorry, but we have no one by that name staying with us."

"Then I would like to speak to a representative of SHR Laboratories."

"Madam, this is a retreat for people that need rest. It isn't a scientific facility."

"In that case, SHR Laboratories is in deep trouble. If they are not using this facility, then they are guilty of fraud and breach of contract regarding the mutual provider contract they signed with the Sandburg Psychiatric Clinic. So which is it, Mr. Gatekeeper? Is SHR Laboratories at this address, or are they fraudulent? Do I have to come back with the police to find out what happened to Sheryl Ferguson?"

"Sheryl Ferguson is recovering from a severe trauma and cannot be disturbed."

"At least that answer is more honest. I will leave for now, but I will demand that SHR Laboratories make her available to me very soon, or I might assume the worst is happening to her."

"Who is doing the query?"

"Anita Morales Jefferson of the Romulus Summit and tell Ms. Rutherford that it's the girl she used to call her second little sister."

Anita turned around and started back down the long drive when she saw a silver Cadillac Escalade approaching. The sun was at the proper angle to allow her to see it was a young lady behind the wheel. It was a young lady with a very familiar face. She slowed and slid her window down. She could see that the woman had her window down also. Anita nudged her car so that it forced the Escalade to maneuver around her, and then she slowed. When the Escalade slowed to get around her, she yelled, "EMILY," out of the window.

The Escalade stopped for a second, and Anita could see the reaction on the young woman's face, and that was all she needed to know. She pulled away, and the Escalade picked up speed towards the gate.

As Anita drove away, her feelings were boiling over. Tears were in her eyes, and her heart was racing. She had just convinced herself of the impossible, and she was trying to deal with the implications. Her dearest friend from her childhood had returned, but in a way that makes her story Pulitzer material if it could be proven.

In a small hotel and casino well off the strip in Las Vegas, Mickey Hardstone sat on a stool drinking a beer. His manager came in and sat beside him. Mickey was not at all happy with him, and he started right in on him, "Oh, look, there is the smartest manager in the business. He cleverly got his client booked at probably the worst venue that has ever existed in Vegas."

Sammy Litzsinger replied, "Hey, it's Vegas, isn't it?"

"It's part of Vegas that only drunks and losers see. They're barely paying me enough to cover my bar bill."

"Look, Mickey, it's the best I can do, okay? If you think you can find someone that can do better, then cut me loose."

"Well, you certainly can't do any worse. What do you want from me?"

"I just got a hold of a copy of a recording. It is a rehearsal for a Barracuda tribute play being done in Romulus, Michigan."

"So, do you think they would pay me to show up? Who's putting it on?"

"It's a local radio station, KWTZ."

"It's a local radio station? How are they going to pay in coupons for the carwash?"

"No, Mickey, you've got to listen to this. There is a buzz starting about this little play. They say they have two look-alikes from Burbank. They look just like Freddie MacArthur and Emily Hicks, and the music is freaking amazing. Just listen to it."

"Wait a minute," Mickey had a realization, "Romulus, that's where both of those bitches were from, both Hicks and Betty Eveready. I don't want any part of that place. They're the ones that killed Barracuda."

"Mickey, just listen to the damn recording. The buzz is that this play may be picked up on the circuit. How would you like a steady gig? How would you like to tour again?"

"Tour, I haven't done that in over thirty years."

"Listen to the recording, Mickey. They may just need a little push to get them out of that Detroit suburb and on the road, and your name may be all that they need."

Sammy left the bar. Mickey got the recording on his phone, and he sat in a booth in the back of the bar and listened. When he heard Freddie talking, he said out loud, "Holy shit! That's my boy. That's my brother. That's Freddie!"

He listened to the dialog and especially the music, and he was blown away. It was like he was listening to a Barracuda practice session from forty-four years ago. Then he heard them talking about the original song written by a guy named Frank McAlester. A girl began to sing the song. He listened, and he listened, and then he once again spoke to no one, "Wait a minute. Wait a damn minute. That is no original damn song. Freddie wrote that song. These people are going to pay."

He got out his phone and called Sammy. Sammy answered, and Mickey said, "I'm going to Romulus, Michigan. I will do the gig tonight and then tell them I got the plague or something. And find a Michigan lawyer, one of those guys that gets paid if they win."

Sarah had greased the wheels that allowed Steve's introduction to NASA to be met with a receptive attitude. He was put in touch with the team, examining the data on what they were calling the event. They passed data to each other over a secure link. The NASA data confirmed the movement of the anomaly, and it added more information about the anomaly's reaction to Earth's gravity well. Finally, the NASA scientists had to agree that it was logical to come to the conclusion that they were witnessing a time-distorting tachyon field for the first time in history. They told him that if SHR wrote the report that NASA would support them.

This was such a powerful moment that the SHR scientists had to suck in their breath. They were going to do it. They were going to announce to the world that time distortions are a reality. They still had so many questions. Could someone have gone the other way and gone back in time? There is no reason to think that such a thing should be linear. There was also no reason to think that such a thing could exist, but it did exist.

The scientists were still hyperventilating when Sarah came into the room. She said to all of them, "From the look of astonishment on your faces, I would say something extraordinary happened here recently."

Steve tried to form the words, "Sarah, their data supports our conclusion. The NASA scientists examined our data, and they agreed. They are willing to support any report we write about the anomaly. This is a breakthrough with so many implications. If we can get the hard science done and done right, this could be Nobel Prize stuff!"

"That's fabulous, you all have done an amazing job, and you deserve the Nobel Prize. As for the implications, there are many, but I will not have your work suppressed to avoid dealing with them."

Steve guessed, "You're talking about Emily and Freddie."

"Yes, and Sheryl, the world will have to know who they really are. It will turn their lives upside down again. I can insulate them, but that wouldn't give them the lives they are building. We'll work that out. Write your report, and we'll get it to the world."

As Sarah left the scientists, Emily walked into the science area, looking for her. She was white as a sheet. Sarah took one look at her and asked, "Emily, what's wrong?"

"I just made a terrible mistake. I was driving up the driveway, and a car was coming down."

Sarah interrupted her, "It was Anita."

"Yes, I didn't know who she was. She had her car in the middle of the road, so I slowed down to get around it. When our windows were side by side, she yelled my name, and I reacted. Sarah, she knows it's me."

Sarah started thinking. She told Emily, "It's okay. The time is coming when you will be able to tell the world who you really are."

The thought of doing that made Emily nervous. She asked, "What about the show? What about our friends? We've become close to those people. How are we going to tell them that we've been lying to them this whole time?"

"They will understand."

"We still have time. Anita may feel she knows, but she can't write a story on her feeling."

"What was she doing here?"

"She was looking for Sheryl."

"Then she does know, and she has some proof."

"Not enough. Let me see what I can do. I can stop her if I have to. I probably deal with or have a connection to most of the businesses that advertise in the Romulus Summit. A story won't do her any good if she has nowhere to publish it."

"No," Emily cried, "you can't do that. Anita and I dreamt the dream of breaking the big story together. I can't be a party to crushing her."

"I don't want to. I remember those days, and she remembers. She told the gate guard to remind me that she was my second little sister."

"She was, Sarah, she was. We were always together. Her mom loved me, and Mom loved her. We couldn't have been closer. When we got accepted to different colleges, we were heartbroken. You can't hurt her."

"I doubt the effort would do any good. She is a powerful woman in her own right, and she would probably get around anything I did without breaking a sweat. This puts a time limit on your life as Beth Richards. We need to talk more. Where's Freddie?"

"He's with the band. I don't know how he's going to take this. He has been so happy working with those guys. They are planning to cut an original CD."

"Well, we'll have to talk it all out."

Cindi finally got the results back from her friend, and they were what she expected. She now believed she had everything she needed to expose Beth Richards and Frank McAlester. She wasted no time.

She gathered everything together, and then she called Anita Jefferson. Anita answered the phone, and Cindi got to it, "Ms. Jefferson, this is Detective Cindi Baveroski, and I have some information about Beth Richards that you have to see."

"Well, detective, you must have some skill. I try to make it a bit difficult to get my personal number. What is this information, and why would I be interested?"

"Ms. Jefferson, I know that you have been as curious as I have about the similarities between Beth Richards and your old friend Emily Hicks. Of course, Richards looks exactly like the Emily Hicks of 1973, so that makes this all impossible, or does it?"

"What makes you think the impossible is possible, detective?"

"I don't know how it is possible, but I am convinced that Beth Richards is Emily Hicks, and I have clear proof of that fact."

"What is your proof?"

"I have to show you. Can we meet somewhere where we can sit and talk?"

"How about meeting at Lester's on fourth; they make a great Harvey Wallbanger, and I think I can use one."

"See you there."

The women met, and Cindi laid out what she had. The final thing she brought out was the voice print analysis. Anita was impressed, "Well, you sure did the leg work on this detective. What made you dig into this? Are you part of the team that tracked and caught Betty Ann Rother?"

Cindi embellished a bit, "I was initially, and that got me started. After that, I couldn't let it alone."

"Was the voice print comparison useful to the case?"

"It wasn't part of the case. During the prosecution of the case, we ended up with voice recordings of Emily and Beth, and I was able to get the analysis done."

"Okay, this sounds like off-the-books stuff. I will ask no more about it. May I quote you stating your suspicions in my article?"

"Oh no, I was hoping that I could be an anonymous source."

"You can be. But I'm afraid if I use this material, it won't be hard for people to figure out where it came from."

"I understand; I want this to come to light."

"Okay, detective, it will. This is the icing on the cake, so to speak. I will be putting it all together soon.

As Cindi left the bar, she thought, "Stick that up your ass, Barry Batali."

It was late, and Emily and Sarah surprised Freddie by being up and waiting for him. They told him the situation, and he had to sit down and think about it. He was angry, and he tried to sum it up, "So first, we couldn't use our real identities because everyone would think that we were nuts. So we worked hard to get used to new names and new lives. We've lied to everyone we've met and everyone that we now call a friend. We work hard on doing something we never did before, and now we have to throw all of that away and start over."

Sarah didn't think coddling would help, "That's the way it is, Freddie. Anita will publish the story. I could stop her from doing it at the Summit, but that would only delay her a short time. This is the story of the century. People have traveled through time. An entity has been proven to exist that distorts time and exists at two times simultaneously. Freddie, even if Anita couldn't prove it, we would still have to tell the world."

Emily tried to help, "The only reason we couldn't be ourselves was that no one would believe us. Now they will. We don't have to pretend. We'll work it out with our new friends, and now we can contact our old friends."

Freddie smirked a bit and said, "Are you kidding? We won't be able to do a damn thing. We will be time travelers. We will be hounded everywhere we go."

Sarah was determined that that wouldn't happen, "Not if I can help it."

Freddie was convinced, "I know what it's like. People think rockers hung around hotels drinking and going crazy because that's what we wanted to do. It was the only thing we could do. We couldn't go out and get a burger or go see a baseball game. There was chaos every time we showed our faces in public. You become a prisoner of your own success, I know."

Sarah answered, "I know a bit about that myself, and I also know how to deal with it. Freddie, you wanted your new band to be successful, didn't you?"

"Yeah, of course; I want us to be successful."

"Well, weren't you hoping to return to that prison you were talking about?"

Freddie had to smile, "I guess you got me there."

Emily patted his hand and said, "We'll work it out."

Then she turned to Sarah and asked, "Can you get Anita's personal number; I want to talk to her."

Sarah answered, "Yes, of course, that's the best thing to do. We know that she knows about Sheryl Ferguson. I had Barry contact the Michaels' family; they said Anita had been there, so she also knows about Skipper. In fact, she learned about Sheryl from them. She is very close."

Freddie added, "If she ran into Detective Baveroski, she might have all she needs."

Sarah finished her thought, "And that's why we should make her an offer. She may have enough to prove that the event happened, but she has no information on the event itself. We can give her exclusive rights to report that information. Frankly, without that, her story is an interesting and exciting speculative piece. With that, her story is historic."

Freddie got thoughtful as he said, "Now all we have to do is figure out how to tell everyone at the theater and radio station on Monday if the story doesn't break by then."

Sarah suggested, "Emily, you need to call first thing in the morning."

Freddie added, "I want KWTZ to get in on this somehow."

Joey, "The Jet," Jefferson, former all-pro wide receiver for the Dallas Cowboys and longtime ESPN NFL commentator, finished getting ready for bed and joined Anita in the bedroom. He talked excitedly as he entered, "I've called the girls and told them to get their families here as soon as they can. I want us all together when your story breaks."

Anita was only half listening. She mindlessly answered, "Yeah, that's a good idea."

Joe looked at her and waved his hands, saying, "Hello, Anita Morales Jefferson, the greatest reporter of all time. You are about to break the story on one of the greatest events in the history of the world. You have proven that people have traveled through time. Your own childhood friend has returned. I would think it would warrant a bit more excitement."

"It does, Joe, and I am excited. I guess I'm also a bit in shock. I saw her. I saw Emily. She was as young and as beautiful as she was the last time I saw her. If it happened to her like it happened to the dog, there was a flash, and she skipped forty-four years. Can you imagine that?"

Joe thought about it for a minute and answered, "It must have been very confusing for her. So much has changed, and all of the people she knew are now older or gone."

"I told you about Sheryl Ferguson; it happened to her too. She didn't have the support that Emily did, and she ended up in a psychiatric clinic. She might have spent her entire life there if Sarah's SHR people hadn't found her."

Joe put his arms around Anita and said, "Your story will help them. They won't have to hide who they are."

Anita said, "It will also make them media fodder. They won't be able to go anywhere without ambitious younger versions of me right on their heels."

"That happens, Anita; it's happened with every story you have ever written. This is a Pulitzer waiting to happen. If you don't write this story, someone else will."

"Oh, I'm writing the story. I'm not that soft."

Chapter 16: Impact

Anita's phone rang early Saturday morning. She didn't recognize the number, but she answered it and then she heard the voice that erased forty-four years of time, "Anita, it's me, Emily."

"Emily, oh God, it is you. I knew we would talk sooner or later, and I have been trying to find the words to help me explain why I have to write about you, Freddie, and Sheryl Ferguson."

"You don't have to explain. We talked so many times about being big-time reporters and breaking the big story. I am actually happy that it is you that will do it."

Anita tried to hold back the tears, "This was your dream also, and it was taken from you."

"It wasn't taken, only delayed. I can still do it; U of M is still there."

"It won't be easy. I am about to take away your anonymity; you won't be able to do anything easily."

"You forget the reach of our big sister."

"How is Sarah? After you disappeared, we lost touch. We just couldn't look at each other without thinking of you. I'm happy that she did so well."

"She is very happy for you also. Anita, we would like to talk about how all of this will happen."

"You can't stop it."

"Oh, we know that, and we wouldn't want to try. We want to give you the other side of the story. We want to give you the answer to how this happened, and that will make your story historic. The SHR scientists are doing all of their work right here at the retreat, and we would like to offer you exclusive rights to publicize their findings. It is really quite remarkable. Can you come here? Sarah and I can't wait to see you."

"Yes, I would love to talk it over and see you both again. I can be there by noon."

"Great, we'll have lunch. It will be cheeseburgers and tacos."

"You remembered our favorite meal. Your mom would make the cheeseburgers, and my mom would make the tacos."

Anita was there at noon, and there were plenty of hugs and tears to go around. Then Anita looked at Freddie and said, "Freddie MacArthur, the maestro of the screaming guitar; I had a poster of you on my wall for years."

Amazingly Freddie blushed a bit, and he said, "From what I hear, you're one badass reporter. I should have your poster on my wall."

Everyone laughed, and they sat down to eat. They did some catching up before getting down to business. Freddie was excited to hear who Anita was married to, "You're married to Joey "The Jet" Jefferson? Man, I sure would like his autograph."

Anita said, "Well, he isn't much of a jet anymore, and he will be thrilled to know you're a fan. We'll get one right to you."

Sarah started, "Anita, you are about to break one of the greatest stories in history. We can help you make it even greater, and all we want is a little consideration."

"I don't need any incentive for that, Sarah. You are family, and I wasn't going to drop this like a bomb, though there is one person that wished that I would. "

Sarah guessed, "You talked to Detective Cindi Baveroski."

Anita couldn't confirm that statement, "I can't reveal my sources. I wasn't going to bring this story to anyone without talking to you first. I had all of those brothers, and I was the only girl in the family. You two were like my sisters."

Freddie had to ask, "What was with the measles question?"

Emily answered, "When we were eight, we got measles at the same time. We were out of school, and no one could play with us. Anita lived three blocks over, so our mothers took turns shuttling us from one house to the other so we could play together. After that, we were inseparable. We were best friends from then on."

Anita said, "She is being modest and not telling the whole story. We had just moved to the neighborhood from Texas. We had only been in the United States for a few years. My English was barely understandable, and most of the kids made fun of me. Emily never did, and she was one of the few in school that tried to break the language barrier to be my friend. The Hicks family was the first family to really welcome the Morales family to the neighborhood. I will never forget that. I would never hurt the Hicks family, so I want to do this the best way we can."

Sarah smiled and said, "That's wonderful, and believe me, what we can give you will take your story to the next level. We just need you to delay the release for a few days."

Freddie added, "We need to have KWTZ in the loop somehow."

Anita was thankful, but she was also mindful of business, "Only after the fact. I still require exclusive rights to the story. How about this? After I break the story, I will go to KWTZ and sit down with their news staff. They can be the first to interview me."

Freddie was very happy with that idea, "That will be great."

Anita was now down to business, "Can you tell me a bit of what your scientists have found? I would like some idea in terms that I will understand before I talk to them."

Sarah explained in general what they had found, and Anita said, "I won't be delaying just for you. I will need a least a week to get all of this new information down, collate it with what I have, and create a coherent presentation. I won't be putting anything out until then."

Emily added, "There is another whole story. That's the tragic story of Sheryl Ferguson. Her story deserves to be told. Her husband died in prison because everyone thought that he killed her."

"Yes, I know, and I haven't forgotten about her. This is all too big for one story, and Sheryl's story will be told as part of the series."

"She's staying with my mom in our house on Craig Street."

Anita got far more than she needed from the scientists. They asked her to emphasize that they were just writing the initial report and that none of this had even been recognized as a theory. Anita agreed.

When she left, Sarah, Emily, and Freddie took a breath. Freddie said, "I'm sure glad that it worked out so well. It's great that you all were such good friends."

Emily's smile was soft a melancholy, "It was great seeing her again, but it also reminded me one more time about how much I've missed. Just like I missed Sarah's climb to success, I also missed hers. She's now old enough to be my grandmother; in fact, she is a grandmother."

Freddie agreed, "That is one thing about this that we can't change. Forty-four years are gone. I felt it when I looked into my brother's face and into Rick's face. We will always have reminders of that fact."

The weekend went by, and Emily and Freddie were trying hard to find the words to explain to their friends what was about to happen. During the first half of the week, they thought they knew what they would say, and then it was hard for them to keep it to themselves until they got the word from Anita.

On Thursday night, Anita called and told them that she would present the story to the Summit the next day. The story was so big that she was sure the Summit would want another day to prepare for the coming onslaught. Friday morning, they set out a bit early and stopped at the radio station. They asked for a meeting with Tony and Art.

Everyone sat down, and Art asked, "Is there something we can do for you? Is there a problem with the show?"

They decided that Freddie would start the discussion, "No, the show is going great. It was a super idea to put this together. We want to talk about something that is going to happen tomorrow. When it happens, it is going to put KWTZ in the middle of a, not a national, but a global spotlight."

Art was shocked, but Tony wasn't. He smiled and said, "Someone finally proved it, didn't they?

And Freddie wasn't surprised at Tony's reaction, "Yes, and your dad was never wrong. He had us made from day one."

Art was getting frustrated, "Will someone please tell me what the hell you're talking about."

Freddie just came out with it, "Art, we are Freddie MacArthur and Emily Hicks. We couldn't say so before because no one would have believed us. Now the scientists of SHR Laboratories have proof of the existence of the anomaly that brought us here from 1973. Anita Morales Jefferson has exclusive rights to the story, and she will release it to the Summit management today."

"Holy shit, we've been working with time travelers? We have been sitting on the solution to one of the greatest mysteries in U.S. history. Is this real, or are you guys just jerking me around for some reason."

Emily finally spoke up, "Oh, it's real, Mr. Williams, and there is a lot more to it. Anita has exclusive rights to the story, but she has agreed to sit down with your news department after the release and give you her first interview on the subject."

Freddie came back in, "We are obligated to keep this quiet until the story breaks, but we wanted you to have time to prepare. Of course, if you want the interview, you will have to keep this quiet."

Art was trying not to hyperventilate, "Ah, yes, we can do that. I'll need to get Bernie and Lisa briefed; they won't say anything until the time comes. I also have to call corporate, but I won't do that until the story breaks. Okay, I need to formulate a plan. This town is about to be overrun."

Tony said, "We need to talk to Roger. This is going to either make the whole play overtaken by events or it may make it a world premiere right at the little Pageant Theater."

As they were leaving their meeting, they heard yelling in the hall. They turned the corner, and Freddie almost ran directly into Mickey Hardstone. Mickey stared at him for a second and said, "Well, they must have done some work on you back in Burbank. You look just like Freddie. Well, you may look like Freddie, but you're not Freddie, and you're not stealing his damn songs."

Freddie looked at his old friend and asked, "Mickey, what the hell are you talking about? The band is a Barracuda tribute band; their purpose is to play all of the Barracuda songs."

"I'm not talking about those songs. You know damn well what I'm talking about. I'm talking about "I'm Waiting for Tomorrow," you claim it's an original that you wrote. I know for a fact that you're full of shit. Freddie showed me the first two verses of that song after our Denver concert. I asked him to write a few ballads for our next album. I've got a lawyer, and I'm going to sue your ass off."

Mickey was surprised when Freddie just smiled and said, "Yeah, I know you wanted some ballads. What you said was that the times were changing, and the band couldn't survive on hard rock alone. You said with the end of the war; people were ready to mellow out a little. You were always the smartest one in the band."

Mickey yelled, "How the hell do you know that? I never told anyone that, and I know Freddie didn't either. We were waiting until after the tour to talk to the guys about it."

Freddie put his arm around Mickey and said, "Come with us, Mickey, we're going to the theater. On the way, we have to tell you a little story."

Mickey was in shock when they arrived, and Freddie was trying to think how he could bring what's left of Barracuda into the show. After Freddie gave the talk, the same shock rolled through the members of the troupe. Roger threw the script down and yelled in exasperation, "What the hell are we going to do now?"

"If this is true, and it better be for your sake, then this play is a moot point. There is no tragedy. There are no lost people."

Freddie countered, "Are you kidding, Roger? There is a tragedy here. Emily and I lost forty-four years.

This is going to be a major draw. Everyone is going to want to see the time travelers. What they will witness is the rebirth of rock and roll, and it will be your play that will make it happen."

"Yeah," Mickey said dejectedly, "with the original young Freddie MacArthur and a new young Barracuda band."

Freddie turned to Mickey, "I've been thinking about that."

Then to Roger, he said, "Can't we add an encore; I'm sure one will be demanded? It will be a surprise encore. The lights will go down, and when they come back up, the band will be on stage along with all of the surviving members of Barracuda. We could start with Mickey singing 'A Dark Night for Walking,' and then we give them a rocking finish with 'She's Got the Devil in Her.'"

Roger thought about it and said, "That just may work. It's up to you guys to get coordinated. You only have two weeks, so you better get Rick in town as soon as you can."

Freddie said, "We will need Rick and Ryan in town."

Roger and Mickey stared at him, and he just said, "It's a long story, and Rick should tell it."

The members of the band finally got over their shock enough to speak. Pete was just amazed, "You are telling me that I've been going head to head on lead guitar with the great Freddie MacArthur?"

"I don't know about great. I don't think I was around long enough for that title, but you did, and you did great. You're damn good on the axe Pete."

"So what now," Jimmy asked, thinking all of their plans had just vaporized.

"So get ready; this is going to be a hell of a ride. We will need to do a lot of talking, but you guys aren't out. In fact, you are in, way in. The next two weeks will tell us just what will happen next."

The article was published, and it hit the world like a hammer. The suburban city was invaded by every news organization on the planet. Sarah tried her best to gear up for the assault on SHR Laboratories. Stock in her companies shot up. Even completely unrelated companies, like cosmetics, thrived.

Sarah hired an army of security people to keep the mobs off everyone working on the show. It was hard for everyone to focus in the crazed environment. Several decided to camp out in the theater instead of dealing with the mobs.

Shelly Hicks, Sheryl Ferguson, and Jessica Bauman now had round-the-clock protection, and Sarah even compensated her mother's neighbors for the constant traffic jam on the small street. Sheryl's recovery accelerated in Shelly's house, and Dr. Stiller was ready to sign the release forms.

The Pageant Theater was way overbooked, and Tony tried to keep some of the focus on KWTZ. Amazingly enough, the station's sudden fame just shifted the focus of the local management's fear. Their news crew was the first to talk to Anita. They also had interviews with Freddie and Emily. The news world praised their work, and now corporate was thinking maybe the station should have an all-news format. There was only one thing that would change their minds, and that was the show.

The theater would be filled to capacity. There were plenty of network news people, and some of those people were music and dramatic critics. They were there to see Freddie MacArthur and Emily Hicks, but it did put them in their seats. If they could be impressed, then the show may take on a life of its own.

It was opening night. The radio station's parent company had negotiated with NBC to cover the performance live. Emily had been nervous about performing in front of a few hundred local people. Now she would start the show in front of a jammed packed theater of notable professionals and maybe a billion people watching from around the world. She thought, "This is a hell of a thing for an amateur with an adequate voice to be doing." She almost panicked, but when the time came, she took her spot. The curtain went up, and the crowd roared when they saw Freddie MacArthur sitting alone on the stage. He played and sang, *"It's a dark night for walking; nothing is going my way. A dark night for walking; it's time to walk away."*

Emily swallowed hard as the light shined on her. The crowd roared again when Emily appeared. Freddie continued to play, and Emily sang, *"It's a dark night for walking; the flags have all been furrowed. A dark night for walking; I think I'll walk out of this world."*

The lights went down, and everyone took their places for the first scene. Then it was time for the band to take their places for the

Chicago concert. The lights went down, and they moved to their spots. They started with "Wrecking Ball". It was hard for Rick Santora to watch from backstage. Bobby Deeds on bass, as Rick, stumbled around until George Fisher, on the keyboard, pretended to whisper something to him. They followed up with "Backstab," and when the lights went down, the applause was so loud that they had to hold the lights down an extra minute so the performers in the next scene could be heard.

Roger's adaptation of the events had been kind to Rick. Everyone knew what happened that night, but he kept the focus more on the dynamics going on in the band.

The scenes went on, and the band brought the house down again with their depiction of the Detroit concert. They purposely left out "A Dark Night for Walking" and "She's Got the Devil in Her."

The midpoint of the show was Pete's big part. He stepped out on the stage, plugged in, and the dueling guitar segment started. By the time both musicians raised their arms in the air, the audience was on their feet. When the music stopped, the applause didn't.

Then it was time for Emily to take the stage. By this time, everyone knew that she would be performing a forty-four-year-old but brand new song written by Freddie MacArthur. She tried to keep herself steady and to remember the hours of rehearsal. She ran behind a cardboard car, and the lights went down. A spotlight is shown on Emily at center stage and a dimmer one on Freddie on upper stage right. He began to play, and Emily started, "I'm waiting for tomorrow; today was not my day. *I'm waiting for tomorrow, when things may go my way. Today started so brightly, but it didn't turn out right. Tomorrow there's a chance, and maybe I will dance."*

The song continued, and the audience was hushed. When the lights went down again, the theater remained quiet. Emily thought, "Oh God, they hated it."

As the lights came back up, the applause started, and it grew thunderous to the point that the scene couldn't continue until everyone quieted down.

Emily and Freddie closed the show the way they opened it, and the audience was on their feet. The cast came out to take a bow, and the audience remained standing and applauding. They left the stage, and Roger made an announcement from backstage, "Ladies and gentlemen, the show isn't over. We have a special treat for you. The band will once again take the stage, and Freddie will lead onto the stage to join the band, the surviving members of Barracuda. Welcome, Mickey Hardstone, Rick Santora, and Ryan Witowski!"

The crowd went crazy as the original members took the stage. Mickey still had his voice, and he sang the full version of "A Dark Night for Walking," and when the band went into "She's Got the Devil in Her," the audience was on their feet, moving to the music.

When it was over, the rest of the cast joined them on stage, and the ovation went on for minutes. Emily had never had such a thrill. She was so excited she could feel her heart fluttering.

The curtain went down, and everyone just jumped in the air, amazed at the feeling they were experiencing. Even Ryan was smiling. Freddie slapped Rick on the back, and he said, "I told you that they would accept you."

Rick was still feeling funny about the whole thing, "Yes, it was good, but they are giving me a pass, and I'm here to enjoy this moment. Sheila Ferretti isn't here. She hasn't been here to enjoy any moments since that night."

"Rick, you paid for your sins, and you came out and did good things with your life. I know you will never forget her, but you have been punished enough."

Sarah came in with Tommy and hugged Emily, and said, "I told you. You're heading for Broadway."

Emily was a bit sober about the whole thing, "I don't know. I wish I could have done it as Beth Richards. Now I'll never know if they were applauding my performance or the time traveler."

Roger said, "You will know soon. New York critics were in the audience, and they promised to write a review. They aren't swayed by anyone's fame. They will give it to you straight."

Sarah came back into the conversation, "I don't know what they're going to say, but I asked Tim to watch the NBC presentation, and he just texted me. He said the NBC poll so far rates the show as a hit 88% to 12%. No politician ever got numbers like that out of NBC. The people loved it."

Just like on Broadway, everyone moved to a large banquet room at the Hyatt and waited for the reviews. Sarah had everything ready, with an open bar and enough food to outlast World War III. It was a grand all-night party that did go a little overboard now and then, but everyone survived in style.

The reviews came in the next morning. All of the local papers did nothing but sing their praises; then came the reviews from New York. Roger read the reviews out loud, "It was a very emotional night with Emily Hicks and Freddie MacArthur on stage. I was thrilled to see them. As for the play itself, it was an amateur undertaking; I could easily pick out a hundred technical flaws. Lines were mumbled at times, and now and then someone seemed lost, but all in all, it was well done for what it was. Roger Mendez's story was said to be accurate, and accuracy is generally the bane of drama. However, the story did flow, and the music came in at good spots. I would say "The Last Days of Barracuda" will not be the last days of Barracuda or of this play. It's a crowd pleaser, and I'm happy for it."

Roger went on to the next review, "It was a special night. Of course, everyone was there to see MacArthur and Hicks. It isn't every day that you can see two-time travelers. Clearly, people were there more to be part of history than to be entertained, but there was a show to sit through. Though it was more like dinner theater than Broadway, it wasn't all bad. The energy of the music certainly was a plus. I would expect at least a limited revival of old rock and roll, and frankly, I welcome it. It will be good to hear musicians play again, even if it is the overly loud type. The acting was, well, at the level, you would expect, but it was very good for that level. The surprise was that Emily Hicks had a passable voice. The song she sang was written by Freddie MacArthur in 1973, and it was delivered not in Broadway style but with great feeling. It was haunting, considering what happened to them. I believe the show should go on, not as a Broadway play, but as a hometown-type production. I'm sure there are plenty of theaters around the country that would benefit from the performance."

The show would go on. KWTZ was flooded with requests for bookings. Their business department wasn't equipped to handle the rush. Whitford Talent Agency could not imagine the gold mine they discovered when they were bribed by Sarah to take on two unknown people that happened to really look like Freddie MacArthur and Emily Hicks. They happily worked with KWTZ to handle some of the bookings.

The show wouldn't be the same. The next morning, actually, it was closer to afternoon, everyone met in the same banquet room for brunch. They were thankful that Sarah had her army of security people on duty. There were people straining the barriers in all directions, looking for autographs and statements.

At brunch, it was clear there would not be a special encore in the show. Ryan announced first, "This was great. I didn't believe I would ever see Freddie again. The truth is I never thought I would see Mickey and Rick either. It was a special time, but I have to get back home. There's a storm moving in up in the mountains, and if I don't get there before it hits, it could be weeks before I see my family again."

Mickey couldn't believe it, "That's it. We have a new train to ride, and you're not getting on board?"

Ryan tried to explain, "It's not my ride anymore, Mickey. This is not the life I want. I have everything I want at home, and I want to get back there."

Rick spoke, "I'm also going home. It's time for me to head back to Virginia. What's ahead for you scares me. That life nearly destroyed me, and I'm not going to give it a second chance."

While everyone else sat and talked excitedly about the future, Sarah got a call. It was from her mother, "Sarah, dear, something has happened to Sheryl. She just collapsed while watching the news. She is on the way to the hospital."

Sarah found the news disturbing. She worried about Sheryl, but she also worried about her mother and her sister. She stepped away to make some calls, and Emily asked, "Sarah, is something wrong?"

Sarah replied, "It's okay; we'll talk about it later. I'll be right back."

Out in the hall, she called Dr. Drexel and asked him to stop by the house and check on her mother. Then she called Steve, "Steve, have you had any indication at all that this tachyon energy is damaging to the human body?"

Steve was puzzled by the question, "No, Dr. Drexel has been working with us, and he hasn't seen any evidence of a problem. Has something happened?"

"Sheryl Ferguson collapsed and is on the way to the hospital. I want a medical staff assembled to look closer into this possibility. Delegate, you have plenty to do, but I want it started."

"I'll see to it. I have an equal vested interest in that effort."

Emily appeared in the hall and asked, "Sarah, what's going on?"

Sarah had to tell her, "Sheryl has collapsed. She's on the way to the hospital."

Emily's first thought was of her mother, "Did Mom see it? How's she doing?"

"She seems okay, but I have Dr. Drexel on the way to check on her."

Emily turned back toward the banquet room, but she clearly wasn't planning to stay there. Sarah asked, "Where are you going?"

"To the hospital. Sheryl needs someone there with her."

"Jessica is with her."

"I want to be there. Sheryl had just begun to live her life again. This is so unfair."

Sarah was relieved that Emily didn't seem to make the connection. Emily didn't think that what was wrong with Sheryl could be wrong with her.

Freddie stood when Emily came in and grabbed her coat and purse. She told him, "Sheryl's been taken to the hospital. I have to be there. Stay here, and you can fill me in on all the news later."

Sarah gave Tommy a nod toward Emily, and Tommy got on his phone. Emily had an escort led by Tim before she got halfway down the hall. Security made a path, and Emily hurried into a waiting SUV.

When Emily arrived, she found her mother and Jessica in the waiting room. As she entered, people started staring and quietly speaking her name. Some began to approach her, and they were immediately intercepted by Tim and Larry. Emily called out, "I'm sorry, but please, not now."

She went to her mother, and Shelly Hicks was visibly shaken. She turned to Tim and said, "Find a doctor. I want someone to take a look at my mother now."

Jessica told her, "I've been keeping an eye on her. I think she's doing okay, but I would be happy for another opinion."

At that moment, Dr. Drexel came in and went right to Shelly. He began to check her out, and Emily felt more at ease.

They waited well over an hour, and then a doctor appeared and came to Jessica. Everyone listened to his report, "Ms. Ferguson is resting comfortably. We have sedated her. I'm afraid we as yet don't understand what is happening to her. We gave Ms. Ferguson an MRI, and the results were difficult to fathom. It seems we can't get much of a picture."

Dr. Drexel introduced himself and volunteered, "I'm afraid no internal scans will produce valuable results. Ms. Ferguson is the Sheryl Ferguson that encountered the time distortion field. The tachyon radiation in her body renders the scan useless."

"I see," the doctor said, "then maybe we need the assistance of your team to help this woman."

"Of course, and we will also consult with the SHR physicists when necessary."

That was the moment that Emily was hit with the implication. She asked Dr. Drexel, "If this has to do with the tachyons, does it mean that Freddie and I will get sick also?"

"It's too early to make those kinds of guesses, Ms. Hicks. Let us work the problem."

Emily demanded, "I want to see Sheryl."

The doctor answered, "She is heavily sedated. I don't know if she will be aware of you."

"I'll be with her," Jessica said.

"I know Jessica, but I want to be there too."

KWTZ's parent corporation was overjoyed. The station was now the center of the radio world, and they were rushing people there to capitalize on the newfound fame. Tony described himself with a description that was so old that many people didn't get it, "I'm busier than a one-armed paperhanger."

It was going to take time to get everything organized. The original contracts had everyone getting a percentage of the profit of the show, with Roger getting a major share. No one knew what that would mean. The profit was huge, considering the budget that was used to put the entire show together. Then there was the compensation from NBC for their televising of the show and subsequent reruns. KWTZ corporate did quickly set that deal up, and they would receive a major portion of that windfall, but the station and the principles also got a share.

After a week of what seemed to be chaos, the enterprise began to get organized. People began to receive compensation notices. Jimmy looked at his, and he freaked out, "Holy crap! When we signed on for this show, I thought it might get us a couple of station-promoted gigs and maybe some beer money. Damn, I can buy a Corvette with this payday."

Freddie warned, "This is one payday. We know more are coming, but we have to take a look at our contracts. Fortunately for us, and thanks to Emily, we are backed by one of the most powerful law establishments in the country. We won't be screwed. Still, be careful. I know how quickly big money can go."

There would be negotiations and paperwork. This allowed everyone to take a break for a few weeks. Frank and Beth didn't have that kind of a break. Every news and talk show in the world wanted a piece of them. Sarah offered to get them a top-flight Hollywood agent, but they decided to stick with Amanda Janloan. Amanda was a junior agent at Whitford, and they dumped Freddie and Emily's accounts on her. The company got their money, and they thought it was just a matter of paperwork to prove that Freddie and Emily were legit.

Amanda called Freddie and asked him to put her on speaker so Emily could hear. She said, "Hey guys, that is all so amazing. I feel proud being connected with you, even in this small way."

Freddie answered, "You put in all the right words for us. Without you, we wouldn't have had the proper in, and we may not have gotten this gig. You were more than a small part."

Emily added, "We would like you to continue. There is a lot going on, and we would like you to help us get a handle on it."

Freddie jumped back in, "And that includes the whole band, except Mickey; he has his own agent."

Amanda was thrilled, "I am way down on the totem pole around here. There are far more experienced agents that may be able to help you more."

Freddie asked, "Who was willing to help us when this all started."

Emily answered, "That would be you, Amanda, and we want you now. We know you can do it. Field the offers and order them a bit for us, and we'll let you know what we want to do."

Amanda almost broke out in a giggle, but she controlled herself. She said, "Of course, I'll keep you posted."

When she wasn't going from talk show to talk show, Emily spent time at the hospital. Sheryl had slipped into a coma. Emily just sat there holding her hand. Sarah came in and pulled up a chair next to her sister. Emily asked without taking her eyes off of Sheryl, "What are the doctors telling you?"

Sarah knew it wouldn't do any good to try to hide the truth from Emily, "They are saying it is some form of malignancy. They've never seen anything like it before."

"Then it was caused by the tachyons."

"We don't know for sure, but that is the most likely cause."

"Then Freddie and I could be next."

"Emily, I can't say no, but Sheryl was exposed to the tachyons at a level at least a hundred times more than you, and she wasn't protected by a car going sixty miles an hour."

"You're right. I promise I won't obsess over it. I just hope they can help her."

"Steve has his team working with the doctors. If it is a tachyon problem, it will take a particle physicist to be part of the solution."

Emily had to muse just a little, "I bet Steve is wondering what happened to his retirement."

It was decided that it was too close to the holidays to make any headway. Everyone took some time to be with their families as much as they could. The Barracuders Club promised the band to double their rate if they played one set, triple if Freddie came along. Freddie and, to the club's delight, Mickey Hardstone also wanted to be there. The club suddenly had a huge cover charge, and the beers were some of the most expensive in town. The cost didn't slow down the crowd. The club was jammed with a crowd standing outside.

Jimmy still hadn't gotten over the thrill. He, Freddie, Mickey, and the band arrived in big SUVs. When Jimmy stepped out to cheers, he just jumped in the air with happiness.

The band rocked the house, and Freddie and Mickey were as excited as the newcomers. This was what they lived for. Freddie and Pete repeated their dueling guitars, and a hundred phones got the video.

The place was going crazy, and Freddie called out to the manager, "Hey, Jackie, we're going to take a short break. Why don't you get all of these nice folks a drink and put it on my tab."

The screaming and cheering were now so loud that conversation was impossible. Fortunately, the bar was big enough to have a backstage. When Freddie got back there, he could hear his phone ringing. He pulled it out, and it was Amanda calling.

He told the band, "It's our agent. I'll put her on speaker."

Then he answered, "Yes, Amanda, you're on speaker with the band and me; what's up?"

Amanda was very excited, "Freddie, I just talked to a representative of Heart. They want Barracuda Rising to open for them at their show at the L.A. Colosseum in February! Even though you are opening for them, Heart wants to come out first and introduce you by playing their big hit 'Barracuda,' isn't that incredible!"

Jimmy and the boys went crazy. They were jumping up and down and hugging each other. Freddie answered, "From the reactions of the boys, I would say that was a good thing."

"A good thing, you have not only been offered a gig with one of the best bands ever, but they are also going to open the show with a tribute to you."

Jimmy was so excited he grabbed Freddie's phone and said, "We want it. God, do we want it."

He handed the phone back to Freddie, and Freddie said, "Yes, we definitely want it."

Amanda was as excited as they were, "Wonderful, I'll get started and get you the details."

Once they were off the phone, Jimmy took in enough air to explain, "Heart is one of the greatest bands of all time. It would be like the Rolling Stones asking Barracuda to open a show for them when they were first starting out. You just missed them. They started getting popular around 1975, and they were huge in the eighties. You will love their music; it is just amazing. Ann and Nancy Wilson are musical geniuses. As a small side note, I've had the hots for Nancy Wilson since I was ten."

Freddie turned to Mickey and said, "You've got to get a hold of your agent and tell him to call Amanda and get in on this deal."

Mickey said, "I already got to him. I'll be with you, brother, and Jimmy is right; that is one kick-ass band."

The band was almost too excited to return to the stage, but they did a second set for free.

Freddie couldn't wait to get home and tell Emily. When he told her, she hugged him and said, "That's great, Freddie; you'll be back on top before you know it."

The words were there, but the emotion didn't fit the words. Freddie brought her out to arm's length and asked, "What's wrong?"

She looked up with tears in her eyes and said, "Jessica called me. Sheryl Ferguson is gone. She died about an hour ago. I was too damn busy to get to the hospital today. Today of all days, I was too damn busy."

Freddie held her while she cried.

The next morning Roger was upset, "You have to coordinate with us before you make a booking. We could have booked the play somewhere during that time."

Jimmy just said, "It's Heart, man. Do you think we were going to hesitate?"

"Fine, just try to coordinate with us next time."

Roger called the meeting to order. "Ladies and gentlemen, I have an announcement. Our first performance on the road will be local. We will open at the Redford Theater on Lahser right here in Detroit."

Sherry was surprised, "The Redford Theater is one of the best in the country."

"It's not Broadway," Roger answered, "but it is definitely big time, and with the big time come changes. KWTZ's parent corporation is not in the show production business, and they don't want to be. They have had an offer from a New York company to take over the production of "The Last Days of Barracuda," and they are going to accept. We will do the work to prepare for the Redford Theater, and then the production will be moved to New York. Once they have full rights to the production, they will make all of the decisions, including hiring and firing."

Sherry said what Roger wasn't saying, "You are saying that means they can replace some of us with performers they think are better."

"Yes, Sherry, that's what I'm saying. None of us wants to see that happen. We've been a family from the beginning, so it is up to all of us to make the Redford performance more professional and less dinner theater."

Emily asked, "What about you? Are you still going to be our director?"

"No, that was just a job I took as part of the deal with KWTZ. For a little promotional gig in Romulus, I thought I could handle it, but now I am way out of the league. You all deserve a professional director, and you're going to get one. I will go back to being the writer and a technical consultant, which is all I want to be."

Chapter 17: A Dark Night for Walking

The holiday break was over. The troupe got back together on stage at the beautiful Redford Theater in Detroit. People wandered around the huge stage and stared out at the grand auditorium until Roger began the meeting, "Yes, everyone, take a minute to get used to this magnificent theater. Then we have to get to work. We have just over two weeks to improve our performance. I have requested details of the critique, and the New York critics graciously provided them. We have a lot of things to work on.

I will have to call out some of you for personal criticism. You have to take it for what it is. Don't get your egos bruised. Believe me, the New York director will rip your ego out, tear it to shreds and drag it through the mud. Besides, I believe we all need to be brought down to Earth just a bit."

Work started, and, as Roger predicted, it wasn't all that much fun for any of the cast. No one escaped criticism, not even Freddie and Emily. Everyone sucked it up and tried to improve.

A few days later, Freddie made a few calls, and then he was ready to voice something that he had been thinking about. He called a meeting with Mickey and the band; There were a few things that he thought better be made clear from the start. He started the meeting, "Guys, the New York types will be all business. Mickey and I have dealt with them before. They will run your lives if you let them. I have access to some damn good lawyers, and I think we had better have our own contract drawn up ahead of time."

Jimmy asked, "What exactly do you think we should make clear?"

"This is a show production company. They will expect us to give our lives and our souls to the show. The show is very important, and I would not want to let any of our friends down, but my dream is to take this band to the top. We have our own schedule. We have to be ready for the Heart show in February. That means we need our own time to rehearse, and we don't want someone telling us to cancel our plans."

Bobby cheered, "You're damn right we don't. Bring out the big guns, Freddie."

Barry found himself caught up in a tale of the time travelers. Tony had told the press that it was Barry who first suspected the impossible. That brought the army down on Barry. They wanted the whole story. When they brought Barry back together with the Dermot family and the Michaels family, Rebeca Michaels tearfully announced that Skipper had died. She said she was told it was some kind of cancer. Barry didn't want to pass the news to Sarah, but he felt he had to.

When Barry called, he could tell that Sarah was clearly upset. She asked, "When did Skipper die?"

"Two days ago. The vet said he had some kind of cancer that he couldn't identify."

Sarah was now wringing her hands nervously, "We need the body for study. Do whatever it takes to get it."

"They buried Skipper right in their backyard. I should be able to get it."

"Compensate them, this is a loss for them, and I don't want them to think that we don't know that."

"I'll be sure to do that."

When she got off the phone, she held it to her chest, softly cried, and she said to no one, "Emily, I can't lose you again."

Steve had returned home for the holidays, and he wanted a few weeks to be with his family. Freddie and Emily spent Christmas with Sarah and New Year's with Steve and Freddie's family in Virginia. After they returned, Steve just wanted a quiet time with Cathy. Sarah hated to call him, but she knew he should know. When she got him on the phone, she just came out with it, "Steve, Skipper died two days ago."

"That was the dog that went through the anomaly."

"Yes, two that were captured by that thing have now died. I'm sorry to bring this fear to you, but you needed to know."

"Yes, I did. I will return to the lab immediately."

"No, Steve, spend a few more days with your family. I don't think rushing back is going to make much difference. Freddie and Emily still seem unaffected; their exposure was far lower than Sheryl or Skipper."

"Let's hope it stays that way. I will see you next week. Hold on, Sarah; we will try to figure this out."

"Should we ask Emily and Freddie to come in for an examination?"

"I would say yes if I thought it would do any good. Catching this thing early will not help. Whatever is going on, it is going on at the sub-atomic level. We are just beginning to observe activity at that level. We still have no idea how to affect it outside of a collider."

With a week to go before the performance, the cast began to get the paperwork to fill out and sign. This paperwork was the start of the transfer of control of the production to the New York production company. When Roger handed the papers to the band, Freddie let Jimmy make the announcement, "We're not signing anything until these New Yorkers understand our priorities."

Roger stopped, looked at Jimmy, and put his hands on his hips, "Oh, now you have priorities? One shot of success, and now you're a prima donna?"

"It's not him," Freddie said; "it's all of us."

Mickey added, "Including me."

Jimmy explained, "We're a rock band caught up in a stage show, but we are a rock band first. We want to stay with the show after this performance, but we can't be a slave to the show. We have to prepare for opening for Heart. This is a big deal. We will perform classic Barracuda tunes, but we are also introducing some of Freddie's original tunes. That's what we really want to do."

Roger was surprised, "This show has taken a bar band and made them into something that they had no right to be and now you think you can just drop us by the wayside on your way to fame and fortune."

Bobby, always being the excitable one, yelled out, "Fuck you, Roger, we're rockers!"

Freddie tried to calm things down, "We don't want to leave the show. We know how hard everyone has worked for this, and we love doing it, but we also love owning the stage. We have had some papers of our own drawn up. We think they are very fair. We just want a little freedom and a little say in scheduling to allow us to pursue our first love."

Roger was still angry, "Well, thanks guys; you may have just had the whole cast kicked to the curb. The New York people won't put up with this kind of shit. If you present these papers of yours, they just may decide the whole deal is not worth the effort."

Just two days later, the band was informed that The Universal Recording Studio would be releasing a soundtrack of the show in Romulus. The cast was told that the demand was high for the raw performance featuring Freddie and Emily in their first appearance. Mickey's mind for business had been reenergized and he went to Freddie and they made contact with The Universal Recording Studio. Freddie offered them the Barracuda Rising's demo CD. They accepted the CD, but they didn't make any promises. They said they would wait to see how well the selections were received when they were played at the Heart concert.

KWTZ was not the same little radio station that they were. The corporation had rebranded them and they were going into syndication. They were now labeled as the cradle of the rock and roll revolution. They had a two-hour segment at night where they presented fresh rock and roll from bands all over the country. A concert was being planned called The New Rock Jam featuring new rock bands and headlined by Barracuda Rising.

It was show day in Detroit. The cast was still nervous, but they were also confident and bolstered by their previous success. This time there was no wandering around and the projection of their voices was considerably better. The audience was on their feet and moving to the music more than they did in Romulus. The cast began to have fun with their parts and the band was more energetic than ever.

Roger was very happy with the show, but he was also nervous. No one had heard a word from New York since they received the papers from Barracuda Rising. The show ended with a great ovation. Everyone returned to take a bow, and it was over. The reviews showed technical improvement, but the enthusiasm for the show had waned. The time traveler story was getting old, and though people were still fascinated by it, it was no longer on the top of the news cycle.

This would be a turning point. They would either continue to play grand playhouses like The Redford Theater, or they would start working the hometown theater circuit. That was entirely up to New York now. Everyone went home feeling good about the play but wondering about the future.

As Freddie and Emily made their way home, Freddie said, "I'm sorry if we've caused so much trouble for everyone."

Emily didn't know how to think about it. She really didn't know how she personally wanted it to turn out. She answered Freddie, "It would be a shame for people like Roger and Sherry if this didn't work out. This was their lives. This is what they want to do. I don't know if this is what I want to do. I have loved it and all of the attention, but I don't know if I am really a performer. I look at Anita, and what she has accomplished, and I'm jealous. I have everything I could possibly want. Sarah told me that she had signed papers making me the heir to everything she has. I have had fame, but with all of that, I am still jealous of Anita. She did what we wanted to do. She fought through the man's world of the seventies and the eighties to get on top. I haven't done a damn thing for myself."

"You worked as hard as anyone on this show."

"We were lucky to fall into this, and we were backed up by Sarah every step of the way. There wasn't a time that we were risking our future on this show; some of the others have."

"I understand that, and that's why I am feeling sorry, but the boys and I can't give up our dream."

"And I understand that, and I am happy that you have a dream. I just wish I did."

The days went by, and everyone waited for some response from New York. The band now rented a space in a local strip mall and jammed after the other stores were closed. They had just finished going over several of their original tunes when Roger appeared at their door.

They let him in, and he announced, "New York has seen it your way. Here are your new contracts, have your lawyers look them over, and hopefully, you can sign them, and we can all get back to work. You will have to designate someone to go over scheduling; they're not going to want all of you marching into their office."

Freddie said, "We will let our agent Amanda and Mickey's agent Sammy handle that; they will know what we want."

"Fine, let's just please get this done as soon as possible."

Roger left and the band let out a great cheer. They hugged each other, and Pete said, "I believe it's time for some dueling guitars."

The band almost ran to their instruments and played with an energy that they had never had before. When Freddie and Pete threw their arms up in the air, Freddie was suddenly struck with pain that surged through his body. His eyes opened wide, and he dropped to the floor in an insane combination of static and music.

Everyone started yelling, and it was Jimmy that got on the phone first.

The waiting room was crowded with all the people Freddie had touched since he reappeared in 2017. Sarah's security and the police kept the horde of reporters and well-wishers at bay. Only one reporter was there, and her notebook and recorder were put away. Anita and her husband Joe sat with Emily and Sarah. It had been over an hour since Freddie was taken in, and everyone was on pins and needles.

Steve was there, and Cathy was on the way. His sons had to work things out with their jobs and their families, but they were expected soon.

Pete was very upset. He yelled out, "This is so fucking unfair."

Everyone looked up, and he said, "I'm sorry for the language, but I just can't help it. I was out. KWTZ didn't need another lead guitar player for this gig. It was Freddie that came up with this whole dueling guitars thing. He has given me all of this, and now this is his reward? It's just so unfair."

Emily cried and spoke softly, "He saved me from those people in Detroit, and he wanted to get me safely home. He is in there because he wanted to help me."

When the doctor came out, the news wasn't good, "Now that we know what to look for and SHR Laboratories has given us the equipment to use, I'm sorry to say that Mr. MacArthur is suffering from the same malignancy that took Sheryl Ferguson. It is like nothing we have ever seen. It attacks all parts of the body at the same time. In that respect, it is similar to Gama radiation poisoning but it is not the same. He is resting now under heavy sedation."

There was no stopping the effects of the alien energy. Freddie had fallen into a coma. Steve and his colleagues worked night and day, but they could not do years of study in just a few weeks. Back at the retreat, Emily was tested over and over, and there were no signs of destruction in her body. She just cried, "Why, why did you take Sheryl and Skipper? Why is it torturing Freddie, and still, I'm spared? Why would it do that?"

Steve and Dr. Drexel were with her. They were trying to understand that very thing. Steve was trying to work it out by talking it through, "You encountered the anomaly at the same place, at the same time. You had the same protection. You drove through it, so you both encountered it at the same speed. What could possibly make a difference? It could be genetic. Emily, you just may be resistant somehow."

"No, I don't want it to be that. There has to be . . ."

"Did you think of something?"

"When I saw this blue thing in front of the car, I yelled to Freddie, and then I threw myself down. I was so afraid of going through the windshield that I jammed myself under the dashboard."

"Did you see the flash?"

"No, I only saw it when it was blue. I was jammed down there with my eyes closed."

"Then you were more protected. You didn't experience the flash at all. That may be the key."

Sarah let out a breath. Until there was a logical reason why Emily was clear of the effect, Sarah was scared to death. She hugged her sister and said, "Freddie loves you. He will be so relieved that you will be spared."

Emily and Sarah returned to the hospital. Steve and Cathy were there. All of the cast, Tony, Barry, and Roger, all took turns holding a vigil in Freddie's room. Ryan and Rick returned, and they were with Mickey. Emily took her place by his side, holding his hand. She tried to keep her voice steady as she talked to him, "There is so much love for you here and so much more pouring in from around the world. You are more than a rock and roll icon or a time traveler, you're a good man, and that's why they love you, and that's why I love you."

The moments of quiet vigil went by. Then on the first of February at seven ten in the evening, his vital signs just faded away. Freddie MacArthur was gone. Emily just fell on him and wept uncontrollably.

All that knew him felt their world get a little darker. It would be a dark night for walking all over the world.

The New York production company suspended plans until they could reassess the value of their investment. Jimmy and Mickey swore they would keep the rebirth of rock and roll alive, for Freddie and Heart agreed. They would do the show with Pete on lead guitar. There would be a solo in the introduction to "Rabble Rouser." There would never be a dueling guitars segment to that performance again.

Freddie would be laid to rest in a special area created just for him on the grounds of the retreat. Tommy made sure security was tight and that Freddie's family and friends were not disturbed. Shelly Hicks was under the constant care of Dr. Drexel, and she held on to her two daughters during the ceremony. Several people spoke of the man Freddie MacArthur was and how he touched their lives. Pete started, but he couldn't finish his tribute. Finally, it was time for the final tribute. Mickey wanted Emily to sing with him, but she just couldn't do it.

Pete played an acoustic guitar, and Mickey sang:

"It's a dark night for walking; nothing is going my way.

A dark night for walking; it's time to walk away.

*It's a dark night for walking; the flags have all been furrowed.
A dark night for walking; I think I'll walk out of this world."*

Made in the USA
Columbia, SC
22 July 2023